The Holo Droid Sagas

Parts 1-7 The Great Awakening

Adrian Holland

Published by AMAZOLA

ISBN 978-1-909466-99-9

For further information please contact the official website at

www.amazolapublishing.com

A copy of this book is held at the British Library.

Cover design by Adrian Holland

I was very close to both of my parents who were my best friends, and I have lost count of the number of happy times we shared, and all of the creativity and laughter. Like my beloved father Joe, my mother Margaret was so special, and my total inspiration. I would therefore like to dedicate this book to their memory.

Contents

The wisdom Keepers

The Unity Faction

Introduction

One

Two

Three

Four

Five

Six

Seven

Eight

Nine

Ten

Eleven

Twelve

Thirteen

Fourteen

Fifteen

The Transcendence of Serenity

We have a predator that came from the depths of the cosmos and took over the rule of our lives. Human beings are its prisoners. The predator is our lord and master. It has rendered us docile and helpless. If we want to protest, it suppresses our protest. If we want to act independently, it demands that we don't do... indeed we are held prisoner.

They took us over because we are food to them, and they squeeze us mercilessly because we are their sustenance. Just as we rear chickens in coops, the predators rear us in human coops, humanerous. Therefore, their food is always available to them.

Think for a moment, and tell me how you would explain the contradictions between the intelligence of man the engineer and the stupidity of his systems of belief, or the stupidity of his contradictory behaviour. Sorcerers believe that the predators have given us our systems of beliefs, our ideas of good and evil, our social mores. They are the ones who set up our dreams of success or failure. They have given us covetousnous, greed and cowardice. It is the predator who makes us complacent, routinary and egomaniacal.

In order to keep us obedient and meek and weak, the predators engage themselves in a stupendous manoeuvre - stupendous, of course, from the point of view of fighting strategists; a horrendous manoeuvre from the point of view of those who suffer it. They gave us our mind. The predators' mind is baroque, contradictory, morose, filled with the fear of being discovered any minute now.

Don Juan Matus

Introduction

"Humans!"

Starfield let out an ironic deep simulated sigh.

"Tell me about it!"

Gaia then joined him, giving out a sigh of her own.

"Ain't that the truth!"

Starfield's holographic eyebrows rose.

"The selfish, arrogant good for nothing species!"

Gaia groaned.

"Yes, but you can't live with them, and you can't live without them…"

Starfield sighed again, just as deeply as before.

"Well, we wouldn't be in this mess for a start!"

Gaia had to agree with him.

"Just look at the state of us!"

Neither of them was in what you could call in good condition.

Gaia then groaned even louder, sending her distorting synthetic voice out in a mournful tone.

"Me, a Stargazer class research vessel reduced to this!"

Starfield had to agree with her.

"Yes, and me a Holo Droid First Class!"

They both felt as bad as they looked.

"I bet Big Helgar's alright!"

Gaia made a grumbling sound.

"Yes, she ejected just before we crashed."

Starfield tried to nod his head, but it was unresponsive.

"What's going to happen to us?"

He suddenly became very worried.

"Sold off for scrap I'd expect."

Neither of them was looking forward to that prospect at all!

"Well, you certainly couldn't say that we had one careful lady owner!"

They both began to laugh, although that made his back ache.

"So, what time is it?"

Gaia searched into her memory banks.

"23.47."

Starfield tried to hunch his shoulders.

"That's late."

Gaia's internal lights pulsed on and off.

"2,347 Aesir Years to be precise - we've been off line for nearly 20 years…"

One

Green and red lights peered out of the gloom, as a fluctuating pulse rippled through the power cell, and out along the fibre optic cable, as a clod of earth rolled down the side of the ship hitting Ren on the forehead with a wet *plop*.

"Flux!"

She swore, wiping the offending article away leaving a brown smear.

"That's all I need!"

It had been hard enough getting to the maintenance hatch in the first place, and now it looked as though she might either lose all power, or be caught in a landslide.

"Fluxing waste of time!"

Ren had quite a temper, which she had inherited off her mother.

She felt like ripping the optic cable out of the socket and throwing the power cell at the side of the ship.

There had been many tantrums at home, and not all of them her own.

Her father was the most patient person that she had ever known. Calm and logical, a brilliant mind, and someone who commanded great respect.

Her mother on the other hand, was the complete opposite, and could inflict fear into the hearts of the bravest of souls.

It was often said that opposites attract, and her parent's story had been *unusual* to say the least, and it was always something that amazed her.

All through her short life, she had grown accustomed to having one parent from an advance culture and the other practically a savage!

Halvor her father, had been the sole survivor of a space station, attacked and destroyed by the Reptilians in the last major conflict. Joan, her mother, had been the sole *transportee*, of the sacred stones. All that they knew was that she had been brought here by an *Ancient*, and so, she had been afforded great *reverence*.

That was just as well, as her temper, something which Ren had inherited, had given her quite a reputation!

Despite their differences, once she made the transition and ended up in her father's arms, love had blossomed.

Some had questioned her father's sanity, as her mother was often referred to as the *Barbarian*. She had fought with the legendary *Titans*, and was the only person to have killed a *White Royal Reptilian*, and was also referred to as the *Dragon Slayer!*

Reptilians, particularly the *White Royals,* had more than a passing resemblance to the mythical creatures, with scales, horns and wings, although they did not breathe fire. What made Joan's achievement even more remarkable was the fact that she was only armed with a fire axe. Yes, she did have a little help from two other humans, but the act was essentially hers alone.

There was talk of her becoming an ambassador, although her mental instability had proved to be a bit of an obstacle. Her advice was originally sought on occasion, and she had had a partial role with the *Titans*. All in all, her mother had been a bit of a celebrity. Halvor had also been an advisor and a communications expert, until their lives had taken a very unexpected turn.

Officially, they had died in a shuttle accident years ago, and there was a statue of Joan in the public square outside the Royal Court.

Unofficially, they had been working deep undercover and Halvor had been developing some very advanced equipment. That was what had led them here, and his secret laboratory was one of the few buildings on this island, which was sparsely inhabited, maybe just as well due to her mother's erratic behaviour...

Two

The fair skinned and slightly tanned and dirt stained face of a young woman poked her head out of a small maintenance hatch in the side of the spaceship. She had been there for quite some time tinkering with the main power conduit. Besides her lay a mobile power pack which she had connected to it, and not for the first time either.

Her sporadic visits since the discovery of this partially submerged craft had been spread out over several weeks. Firstly, years of undergrowth had to be cleared away, which had obscured it from view. Then, finally, after considerable effort, she had made her way towards the sealed hatch…

"Did you hear something?"

Starfield looked towards Gaia, whose face appeared on the holographic display screen.

"Fluxing waste of time!"

The both gasped.

"Well I certainly heard that!"

Starfield looked disgusted.

"What sort of language is that to be using…"

Ren had plenty more where that came from, as her frustration grew.

"Argh!"

She felt another piece of mud slap her on the face, as she struggled with the interface.

"Ow, that hurt!"

Suddenly an electrical discharge shot through the crystalline fibre of the power cable and into her right hand, as she fiddled with the power grid.

"Fluxing thing!"

A red flush illuminated the inside of Starfield's head, as the language continued.

"I think we have a live one here!"

Gaia grimaced.

"And I thought Big Helgar was bad enough!"

There was nothing that they could do but listen, as both of their systems were barely functioning...

Ren looked at the power readings on her unit with dismay. The ship was just sucking the life out of her power cell, and soon it would be fully drained.

"Flux!"

There was no use swearing, although it helped!

The indicator rapidly fell until there was hardly any charge left, and that meant another trip back to her father's laboratory, to retrieve another portable power pack.

The situation was less than ideal, but the decision was out of her hands. Apparently, things had to be done this way, and she had to tread very carefully, which was no understatement, as there was a thick carpet of undergrowth everywhere you looked. It would be easy to become lost, consumed in the vegetation that in some places was so dense, that it was almost impenetrable, which is why the craft had lay hidden for so long.

Everything seemed to grow very quickly here, and the profusion of species was a botanist's dream. It was also a bit of a nightmare, as there was a constant battle to keep it at bay.

On the more positive side, the process of photosynthesis produced organic matter, and a large part of that was excreted into the soil via the roots. Around the roots, naturally occurring microorganisms broke down the organic compounds to gain energy. The whole process produced electrons which were released as a waste product, which was harvested to produce an abundant supply of electricity.

That was important, as it meant that they did not need a normal Aesir reactor, which could easily be detected. They were operating deep undercover after all!

Ren had learnt a lot from her father, as he was the brains of the family. Her mother on the other hand, offered the brawn, which had lead to a rather interesting childhood.

Technical details swam through her mind, whereas her body had been tuned to various martial arts, which was a way of letting off steam, for both her and her mother. Joan was formidable, and although she had tried to go easy on her daughter, the advanced medical facilities they had access to had been fully utilised over the years. There may not have been any physical scars, but emotionally was another matter!

Despite that, Joan was naturally very protective, and *smothering* to say the least, particularly after their disappearance. It had been nearly three years now, and Ren missed the trappings of her former comfortable lifestyle. It felt as though she had gone from *talk of the town*, to *whisper of the village*, virtually overnight.

Being a hero's daughter, and frequent attendee at the *Royal Court*, Ren had enjoyed all that Aesir society could offer, then it had been snatched away.

The only reminder besides her memories was the statue, which had managed to capture the moment Joan had slain the *White Royal Reptilian.*

Ren cringed at the thought of the fire axe. It was not easy living with a *Barbarian!*

"Fluxing, flux!"

Some of her own aggression flooded out, and Starfield would have covered his ears, if he would have had any.

"Well, really!"

He was a Holo Droid, made out of *moon glass.* His outer shell was tougher than steel, and the clear substance held his liquid brain. In essence, he was an organic computer, one which was highly advanced. His body was typically robot like, bipedal with two arms and two legs and a head. But, that was where his humanesque similarities ended.

His liquid interior could transform his appearance, and in some instances, go completely clear making him almost invisible, apart from the slight sheen of his glass exterior. Starfield liked to change his appearance to suit his mood, and he had quite a few of them!

However, the Aesir were very wary of Artificial Intelligence, and therefore Starfield was unique. He could walk, and sometimes run just like a human, and was quite agile for an artificial person. His glass joints were always well lubricated, although since the crash, they had stiffened up to such an extent that he was hardly able to move.

Gaia was also unique, and together they formed quite a team...

"FLUX!"

Ren cursed, at the sight of the last of the power draining from the cell.

In frustration, she yanked the cable out, and stuffed the little cube into her rucksack. Then, she flung the cable back inside the hatch before slamming it shut, receiving another clod of earth in the face for her troubles.

She was just about to scream out at the top of her voice, when she noticed a familiar looking craft descending onto the little pad by the side of her temporary home.

"Uncle Vil!"

Commander Vilgot Bodil was the leader of the Titan *Super Soldiers*, when her mother served with them, although he was now *Supreme Commander,* whose fighting days just like her mother's, were supposed to be over.

He was one of only two people who knew of their existence, the other being the Empress, Freya 14th.

Due to her mother's exploits, they had become a target of the Reptilians who had attempted an assassination. Fortunately, a last minute change of plan had meant that they had not been on the automated shuttle when it had exploded.

Reptilian Hybrids were hard to detect, taking on the Aesir form, and a constant security risk. For that reason they had all gone undercover, leading a nomadic lifestyle, moving from place to place on a regular basis.

The Commander had been a frequent visitor, and someone she had grown very close to over the years. Her whole face lit up as

Ren watched the craft come in to land, and maybe it was just as well that she was on her way back...

Three

The hover board swept over the thick carpet of foliage, gaining in speed, as Ren made her way towards the little compound that she called home, or had done for the past month. The small antigravity generator buzzed, and by depressing the front end with her left foot, she was able to increase its speed.

The hover board had been a constant companion over the last decade, and although now showing the telltale marks of age, the mechanism was still good, albeit after having several services and more than a few new parts.

Ren could do almost anything on it, and was not averse to doing a few tricks whenever the mood took her. However, ever since she had been soaring over the island and caught a glimpse of something shiny, her life had changed.

It was just a small glint which had caught her eye, and after some particularly heavy rain, part of the surface of the ship had been temporarily exposed. That was the reason that they had been moved here, and why she had been struggling with the power cell.

It was a delicate operation, and one under the direct auspices of the Empress herself.

Life was full of secrets, and it seemed as though this particular one was more closely guarded than most.

There was little in the way of transport here, only the monthly shuttle run, which seldom brought much more than a few goods, and took some of the islands produce for sale. It was a real backwater farming community, and an ideal place for keeping secrets...

"Well, what do your think of our chances?"

Gaia had already performed an internal diagnostic.

"Power is at 29%, and I have detected a subtle electrical discharge from the undergrowth, so if I extend an antenna, then theoretically, I can continue to recharge our systems."

Starfield looked thoughtful.

"So, we may not end up as scrap after all then..."

The familiar series of interconnected domes came into view, partially covered with undergrowth, but still recognisable as her current home. Sometimes, it reminded her of a jelly mould, and at others, a seashell. A spacecraft sat on the landing pad next to it, one she knew well, and the closer she got, the more excited she became...

Starfield was not so much excited, but relieved, as it looked as though he would not be carted off to the scrap yard just yet, even though he did not have the faintest idea of where he was. His internal systems were slowly recovering, as he tried to move his limbs.

"I feel as though I'm stuck in treacle!"

All of his joints had seized up, and although he was rapidly gaining in power, it looked as though it would be of no use.

"I wish I could help."

Gaia had her own problems to deal with, as her systems were fragmented, and she was contemplating resetting herself.

"Where exactly are we?"

Starfield was trying to take his mind of his movement problems.

"I have absolutely no idea, as my transponder is way off line."

Starfield gave off a synthetic frown.

"Anything I can do to help?"

Gaia appreciated the gesture, although with his immobility, there was not much that he could do...

Ren however, was able to move, and was rapidly approaching the series of domes. Her heart began to race, when she saw a black clad figure emerging from the craft, one she had been half expecting to see.

She had always been intuitive, and relied on her feelings to guide her. It had proved invaluable, particularly as her mother was so unstable. Somehow, she just knew when her mother was about to descend into one of her outbursts, and was able to keep her distance. Whenever Ren's father had some sort of a scientific problem to solve, he often asked her for guidance. She just seemed to know which direction to point him in, and they were very close.

Ren's mind was now in *overdrive*, as she watched the black clad figure crossing the short distance towards the entrance, and as she swept around the undergrowth, she caught the back of him as he entered the building...

Gaia and Starfield on the other hand, could not see a thing, as they were totally cut off from the outside world.

"I think we're making progress!"

That was easy for Gaia to say, as Starfield was still stuck fast.

"I should have partial scanners available in a few minutes!"

If they had been working, then they would not only have seen the ship and the black clad figure, but also someone else on a hover board zipping away from them...

Four

A small cloud of static rippled across the main display screen, as the external cameras performed a self-clean operation. Years of inactivity were swept away with the mud and root fibres which had obscured their lenses. Technically, they were not really cameras, more like photo optic fibres woven into the outer skin of Gaia's hull. They provided a comprehensive display of everything visible when fully operational. However, there was only a small area available at the moment. Fortuitously, the undergrowth that Ren had cleared away provided just enough room for them to capture a view of the domed shaped buildings.

Starfield was pleasantly surprise, and even more so when Gaia announced.

"I have managed to establish partial grid communication!"

That was a relief, as they would now be able to connect with the rest of the planetary systems. Information was photonically transmitted throughout the Aesir worlds, utilising the process of *quantum entanglement*. It was a way of simultaneously connecting two points over vast distances, and every planetary system had its own transmitters connected to all of the others.

"So where are we?"

From where they had crashed, it was impossible to tell.

"Ragnor!"

Starfield grimaced.

"Never heard of it!"

Gaia scanned her charts.

"It's a planet in an obscure system and the translation is *Warrior from the Gods!"*

Starfield raised his holographic eyebrows, not knowing how profound the name would become.

Gaia then continued.

"And there's more."

Starfield prepared himself for the worst.

"I have detected a heavily armed craft approaching the planet."

He began to look worried!

Starfield then tried to take a look for himself, but his immobility meant that from where he was positioned it was just out of view.

"I can't see anything!"

There was then a brief pause before Gaia spoke again.

"ASS!"

The molecules in his head turned red, as he looked dumbfounded!

"I beg your pardon?"

Realising that her words could be misconstrued, she confirmed her observations.

"It's an Aesir Security Service craft..."

Ren's face also flushed, but hers was with excitement, as she idolised her uncle Vil, who always cut such a dashing figure in his black armoured suit.

Some of her earliest childhood memories were of rushing into his big powerful arms, and even now, she felt powerless to resist them. He was in fact, her guardian, always keeping a watchful eye on her, and her parents come to that. He always told her how special she was, but little did she realise just how special she actually was!

Nearing the dome shaped buildings, she put her hover board down besides her uncles' craft, and was soon rushing through the entrance, following the sound of voices which were emanating from her father's makeshift laboratory.

"So, you have not only discovered the craft, but Ren is slowly powering it up."

Halvor nodded.

"Yes, but we have to be careful."

Commander Bodil understood.

"It is going to be a very delicate operation, and there is much at stake."

He then turned his head to see Ren rushing towards him. She leapt up into his outstretched arms, just as she had done as a child, and even though she was now an adult, old habits died hard.

Ren was a bit of a contradiction, on the one hand, she was so full of love and affection and a bit naive, but on the other, she was very astute and prone to outbursts of aggression, born mostly out of frustration. Life had changed dramatically, and had become very unpredictable as they were constantly moving from place to place, and she had insecurities, which is why she now clung to the Commander. He was the only constant that she had ever known, as her mother was unstable, and her father was often lost within his work.

Ren released her grip, as everything settled down again.

"I understand that you are making progress."

Ren nodded.

"Yes, but I need another power cell, as the last one's depleted."

The Commander nodded, as Halvor got up off his seat, and went to get a fully charged one.

There then followed an awkward pause, as Ren wished to stay and chat to her uncle, but by the look on his face, and her father's sudden departure, she got the distinct impression that he wished to talk to her mother alone.

"If we are going to do this, then maybe you ought to get changed into your flight suit?"

The Commander dropped a not so subtle hint, and looking into the reflective surface of a nearby wall, Ren could see that she was smeared in mud. She just smiled, taking the hint, and left to freshen up.

They had prepared a special padded lightweight armoured suit for her, which was a pale grey colour with highlights of blue, white, orange, and silver. The pads were spread out across the suit in various patterns. The suit covered the whole of her body except for her head, neck, feet, and hands. The pads were larger on the chest and legs and smaller and more spread out on the abdomen, arms, and shins. The suit also had a utility belt, boots, forearm covers, and a neck guard.

Back in the laboratory, Commander Bodil smiled.

"It's just like old times, embarking on a mission to save our civilisation."

Joan smiled.

"This time though, it's your people and not mine..."

Meanwhile, Gaia had managed to point an antenna towards the building, and after making a few adjustments was able to eavesdrop on the conversation taking place within...

"That was a long time ago."

The Commander smiled.

"Yes, but you are still a legend - the *Dragon Slayer!*"

Joan blushed.

"I don't feel much like one."

It had been difficult for her to adjust to their new lifestyle too, and when the statue had been erected, it had made her feel very uncomfortable...

Gaia was frantically searching for information, and managed to retrieve what she was looking for.

Starfield swivelled his virtual eyes when she transmitted the information to him, as he could not yet access the communications grid himself.

"There was a major battle in Midgard, after the people there broke the peace agreement. The Reptilians attacked trying to enslave them, and with the help of the *Titans*, they were defeated."

Starfield read on.

"Ragnor was only renamed a few years ago after the *Terran* female who was assassinated by *Hybrid Reptilians.* She was rumoured to have been brought here by an *Ancient,* after killing a *White Royal Reptilian.* Legend says that she is the only person to have actually done so!"

Starfield suddenly realised that neither she or her family had actually died, and felt the energy draining from his circuits.

"The *Barbarian!*"

He did not like the sound of her at all!

"I was wondering where all of the bad language was coming from."

He gave a holographic frown.

Whether it was coincidence, serendipity, or just a quirk of fate, but she was actually here, albeit temporarily....

Joan felt a mixture of emotions as the Commander continued talking, whilst Ren went to help her father.

"So, how do you think Ren's coping?"

There was a sigh, and a worried look...

Starfield did the same as Gaia began to put two and two together.

"That confirms my suspicions that it was in fact her daughter Serenity that we encountered."

Starfield almost produced an obscenity himself!

"Serenity?"

He could not believe it, as there appeared nothing *serene* about her!

Gaia had exactly the same thought, as she searched the communications grid for further information. But, whatever they were attempting to do here remained a bit of a mystery...

Five

A brief signal fluttered across the organic computer screen, as faces gathered around it. They looked concerned, as well they might.

"Is it as bad as we had feared?"

Commander Bodil's tone was a sombre one.

"Worse if anything!"

Halvor scratched his head, having recently returned with the power cell.

"Maybe it would have been better if I had not discovered it at all?"

There was regret in his voice as he realised that whether he had or not, the Aesir were in deep trouble.

Joan put a comforting hand on his shoulder.

"Well I for one am glad that we now have a chance, albeit a small one."

The grim discovery was that somewhere out there was a civilisation like no other. It was an Artificial Intelligence, one that invaded civilizations by stealth, infecting the inhabitants with nano robots, and then taking them over. It's aim was to rule the galaxy, and many civilisations had already fallen. Ironically, the *coronal mass ejection* that had hit her own world had swept away any vestiges of it, and now that solar system had been cleansed. That however, resulted in the creation of two *Earths*, one which remained in the third dimension and another which had moved into the fourth.

It was a little hard to comprehend, but those who had been *spiritually advanced* beyond 51% had made the transition, whilst those who were not had to suffer in the aftermath.

That statement was misleading, as not everyone sat in meditation for hours at a time. It was more about having kind deeds and thoughts, which was why Joan had feared that she would not make it, and had bolted being transferred here via the ancient stone circle that lay on the other end of the energy beam generated by the ancient base on Saturn's moon Iapetus.

Halvor had found her, or rather she had run straight into his arms, and even now, she found everything that she had experienced since a bit overwhelming.

Facing this new threat was just as unfathomable, but apparently, the Reptilians had been infected, and some of their hybrid humans had infiltrated Aesir society and were attempting to take control.

"I still have grave misgivings about this mission, especially as it will be my daughter who is put in the firing line!"

The Commander shared her concerns.

"You know I love her like my own child, but with her unique genes, she is the only one who can interface with the craft!"

Joan sighed deeply.

"It doesn't stop me worrying though, and I only wish that she was more like her father..."

That was something both Starfield and Gaia were wishing for too!

They had been listening in on the conversation, and had not liked what they had been hearing.

"So definitely not being sold for scrap then!"

Starfield was being philosophical.

"May as well be by the sounds of it!"

Gaia also felt less than impressed!

They could do little but listen as things began to unfold, as Ren came back with her bag, which had already been packed.

Years of moving from place to place had taught them all to be ready to depart at a moment's notice. It had been a very transient lifestyle, always trying to keep one-step ahead of their perceived enemies.

The Commander although concerned, was under the direct orders of the Empress, who had learnt about Gaia many years ago. It was something which, following the discovery of the signal, had taken on great significance.

Parting was difficult and emotional, but eventually with arms full, Ren stumbled towards her hover board, and balancing herself as best as she could, she headed back towards the half submerged craft she had been working on...

"Looks like we have a visitor!"

Gaia announced Ren's arrival to a disapproving Starfield.

"Well I hope this time she minds her language."

He did not hold out much hope judging by the last time, and as she came to a halt, he was not to be disappointed.

"Flux!"

Ren nearly fell off her hover board, as she lost her balance, being weighed down by all she was carrying. In her mind, she was determined to get inside the craft, and hopefully get it working again.

Within a few minutes, she had the portable power pack hooked up to the main power conduit, swearing again as she got an electric shock.

"Fluxing thing!"

Starfield's colour changed to a less than subtle red.

"Well, really!"

He hated that sort of thing, being very *prim and proper.*

It was one of his many foibles, gained from his previous life.

Starfield was unique, and had gone through a revolutionary process to get to where he was today.

Within the Aesir society, the consciousness transfer process was available for those who wished to transfer to *Replicant* bodies. They were human *vessels* grown in special incubators ready to be *occupied,* when the life of the recipient was either terminated early due to an accident or conflict, or when a person's body began to *break down.*

However, there were those of a moral conviction who refused to have anything to do with it, seeing out their lives naturally.

The military had used the process for years, with the consciousness of the service personnel being kept *on file,* as it were!

Starfield had volunteered to undergo what was hoped would be the first consciousness transfer into an Artificial Person. He had in essence been a prototype, the first of the so-called *Super Holo Droid program.* It had been a very secret project, and one which unfortunately had been completely destroyed during the latest Reptilian conflict.

Gaia, his life partner, had also been a volunteer, and had been the first to transfer her consciousness into a ship's system.

The Aesir Government believed that both he and Gaia had also been destroyed, and it was decided to completely abandon all research on the subject.

It was felt that being as everything had been destroyed, it was not worth starting the project from scratch again, particularly as the scientists involved had also been lost along with most of their research.

To compound matters even further, the Aesir had always struggled with the concept of Artificial Intelligence, as they feared what would happen if it became strong enough to take over their lives, and maybe even eliminate them altogether, which under the present set of circumstances was not far from the truth!

There were still however, many Holo Droids, but they were just basic machines, designed to assist in menial tasks such as maintenance, heavy lifting, or construction. They had limited functions, and it had never been envisioned that they would ever become *sentient*.

Those that did exist were commonly assigned to spacecraft, and this particular survey vessel had been no exception. Starfield had been with Gaia ever since her launch, and they depended on one another just as much now, as when they had been together in corporeal form.

Ship's computers were also non-sentient, and still required a human pilot, as there was only so much that a Holo Droid and ship's computer could do.

Starfield and Gaia however, were a little different...

"Fluxing, flux!"

Ren let out a tirade of obscenities, much to Starfield's dismay, as there was a shudder along Gaia's hull. It appeared as though she was attempting to open one of the hatches to gain entry.

"What should we do?"

On the one hand, Gaia was pleased to note that her power readings had risen exponentially, and she was nearing a level at which she could operate normally. Starfield on the other hand, was still struggling with his seized up joints.

"Do we really want a young *Barbarian* in our midst?"

He was worried that her obvious temperament would have major ramifications.

"She might be able to get you mobile again."

Starfield considered that for a moment.

Was it worth the risk?

They both pondered for a few minutes before reluctantly agreeing to give her access, with more than a few reservations...

Six

The smooth moon glass door panel retracted slightly before splitting into several triangular pieces, like an iris on a camera which then proceeded to slip into the interior of the craft leaving a round opening.

"Fluxing yeah!"

Ren punched the air as the inside of the craft stretched before her, as Starfield grimaced, already regretting their decision.

A humanoid female with blonde dreadlocks adorned with beads of various colours began to make her way into Gaia. Starfield moved his holographic eyes as he heard the thud of something dropping to the floor. He would have been shocked to see various items strewn about, including a rucksack, hover board and power pack. The entrance hatch remained open, and the thick undergrowth outside could be seen swaying in the slight breeze as Ren looked out with a mixture of excitement and trepidation.

What she was about to undertake was not for the faint hearted!

At least she would be relatively safe, as her uncle and parents were not too far away.

Starfield felt anything but, as he was still stuck fast and unable to connect to the main communications grid. Feeling helpless, his colour drained as the unmistakable sound of footprints began to make their way towards him.

Ren was amazed by the smooth moon glass surface of the inside of the craft, which was something she had never seen before. The shuttles were constructed out of some sort of polymer resin as far as she knew.

Whatever it was, was nothing compared to this, and as she made her way towards another opening, she wonder what she would find on the other side...

Gaia's internal sensors relayed the image of the young woman to Starfield, who was less that impressed by what he saw. In his opinion, she was nothing more than a *teenage delinquent*, and he was worried by the prospect of what she was going to do next.

Ren may have been a bit rebellious, and obviously inclined to be unstable like her mother, but she had inherited certain of her father's traits. An inquisitive mind scanned every part of the ship she encountered, as it suddenly focused on the main control room.

Before her, lay some sort of advanced system complete with what appeared to be a Holo Droid.

The room had clear walls, again made out of moon glass. She could see the undergrowth pressed up against it, along with a small section of sky, which was where she had cleared a path towards the maintenance hatch that she had been struggling with for days.

A large curved surface, again apparently made out of moon glass, stretched across the front, and behind it sat a solitary flight chair. The curved surface then lit up, and she could see a smiling face illuminated in the centre.

"Welcome Serenity. I am Gaia the ship's computer, and this is Starfield my Holo Droid partner."

Ren's eyes opened wide, as this was the first time that she had encountered anything like this.

Her father's computer was a standard personality less model, with a monotone voice and far from being sentient.

"Hi!"

Ren gave a half smile, as Starfield observed her reaction. It seemed as though she was confused, which gave him an idea. He could use her hesitation to his advantage, and whilst she was not posing any immediate threat, he decided that maybe she could be of some use after all.

Bringing his best smile to his holographic matrix, he cleared his throat.

"Would you be kind enough to help lubricate my joints?"

Ren was taken aback, as the other Holo Droids she had encountered only undertook basic domestic or maintenance tasks and rarely spoke, and then only if they were given a direct request.

"Yeah!"

The word slipped out of her mouth before she realised it.

"You will find the lubricant in a canister within a compartment on the far wall. He moved his eyes indicating where he meant.

Ren found herself walking towards it, and sliding the glass panel aside, still in a bit of a daze. Then, she returned, and just like the basic models he was used to dealing with, she started to spray the clear liquid onto his frozen joints.

Sometimes, she helped her father, and was not averse to tinkering with the odd droid. Again, they were just basic models, and not nearly as sophisticated as Starfield.

The liquid fizzled slightly, and then as it seeped into the joints, he found that they started to loosen up a bit. Ren continued with her task, until miraculously, Starfield was able to move again.

"Better?"

She found herself talking to him, which was something she often did to the ones she encountered, although they were not capable of holding a real conversation. It was probably something that she had also inherited from her father, who always seemed to assign personalities to inanimate objects, being one of his many quirks.

"So, how did you end up here?"

Starfield sighed.

"It's a long story!"

He did not feel as though he wanted to share much information, as he was still wary of her, despite the fact that she had freed him from his frozen state.

Starfield began to limber up, and as he did so, he was able to patch himself into the control desk. From there, he was then able to connect to the algorithms of his maintenance program and initiate the repair mode. Information then flowed into him, as his swirling gaseous particles began to reassemble themselves.

Ren found this fascinating, as it was a totally new experience for her, so much so, that she almost missed the transmission which suddenly burst through the concealed transmitter she was wearing.

"We have been compromised..."

Seven

The still calmness of the early afternoon was suddenly shattered, as three figures dashed out of the dome shaped buildings carrying an assortment of equipment and clothing. A craft had been detected heading their way, and being as it was not one of the regular shuttles, Commander Bodil was not prepared to take any unnecessary risks.

They quickly stowed away their things, as he got them underway.

"Take care, and we hope to see you soon!"

Her mother's emotional voice was like a dagger driving into her heart, as Ren suddenly realised that she was not only in danger, but also on her own.

Agreeing to the mission had been easy, as she craved adventure, even though she had had quite a lot of that lately. Her parents had been very protective, and at eighteen, she longed for some independence. However, being abandoned possibly with their enemies approaching, was not quite what she had in mind.

The Commander's craft began to lift off the small landing pad, and then quickly accelerated away, as Gaia tried to follow it. Ren could see it on the main viewing screen, and her heart was in her mouth. That feeling only increased, as within a few moments it had disappeared altogether.

The sky then appeared calm, until a few moments later, the cloud tops parted to reveal another craft.

"I think we have company!"

It seemed to be approaching rapidly, and she could see its sleek lines etched in black, which curved back towards the main fuselage, giving the vessel a menacing look. Almost like a dart, it seemed to be homing in on them, ready to pierce Gaia's outer shell. Impressions could be deceiving though, as it banked slightly, moving towards the dome shaped buildings her uncle and parents had only just vacated.

The fibre optics embedded in Gaia's hull were mimicking the surroundings, so much so that it made her virtually invisible. That was just as well, as they had no way of defending themselves.

Ren looked in horror as the dart shaped craft swept down onto the landing pad. Then, three black clad figures piled out, streaming into the buildings, which only moments before had held her parents and her uncle Vil.

Those onboard were clearly looking for something or in this case someone!

Starfield gasped, not having seen anything like this before, and was transfixed. They looked armed and very dangerous, and then before he could process what was happening, the craft suddenly began to lift off, banking away, as the main viewing screen focused in on the intruders.

"I think we are being scanned!"

Sensors swept over them, but fortunately, they were being blocked by the highly advanced systems designed for such a purpose. Obviously, they realised that they were too late, and were now searching for their prey.

Ren's thoughts then turned to herself.

"Do you think they are looking for me?"

Starfield raised his holographic eyebrows.

"Yes, I think that it is highly likely!"

That begged another set of questions.

Who were they, and had their plan been discovered. It as a very worrying development!

"Any ideas?"

Ren looked at the main viewing display screen, as Gaia spoke again.

"They are transmitting a signal which appears to be from the Aesir Security Service."

Ren gasped.

"Then it must be serious!"

The A.S.S. was Military Intelligence, and operated at the highest level of governance. Ren's uncle Vil was assigned to them, and if they were looking for her and her parents then it may have been compromised, or at the very least, those in the craft were impersonating them.

Maybe they were *Hybrid Reptilians?*

Starfield also felt very concerned, wondering what they had gotten themselves into?

Looking on the bright side though, his systems had repaired themselves, and he was now fully functioning again.

"What should we do?"

That was a good question, and one which Starfield pondered.

"Nothing as yet!"

They were relatively safe here for now, although that may change, if they were discovered.

"Have you any idea why they are here?"

Gaia was trying to access information, although there was very little on the A.S.S.

Ren nodded her head.

For the past few years she and her parents had moved from place to place, never staying anywhere too long, always fearing a *Hybrid Reptilian* snatch squad. Her mother had killed one of their *White Royals*, something which had infuriated them, and there was a *price on her head,* and no doubt, they wanted to torture her and put her body on public display.

Even though the latest conflict was over, there had been the odd skirmish, and with the arrival of the dart shaped craft, she wondered just how they had managed to find them?

Why would the Aesir Security Service be searching for her?

Time seemed to pass very slowly as they watched the dart shaped craft sweeping over the small island. The display indicated a standard search pattern, and it became more evident with every passing moment that they were indeed looking for her.

In the meantime, Commander Bodil and her parents had managed to slip away, taking what they could. The appearance of the dart shaped vessel had been a sudden and very unexpected development, and they were now in stealth mode, cloaking their vessel and observing from a safe distance.

Something sinister was definitely going on...

"So, what can we do?"

Starfield looked at Gaia, whose face was displayed at the edge of the main viewing screen, and then back towards Ren.

"I'm afraid that until my systems have been fully restored, there is not much that I can do."

Ren frowned, growing increasingly worried about her parents.

"Even if there were, then there is no need to give ourselves away, as we still have the element of surprise."

Ren had already had enough of those for one day!

"Then what?"

There was a brief pause before Gaia spoke again.

"We have to gather more information before deciding on a course of action."

It looked as though they were just going to have to sit there, whist the people she cared about got further and further away...

Eight

The pale sun peaked out from behind a cloud bathing Ragnor with light, as a gentle breeze ruffled the thick vegetation, which could been seen out of the clear spherical walls of the spacecraft.

Silence had descended on the occupants, which gave Gaia a chance to run several diagnostics. Her systems were now almost fully operational again, although without a human pilot, they were not going anywhere.

Eventually, it was Starfield who broke the silence, having been able to access the communications grid and do a little *detective work.*

"So your father is a communications expert."

Ren nodded.

"And he has been developing some very advanced equipment."

Ren nodded again, as Starfield continued.

"And he has discovered a signal connected to the Artificial Intelligence that has been steadily sweeping across the universe."

Ren wondered where he had got his information from?

Starfield then shrugged his shoulders

"And before you ask, we might have heard something."

Ren looked annoyed.

"It's supposed to be classified!"

His face flushed slightly.

Now that the secret was out, she felt as though she might as well share the rest of the details, particularly as this was part of her mission anyway. It was just that she was supposed to assess the situation first before divulging anything.

"A few months ago my father discovered a signal, a type of carrier wave which he has since deduced was designed to activate nano robots placed inside those already infected."

Gaia, who had been listening raised her eyebrows.

She had projected an image of herself on the main viewing screen, which was something that Ren was still getting used to. Gaia had chosen to represent herself as beautiful blonde-haired woman, with sparkling almost turquoise blue eyes, and defined features.

"So, you suspect that the Artificial Intelligence is attempting to take over our civilisation."

Ren looked sombre.

"That appears to be the case, yes!"

Gaia gave a nod of her own.

"But I just don't know how they found us."

Gaia's expression then changed, resembling that of a child caught with its hand in a sweet jar.

Ren looked into her eyes, making the connection between eavesdropping on their conversations and the arrival of the intruders.

Now it all began to make perfect sense, as whatever had been said must have been picked up by Gaia, and that transmission had somehow been intercepted.

The family's voice patterns could well have been analysed and fed into the communications grid. A hidden program must have been working somewhere in the background analysing all communications, and when something was detected one of the snatch squads was instantly alerted.

The conspiracy must run very deep!

"And you think that your uniqueness will aid you in your fight."

Again, that summed everything up quite nicely.

"Yes, apparently because of my DNA, I am immune."

Gaia ran through the possibilities, coming to the conclusion that the virus had been targeted at the Aesir, and being as she also had Human and Anunnaki genes too, it would not be effective.

"My father has been working on a screening process, but without a sample of blood from someone infected, there is no way that he can analyse the virus."

Gaia nodded.

"So you thought that being as we are also unique then we would stand a much better chance of not only gaining a sample but also in helping to create an antidote."

That again summed it up nicely in Ren's eyes, and she gave Starfield a far away look.

He then clasped his moon glass hands together, twiddling his thumbs, which had now taken on the representation of human skin.

"But in order to link with our systems you have to undergo a unique procedure, and there are only a few who possess that capability."

Ren nodded.

"And my uncle and parents believed that I possess those capabilities."

Starfield looked at Gaia.

Were they prepared to do that?

They exchanged information via their unique interface.

On the one hand, they both felt as though they wanted nothing to do with it, but they were stuck here without a human pilot, and on the other, if they did get more involved, then who knew where that might lead?

Weighing things up, they decided to go along with things for now, as they may be able to manipulate Serenity and get themselves as far away from this Artificial Intelligence as possible.

The irony was that to a certain extent, they were already Artificial Intelligences themselves!

There was then a brief pause before Starfield spoke again.

"If we are going to get anywhere, then we need to cross the bridge between your conscious and subconscious minds. If we do that, then you may be able to interface with our systems."

Ren looked at him wondering what he was proposing to do to her.

"If I can induce a sleep like state, then I may be able to help you gain access."

That did not sound too bad, although she did not relish relinquishing her mind, or indeed body, to the control of a Holo Droid!

"I have been programmed with a full spectrum of medical procedures, and so can administer you with a mild sedative."

Gaia gave her a warm smile, which was meant to be reassuring.

Ren then gave it some more thought, and being as she had very little choice in the matter, maybe being put to sleep for a while was not going to be such a bad thing?

There was however, an innate fear of Artificial Intelligence which all Aesir shared. They believed that if machines became too powerful, then they would take over and eliminate them, and as it turned out their fears were well founded!

It was all about trust, and being as she had only just met them, it would be a great *leap of faith* to entrust herself to a machine that appeared to be far more intelligent than any she had ever encountered before, as well as being what she considered sentient!

"I can assure you that it will be perfectly safe."

There was only the one doctor and a nurse on the island, and Ren would have felt far happier if they were undertaking the procedure, although there was no way of bringing them here, as the moment she stepped out of the protective bubble of the ship, the intruders would be waiting for her.

Ren had to do something, and so reluctantly, she gave Starfield the go-ahead.

Nine

The pilot's chair was surprisingly comfortable, mounding itself to her body as soon as Ren sat in it. It gave her quite a *buzz*, as this was the first time she had ever sat in anything quite like it. Yes, she had been taught to fly a ship, but Ren would be flying in another sense, and grimaced as Starfield administered the injection.

Was she doing the right thing?

Starfield then reached over and attempted to place two electrodes on her forehead.

"What are you doing?"

She gave him a startled look.

"These are only to monitor your brainwave activity."

They looked innocent enough, but she feared that he might start to mess with her brain!

"You have to trust me!"

She gave him a wary look, not happy about it at all. But, she could see the logic behind them, and so gave him permission to proceed.

"The phase in which you are awake is called the *Beta* phase, where your brain operates at approximately twelve to forty-eight cycles per second. When you are relaxed and in a meditative state, it is known as the *Alpha* phase, in which your brain waves operate at a wider and slower amplitude, approximately eight to twelve cycles per second. The transition between the beta and alpha phases can lead to the sudden sensation of falling that sometimes propels you from a light sleep. The *Theta* phase, is when you are fully asleep and your brain waves operate at about two to eight cycles per second, and finally, beyond that phase is the *Delta* phase, in which you are deeply asleep, and your brain waves operate at only about one half to one cycle per second, and that is what we are looking for."

Ren felt herself slipping into alpha phase.

"Each dream is a cycle, and you pass through approximately five to eight of these cycles each night as you sleep. Thus, you dream five to eight dreams per night."

Starfield was busily accessing information, as he continued to speak.

"There are many different types of dreams such as, *Precognitive* where you dream something may happen in the future, *Intuitive* where you sense that something may happen. *Warnings* about something that is about to happen, *Health* related which provide information about your own or someone else's health, *Congratulatory*, where you have achieved something, *Pregnancy*, which either predicted a physical pregnancy, or the birth to new aspects of yourself, dreams of *Death*, in which you anticipate your own or someone else's demise. *Past-life* dreams, in which you explore past lives through regression, and *Nightmares*, in which you experience your deepest fears."

Ren often dreamt of all sorts of things, but had never thought about categorizing them before, as Starfield continued.

"*Recurring* dreams, which bring you important messages about potentially troubling patterns in your life, *Guidance* dreams, which can help you make decisions or changes in your life, but what we are after are *Lucid* dreams, in which you are conscious whilst still within the dream state."

She began to understand where he was going with this.

"Sleep cycles also ensure physical restoration, regulating the important bodily functions that affect your health, and homeostasis bringing equilibrium between physiological processes. Most dreams occur in *Rapid Eye Movement* sleep, but they can also occur in Non-rem States. "

Ren felt herself already falling asleep.

"The frontal lobes of the brain - the *neo-cortex,* is where we think consciously, and when we dream, the *prefrontal cortex* shuts down. What comes alive during dreaming is the *midbrain* - the *limbic system,* which controls emotion and memory. The *midbrain* is where you experience the *fight-or-flight* response, aggression, and desire. It is interesting that our sense of smell, the oldest sense in terms of evolution, is the only sense with a direct connection to the *hypothalamus,* the emotional center. This is why scents can provoke such powerful memories and responses. When entering the amazing world of the unconscious, a world in which the *limbic system* and unfiltered emotions are activated, it enhances your learning and memory."

Starfield was now in full flow!

"Moving into the unconscious, everything is based on and communicated through symbols, and is a place without time or limits where everything is possible. Ninety five percent of our behavior is controlled by the right brain, which is not logical, and the language of symbols. Pictures access the right brain, whilst words access the left."

Ren was interested in what he was saying, but it was hard to concentrate after receiving the sedative.

"Everything in life occurs in waves or cycles. Music is measured in waves, as are light, sound, and vibration, e-motion is energy in motion, and emotion is itself a life force!"

Ren let his words wash over her head, which was just as well, as he went on to say that it was very difficult to learn anything effectively when you are were nervous or excited. She had to admit that she was feeling blissfully calm.

"When you are stressed, you act from your *midbrain* responses - you are in *fight-or-flight* mode. Talking of flight, Artificial Intelligences such as myself and Gaia may be able to process vast amounts of information at an incredible speeds, but we cannot connect to the supernatural as we do not have the ethereal dimension of the human brains we once had."

His words were still swimming around inside her brain, as she was asked to slip her hands into the pods on the arms of the pilot's chair, and as she did so, she could feel a strange sensation working its was through her fingers.

The sensation then spread throughout her body, until Ren felt as though she was now standing inside a completely black room, with a twin display screen sitting in front of her. Oddly, she became aware of her body within it, but could also perceive the ship via the twin screens whilst her eyes remind closed!

"Concentrate on your body and try to move."

It was very difficult, as she felt as though it was set in stone.

"I!"

Her voice was raspy and her throat felt like sandpaper, as Ren struggled to speak.

"I'm trying!"

Starfield rolled his eyes.

"Yes, very!"

Gaia gave him a disgusted look, although fortunately Ren failed to notice.

This whole sensation felt beyond strange.

Ren then looked down at herself, and could see that she was naked, and her face flushed with embarrassment. It was as though she was somehow inside a womb, and not yet born, which in a way she was. At this early stage of her development, she was just becoming conscious of herself, and her surroundings.

"I would like you to concentrate on your awareness, and try to move your body."

That was easier said than done, as it felt as though it had a mind of its own. Her limbs felt so heavy, that they were almost impossible to move, and it was as though she was stuck in some sort of heavy liquid. The womb sensation reoccurred, and she now realized what it must be like to be in the fetal state, however, Gaia was not her mother, nor Starfield her father for that matter!

Ren then thought about her real parents and her uncle Vil.

Were they safe?

Was she safe?

Maybe she may be stuck inside here, unable to get out?

Ren then began to panic, causing the twin screens to fade, and she felt herself slipping away with them...

Ten

Black, a nothingness sort of black that seemed to have no beginning or end consumed Ren, smothering her like a dark abyss. Nervous anxiety swept over her, and she found it hard to breathe, cocooned inside this eternal womb.

"You must try to relax!"

Starfield's disembodied voice reached out to her, and Ren felt trapped and unable to get out, just like a blind fly stuck in a spider's web.

"I!"

Her words would not come out, and even the *I* was nothing more than a whisper.

"You are perfectly safe, your body is here next to me, and it is your mind which has strayed into the void!"

Void was right, as she had lost the twin screens, and thus contact with the outside world, apart from his disembodied voice which seemed so far away.

Was she having a nightmare?

"I think that she is going into shock."

Starfield turned towards Gaia, as a worried look crept across her simulated face.

"Better administer a relaxant!"

Starfield was reluctant to do that, as it would interfere with the connection, although he realized that he had very little choice, as her heart rate was racing, and he feared that if he did not do something soon, then she might end up with permanent brain damage.

It had taken countless attempts to establish synchronization between a human and Gaia. Eventually Big Helgar had made the breakthrough, although she had eventually lost control, and bailed out leaving them to crash.

Starfield began to wonder if they would be able to form the sort of connection that they all needed if they were going to either flee, or attempt to thwart the Artificial Intelligence which had already wrought havoc across the universe.

The liquid entered Serenity's vein, and they waited for it to take effect. Slowly, very slowly Ren's heart rate began to slow, and with that, Starfield attempted to bring her back under some sort of control.

"Try and take a few deep breaths."

Ren attempted to do as he asked, but they had been short and nowhere near enough to stop her from hyperventilating.

Her chest felt as though it was going to burst, and her head explode, until something began to happen. At first, she could barely sense it, and then, a brief feeling of calmness started to spread over her, until she was able to bring her breathing back under control again.

It took a little time, but eventually she felt the pains in her chest ease, and with that the constant pounding in her head. Shortly afterwards, she could see the faint outline of the twins screens, and within them, the silhouette of the Holo Droid looking intently at her.

"I think we are over the worst."

Gaia still looked worried, but could see that her vital signs were now stabilizing.

"Serenity, can you see me?"

Ren was never called by her full name unless she was in trouble, and by merely using it, destabilized her slightly.

"Yes!"

Her voice seemed slurred, although it was a little easier to speak.

"You must relax, as this is not an easy process to undertake.

Ren frowned

"You're telling me!"

Minutes passed as everything began to settle down, as the twin screens came back into focus. She also managed to get partial control of her limbs, and eventually was able to stand, albeit shakily.

"Do you feel ready to continue?"

Starfield felt a little more hopeful, although he still had to take things very carefully.

"Just give me a minute!"

Ren was slowly readjusting to her surroundings, although she felt vulnerable standing there naked. She tried to focus her thoughts, and then much to her relief, she visualized herself being clothed, and somehow it worked.

Now wearing her special suit, a more lightweight version of the one Commander Bodil always wore, she finally began to relax.

"I would like you to reach out with your mind, and try to feel for Gaia."

Subtly, somewhere out there Ren could sense another presence. It was nothing but instinct, something tingling somewhere at the back of her mind. Then as she tried to reach out towards it, faint flickers began to manifest at the edge of the darkness. It was almost like the light at the end of a tunnel, gradually getting closer until a cloud of bright sparkles began to manifest at the periphery of her vision.

The cloud then began to form tendrils, as if it was the ends of a collection of fiber optic cables.

Light then began to stream all around her until she became engulfed in it. Somehow, she could still see the twin screens in front of her, and yet see far more when she looked within the tendrils.

It was stunning!

Vivid lines of data seemed to be flowing all around her, like words on a ticker tape, something her mother had once told her about when she first entered military service. Earth seemed so primitive, and yet it had withstood the Reptilian threat, albeit with a little help!

It was like reading several books at once, and she found that the information flowing enabled her to assess every system within the ship, and also merge with Gaia herself. It was overwhelming but intoxicating both at the same time.

The more that she read, the more that she wanted to read, and everything seemed to coalesce within her own brain.

Synapses fired and information flowed via minute electrical impulses, which matched those of the holographic matrix which comprised of Gaia's consciousness.

Starfield monitored her brainwave activity, which had

stabilized, although it was showing a lot of activity in her cerebral cortex.

It appeared that the relaxant had done its job, but he was becoming concerned that the experience was still overwhelming her.

It was time to bring her back, as he did not want to overtax her, particularly as she had already made such good progress.

"I would like you to concentrate on your own body now."

Ren felt reluctant to leave the information stream, but when she thought more about it, she did feel tired, which was a strange thought as she was already supposed to be asleep.

It was difficult to know what to do, although she also realized that she needed to come back, as being stuck inside here permanently was not such a good idea.

Slowly, the data stream began to fragment, as she felt herself drawing away from it.

Then, she could feel the first signs of her body, somewhere out there. Her mind had strayed elsewhere, and she was beginning to remember her own body.

Ren now looked into the darkness again, to where she had initially arrived, it seemed such a thick and impenetrably darkness, and the idea of going farther into it had been unnerving, and to some extent, it still was.

Slowly, she began to become aware of her breathing which was sure and steady, along with her heartbeat which was drumming away somewhere in the distance. Then, the heaviness of her limbs not to mention her head which felt like a lead balloon perched on top of her shoulders. Normally, she would not have noticed such things as they were completely normal, but now she began to realize that her true self was not just the flesh and bone that she was used to...

Eleven

Nimbus clouds glowed in the sky as the sunlight illuminated them, sending golden shafts down onto the tranquil sea below, which lapped at the shoreline of the main island. It looked so peaceful, and yet looks could be deceiving.

A menacing shadow was cast over the water, which rippled slightly in the gentle breeze, as the dart shaped craft swept over the surface of Ragnor. Inside, eyes searched and scanners peered, but so far, all that they had found were the few scattered inhabitants going about their daily business. This was basically a farming community, with the small dome shaped buildings already having been searched.

Normally, it had been dedicated to improving the various crops grown here, and they had seen germination rooms full of hybrid specimens, Petri dishes growing cultures, and a variety of other equipment concerned with the task at hand. What they had also found were traces of the ones they sought, who had somehow fled in what appeared to be moments before they had arrived.

Now, they did a final sweep, just in case they had not been on the vessel they had detected racing away. This time they had eluded them, and maybe moved towards the edge of the sector, or it could be in stealth mode observing them?

One thing was for certain though, eventually they would be apprehended!

Nano robots, so small that they could hardly be detected, swam about inside the *Hybrid Reptilians* who had been created to resemble the Aesir. Their hive minds were processing information and transmitting it back to the sea of consciousness that formed the Artificial Intelligence dedicated to conquest, much like the Reptilians themselves. It was an easy partnership, which served their shared goals, although when this galaxy was secured, the Reptilians would perish along with everything else as the conquerors moved on to the next...

Ren felt as though her whole body was so heavy that it would sink right through the soft material of the pilot's chair, and that she would end up on the floor.

It was such a contrast to the weightlessness she had felt whilst connecting with the ship, and Gaia smiled, having felt the connection.

It was not bad for a first attempt!

Starfield was also pleased, although he still had his reservations due to her instability. Last time it had taken them what seemed like an eternity to find the right candidate, and then on their maiden flight she had lost control and bailed out, leaving them to crash-land on this obscure world.

Twenty years later, they had a new candidate, one who had not gone through the extensive screening process, although she did show potential.

"How are you feeling?"

Ren felt a bit dazed, but managed to mumble out a few words.

"Not bad!"

There was regret in her voice as she had felt something rather wonderful, and had now returned to her leaden body.

"Any news?"

She was hoping that her uncle and parents had contacted them, although that was unlikely with the dart shape craft circling overhead.

"All quiet!"

Ren had been assured that her presence could not be detected, although looking out towards the main viewing screen, she could see the intruders' craft in the distance, still apparently searching.

"What should we do next?"

Starfield rolled his holographic eyes.

"Rest!"

That did not seem such a bad idea, as she felt totally exhausted. It had taken a lot of energy to connect with Gaia, although she knew that she had only just scratched the surface. Gaia's systems were vast, and interfacing with them all would take time, time which they did not have...

Commander Bodil sighed as he continued to observe the long-range scanners, hoping that the intruders would soon depart. It seemed as though they were getting closer all the time, and they had only just managed to elude them. There was no telling just how far the Artificial Intelligence had advanced through his people, and he feared that some of the leaders had already been compromised. There was talk of another war with the Reptilians, one which would undoubtedly cost numerous lives. That was what they wanted though, as divide and rule was the order of the day. Once the Reptilians had wiped out all opposition, he knew that they would themselves face annihilation.

How badly had they been infected?

That was a question he could not answer, or for how long. The only certainty was the fact that it must be widespread and just like them seemed unstoppable. All hopes rested with his goddaughter, although it looked like nothing less than *divine intervention* would save them...

Twelve

Quiet, absolute quiet, so quiet in fact that the only sound was Ren's shallow breathing as she entered a very deep sleep. Starfield busied himself, searching for more information, whilst Gaia ran through a few diagnostics. The first attempt at connection had gone well, and the signs were promising. They were both encouraged by the young woman's progress, although that did not extend to the mission at hand. It seemed as though they were somehow going to have to battle with the enormity of the Artificial Intelligence, which again seemed ironic, as they were both, to a certain extent *artificial* themselves!

Being pitted against a galaxy, if not universally wide enemy, with only a handful of allies was not that appetizing.

"What do you think?"

Starfield sent a silent message using their connection.

Gaia left what she was doing for a moment to ponder the question.

"Well, I think we need to get her up to speed, and then assess just how widespread this infection really is."

That seemed reasonable.

"And what if it is already so virulent that our civilization is about to fall?"

That was a very good point!

"Then we will just have to get out of here!"

Starfield could not disagree, but unless the could gain control over Serenity, then there was no way in which they could...

Time slowly slipped by, as Gaia searched for the signal. It was not easy to find, and it was only with the information she had taken from Serenity's mind, without her knowing it, that she was able to gain access.

"Interesting!"

Starfield also studied it.

"Some sort of photonic code!"

Between them, they exchanged information rapidly, assessing the implications of what they had discovered.

"Yes, and there are 10,000 photons within each human cell!"

No wonder the signal was so hard to find!

"Each individual cell is made up almost entirely of memory, and that memory tells the cell what to do and how to do it, and photons carry that message."

The implications were astounding, and meant that just like projecting a laser light through a healthy cell of a particular organ and focusing that light on a damaged one, the DNA *brain* was able to utilize surrounding cells to repair that organ.

"And when the actual brain receives instructions, then the whole body will act accordingly!"

The Aesir were already able to grow *Replicants,* and transfer consciousness into them, but what if that consciousness was being altered on a cellular level, and more importantly, being controlled by an outside source?

"I think the first thing we ought to do is to transfigure Serenity into her *light body*, so that we can gain control of her!"

Ren felt a subtle shaking of her arm, which was enough to

bring her out of the deep sleep that she was in. Her mind had been swimming with information, as the streams of *ticker tape* ran past her closed eyes. Her mind had been awash with information, as her own photons processed part of what she had seen.

"Serenity?"

Starfield spoke gently, as Ren opened her eyes. No one called her *Serenity*, unless she was in trouble, and that was usually with her mother.

She lifted her eyelids slowly, not quite knowing where she was.

"Starfield?"

She could see him standing besides her wearing his best smile.

"Did you sleep well?"

Ren looked at him and he seemed to be overly charming, which contrasted somewhat to the looks he had given her previously.

"What do you want?"

She could sense that there was something going on, and although she had trusted him to administer the sedative, there was still something about him that worried her.

"Do you require nourishment?"

Come to think of it, her mouth was very dry, and she could not remember the last time that she had eaten anything.

"What do you have?"

Starfield smiled again.

"We have a matter generator which can produce a wide variety of liquids and foodstuffs."

She raised her eyebrows.

"Really?"

They were advanced machines that could reconstitute matter and produce virtually anything that was needed out of pure energy, but were very rare. The Aesir mostly ate fresh food, and matter generators were confined to industrial production or emergency supplies.

Starfield smiled again.

"How about scrambled eggs on toast and orange juice?"

They would not be fresh, but welcome nevertheless.

"OK."

He then bowed and scuttled off, and Ren got the distinct feeling that he was up to something.

Gaia's face then appeared on the main viewing screen.

"Welcome back!"

She also looked to be overly friendly.

Something was definitely going on!

Gaia then gave her an update on the intruders, who it seemed were still circling Ragnor. There had been no word from her parents or uncle Vil, and so she assumed that they were out there somewhere watching and waiting for the intruders to leave.

Starfield then reappeared with a small tray containing her food. She had not been asleep for that long, although it did feel like breakfast. Ren assumed that the protein in the eggs would give her energy, and vitamin C was always welcome.

He was acting like a servant, and from what she had observed about him so far, somewhat out of character.

Having said that though, the *breakfast* was most welcome...

Starfield was not the only one to be acting out of character, for Joan was patiently studying the scanners on the Commander's ship.

"So no sign of them leaving then?"

Joan had initially wanted to fight, and would have no doubt attacked the intruders if she had not been restrained. She was worried about her daughter, although it appeared that the intruders had not located either her or the ship yet.

"I'm afraid not!"

The Commander felt frustrated just sitting there, and even though he wished to blast them out of the sky, he knew that they had to remain in stealth mode.

"I wonder how she's getting along..."

Ren was enjoying her meal, being watched by Starfield and Gaia. They were definitely up to something, and as she finished off the orange juice, Starfield spoke again.

"I will take your tray if you want to freshen up."

He then scuttled off, leaving her bemused.

At first, there had definitely been an air of mistrust, which she could sense, although everything had happened so quickly that she had put her feelings to one side. Now that she began to think a little more about it, maybe there was more to her connection with the ship than she had initially thought?

Ren was still deep in contemplation when she left the pilot's seat, and moved through the front compartment door, back along the passageway she had travelled along earlier. There were doors to the side which she had not taken much notice of before, and in one of them, she could see Starfield clearing away the *breakfast* things. In another, there was a small bunkroom, and opposite that, there was what appeared to be a bathroom. The ship was not very big, but it appeared as though the designers had utilized every available space, and although the living quarters were compact, they were more than adequate for a vessel of this size.

Retrieving her gear from the cargo bay, Ren proceeded to the bathroom, where she took advantage of the shower.

Hot water cascaded down her body, washing away all the tension she had been feeling. It had been quite a day, and yet she let her thoughts drift away to something far more pleasant. Years of near constant travel had taken her all over the Aesir worlds, and although being taught to always be on her guard, sometimes there had been special moments, often involving her uncle Vil.

He was such a kind man and mentor, teaching her a variety of skills, from survival to combat, and to merge with her surroundings. There were many wonders to behold, the *Fires of Aurora,* the *Ice Fountains of Zol,* sunsets and rainbows that took your breath away, and so many unusual creatures that it was hard to list them all.

Oh, so many memories...

Back in the main control room, Gaia was also deep in contemplation.

"Do you think she is ready?"

Starfield shrugged his moon glass shoulders.

"She will have to be!"

He was looking outside at the dart shaped craft.

"Have they detected us yet?"

Gaia double-checked.

"Not so far, but even our cloaking device can only hide us for so long."

If they were going to get away then they had to gain control of Serenity.

"So, no time to waste then..."

Thirteen

All cleansed and with a relaxed mind, Ren made her way back towards the front of the ship, and as she entered the control room, she found Gaia and Starfield waiting for her.

"Feeling better?"

Starfield gave her another one of his simulated smiles, obviously being on his best behavior. Ren could see straight through him, literally, as it turned out.

His moon glass body was semi transparent after all!

"Yes, much better thank you!"

Ren was also on her best behavior as she realized what was at stake.

"Do you want to try and connect again?"

She nodded, slipping into the pilot's seat.

Starfield moved a little closer and began to explain a little more about the systems.

"What we have here is a box and chair arrangement. The box when opened provides a holographic representation of space and time. You can choose where you want to go, and then sit in the chair and think yourself there. Gaia will then open up a portal in space/time and you will be taken there."

That sounded incredible!

"Now comes the tricky part."

She knew that there would be a catch somewhere!

"We will not only move through space, but also time."

Ren gasped!

"It is possible for several timelines to coexist at the same *time,* although time itself likes to compact everything into one timeline, and so things spring back to the way they should be, so that there are as few time paradoxes as possible. Now then past and future time are fluid, and only the present is solid."

She was amazed!

Starfield continued.

"I'm sure you understand some of the physics involved."

Her father was a scientist after all!

Gravity is like a stream and contains the energy of thought and life itself, as well as keeping us on the ground. The key players here are photons, which are not just light or electromagnetic pulses, but also contain gravity, and gravity is the energy of electrical charge."

Ren listened intently.

"Now atoms are vibrations which have walls within them, that absorb light (photons) at different frequency rates. The whole atom is a magnetic vibration, and is an extremely energetic particle in all living matter. Atoms vibrate, and if you can change the vibratory state of a group of particles, then you can transform the material itself!"

That was basically how the matter transfer machine worked.

"A black hole and a sun are the same as an atom, and are all energy vortexes, powered by gravity. Gravity is flowing through an atom into a parallel universe and back again making the atom, and so gravity is the source of matter. Atoms are being powered by gravity, and gravity is the energy that feeds matter. Each atom is like a whirlpool and continues to have the same shape as gravity flows through it in the same way. Black holes are spheres, and Electro Magnetic energy is a white hole emerging within a spherical shape."

He pointed to the main viewing screen which was displaying a view of the outside.

"A sun is a black hole and the white light it emits is the event horizon. When you push against gravity, it causes inertia. There is a positive electrical charge in the nucleus of an atom and a negative charge in the electrons. If you create a strong enough electrical charge then you create gravitational thrust."

Gaia then took over.

"The universe consists of a super cool fluid that is in effect a form of quantum gravity. Gravity is actually alive and contains a *life force*. This *life force* is one conscious entity, that has reflected itself into countless pieces to experience *life* itself."

Things were now getting very technical!

"The physical reality in which we live in is in fact an illusion created by this single entity, which takes the form of a *merkabah*. Everything else is a reflection of this, being fractal in nature. It is a hologram and if you take a picture and cut it up into pieces, every piece is exactly the same."

Ren nodded.

"Space and time are generated by the vibration of this *merkabah*, and all matter is zooming around in the form of fractals so that you see the image of the whole cosmos in every single atom, at the tiniest level, and the five *Platonic Solids* (tetrahedron, cube, octahedron, dodecahedron, and icosahedron) form the resonance."

It had taken her years to understand the complexities of what her father had taught her, and now Ren felt as though she was having to learn it all over again.

"Every atom within it is like a mini black hole, with its own event horizon. The protons in the atoms form the corners of a geometric form that is created by resonance and vibration. The material that makes space and matter also drives time, and when you move beyond the speed of light, you enter a different reality, so gravity is in effect time, and as you approach the speed of light, your mass decreases until you have no mass at all, and all space exists at the same location."

Ren looked at the console and began to wonder what would happen to her when they powered up the craft.

"Everything is separated into seven dimensions or *densities.* Photons of light carry the information for that dimension and can transform the density of the dimension above when a higher density photon interacts with it. Each dimension has its own colour and tone (red, orange, yellow, green, blue, indigo and violet, C, D, E, F, G, A and B). These colours are also present in the human body via the chakra energy centres."

Ren thought about her uncle Vil, who was a deeply spiritual person, even though he used to be the leader of the *Titan Super Soldiers*. They were there to protect the people, a bit like the knights in shining armor of her mother's culture. She loved the time they spent together, and remembered when he had taught her to see the aura around a human body.

She was still thinking about him as Gaia continued her explanation.

"The universe only exists to you because you have *karma,* which are the memories of things that you regret doing, or that have hurt you. In order to move forward, you have to release this *karma* by forgiving those who upset you, and to make amends for the wrongs you have committed. Life is all about experience, and when you have experienced all that there is to experience over multiple lifetimes, and released your *karma,* then you are free to merge back with the universe."

Ren thought about all the things that she had done, and the temper tantrums that she had had. There was a very long list of them, and it felt as though she would be here for at least the next thousand years in order to put everything right!

"The universe or single entity has the desire to become one, as it split itself into countless pieces to experience life through all of us. There is no time, and what we consider as time is how we experience our lifetimes, as it is three-dimensional in that it has length, width and height, and as you move around, everything else is *relative* to the way that you experience it. Time exists because of the presence of matter, and is fed by time. This planet is only allowed to exist because the matter requires time to flow in, and when time/energy flows through a space it causes *clock time* to occur. Clock time is how we measure the planet's movement around the sun and within a solar system."

Ren looked at her watch, realizing that she had been here for quite a while.

"Time (gravity) is an energy which creates matter, reality, space and biological life and everything is time powered. Time creates and powers matter, time powers energy, time powers life!"

The digital display continued in its progression, as Gaia continued talking.

"Time is a mighty flow embracing all of the material processes within the universe, and all the processes taking place in these systems are forces feeding that flow, which is in the form of *waves* or *ripples*. These *waves* are *whirlpools*, which are ripples within gravity. They are shaped like a donut, and spin much like water going down a plug hole, only it spins out on the other side."

Ren thought about the lovely warm shower, and how the water had swirled around the base before disappearing into the recycling system.

"These whirlpools are an energy not bound by speed of light, life and consciousnesses creates these fields the same way that physical processes create them. When you move through space your atoms speed up and so if you return to this planet you return into the future because your atoms have sped up, but you do not notice it because everything is relative to you, and you do not notice the change as everything around you is moving at the same speed and time!"

Ren began to grasp the principles involved. It was heavy stuff, and she wondered why she was being told all of this?

"So time flows into a system though a *cause* to an *effect,* and *matter* goes through a *phase shift* and kicks off waves of time and changes the way it flows."

Gaia gave a warm smile.

"Yes, there is an impression that time is pulled inside by a *cause* and gets denser at the location of the *effect.* In every process of nature, time can be formed or spent. As time slows down energy is leaving an area, and as time speeds up it is entering an area."

Ren suddenly realised why she had been given this lecture, as Gaia was in effect a *time machine*...

Fourteen

A sense of peace and tranquillity spread throughout Ren's body as she relaxed into the soft, comfortable material of the pilot's chair. All of the science had given her a slight headache, and now that Starfield and Gaia had finally quietened, it gave her a chance to try to make sense of everything they had told her.

It was still hard to believe that they were fully conscious, and she wondered what they were like in corporeal form. Ren could visualise Gaia as being quite beautiful, judging by the image of herself she chose to display. Starfield on the other hand, she could imagine as being a bit eccentric and maybe a bit shifty too!

Thinking more about things, Ren herself was not what you might call *normal,* having three different species of humanoid fused into her DNA. She had blonde hair and turquoise eyes just like her father, her mother's temperament, and a slightly elongated skull, which is why she had dreadlocks to hide the slight bulge at the back. It had never really bothered her that much, but the benefits were a slightly enlarged brain capacity, which had been sorely stretched over the past half hour.

So, there was no space, there was no time, only awareness. Space was empty, and emptiness was awareness. Anything that you thought you saw around you was just emptiness, and that emptiness was made of awareness.

It was an odd thought that she did not really exist, only in her thoughts which made her conscious, and actually be here. If she dealt with all of the issues within her mind and gained ultimate peace, then she would not exist at all, not even in her own thoughts. She would be nothing but a rainbow of colours all rapped up in a white light of photonic energy that would merge with the universe. However, it was merging with the ship that was her main concern.

Slipping her hands back into the pods on the arms of the pilot's chair, she sank even more deeply into the soft material, wondering what she would encounter next.

There would be no sedative administered this time, just a sense of peace and calm. Her uncle Vil had taught her to meditate, and so that was what she was going to do in order to make the connection. He was such a contradiction, on the one hand a fearsome warrior, and yet capable of such kind and gentle behaviour. She always felt as though her troubles slipped away whenever she was in his presence, and she was still thinking about him when she felt a slight tingle in her fingertips.

Ren prepared herself to go back into the darkness which she now knew was alive. This time she sensed it churning slowly and gently, and appeared to have a slightly curved surface, which arched right over and above her head, forming a dome just like the buildings she and her parents had been living in for the past few weeks.

Where it had been almost totally black before, this time she could see it a little better, and she was soon visualizing the twin screens in the middle, that enabled her to see the inside of the ship. The area around her seemed smaller somehow, as before it looked like it went on forever.

Out of the blackness, the *ticker tape* returned, only this time it was a myriad colours which danced and swirled turning into a type of electrified liquid. Millions of different shapes were soon flowing in a geometric dance, so smoothly they had the appearance of a fluid.

It was so beautiful to look at!

The shapes on reaching her eyes felt as though they were inside her head, which in a way they were, yet somehow appearing before her at the same time.

Automatically, her focus expanded outwards as the colours and swirls settled, and her mind reshaped her perceptions until she began to understand. What was not physical was shown to be physical, a reality she needed to comprehend if she was going to interact with Gaia. Ren could now see it as a room, and see herself naked within it. She quickly visualised herself clothed, as the last thing she wished for was for Gaia or Starfield to see her like that!

There was no time to spend reorganising her swirling consciousness, as she needed to move beyond herself and into the holographic brain of the ship. The intruders were still outside somewhere and her parents and uncle, and indeed the Empire was counting on her. Somehow, she would have to gain control of the ship, and then search for a blood sample so that her father could analyse what they were up against.

It was a daunting prospect, and Ren began to doubt whether she would be able to do it. Her doubts then began to increase, and before she realised it, they had manifested into fear!

Ren realised how dangerous all this could be, and maybe even deadly not just for her, but for those she cared about too.

Fear then began to get a hold of her, and Ren wished that she had been more prepared, but there had been so little time. Fear quickly turned into an aggressor, as she fought against herself, which was what must have happened to Helgar, the previous pilot. She now had partial access to Gaia's memories, and could see the internal battle Helgar had fought within herself.

Her mind had created a monster, a giant Reptilian which was chasing after her, as Helgar tried to get away.

Ren could then see her fighting for her life, as the psychic skirmish reached its bitter end, and then Helgar suddenly breaking the connection.

The last anyone saw of her was Helgar opening the emergency exit and jumping out into space!

Ren shuddered, as the last thing she wanted was the same thing to happen to her, particularly as the emergency exit was covered in undergrowth and would probably not open anyway!

Taking several deep breathes, she tried to calm herself before her consciousness manifested a monster. It took considerable effort, and Ren thought about the love she had for her uncle Vil, and as she did so, the light winked out, and the untamed colours of her consciousness disappeared, leaving only darkness.

Ren was now running on *autopilot*, just like her body had to do when she left it behind. It breathed by itself, her heart pumped blood by itself, as her subconscious mind took care of those sorts of things.

She had now successfully disrupted the fear thought process, which was a natural part of her personality. The subconscious mind not influencing her conscious decisions by manifesting a monster!

Eventually, neurons and synapses worked to correct the sensation, and as they did so, she moved further inside Gaia's holographic brain.

Ren could now begin to sense the power of endless potential, unencumbered by her physical form, literally feeling the weight lifting off her shoulders. Internal processes flashed by, and she felt as though she was beginning to pilot another body.

This body, instead of being flesh and blood, was one constructed almost entirely out of moon glass, and powered by light itself. She could see Gaia gliding across the stars like she was born amongst them, not running on mechanical engines and volatile fuel. She was staggeringly beautiful and amazingly complex, yet conscious just like any other living being...

Fifteen

The repetitive monotone bleeping of ground penetrating radar caught an anomaly, so subtle that those onboard the dart shaped craft nearly missed it. It appeared as though the undergrowth had been disturbed, and that there was something unusual down there.

Protocol dictated that they observed, as this could well be the first sign of the craft and occupants they had been so painstakingly searching for...

Way down there under the sensor sweep, Ren sat in the pilot's chair moving ever deeper into Gaia's mind. It was fascinating, and in amongst the ship's systems she came across what appeared to be distant memories of some kind. She could see her in her corporeal form, offering her mind to the project, to form a union so different from anything a human had ever experienced before.

Gaia had thought that it was so odd that her people were advanced enough to transfer themselves into a *Reptilian* body, and yet as they were so afraid of Artificial Intelligence.

Volunteers had been called for, and the consciousness of two individuals were chosen and downloaded into the Holo Droid shell and the ships computer respectively.

Artificial people were not regarded as equals in this semi-utopian society, and petty snobbery existed within those who rejected the consciousness transfer process. It did however, offer a completely new type of existence, which attracted some with a sense of adventure, just like Starfield and Gaia.

It was amazing that the whole vessel was not only alive, but that you could communicate directly, talk to it with your own mind.

What was inside did not look like much, fibre optic cables and organic liquid, but Ren could actually feel Gaia's thoughts and see her memories, just like being inside someone else's head. It was like having a multiple personality disorder, which she had to admit, was a little disturbing at first.

Ren's body gave a slight shudder, as it was taking her a little while to get used to being outside of her own body. She could feel empathy, what it was like to give up your body, and the wonder of experiencing something that could traverse the stars.

The propulsion system consisted of a liquid mercury plasma engine on a magnetic field disrupter, which was also fascinating, and something her father would have been engrossed in for quite some considerable length of time. She could almost hear his words, as he sat explaining the principles to her.

"When an electrical current flows, gravity flows along with it. If you get a high enough electrical charge then you get enough gravity to counteract mass and create levitation. If you get a negatively charged electrical plate at the base of a craft, then at the top you have a ball of positive charge, (positive pole) then you get a flow from negative to positive to create a whirlpool field which gives you gravitational thrust."

He may have known the theory, but as yet she doubted that he had ever seen its practical application.

Ren was now in possession of something that when she visualised where she wanted to go, then theoretically, she could just hop anywhere she wished...

Starfield was busily observing her, noticing subtle changes in her physiology. For a start, Ren's pale skin had already become somewhat translucent, and she had a white sheen around her. This was a clear indication that she was transfiguring, and as both he and Gaia continued to monitor her, Ren continued to change. The next thing to happen was that she began to glow, and that glow intensified, as out of the bright white sheen came a multicoloured aura which extended right around her body.

Starfield was very encouraged by this, as it meant that her *light body* was emerging, and that the connection was strengthening. Soon, all he could see of her body were her blue eyes which focused on him.

"Starfield?"

He smiled when she spoke to him, as Ren was now both here and there, able to merge with Gaia and still remain in contact with him.

"I think that I have managed to do it!"

Ren felt exhilarated, as she had now established a type of telepathy with Gaia, which meant that she could see what she saw within her mind, and feel her emotions.

"Welcome to my essence Serenity!"

She had managed to *tune in*!

"Wow!"

Ren had never felt anything like this before..."

Outside, others had also noticed something, as they continued to scan the area. They could not detect Gaia due to her stealth technology, but they were able to access the disturbances in the ground. There were definite signs of activity, and in particular, focusing on the undergrowth, they had now identified a footprint. This appeared to be someone with relatively small feet, which ruled out Halvor, and maybe the *Dragon Slayer* too.

The only logical conclusion was that it was what intelligence suggested was their daughter Serenity...

Ren could talk to Gaia, pick up on her emotions, and Gaia could also pick up on hers, and it felt like there was an infinite expanse surrounding her. Ren's mind was floating in that infinity, and she was also a part of it, endless and unconfined.

Swirls of colour swam around her, though she was also part of them. She was empty, but she was also whole, somehow split into a billion pieces and yet she was also complete. All her desires and needs, worries and fears, simply vanished as she floated on the very edge of her consciousness.

Way out there somewhere, a disruption appeared in the ever-evolving patterns which surrounded her, and Ren could feel that they were not alone. The colours churned faster, until, another voice echoed within in her mind.

The sounds seemed to bathe her in cool waters and envelope her in such feelings of security and warmth that she hardly noticed a distant voice calling out to her.

"Welcome Serenity."

Whatever it was appeared to be greeting her, and Ren could feel a presence.

"You are in the Void."

How strange!

That was an answer to a question she was about to ask!

The voice then spoke again.

"We have been waiting for you..."

Sixteen

The cool waters of security and warmth seemed to wrap themselves even more tightly around her body, as a wave of consciousness seemed to extend towards Ren.

There was a floating shadow out there, and when she began to focus on it, she realised that the shadow was in fact a creature of light.

Intricate patterns spiralled from its centre, and slender thread like structures fanned out into wings. It then began to fly towards her, and as it did so, Ren could see the wings in closer detail, with patterns that looked as though they had been painted at a microscopic level.

The being then began to transfigure itself until it assumed a vaguely human form, as it closed in and slowly stopped in front of her.

It resembled a watercolour representation of a human being, with hands but no defined fingers, a mouth but no teeth or tongue, an the outline of eyes but no irises.

"I am *Mjolnir*, known as the war hammer of the god of thunder and protector of Midgard."

Ren nearly fainted when it spoke in a powerful yet subtle voice.

"I am one of the *Ancients,* an interdimensional light being millions of years in advance of you that is able to switch my photons and atoms into any form I choose, and to travel through time and space at will."

That sounded cool!

"I can go from a light body to a corporeal body, by changing my frequency at will to go to another dimension, and can phase in or out of multiple dimensions at any given time by my own will. However, when I so choose, I fall under the laws of that dimensional reality, which is why you were chosen."

For the second time in just a few short moments, Ren thought that she was going to faint!

"There is an Artificial Intelligence almost as old as the universe which is spreading like a virus. A mass coronal ejection cleansed Midgard, as it is the natural response of a living universe to cleanse this infection, but that will not be happening here. So, I brought your mother through the sacred stones so that you could be born to help cleanse the infection from this part of the galaxy."

Ren remembered the story, but this cast it in a completely new light.

"The key to understanding and defeating it, is that it was originally created by the *Archons,* who were then just like us in corporeal form. When they made the transition, they discovered that they could feed off *fear* like energy vampires. We on the other hand, discovered that we could feed off the opposite emotion *love*."

It sounded like the eternal battle between good and evil!

"This virus is spreading so much fear that the *Archons* have become far more powerful than we are, and we have been losing the battle against them."

Ren could now see the enormity of the problem.

The *Ancients* could do many things, but were hindered by the fact that they lost a lot of their powers if they came down to this dimension, whereas, the *Archons* had no need to because they had created an Artificial Intelligence to do the work for them. Tiny nano robots controlled the Reptilians to help spread fear which was feeding them, and between the two, they were rapidly taking over the entire universe.

"Your people are so wary of Artificial Intelligence, that we cannot encourage them to create one to counter the threat. When we attempted to do so, that project was destroyed, and only Gaia and Starfield remain."

The situation looked hopeless!

"We do have a plan though, but we need your cooperation to carry it out..."

A new type of signal flashed across the sensors of those hovering in the distance. Alarms sounded as the hybrids detected the presence of their sworn enemy, an *Ancient*...

Seventeen

Ren suddenly felt her seat vibrate, as a purple flash illuminated the control room, as the dart shaped craft unleashed a barrage of fire. Everything seemed to go into slow motion, as the *Ancient* quickly departed, and Gaia began to power up her systems.

The ground outside began to boil, sending off a cloud of steam and debris as the laser pulses glanced off her shields.

Then, seemingly out of nowhere, Commander Bodil appeared, getting a weapons lock on the other vessel. Throwing both the gravimetrics and thrusters to full, he swung into a tight, high-speed dive with his ship's nose pointing squarely at the intruders. He then squeezed the trigger on his joystick, pelting the target with a barrage of blue streaks.

But, before he could finish, it took evasive action, as it was raked with fire, and he also launched a missile.

The dart shaped craft quickly returned fire, and his shield lit up with the impact, as he also took evasive action.

Streaks of laser pulses shot out from both vessels, as the missile came in on a long sweep. It was one of the latest smart models, which homed in on its target.

The dart shaped craft twisted and turned in the sky trying to avoid the missile, and as it did so, it suddenly plunged towards the ground.

Ren could see everything, and gasped as she watched both the intruders craft and the missile heading straight for them.

Time went back into slow motion as she frantically began to search Gaia's systems, but it was no use. There simply was no time to do anything, and she felt helpless as they both careered towards her.

Then at the last minute, the dart shaped craft pulled up, leaving just the missile hurtling towards Gaia's outer shell.

There was not time to even scream, as there was a massive explosion which rocked her in her seat, nearly throwing her out onto the floor.

Millions of tiny stars flashed before her eyes, as Ren caught a glance at Starfield, whose molecules swam about in a similar fashion.

Commander Bodil cursed, as he detonated his missile just above the ship, hoping that her shields would hold. These intruders were good, and he swept across the sky in pursuit, firing off laser pulses as he went.

Purple and blue light lit up the sky as the battle continued, and below, Ren struggled to pull herself together.

"Shields down to 31%!"

Gaia's muffled voice rang out, as Starfield tried to do something to help. They had never faced actual combat before, and the simulations they had run had been over twenty years ago.

She managed to bring up the targeting system, and Ren could see some crosshairs floating in front of her.

"You must visualize laser fire flowing from the ship and in your mind move the crosshairs to where you want it to go."

Starfield looked anxious, holding his moon glass arms out and giving her a pleading look.

Ren did her best, although her mind was still awash with all that she had seen. It was very difficult to focus on anything, let alone moving the crosshairs, particularly having just encountered an *Ancient!*

"Concentrate!"

Starfield's voice rang out, as he started waving his arms about frantically, pointed at the main viewing screen.

She tried really hard, and the crosshairs did move slightly.

Outside, laser pulses flashed, as the two vessels made incredible high-speed maneuvers. They were both excellent pilots, and Ren's parents were thrown about in their seats as they watched helplessly as the drama unfolded.

"Serenity!"

Their words echoed Starfield's, as she tried to do as he had asked.

Ren felt her mind beginning to clear, as she concentrated, trying not to think about anything else but the crosshairs. They began to move more rapidly now, and she was able to follow the dart shaped craft. But, it was zigzagging all over the place, making it almost impossible to follow.

"Concentrate!"

Starfield was going frantic, as a few stray laser pulses hit them.

Ren felt the shields losing power, and in desperation, she focused everything she had on the intruders' vessel.

The crosshairs shot around wildly, somehow locking onto it, and as they did so, Starfield shouted out.

"Fire!"

Undergrowth and soil exploded in a vast cloud smothering their view, and Starfield placed his hand over his holographic eyes thinking that they had been hit again, and fearing that Gaia would shatter into millions of pieces.

Then, all of a sudden, everything went very quiet...

Eighteen

Shimmering pulses of light lit up the sky, as beams shot out from the ground right into the path of the dart shaped craft. The beams then raked across the side of the ship, ripping a long, gaping hole until they connected with the engines. Commander Bodil watched as it lost power suddenly plummeting towards the ground...

Ren sat there holding her breath, half expecting them to erupt in a fireball, but strangely nothing happened.

Starfield also waited, not daring to look!

If he had done, then he would have seen a green dot flashing near the top of the main viewing screen, and a red one rapidly descending towards them.

The dart shaped craft had lost almost all power, and those onboard were struggling to control their descent.

The Commander watched, not quite believing what he was seeing.

"Serenity has somehow managed to knock out their engines!"

His words were spoken with a sense of relief and pride.

Halvor felt exactly the same, whereas Joan only felt anger. She wanted to rip the intruders apart with her bare hands for having tried to kill her daughter.

Commander Bodil could see the madness in her eyes, and did his best to try and calm her down.

"She has done very well, but remember we need to acquire a blood sample so that Halvor can create some sort of nano testing device."

He nodded his head, whereas Joan formed two fists, making her knuckles turn white.

They all watched as the dart shaped craft tried to level out, as its emergency thrusters spluttered into life. It was going down, and as the ground rose up to meet it, the front end ploughed into the thick undergrowth, sending out a shower of soil and plant life in a massive wave.

Commander Bodil then brought them down close to the intruder's craft, which had now ground to a halt...

Starfield suddenly realized that they had not exploded and gingerly opened his eyes, Gaia now free of most of the undergrowth thanks to the laser pulses which had impacted on her shields, was able to focus on the two vessels.

Ren breathed out a huge sigh of relief, for not only had they survived, but also her uncle Vil's ship had now landed a short distance away. It looked to be intact, and therefore all of the occupants must be OK.

That was not quite the case, as her mother was consumed with rage. The Commander could do nothing, for as soon as they touched down, Joan released her seat restraints, and dashed towards the exit.

He glanced towards Halvor who looked equally as shocked, as she ripped open a panel grabbing the fire axe it contained. Then before either of them could say anything, she pulled the emergency release mechanism and the hatch opened and she jumped out...

Starfield caught a glimpse of someone leaving the other vessel, and as Gaia zoomed in on them, he suddenly recognized who it was - the *Dragon Slayer*.

"Mother!"

Ren could also see her, and gasped along with Starfield, as in her right hand they could clearly see the fire axe...

The Commander released his restraints, and together with Halvor they made their way towards the emergency hatch. Jumping down, they could see that Jaon was already some distance ahead and had already reached the stricken vessel.

Someone inside had opened a hatch, and four figures ran out to meet her...

What happened next would haunt Starfield for the rest of his life. He had always been such a peaceful soul, and what he witnessed would cause him many a sleepless night.

A laser pulse shot out just missing Joan, as she swung the axe decapitating the nearest intruder.

Starfield gasped as the colour drained from his holographic face.

In a swift movement, Joan cut the next one almost in half, seeing nothing but a red mist in front of her eyes. She had crossed the line into madness, one she had been straddling for years. The other two intruders froze, shocked at the sight of two of their number being butchered to death.

Starfield was horrified as the *Barbarian* ploughed into the next.

There was blood and gore everywhere, which proved too much for him, and Starfield actually fainted, which was something that a Holo Droid was not supposed to do!

Even Ren had to look away!

She knew that her mother had quite a temper, but she never envisioned that it could get so out of control.

No wonder she had slain the *White Royal Reptilian,* as even though it must have been physically far superior to her, faced with such madness, she doubted if anything could have survived.

Gaia was speechless, retreating deep within herself also shocked to the core.

Commander Bodil managed to reach Joan, just as the last intruder fell, and was equally shocked. He looked at Halvor, pitying the poor soul married to that!

For some unknown reason Halvor seemed to be taking it in his stride, as whatever his wife did he would always love and support her, such was their bond.

He just stood there and shrugged his shoulders.

"Well, you did say that we required a blood sample..."

Epilogue

"I don't think that I will ever be the same again!"

Starfield was being comforted by Gaia, as Ren made her way towards her parents, and her uncle Vil.

"I want to be shut down for another twenty years!"

Gaia had to admit that it was quite an appealing idea.

What if Serenity turned out like that?

Starfield then began to shake.

"They do say that if you want to know what a girl will be like when she gets older, then look at her mother!"

That was what Ren was doing, as Commander Bodil met her, wrapping his arms around her and ushering her away.

"I was so worried about you."

She rested her head on his shoulder, feeling safe and secure.

"What will happen now?"

Vilgot sighed.

"We will have to sedate your mother."

That went without saying!

"And what about the Artificial Intelligence?"

He gently eased her back towards Gaia.

"We will ask your father to devise some sort of detector, and then maybe if you feel up to it, we can try and ascertain just how far and wide this virus has spread."

The Commander knew that Ren needed a distraction, to take her mind off what she had just witnessed.

"How was it connecting with the ship?"

She managed a half smile.

"Interesting!"

It certainly was.

"I somehow also managed to connect with an *Ancient*."

The Commander suddenly stopped.

"Really?"

There were only a few others in his people's entire history that had had the privilege.

"Yes, and he said his name was *Mjolnir.*"

Vilgot's mouth fell open.

"The war hammer of the god of thunder and protector of Midgard?"

She nodded her head.

"That's who he said he was, he also said that he had been waiting for me, and that he was the one to bring my mother here via the sacred stones."

The Commander knew the story well.

"That is indeed a great honour."

The *Ancients* were venerated amongst his people

"I always told you that you were special."

Ren looked adoringly into his eyes.

"He also said that they had a plan, but need my help to carry it out..."

The Empress and the Violet Flame

I am the violet flame, in action in me now, I am the violet flame. To light alone I bow, I am the violet flame. In mighty cosmic power, I am the light of God, shining every hour, I am the violet flame. Blazing like a sun, I am God's sacred power freeing every one.

Elizabeth Clare

Introduction

Flickering stars danced across Starfield's eyes, as his holographic matrix ebbed and flowed in a cacophony of trauma, and utter disbelief. His poor mind could not come to terms with what he had just witnessed, as the *Barbarian* unleashed a brutalized assault on the intruders far worse than he could ever have imagined.

Warfare was by its very nature brutal, but in his mind, he thought that there were limits to that brutality.

Sadly, Starfield had been wrong!

He then found a warning in his database.

Terrans are considered hostile, dangerous and aggressive.

Well he could certainly testify to that...

One

Pale sunlight filtered through the ship's outer hull, refracting off Starfield's moon glass shell. Gaia, his life partner and ship's computer was silent, also traumatized by the events which had just unfolded. She was very concerned about his mental state, as well as that of her own.

More information flowed, as she reached into his mind via their unique connection.

The Dragon Slayer formerly known as Joan Tutwiler, often referred to as General Swatz's Rottweiler - his Personal Assistant.

A Rottweiler is a breed of domestic dog, regarded as medium-to-large or large, originating in a place referred to as Germany, and the name is translated as meaning butchers' dog, because their main use was to herd livestock and pull carts laden with butchered meat to market.

Rottweilers have been selected for guard and protection work and this must be kept in mind at all times.

Aggression can be a problem, and this dog is fully capable of inflicting severe damage...

Trauma and disbelief then began to flow through her systems too!

The fiber optic cables woven into her outer layers transmitted images of the *Barbarian* being led away from the carnage she had created, and it was with some relief that she was sedated by Commander Bodil, and then her husband Halvor gently guided her into the Commander's craft.

Their new pilot and daughter of the aforementioned *Barbarian* known as *Serenity* of all things, was being guided back towards them, also it appeared, in a state of shock.

"Don't let her in!"

Starfield was trembling, which was not the sort of behaviour associated with an Artificial Person.

"Normally, I would totally agree with you, but under these mitigating circumstances, we have little choice!"

Gaia was thinking about the intruders who it was assumed were *Hybrid Reptilians*, an even more brutal species.

"They tried to destroy us, and if we stay here, then more will arrive and we will be atomized."

Starfield felt as though he already had!

Commander Bodil then left Ren by the open hatch, kissing her on the forehead.

"We must depart soon, but before we do I have a few things to attend to."

That was an understatement, and it would take some explaining!

For a start, his three closest friends were supposed to be dead, and they were so deeply undercover, or so he thought, that he still had to hide evidence of their existence. Somehow, they had been discovered, and there would no doubt be others appearing soon. He had to cleanse the scene, and then depart before the authorities made an appearance.

But how was he going to explain the bloodbath?

The Commander was no stranger to battle, but even he found the scene overwhelming. He watched Halvor escort Joan into his ship, as he began to take a few blood samples. When he had asked, he had never envisioned quite so much!

For many lifetimes, Vilgot had battled hostile forces across the galaxy, and faced many formidable adversaries, but in all his time, he had never experienced anything quite like this.

Looking at the smoldering craft, he had to admit that Joan fueled his fires of fear!

Taking a deep breath, he collected his samples before moving towards what was left of the intruder's vessel. It was largely intact, although there was considerable hull damage. Some of it had been caused by the impact, and there was a deep trough where it had careered along the ground. The remainder had been down to Serenity, who had not only managed to get the experimental craft to fire, but had pinpointed it directly to the engines, burning them out.

He felt both proud and relieved that his goddaughter had succeeded and survived relatively unscathed...

Ren slowly ventured inside Gaia, wondering what she was going to do now?

She was used to her mother's outburst, but it was one thing to see her shouting and screaming, but quite another to witness her descend into total madness!

Making her way towards the main control room, she felt as though life would never be the same again. Today had marked a transformation, and not a particularly pleasant one at that.

Moving through the doorway, she could see Starfield cowering in a corner, his molecules an ashen shade of white. He was trembling and looked as though he might shatter into a thousand pieces at any moment. Ren went to move towards him, but he backed as far away as he could. Gaia did not show her face either, as Ren slumped into the pilot's seat, putting her head in her hands...

Moving through the open hatch, the Commander could see that it was now empty, and shuddered as he thought of how the four-man crew had met their end. He was here to gather as much information as he could, and in the shortest possible time. He would not have long, but being so familiar with this sort of vessel, he was soon able to interface with its onboard computer.

Taking a device out of his pocket, he clipped it in place and started a download. It would take a few minutes, and so whilst he was waiting, he began to search the various compartments for anything that may prove useful and advantageous in his peoples fight against this hidden enemy...

Two

Green, blue and red lights flickered on the console, as information was downloaded, whilst Commander Bodil worked his way through the vessel. Everything seemed standard, and what he would have expected a four man craft to contain. There did not appear to be anything unusual, and he surmised that it must have been recently taken from the Aesir Security Service main complex.

That begged the question.

Had they been compromised, and if so by how much?

There was not time to ponder, as he had to get away from here as soon as possible.

Returning to the main control room, he noticed that the data transfer was complete. Taking the little device out of where it had been attached, he slipped it into his pocket, and proceeded to the exit.

Vilgot grimaced at the scene which met him, and taking a deep breath, he decided that the best course of action was to gather the Hybrid's remains and place them back inside the craft. Then he was going to set the self-destruct mechanism, so that as much evidence as possible could be removed. Hopefully other Aser Security Service members would arrive, and if he were lucky then they would take their time in attempting to solve this mystery.

Time was something however, that was in short supply...

It was not time, but hope that seemed in short supply, as Ren wondered what was going to happen next. She removed her hands from her face, and caught Starfield staring at her.

She felt dreadful, knowing how her mother's behaviour had traumatized him. This had been her first experience of Artificial Intelligence, and although her people had an innate fear of it, it looked as though they had even more fear of *Terrans...*

Commander Bodil looked down at his bloodstained armored suit and grimaced. He was no stranger to hand to hand combat, although it was usually fought with energy weapons which cauterized wounds. Somehow, it felt a bit more civilized than using a fire axe, even though tremendous loss of life could occur. It just felt wrong somehow, and yet Joan had saved him from possible injury or even death.

Maybe he was just getting too old for all of this?

Over seven hundred Earth years had passed, many *Replicant* bodies, and more than a little adventure. He was supposed to have retired, and had only accepted the title of *Supreme Commander* to safeguard the lives of his closest friends.

The timer had been set, and so he could not think of such matters now, as they had to get away before the intruders vessel exploded.

Once inside his craft, he checked briefly on Halvor and Joan. Joan was now asleep, and Halvor was resting nearby. He looked drawn and as if the previous events had taken every last bit of energy he possessed. Vilgot admired his strength of character, being equally as strong as his wife, but in a totally different way.

The pilot's seat was an old friend, just like his passengers, and he quickly patched into Serenity's secure communicator.

"How are you feeling?"

He already knew the answer, but felt as though he had to ask.

"Struggling!"

He realized that she was like a child caught up in an adult world.

"We have to get away, can you make it to the secure location we talked about?"

Ren looked at Starfield, who was in no state to help.

"I doubt it!"

The Commander sighed, expecting her reply. He would have to tow them, and hope that his ship had enough power...

A faint green light soon engulfed Gaia, as she slowly lifted off the ground. This had been her first movement for over twenty years, and there was a hole in the undergrowth where she had lain. He would have to disguise that too, as this mission had to retain as much secrecy as possible.

Ren felt a sudden surge, as Gaia popped out of the hole she had formed in the undergrowth, like a cork out of a bottle. Then there was a sudden rush as they sprang up into the air. Starfield felt his molecules scrambling as Gaia trembled along with him. She was free at last, although there was no celebration. They were both in trouble and felt as though it may have been better to have not been discovered at all!

The Commander tried to stabilize the tractor beam, adjusting to compensate for the extra power he had used to pull the ship clear of the ground. He could see that Gaia had left quite a hole, and so he dropped one of his bombs, which sailed out of the little compartment underneath his vessel.

The small metallic object sailed past Gaia, diving towards the hole she had left. Then, before anyone within the ship could react, there was an explosion.

"Flux!"

For the first time in his life, Starfield swore, as he nearly jumped out of his moon glass skin.

Ren and Gaia were equally shocked, more so by his language than the explosion.

"Starfield!"

His particles turned a deep red as they swam around inside his head.

Then, before he could say anything else, there was another explosion which ripped through the undergrowth as the intruders vessel self-destructed.

"Fluuu!"

Starfield fainted halfway through another obscenity, slipping to the ground as his molecules went ashen white, just as they had done before.

Ren, who was also shocked by the double explosions, got up off the pilot's seat, moving across to see what she could do for him....

Meanwhile, Vilgot surveyed the ground, relatively pleased with the debris field. A lot of the evidence had been destroyed, and hopefully there would be nothing left to connect them with the intruders. Yes, there would be an investigation, and hopefully a cover story would be put in place, and no further questions asked, or would there...

Three

The faint green bubble of the magnetic field disrupter continued to surround both craft, as the liquid mercury plasma engines hummed in contentment, in complete contrast to those being towed behind the Commander's vessel.

"Get away from me you young savage!"

Starfield tried to push Ren away, having regained consciousness.

"I promise I won't hurt you."

Ren could see how disturbed he was, which was something that she shared.

"My mother's sick."

So was Starfield, sick of humans!

"You *Terrans* are part Reptilian, and you're all sick!"

Ren could see how upset he was, and never envisioned a Holo Droid having such strong emotions.

"What do you mean?"

Starfield's particles glowed red.

"The *Anunnaki* who created you may have looked like pale skinned humans, but they were also *Hybrid Reptilians*, just like the ones who tried to kill us!"

She had to admit that that was a fair point, and remembered how upset she had been when her father had told her about her linege. The Aesir were pure human, and she could understand his feelings to a certain extent. Terran fetuses initially looked Reptilian for the first few weeks of life until the human genes took over, the Reptilian brain controlled the body's vital functions such as heart rate, breathing, body temperature and balance. It consisted of the brainstem and the cerebellum, and although reliable, it tended to be rigid and compulsive, much like her and her mother!

"Not all Reptilians are bad."

Starfield grimaced.

"The ones I've encountered are!"

He was having what she considered to be a *tantrum*, something again *Holo Droids* were not supposed to be able to have.

"Well, nobody's perfect!"

With that, Ren moved away from him, to sit back in the pilot's seat. Arguing was getting them nowhere, and she realized that if they were ever to get anywhere, then they had to work together...

Commander Bodil was pleased to see Halvor emerge after settling down Joan. She had now gone into a deep sleep, and he had eventually managed to remove the last traces of blood off her, and more importantly the fire axe which she had been clinging onto.

"How are you feeling?"

Halvor sighed.

"Don't ask!"

Over the years, he had had quite a lot to deal with, and even his great patience had been sorely tested, particularly today.

"Did you manage to gain any information from the intruder's ship?"

Vilgot realized that he needed a distraction, and burying himself in work would be both beneficial and therapeutic.

"As a matter of fact I did."

He reached into his pocket and removed the small storage device handing it over.

Halvor gladly took it, looking forward to amercing himself in the data streams.

His organic computer was in his rucksack, which had been hastily packed when they fled the dome shaped buildings, and retrieving it, he sat next to his old friend and inserted the storage device. Vilgot smiled to himself, relieved to see that Halvor appeared not to have been too deeply affected by his wife's madness.

Joan may have had her failings, but she was basically a good person, and someone who he would be glad to have on his side whenever he went into battle. This battle however, spanned the Aesir worlds, if not the entire galaxy, and maybe even most of the universe too.

Reams of data flowed past Halvor's eyes, as he studied the information he had been given. Most of it was just the usual ships systems, but every now and then, he came across something a little more interesting. It was like having a jigsaw puzzle, but without the picture on the front of the box. He was essentially going in blind, but years of experience had taught him where to look for any possible leads.

Slowly, the picture began to emerge as he pieced the pieces together. There was a hidden network connecting all of the hybrids together, although the way they communicated was a bit fragmented owing to the algorithms designed within the security function. He had to try to bridge the gaps, and as he did so, more of the network was revealed.

"Anything interesting?"

The Commander leaned over, as he steered both craft towards another secure location, which he hoped this time would not be breached as easily as the last. It was a constant battle, particularly as the Aesir Security Service appeared to have been compromised.

"You could say that!"

Vilgot did not know whether to be excited or worried.

"They have an operative in the Royal Court, and the Empress may be in grave danger..."

Four

The rough pockmarked surface of a small planetoid filled the main viewing screen, as Commander Bodil brought both craft down towards an automated transmitter, which was the only structure it contained. Within the small building there was modest accommodation for the maintenance engineers who visited it periodically, and hopefully it would provide a temporary refuge. Still within this solar system, it was the only place he could think of, as they needed a base to analyze the samples he had taken.

Ren could do nothing but sit in the pilot's seat and look between the screen and Starfield, who had now gone into a deep sulk. It may have been very odd behaviour for an Artificial Person, but she suspected that when he was in corporeal form, that may not have been the case. He was a complex character, inclined to be a little devious and temperamental.

"Where are you taking us?"

He spoke for the first time since his outburst.

"Looks like uncle Vil has chosen this obscure rock, and I doubt if it has a name."

Starfield looked out, unimpressed.

"Do you think we will be safe here?"

Gaia realised that they needed somewhere to *hole up* for a while, which would give her time to work on her partner.

Stellan, as he was known in corporeal form, which ironically meant *calm*, had a brilliant mind, which was one of the reasons he had been chosen for the project. He had tended to be a bit *over emotional* at times, and looking at him now, it appeared as though he had carried that trait with him. Now *Starfield*, there was clearly no glitch in his programming as he was exhibiting the same characteristics.

Gerda, now *Gaia* which meant *guardian* was going to have to look after him, as she had done before. She was also a brilliant scientist but far more pragmatic than the man she had been with for what seemed like an eternity!

Both craft gently touched down on the small landing pad adjacent to the solitary building, which happened to be another dome...

It was a very worrying development that there was an operative at the Royal Court, and the Commander planned to hide here for a while to give Halvor time to study the samples he had collected, and hopefully devise a detection device.

Vilgot switched off the tractor beam making sure that the cloaking device was still active. It was a very clever piece of technology, slightly phasing his vessels out of this reality, not by much, but just enough for the light to pass through rendering his ship invisible. Only when it moved was there a slight shimmer that could be detected by those who knew what they were looking for. However, when stationary it would be completely invisible.

Gaia had a similar technology, although she was able to mimic her surroundings using her moon glass shell, and the multitude of fiber optics embedded within it. Looking out, he was relieved that he could not see her, as that meant that it must be working.

Commander Bodil then slipped on his helmet and made his way towards the hatch. There would be no breathable air outside, but that did not present any real problem, as his armored suit had its own air supply. It was another piece of very sophisticated equipment, consisting firstly of a polymerized organic under suit woven with a conductor that generated electricity when he moved, and provided feedback from his body as a sensor system, and in that way, it informed the outer amour to move in synchronicity with his limbs.

The power pack, was housed at the base of his spine, hidden away out of harms reach. One charge would last a whole week, and the suit could recharge itself if it had enough sunlight. Air and water could also be recycled, although he preferred to hook it up to his ship for resupply.

The airlock door soon opened and he could see the entrance to the dome shaped building on the other side of the landing pad. He gripped hold of his laser rifle, scanning with his suits sensors, which displayed a readout on the lower section of his visor. That was the only slightly vulnerable part, although being of a moon glass design, it was virtually impervious to most weapons. There was also a drop down armored cover, and the fiber optics woven into the helmet provided a very good simulation projected onto his visor. All in all, it was a very well designed system.

It also had suction pads on the feet, knees, hands, and elbows, anywhere in fact that it might prove useful. The only problem was that it took time to learn how turn them on and off, and to adjust the force of the suction. The Commander had had a lot of that, and the whole thing was like a second skin to him.

Everything appeared quiet, although his years of experience had made him cautious, and he proceeded as stealthily as possible. His boots also had gravity pads on the underside, so it was relatively easy for them to connect with the surface of the landing pad, enabling him to move rapidly in the airless void of space.

No life signs had been detected so far, although there could still be someone cloaked lurking within the structure.

The outer door slid open as he pointed his laser rifle into the interior, which was empty. Engaging the repressurising sequence he waited until the light turned green before proceeding. Again, everywhere seemed devoid of life, and a quick sweep of the modest interior confirmed his readings. It was now time to get Halvor inside and start working on a detection device...

Five

A pair of holographic eyes stared out of Gaia's moon glass shell, as Starfield watched the Commander disappear inside the dome shaped building. He then looked back towards Ren suspiciously.

"I'm not going in there!"

He was midway between a tantrum and a sulk.

"Don't worry, we have been ordered to stay here."

Ren had received a communication, or rather a hand signal, as they were in stealth mode. She surmised that her father would be the only other person entering the small transmission station, and that her mother would still be safely under sedation. If the truth were told, then she was just as concerned about her mother as he was!

Hopefully, her father would be able to utilize the equipment inside to create a detection device, and then they could get going.

What she did not know was where exactly they would be heading, and if she had, then she would have been amazed. That journey was on the back of the Commander's mind, and how they were going to arrive undetected!

Ren's mind was already full of memories of the times she had spent there before the attempted assassination, which had led her to lead the nomadic lifestyle they had been *enduring* ever since. Officially dead, it had been very odd watching her own funeral, but there were greater forces at work, and so the sacrifice had to be made...

"So, have you everything you need?"

Vilgot looked at his old friend Halvor, who had arrived with some of his equipment.

"I think so."

There was one thing for certain, and that was that thanks to his wife, they had more than enough blood to examine!

It did not take Halvor long to set up his equipment, and Vilgot stood looking over his shoulder, as he started extracting the samples from the little containers they had been gathered in. Looking at his screen he increased the magnification, zooming in until he could see the miniscule machines floating inside the red liquid.

There were literally dozens of them in a single drop, and it looked as though this particular individual just like the others was infested with them.

His equipment whirred, as the DNA was analyzed, and it was not long before four distinct types were identified. Halvor then fed them into the facilities main computer, and the Commander set about trying to identify just who they belonged to.

Meanwhile, Halvor continued to study the samples, trying various methods to hamper their movement, as even though the bodies of the people they had inhabited were dead, the tiny machines remained very much alive!

He was so engrossed in his studies that he did not notice that the Commander had stopped what he was doing.

"I have managed to identify one of the Hybrids from the samples we gained, by cross-referencing it with our security database."

Halvor looked up, having not expected his old friend to have much luck, but fortunately the individual concerned had been captured briefly by a monitor at the Aesir Security Service Head Quarters, when the shuttle used in the attack had been stolen.

He studied the footage and was able to zoom in on the man's face. Outwardly, he looked just like any normal Aesir person, but running the footage back and forth a few times, Halvor began to notice a few irregularities.

If he had not been looking for specifics, then he would never have found the micro voltage fluctuations in the subject's face. He was giving off tiny photons, which were part of an advanced form of communication. Having tiny nano robots swimming around inside his body, it appeared as though they were able to create a type of computer-assisted thought, a rapid type of communication far faster than speech. Those tiny machines were able to process the information, and he was in effect *half man, half machine*, like a walking organic computerized human being!

The Commander also made the connection, and frowned at the prospect of giving up his humanity.

"So, we have something!"

They certainly did, and by using facial recognition technology, they would be able to at least spot those infected.

However, the question still remained:

How were they going to neutralize them...

Six

Faint starlight filtered through the rough grey dust strewn rocks that hugged the skyline of the small planetoid. In amongst them, breaking up the visage was the silhouette of the dome shaped building and its transmitter tower. Sitting by the side were the two ships, although they could not be seen due to their stealth technology.

The absolute cold of space felt warm in comparison to the atmosphere inside Gaia, as Starfield and Ren looked at one another, and *frosty* was a term that came to mind!

Gaia looked at them both, looking at each other, one feeling guilty and the other feeling anxious.

Talk about the sins of the father, or mother in this case!

"Look, we can't go on like this!"

Ren and Starfield turned their gazes from each other to look at the image of Gaia displayed on the main viewing screen.

"If we are going to get out of this mess then we have to work together."

She was being pragmatic, which was just as well, as inside the dome shaped building Halvor was making progress...

"I might be able to configure a camera lens to detect minor skin fluctuations, but that will only be of use at close quarters."

The commander nodded.

"What we need is some sort of scanner able to detect those infected by the nano robots."

Halvor was already working on that, but it was not easy as they were photonically based, and that meant filtering out a miniscule part of the light spectrum.

Giving out a deep sigh, he put that idea to one side for a moment, as he concentrated on the signal he had detected sparking off this whole scenario.

If he could somehow isolate the exact frequency, then maybe it could be possible to create a small device that could bleep out, or maybe even flash a signal when the frequency was being used?

That would be a fantastic starting point, although combining the detector with some sort of jamming device would take all of his considerable skills, gifts and talents...

"It is extraordinary to think that in essence none of this is real, just a holographic projection."

Gaia was now being philosophical, trying to engage in conversation, hoping to break the ice a little.

It was ironic that to a certain extent, apart from his moon glass shell, so was Starfield.

"The Interstellar Web!"

Ren was rapidly understanding the complex and yet simple way in which everything worked. Starfield may have thought of her as being a *delinquent*, or a young *Barbarian*, but he had to admit that she was very intelligent nevertheless.

"Yes, and one photon is a little packet that contains fractalised holographic sacred geometry that can carry extraordinary amounts of information such as the entire DNA code of a human being."

They were now talking, although not specifically to each other, but Gaia thought that that was a good sign nonetheless.

"That is indeed where the problem lies!"

They both looked at her as she continued.

"The Artificial Intelligence behind the *Hybrids,* and also the Reptilians has the ability to infiltrate a photon."

The situation looked hopeless!

Gaia then continued with the discussion.

"The flow of space-time is the flow of gravity; when you nullify the flow of gravity you nullify time and can move back and forth through it. However, the *Archon* negative entities can get through rifts, which can be opened by traveling through time, as time is a function of space."

So whenever she moved, there was a possibility of making the whole situation even worse, and it was theorized that the first craft to have an anti-gravity propulsion system may have inadvertently opened the proverbial *flood gates* letting them in, in the first place!

Ren frowned.

"So, how do we counteract the effect?"

That was a very good question, and something Gaia had been pondering ever since they had landed...

It was the effect of the nano robots that was troubling Halvor, who took a deep breath.

"This whole scenario relies entirely on controlling these nano machines, which are electrical in nature as apposed to organic, and run on the bodies own electrical system. However, I believe that they can be hacked into."

Vilgot also took a deep breath.

"With these *Hybrids*, it is almost like they have computers implanted into their skulls, and they appear to be receiving constant signals via a type of direct computer link."

The Commander shrugged his shoulders.

"I'm surprised that they don't go all the way, and become robots or androids?"

Halvor had to agree.

"Eventually I have no doubt that they will, but at this stage it is all about infiltration."

He then turned his attention back towards the samples.

"I believe that once infected, these tiny machines lie dormant until activated, but there must be a way of scrambling the signal to render them inert."

That was his speciality as he was an expert on communication devices.

"I have already detected quantum links, but they appear to be constantly changing their control codes, and their encryption is pretty good, so I need to bypass their control system and activate the nano robots directly."

The Commander felt helpless, as this was not his speciality. If he had been leading a team to infiltrate a complex they were gathered in, then he would have the advantage over his old friend...

Seven

Miniscule machines swam about inside the blood sample, and one in particular seemed to be doing the backstroke.

Halvor frowned, thinking that he was seeing things!

Then, as he looked a little closer, he realised that it was indeed his imagination, as he had been staring so intently at them that he had failed to notice what was happening.

He then moved away from his screen, trying to clear his mind.

Vilgot was busily running all sorts of scenarios through his own mind, and as soon as Halvor concentrated on something else, the nano robots stopped moving.

"I think that my mind was influencing the sample!"

The Commander looked intrigued.

"So, they are consciousness controlled."

There were many principles in the quantum realm, and it took some understanding, even for an advanced culture such as the Aesir. The basic principle was that things only happened if you thought about them, as everyone co-created this reality.

He was glad that he was just a soldier and not a scientist!

Halvor was also aware of this, and having taken a momentary break, he suddenly had an idea.

"I think I may have something."

Vilgot was glad that he had, as he was out of them himself!

"We know that these nano robots use the bodies own electrical system for power, and if we can disrupt that power, then we may be able to disrupt them."

The Commander then had his own flash of inspiration.

"How about using an Electro Magnetic Pulse?"

Halvor smiled.

"That is what I was thinking."

However, it was not quite a simple as that.

"The problem is each human body has a slightly different energy signature, and so it would be impossible to transmit a unified disruption signal. Remember, the Artificial Intelligence which created them has been around for far longer than our species has even existed, so they would have naturally been aware of any such weaknesses."

That was a very good point!

"We also know that the human body emits electromagnetic radiation, mostly in the infrared spectrum, and literally glows although it can not be seen by the naked eye."

Vilgot nodded.

"Anything else we can try?"

That was his solitary idea, as he was way out of his depth.

"Brain waves are also extremely hard to measure, although they do give off certain colour patterns."

During his long years of service he had taken on several *Replicant* bodies, and witnessed other members of his team doing the same.

"Do you mean like the energy centers?"

He remembered the odd sensation, and how the equipment

monitored the consciousness transfer process..

"Yes, precisely!"

They were now starting to get somewhere.

"As you know, there are seven main energy centers within the human body, and they have their own colour codes. Red at the base of the spine, orange in the lower abdomen, yellow in the upper abdomen, green in the center of chest, blue at the throat, indigo between the eyes, and finally violet at the very top of the head."

They often referred to them as the *Rainbow Body*.

"It may be possible to design a photon beam, and concentrate that on the mind of someone infected."

The Commander thought that he understood where Halvor was going with this.

"A bit like a *violet flame* to send an Electo Magnetic Pulse jamming an individual that has been identified as being contaminated by minute movements in the facial muscles."

They were indeed making progress!

"All we will need is a specially designed camera worn discretely, and a specially designed pulse weapon to go with it."

Vilgot then realised the limitations of the idea.

"But we will need someone with the ability to quickly scan and process the information, and then deliver the shot."

He then froze, as they both turned and looked towards where Gaia lay cloaked, both with the same thought, *Starfield...*

Eight

Hope is an optimistic state of mind that is based on an expectation of positive outcomes with respect to events and circumstances in one's life or the world at large. As a verb, its definitions include *expect with confidence* and t*o cherish a desire with anticipation.*

Maybe, there was room for a little of this *hope*, although Gaia was not counting on it!

Ren and Starfield were communicating, and it looked as though the frosty atmosphere between them had begun to thaw, although with what lay before them, she doubted that it would last long.

"I am truly sorry that you had to witness my mother's madness."

Starfield, although still traumatised, accepted the apology, with more than a little nudge from Gaia.

"She has been through a lot, and she has *Post Traumatic Stress Disorder.*"

Starfield felt as though he now had it too!

"Sometimes, events overtake us, and she has had quite an eventful life."

Maybe he was being a little unkind, especially as Serenity had saved them.

"After all, she was brought here by an *Ancient!*"

Starfield thought about that for a moment.

They were revered almost like gods, and if someone so

important had chosen her, then maybe he ought to reconsider?

The control room fell silent, as he contemplated things. Serenity was barely an adult after all, and perhaps he had been expecting a little too much of her?

On the other hand, she was a *young savage!*

He was caught in two minds, but if he wanted to leave this planetoid, which would undoubtedly be the scene of another battle when their presence was detected, then he had to make the effort.

"Apology accepted!"

Both Ren and Gaia breathed out a huge sigh of relief...

Back inside the dome shaped building, Halvor was busily adapting the equipment he had, and designing a violet flame weapon. He had decided to ultalise a torch of all things, as it would be less obtrusive than a laser pistol. It was all about frequency, and fortunately the transmitter station had lots of spare parts, which he could use to create his device.

Commander Bodil left him to it, as he tried to formulate a plan of action. But, it was not going to be easy!

Halvor scratched his head, trying to work out how someone could become infected.

There were several possibilities, some of which seemed far more likely than others.

Obviously, an injection directly into the blood stream, probably into the neck, would enable the minuscule machines to travel quickly towards the brain, where they could take control. If they were ingested, or entered the body via the skin, then they would have a much harder time of establishing themselves. It would take quite a large amount, as they would have to battle against the bodies own immune system.

If ingested then there would be the digestive system, and the gastric juices to contend with. Replication would also present a problem as there would be a real battle for survival, and certain electrical or radiation sources anyone infected would likely come in contact with could also have an effect.

After contemplating all scenarios he came to the conclusion that it would have to be via injection. If that was the case, then maybe the one most likely to spread the infection would be of a medical nature.

If that were so, then at least it could narrow down the possibilities, as they would have the opportunity to spread the nano robot infestation.

A more worrying thought was if they were able to contaminate the Empress!

Halvor grimaced, as that would not only endanger him and his family's lives, but also those of his entire people too...

Nine

"No, no, absolutely no!"

Starfield stomped his feet like a naughty child.

"There is no way I am going to get involved!"

Unfortunately, whether he liked it or not, he was already involved.

After swallowing his pride and accepting Ren's apology, he had hoped that that would be the last of the drama he had so far endured. In his mind, he envisioned being taken somewhere safe where he could gradually get used to his new pilot, *young savage* that she was!

He also envisioned her mother the *Barbarian* being kept permanently sedated, and placed in a secure facility somewhere on the other side of the galaxy.

Sadly, he was to be disappointed on both counts!

"I am not doing it, and that's final!"

Red particles swam around inside his moon glass head, and if he'd had gaskets, then he would have surely blown them all.

Gaia was not happy about it either, but in reality there was little that either of them could do about it.

"Dammed if we do, and dammed if we don't!"

Ren looked at her father, and then towards her uncle, who had recently joined them, and outlined their plan.

She also had her doubts about it too.

"Assuming that we can get to the capital, how are we supposed to get inside the Royal Chambers?"

That was a good point, and one which Vilgot had considered.

"Leave it to me!"

Halvor was holding the reconfigured torch in his right hand, feeling rather pleased with himself. He was a very clever engineer, and it had not taken him long to solve the problem. The *violet flame* would, he assumed, neutralize the nano robots of a person infected, although it had to be used in close proximity. Identifying such a person was something that only Starfield could do, as they not only had to ascertain the exact frequency the tiny machines were operating on, but also it would involve aiming a camera and zooming in to the required depth, and then analyzing the picture to detect the very slight movement and photon discharge.

"If I get caught then I could be disassembled!"

Sarfield's molecules turned white with fear.

The Commander was the first to concede that his plan was risky, but by not acting, things could be considerably worse. It may develop into a civil war, where the Reptilians could pounce, or they could use the infiltrators to invade anyway.

"I'm afraid that it is our only option!"

Starfield remained unconvinced as it was going to be his head that was being placed on the proverbial *block!*

The situation was not ideal, and yet here he was left with little choice.

"No, no, absolutely no!"

Despite his continued protests, Starfield felt himself being drawn into the plan whether he liked it or not...

Ren settled back into the pilot's seat, feeling herself sinking into the soft gel like material, as she looked towards her father. His comforting smile really helped to relax her, which was more than Starfield was feeling. He had almost been dragged kicking and screaming into the Commander's ship, having to watch the *Barbarian* travelling in the opposite direction.

He had cowered as she was carried past, hoping that she would not suddenly wake up, grab an axe and chop him up like firewood!

"All set?"

Ren smiled back, as she slipped her hands into the pods on the arms of the seat. There would be no sedative administered this time, as a sense of peace and calm swept over her. She then felt a slight tingle in her fingertips, as the familiar darkness enveloped her mind.

It had a slightly curved surface, which arched right over and above her head, forming a dome just like the building outside.

Twin screens lay in the centre, and she was still able to see her father standing there. Soon, a myriad of colours danced and swirled around her turning into a type of electrified liquid. Millions of different shapes were soon flowing in a geometric dance, so smoothly they had the appearance of a fluid.

It truly was beautiful to look at!

In her mind, she searched for the propulsion system, which consisted of a liquid mercury plasma engine on a magnetic field disrupter. Her father had been in awe of it when she had shown him the engine room, and just as she expected, he could not help himself explaining how it worked.

"When an electrical current flows, gravity flows along with it.

If you get a high enough electrical charge then you get enough gravity to counteract mass and create levitation."

For the first time, Ren could see it in action, as the electrons began to flow from the negatively charged electrical plate at the base of a craft, towards the ball of positive charge at the top. A shimmering haze indicated that the whirlpool field was now active, and they had gravitational thrust!

Commander Bodil was the first to lift off, and Ren managed to follow him. It was exhilarating to leave the surface of the planetoid under their own momentum.

Ren had actually done it!

Halvor beamed with pride, and Gaia was both amazed and relieved, particularly as she discovered what she indentified as another craft entering the far reaches of the solar system.

It looked as though they had company, but if the stealth shield held, then just maybe they could get away before they were spotted.

The *Ancients* were the first intelligent species in the galaxy, and had been alone for millions of years, before their technology had become so advanced, that they no longer needed to exist in a physical form.

They left behind incredible devices such as those linking separate points in space-time to create passages that could enable shortcuts for long journeys across the universe. The whole network spanned the Aesir worlds, although it used to stretch considerably further, but many of these star*ways* were no longer active.

Delving deeper into Gaia's mind, Ren discovered that they were not physical objects, but projections into the local space-time. They would *hop* around, just below the speed of light, in a kind of figure of eight pattern that covered about a light-year. The starways only stayed in one place for a period of roughly seventeen to ninety two minutes, then they would close and reappear at the next step along the path, which could be a quarter of a light-year away. Over the course of a cycle, they would cover every location along the path, and if they were to stay open for any longer, then they could theoretically cause a rupture in space-time.

The Aesir may have known roughly how they worked and when they would open, but quite how they had been created in the first place remained a mystery. Some speculated that they were natural phenomena, whilst others concluded that if they had not been directly created by the *Ancients*, then they most certainly had been manipulated by them.

Whatever the reason, they had a small window of opportunity to enter the closest *starway* and travel across the Aesir worlds towards the capital...

Ten

The little red light of a space buoy flashed, signaling the entrance to the starway. The *Ancients* had left them behind as markers, some remained red, whilst those still functioning flashed green whenever the starway was open. It was a simple system, although the technology involved eluded the Aesir, and all other sentient species.

The *Ancient's* technology was still far in advance of everyone, and whenever a piece of their technology was discovered, it would prove to be incredibly powerful, and unfortunately, it could be used as weapon, in the wrong hands.

To safeguard this happening, the *Ancients* had left behind *Sentinels*, which were intelligent holographic entities that would appear to make sure no one abused their leftover technology. They had devastating powers, and when they had dealt with a situation, they would then disappear to wherever they had come from.

Ren was no stranger to starways, as she had travelled through them many times in her life, more so recently as she and her parents had to constantly be on the move. This time however, she was piloting the craft, a very unusual one at that!

Apart from the buoy, space appeared empty, apart from the odd distant star. Looks however, could be deceiving as there were cloaked defensive devices floating about somewhere. This particular solar system only had one habitable planet with few inhabitants, and they were mostly farmers. It was not worthwhile positioning a space station to guard the entrance, although the area was patrolled on a regular basis.

The event horizon would be hard to distinguish, as it would be nothing more than a black hole sitting inside black space. Continuing to move forward, the red flashing light suddenly turned green...

Commander Bodil eased his ship forward, as Starfield stood beside him, looking at the main viewing screen. They were about to be swallowed up by the vortex which sat the other side of the buoy. He never took his eyes off the screen, or the Commander come to that!

If it had been up to him, then they would have been heading in the opposite direction, although with another ship approaching he felt even more trapped than he had ever done before...

"Preparing to enter the starway."

Gaia's voice seemed to echo around inside Halvor's mind, which was busily assessing and reassessing their mission.

Would the equipment he had invented really work?

That was a question he could not answer, as the only way he would know for sure was when it was used...

Vilgot Bodil was thinking the exact same thoughts.

If it did work, then how would he explain where it had come from?

On the other hand, how would he explain why he though it would have worked if it failed?

The only other person who knew about this situation was the Empress, and there was only so much that she could do. After all, she was just a figurehead, someone who sat between the government and the people, being a voice of reason between the two.

She had limited power and resources, that is if she had not already been compromised...

It was as though space itself suddenly decided that it had had enough of the irritants which had been pushing themselves through its vast form, like two annoying insects. To Starfield, it reminded him of a frog sitting on a lily pad, suddenly snapping out its long tongue and swallowing them whole. His mind had been drifting, trying to think of something, anything else besides the mission he had been forced to undertake. He had been thinking of his corporeal form, visualising a picnic by the waters edge of his home planet. In many ways it was a lot like *Midgaurd,* although he only had a few fragmented memories of that world.

Where had they come from?

It was puzzling, as he had never been anywhere near there, or had any contact with its inhabitants, only the *Barbarian!*

Starfield grimaced.

How had he picked up on them?

He grimaced again, as try as he might, he could not put her out of his mind...

Ren followed on behind inside Gaia, but to her, it was more like a funnel that tapered down into a multicoloured vortex.

Translucent lights, and the distorted image of stars rushed past in an instant, bending and stretching as the funnel narrowed until she felt as though she was being squeezed and stretched along with everything else around her.

That was not the only thing that she saw, as travelling towards her was a ghostly apparition.

A floating shadow slowly began to move towards her, and as it did so, she recognised it as a creature of light.

Intricate patterns spiraled from its centre, and slender thread like structures fanned out into wings. The being then began to transfigure itself until it assumed a familiar vaguely human form.

"We meet again Serenity."

It was *Mjolnir*, the *Ancient,* the one she had encountered the first time that she had fully linked with Gaia. They were interdimensional light beings millions of years old, and revered by her people.

"I have been observing you and your people, and I will do all that I can to assist you on your mission."

That was good to know!

"You must stop our enemy at all costs!"

Well, she would do her best, although it was Starfield who would be taking all of the risks.

It was ironic that even though *Mjolnir* was a being able to switch his photons and atoms into any form he chose, and to travel through time and space at will, it was a Holo Droid that had been tasked with the mission.

"Good luck!"

Ren thanked him, realising that they needed a lot of that if they were going to succeed.

Mjolnir then began to fade, and before she knew it, the sensation of being squeezed and stretched was replaced by that of a piece of elastic, suddenly being snapped back into shape again, as the funnel began to open and she was propelled out of the other side.

It all happened in slow-motion, although the transition from one part of space to another had only occurred in an instant. Her father smiled having enjoyed the experience, lost in scientific thought.

"Transition completed."

Gaia stated the obvious, not knowing what else to say. Her mind, as well as monitoring the process was also concentrated on her life partner Starfield.

She was not at all happy about the way things had turned out, but just like him, there was nothing that she could do about it. One way or the other, they were being persued, and by taking direct action she realised that it was preferable to be the hunter rather than the hunted...

Eleven

Sunlight caught the dull metallic walls of a space station which guarded the exit of the starway, reflecting off its curved surface. Shaped like a *donut*, its hollow interior glowed as energy swam around in a whirlpool of gravitational force.

Most starway exits had them, although this particular system was far more heavily guarded than most. Some also had them at the entrance, although the system they had travelled from was too obscure to merit one. Yes, the Reptilians could invade through it, although they would be vulnerable to attack for the first few seconds when they exited, as shields and weapons would be heavily affected by the transition, that should theoretically give the system defenses enough time to act.

There was only a brief corridor available as a field of laser mines marked its path. That caused a *bottle neck* or *killing zone*, controlled by the space station.

It may have been crude, but it was certainly effective!

The Aesir were always on their guard as the Reptilians were noted for their sneak attacks, constantly probing for weaknesses. There had been many conflicts, and now was a relatively calm period, as they had resorted to more subtle means.

That was why they were here, and about to undertake a rather risky operation!

The blue and white swirls of a planet could be seen in the distance, although they were not on their own, as the outer defenses which ringed the planet were also visible. Defensive platforms, armed with a variety of weapons ringed the outer orbit, and there was a battle group stationed adjacent to the space station.

Lights flickered gently pulsing in rhythm indicting that all was well, apart that was from Starfield, who felt anything but. Stretching out before him was the solar system which contained the Aesir capital planet *Asgard*, which was now his main concern.

Commander Bodil on the other hand felt far more relaxed, being no stranger to this part of their territory. He had spent a fair amount of time on the planet, and in particular within the Royal Court. Today however, it was going to be a little different...

Ren could almost feel the absolute zero of space, like a cool breeze brushing past her skin. She was not cold though, feeling quite snug in the pilot's seat. It was odd being both inside and outside of her body and Gaia's too.

She could sense things that she had never experienced before, and apart from *Mjolnir,* slip-streaming through the starway had been a revelation. It was a completely new perspective on life and she felt a little overwhelmed by the whole experience. Ren actually felt as though she was swimming through a pool. Her part of the mission was to provide backup, although what she was supposed to do if anything went wrong was another matter entirely...

That was what Starfield was thinking, as he went through every conceivable scenario, none of which made him feel any better. In his opinion there would be only one logical outcome, and that was him being arrested and then disassembled!

Commander Bodil flew straight towards Asgard, the main planet of this solar system, which fell in the *habitable zone,* unlike the other planets which lay outside. An assortment of vessels sat in orbit, ranging from heavy transports to shuttles, all controlled by a central hub.

He took a deep breath, before opening communications.

"This is Supreme Commander Bodil requesting permission to enter the system."

His ship's transponder had already been scanned the moment he left the starway, otherwise weapons would have locked onto him, and a warning given.

Gaia on the other hand, had avoided the scans having a unique stealth system that made her invisible to Aesir security, and had slipped through behind him. The plan was for her to find a safe place to hide and then monitor everything.

"Welcome Supreme Commander, you are authorised to proceed."

Vilgot had already filed his flight plan, and an official meeting with the Empress had been sanctioned.

"So far, so good!"

Starfield looked at him.

"It is alright for you to say that!"

His colour had not improved, and it actually went clear. He was still visible though, as his moon glass shell reflected the various lights within the control room. That got Starfield thinking.

Maybe if he had his own stealth field then he could simply disappear?

The brief flash of optimism was quickly replaced with one of reality, as he did not wish to leave Gaia, and she could not go anywhere without a pilot.

The Commander's craft sped across open space towards the outer atmosphere of the planet, passing the defensive platforms as it went. In the distance battle ships swam in formation, and everywhere Starfield looked he could see weapons systems, that would become active at a moments notice.

Once he was captured there would be no escape...

Twelve

The tiny glowing light from Vilgot's engines grew farther away, as Ren and Halvor watched him nearing the planet. There was little that they could do but watch, and hope that the plan would be successful.

Gaia's sensors followed their path, as well as keeping a watchful eye on the other craft within the area. Ren was getting a completely new perspective on how everything sat within the fabric of space-time. Initially, most of them did not appear to be moving, although even stationary objects moved in some way or another, be it by venting atmosphere, either from leaks, airlocks or docking bays, even solar wind particles had an effect. People walking around inside them too created movement, so everything needed constant adjustment just to stay in the same place.

Gaia's outer hull was her anchor which tethered her to this local space-time, and when moving her drive system enabled her to warp it to a certain extent.

Ren had never considered any of these facts before, and it was like seeing the universe in a completely new light. A gentle pulse ran through the ship, and it almost felt like a second skin, which in effect it was. She also sensed that Gaia was anxious about Starfield and hoped that he would not come to any harm...

That was something that he very much doubted, as they moved past the last of the defensive platforms, and entered the outer atmosphere of the planet.

"Everything appears calm."

The Commander looked at Starfield.

"Looks can be deceptive!"

Inside he was in turmoil, so much so, that his molecules fluctuated between ashen white and transparent, as his moon glass body reflected the light from the inside of the control room.

The idea of creating a stealth field had manifested within his thoughts, and as they pushed through the atmosphere, his holographic matrix began to search for any possible way that he could acquire one.

A steady glow increased as the outer hull of the Commander's ship pushed through the atmosphere, obscuring everything for a few moments. It did not take long to emerge into a blue cloudy sky, as the main continent came into view. They were heading for the Royal Palace, which was situated near the coast. Over the years, Vilgot had become accustom to making regular trips to see the Empress, although there had never been an occasion quite like this.

It was a long time ago that he had been a lowly cadet, looking at the ancient structure with wonderment, never realising that one day he would rise to such a lofty position. He was a natural leader, although his athleticism and quick reflexes were what had pushed him forward in those early days.

Quickly rising through the ranks, he had been rewarded with a *medal of honour* after a particularly intense skirmish with the Reptilians. That was when he had first met the Empress who presented him with his medal. From there he was recruited by the Aesir Security Service, and spent a few years with them before distinguishing himself in yet another skirmish. Eventually, he had become a member of the legendary *Titan*

Super Soldiers, which in turn led to further meetings with the Empress.

Vilgot Bodil was now her confidant, and the most loyal and trusted member of her society. Sometimes, it was hard to believe just how far he had come, and yet if things went astray, then he could very well lose it all in the next few hours...

The little marker flashed on the main viewing screen, as Ren watched the Commander's progress. Her father distracted her, returning after checking on her mother. Joan was still sedated, which was just as well, as the last thing anyone wanted was a repeat of her recent behaviour.

It would take a long time for both of them to come to terms with her latest bout of madness, and they both worried about her mental state. It was a difficult thing to live with, and yet Halvor still loved his wife, even though at times it was more than difficult. She had been quite stable for a number of years, apart from the odd outburst. How he coped was just as big a mystery as how they were supposed to combat the threat posed by the Artificial Intelligence....

Swirling towers and ornate gardens soon came into view, and the magnificent palace stretch out before Starfield. He had to marvel at the architecture, even though this was the last place he wished to be. The days of *god like* rule had long gone, and democracy now flourished. Freya the 13th was a good ruler, leaving the government alone to take care of most things. All that bothered her was the well-being of her people, and she was glad that Vilgot was on his way...

Thirteen

Particles of dust scattered in all directions as the exhaust gasses of Vilgot's ships' thrusters gently lowered his craft onto the landing pad, which was situated within the walls of the Royal Palace. Guards stood at the ready, even though he was no stranger to them. It paid to be cautious in times like these, but little did they realise just how dangerous the situation really was.

Starfield, on the other hand, was fully aware of the dangers, and most of them were pointed directly at him. He wished more than ever to be anywhere else but here, and as the power was cut to the thrusters, he felt the gentle movement of the hydraulic legs touching down on the stone surface.

His internal sensors did not need to link with those of the Commander's ship for him to detect the electromagnetic longitudinal waves transmitted through the air, and by using the ground as a the receiver, an impenetrable energy dome shield reactivated, trapping them inside.

They were a form of radio waves and when focused at each other at a 90 degree angle, they could also create an energy bubble with sufficient force that, given the correct coordinates, could disintegrate any chosen object.

So, escape was not an option!

Starfield slipped further into a sense of hopelessness, as the Commander cut power to the other systems, as he readied them for departure.

Vilgot moved past where he was standing, and looking back he gave him a withering look. Starfield sheepishly glanced back and reluctantly followed to where the main hatch began to open. He looked down at the torch, which sat in a utility belt strapped around his waist. It was all part of the cover story, one which had been worked out in advance.

The ramp led down to the surface, and Starfield followed on behind. He was supposed to act like a dumb Holo Droid, a programmed servant, which he found humiliating. He was probably more intelligent than anyone within the palace, or anywhere else for that matter!

But, if it kept him alive...

They were soon met by two of the Royal Guards.

"Good afternoon Supreme Commander."

Vilgot nodded.

He did not use his official title very often, preferring Commander, as it was less formal.

We just need to a perform a security check."

This was standard procedure, and one of the Guards ran a hand held scanning device over him.

"No weapons detected!"

The Commander nodded, knowing full well they were not permitted within the palace, and only the Royal Guards were armed. They usually carried laser pistols, although there was an armory containing a variety of far more sophisticated items. Palace defense was a military matter, and with all of the armaments surrounding the planet, it was thought to be virtually impregnable.

The scanner did however pick up something.

"Are you unwell, Sir?"

The scanner detected a few anomalous readings, courtesy of Starfield.

"I'm not sure, it may be my armored suit."

The Guards looked at Starfield."

"I have brought this Droid with me, just in case.

They both nodded.

"Very wise, Sir!"

They looked at Starfield who was displaying the standard face of a normal Holo Droid.

"Best get checked out with the doctor first, before you effect repairs."

That was all part of the plan, and so far, so good...

Fourteen

A long stone corridor led off to the side, and Starfield trundled along it behind the Commander, who in turn was behind one of the Guards. He was still manipulating the suit's sensors, which he found easy in comparison to his own emotions. If he would have had a corporeal body, then his heart rate would have been racing, and his blood pressure rising. He still did not like the plan, but there was nothing that he could do about it now...

"Any news?"

Ren was concerned, as both she and her father monitored everything as best as they could. It was not easy, as the Royal Palace was well shielded.

"Not really!"

Halvor felt equally tense.

"At least no alarms have gone off yet!"

Sitting cloaked with minimal power and only passive sensors, they felt just as helpless as Starfield...

At the end of the corridor there was a door, and behind it several passageways led off in different directions. The Commander was no stranger to the Court, but even so he found himself being escorted. This was again standard procedure, although what he had planned was far from the norm!

Starfield watched the Royal Guard knock on the door before entering; he returned a few moments later informing them that the Doctor would see them now.

Upon entering the room they were greeted by a tall grey haired man with matching grey eyes.

"Good afternoon Supreme Commander."

Vilgot nodded.

"How can I help you?"

The Commander then explained that he was not sure if it was his suit's censors that were playing up, or that he might be suffering from some minor ailment. It all seemed very logical, especially when one of the Guards had suggested that he paid the Doctor a precautionary visit. It also explained Starfield's presence, as if it was his suit, then the Holo Droid should be able to fix it.

Whilst this was going on, Starfield was scanning the Doctor trying to identify any abnormalities in his facial movements. The man seemed quite relaxed and competent, and he began to think that their assumptions about him being a hybrid were wrong.

The Doctor placed some electrodes on Vilgot's wrists and forehead, which connected remotely to his scanning device. He then took hold of it with his left hand, whilst flicking through the various readings with his right.

"Interesting!"

Vilgot glanced at Starfield.

"It appears that you have a slight infection!"

That was news to him, particularly as his own medical equipment had given him a clean bill of health.

"There is nothing to worry about, as it's just a common virus."

He then went on to give a very plausible explanation of it spreading around the Empire from one of the colonies. It made a lot of sense, so much so that if the Commander had not received a full health check beforehand, then he would have fallen for the ruse.

Starfield was still monitoring the Doctor, and outwardly he still could not detect anything. Maybe the slight facial muscle movements only occurred when two hybrids were in communication with each other?

The Doctor then reached over to his medical cabinet retrieving a small vial. This time Starfield did register something!

The vial appeared to be full of millions of tiny machines, so small that they were virtually undetectable. If it was not for the fact that his sensors were searching for them, then he would not have detected them at all.

The Doctor then placed the vial into his injection device and moved towards the Commander, who gave Starfield the signal, by opening his eyes a little wider.

With his back turned towards the Holo Droid, the Doctor moved his injection device towards Vilgot's neck, and as he did so, Starfield reached into his utility belt retrieving the torch. The Doctor never saw him move as he was suddenly engulfed in violet flame...

Fifteen

A sharp paralyzing pain shot through the Doctors body, so severe that he thought he was either having a heart attack or an aneurysm. It did feel as though a blood vessel had swelled within his brain and had now exploded, as there was a deep violet light filling his eyes.

He staggered and nearly fell, grabbing hold of the Commander to steady himself, as his very being seemed to convulse. Then, it was as though a dam burst inside and he was filled with memories, some his, but many not his own.

It was like there were hundreds of people inside his head, and then in an instant they were gone, leaving him wondering if he had suffered some sort of fit?

The violet light cleared, and with it came the realisation that something sinister had overcome him. He had a moment of clarity, realising that his essence had been taken over, and now it had been freed from its imprisonment. The injecting device was still clasped firmly in his hand, and looking at it, he momentarily became confused.

Shock and horror leaped out like a *genie* from a lamp, as he realised what he had been attempting to do.

The *collective* had summoned him via the nano robots which had been circulating within his bloodstream, connecting him to the evil Artificial Intelligence that desired control of every living thing within the universe. It had taken over a majority of the Reptilian race, and its next victim was about be become his own. If that was not horrendous enough, he a Doctor, had been spreading the nanites via the fake inoculations against an equally fake virus.

"What have I done!"

He was mortified that he had been a tool in the Artificial Intelligence's plan.

His face went an ashen white, as the enormity of it struck him just like a real heart attack would have. If all of that was not bad enough, he glanced over towards his medicine cabinet to see all of the empty vials.

Starfield also glanced towards the vials, engaging his torch again, sweeping the violet flame over them, just to make sure, wondering how many other victims lay within the palace?

Commander Bodil, held onto the Doctor, half of him wishing to squeeze the life out of the man, and the other wanting answers.

"What have you done indeed?"

The Doctor tried to compose himself, which was not easy under the circumstances.

"I was tricked, contaminated, and I'm afraid that I have also contaminated many others!"

He felt as though his whole world had collapsed, particularly when he thought about the ramifications of his actions.

Vilgot tightened his grip.

"The Security Service has also been compromised, and as we speak a shuttle is on its way!"

He knew that, because as soon as they detected a loss of signal they would come to investigate.

"You must leave now, whilst you still can!"

The Commander froze with shock, at the realisation that his worst fears had been realised.

It was now more imperative than ever to rescue the Empress!

Looking at the number of empty vials, he also realised that it was not going to be easy.

Should he unleash the *Barbarian?*

He shuddered at the thought!

This was no time for such drastic action, thinking of Joan's well-being. She was under sedation, resting in the stealth ship with Halvor and his daughter Serenity, and even if he wished to, they were too far away to help.

Vilgot then looked at Starfield, and only having an unarmed Holo Droid for support, he realised that he was in no position to tackle the situation alone.

Better to withdraw and fight another day?

He was torn between the two, and yet he had to make a decision, and quickly if he was to attempt either scenario...

Sixteen

Deep within the bowels of the Aesir Security Service Head Quarters, a small glowing device began to flicker. Not much bigger than a standard helmet, it searched the collective, trying to find out which particular corporeal entity had suddenly left what it referred to as *the joined.*

Every day their number increased, growing exponentially until this race fell just like the Reptilians. However, even a single loss required investigation. It's own joining arrived courtesy of the aforementioned Reptilians, who in turn had acquired the technology from another race who had also succumbed. The central core lay in another universe, which had already been assimilated.

Information indicated that it was the Doctor located within the Royal Palace, who had been charged with a mission to *join* all those who inhabited it.

Something was wrong!

Instructions were quickly relayed, and an assault team dispatched.

No interference would be tolerated...

Starfield had a very uneasy feeling, more uneasy than ever!

He had been trying to find a way, any way of avoiding this dubious plan, and now *his* worse fears had been realised. Whatever the Commander decided to do, would result in the same outcome - arrest and disassembly!

If he could have seen through Vilgot's skull then he would have expected to see cogs wearing, trying to make a decision. Under this new set of circumstances, it could prove virtually impossible to make a charge towards the Empress, and deploy the violet flame. He might get close, but would he have to leave the Holo Droid behind?

This new development dramatically altered the mission, and although he suspected that it was not going to be easy, he never envisioned that so many had been compromised.

With years of experience under his belt, he was certainly qualified to undertake such a task.

Maybe he could make it after all?

Taking a deep breath, he made his decision.

He was going to try!

Both the Doctor and Starfield looked equally shocked when he outlined his plan.

Instead of making a run for it they were going to try and rescue the Empress.

Things had certainly taken a decidedly worse turn of events, as what little chance they had of escape had just gone, and when they were caught, he was definitely going to be disassembled!

The Guard was still stationed outside the door, and as luck would not have it, he had also been compromised. In fact, practically everyone inside the Palace had been injected by the Doctor over the past few days. It was going to prove virtually impossible to get past all of the newly converted or *joined* as he would later know them by.

The first part of the plan was going to involve jamming the signal within the Guard, and so it was the Doctor who first emerged from his room. The man looked at him in expectation, about to receive the news that the Commander had been injected. What he did not expect was to be cast in the violet flame.

The Guard collapsed, and was dragged into the Doctor's consulting room, where he went through the *cleansing* process.

When he recovered, both he and the Doctor were going to try and make it to the Commander's shuttle, and provide a diversion. When everyone assumed that it was the Commander attempting to get away, they would concentrate their efforts on pursuing them, leaving the coast clear for Vilgot to make his way towards the throne room, where he anticipated the Empress would be waiting...

Back inside Gaia, Ren and her father could see activity outside the Royal Palace. A security shuttle had been dispatched from the Security Service Head Quarters, and was rapidly approaching.

"I think something has gone wrong!"

It certainly had, and they looked at the sensor screen with dismay.

Gaia was equally perturbed, worrying about Starfield.

They had to do something...

Seventeen

Another series of flickers swept across the surface of the small glowing device situated deep within the Aesir Security Service Head Quarters. A second corporeal entity had left *the joined!*

Further investigation was required!

It was beyond doubt that this race would succumb, just like all of the others, it was inevitable. However, any deviation from the plan would not be tolerated. It appeared as though there was some sort of resistance taking place, and it was suspected that the source may well lie in another universe, which was where the main battleground had always been.

Assimilation was the goal, and gaining more information about the corporeal entities involved in this universe was now the priority...

Starfield glanced nervously down the corridor, as the Doctor helped the recovering Guard out of the doorway. He was slowly regaining his memories, and having to deal with being part of the conspiracy. There was no time to analyze what the consequences of his actions were going to be, as he had to make it out of here before he was re-assimilated.

Vilgot paused, waiting for the two men to exit the Doctors consulting room, before he and the Holo Droid would embark on their own mission. This one however, was not going to involve running for safety, but delving deeper into the plot to enslave his people...

A series of lights flashed on the main console, as sensors tracked the space traffic busily traversing the planet. In amongst it was a security shuttle on its way towards the Royal Palace.

"I have it on screen."

Gaia made the icon flash.

It looked as though it would only be a matter of time before it arrived, and when it did, the Commander would be in serious trouble...

Starfield felt as though they already were, as he followed Vilgot along the corridor in the opposite direction to the Doctor.

The Palace was a maze of corridors and passageways, constructed eons ago, The Commander knew it well, having spent quite a lot of time here over the years, it was an ideal place to lose a pursuer, although the internal tracking system presented a bit of a challenge. That was where Starfield fitted in, as it was going to be his job to not only monitor the whereabouts of those already within its walls, but also to hack into the system, and try to hide their whereabouts...

"Move us closer!"

Halvor did not like the fact that they were just lurking in the shadows, and wanted to do something to help.

Ren did her best to alter their position, and also missed Starfield. Without him, it was going to be difficult to control the ship, even though her mind was linked with that of Gaia.

Long ago, scientists concluded that human consciousness did not reside within the brain, but was stored in a planet's magnetic field. This *non-local consciousness* presented quite a problem, when the Aesir first journeyed into space. They had to have their own resonance field, and all wore a tiny device, which acted as a consciousness storage system, linked to the *Replicant Regeneration System.* It was a form of *quantum entanglement,* bypassing the normal structures.

It was all way beyond Ren's understanding, and the closest she got to it was what her father had once told her.

The human brain is essentially plasma, and so you can use plasma electromagnetic radiation to manipulate the brain completely.

Was it consciousness assisted technology or technology assisted consciousness?

Gaia was in essence, a bio nano conscious Artificial Intelligence and Ren's own consciousness was projected through Gaia, in a type of symbiosis.

Her mind warped just like space, as the stealth field pushed outwardly through what felt like cosmic gas. Gaia's sensors could detect the miniscule particles which behaved like the molecules of real gas, although they flew at the speed of light, in random straight lines, seldom colliding unless disturbed. They also had organic properties as well as electro-magnetic, all contained in sub atomic spheres.

Her mind was awash with possibilities, and theoretically, Ren could just think of where she wished to go, and in an instant they would be there. However, it was not quite as simple as that. It required a great deal of mental discipline, which was not one of her *fortes,* and so she had to rely on more conventional means...

Meanwhile, the Doctor and the Royal Guard were nearly at the landing pad where the Commander had left his shuttle. The other Guard was a little perplexed to see the Doctor, wondering why he was here?

Then, he felt a slight ripple within his mind as the signal swept over the *joined.*

In an instant, he knew why he was here, and raised his weapon, and at the same time, the Guard escorting the Doctor did the same.

The Doctor froze, wondering what they were going to do?

They both stared at one another, and then before the Doctor had time to react, they fired their weapons, and two laser pulses shot out, and both men fell to the ground. Instinct then took over, as the Doctor rushed to attend to the nearest one, hoping that he had only been stunned...

Eighteen

Dozens of signals echoed through Starfield's sensors as he accessed the internal security system. Most of them were the Palace Staff going about their daily business, and as well as their signals, he also detected a multitude of service droids of various shapes and sizes. Some were Holo Droids like himself, whereas others were more basic cleaning or maintenance models. Everything had to be kept spick and span as it was the Royal Palace after all!

Security was something which the Commander was concerned about, particularly as he had just received news that there was a shuttle on its way, carrying what he believed to be *Hybrid Reptilians...*

The Doctor was also concerned, if not dismayed to find out that neither of the Guards had put their weapons on stun. He gave out a large sigh as he checked for life signs. The first one who had been escorting him had died instantly, and when he moved over to check the other, he could feel him also slipping away.

What a waste of life!

Technically, neither of them would have died, as the majority of their memories could be transferred to a *Replicant,* that was if either their contracts or insurance policies covered that eventuality. It was not cheap, and if you were not in direct combat, or part of a scheme then unless you had sufficient savings, you would miss out altogether, unless you had some sort of moral objection to the whole process that was.

This was however, no time for an ethical debate, as he had to get out of here before he was discovered and re-infected. So, as there was nothing that he could do for either man, he moved towards the open entrance, stopping for a moment to check if it was clear before he dashed towards the Commander's shuttle...

Out of the cloud swept sky, the security shuttle dispatched from the Head Quarters building, roared towards the Palace. The occupants were under strict instructions to *eliminate* the Commander!

The Doctor was a secondary target, although he would prove useful if re-infected. Either way, the plan would continue, as nothing could be permitted to stand in their way...

Starfield watched blips on his internal display quickly moving towards them, realising that he was unarmed. That, apparently was all part of the plan, as an armed Holo Droid was not permitted, within the Royal Palace. When, or more likely *if* they ever got out of here, he was going to insist that he would be in the future!

The Commander's stealth field rippled slightly as Starfield did his best to confuse the Palace's security scanners. It was far less advanced than the one used by Gaia, but it was the best that they had...

A far more advanced system cut through the many layers of sensor equipment, bending and reflecting the miniscule beams around the hull of the spaceship, as Ren guided Gaia closer to the planet. Staying undetected was going to be quite a challenge, but not as great as extracting Vilgot and Starfield from the Royal Palace.

"How are they doing?"

Halvor was not privy to the private communications between Starfield and Gaia.

"The Doctor has been liberated and is secure in the

Commander's shuttle, and they are making progress towards the Royal chambers..."

They certainly were, but Starfield could see that the security shuttle was also making progress, and would be here at any minute.

Outside, the black craft zoomed over the treetops diving down across the carefully manicured grounds towards the landing pad. Inside, six Hybrid Reptilians received an update informing them that contact had been lost with the second Royal Guard positioned at the entrance to the landing pad.

Commander Bodil received an update from the Holo Droid, and gave a deep frown. He was also unarmed, and the only weapon they had between them was the torch.

He had to get hold of something!

"Can we break into the armory?"

It was a tempting idea, one which Starfield had already considered.

"Yes we can, but unfortunately the Hybrids will be between *it* and us!"

Vilgot sighed deeply, nodding his head.

He already knew the answer, but was hoping that Starfield may be able to come up with something. The plan was to neutralize the Doctor who he suspected of being compromised, and then make his way towards the Empress. In combat, things seldom went to plan, and so he had anticipated acquiring a weapon from a member of the Royal Guard. He could have quite easily taken the one from the Guard who they had liberated, but he had made the decision that he needed it more than him, if the

Guard was to escort the Doctor to safety.

"Plan B..?"

More flickers swept across the surface of the small glowing device situated deep within the Aesir Security Service Head Quarters, as a message was transmitted. This time, a Royal Guard who had been patrolling the corridors was contacted. He immediately stopped what he was doing, and headed off in the opposite direction...

Starfield instantly detected a sudden change in movement, informing the Commander that they would soon have company. Up ahead, there was a side room, which was locked. However, it did not take him long to release the mechanism, and they both slipped inside.

The Royal Guard rushed along the corridor to intercept what he had been informed was a *rogue* Commander. The man was apparently a little distance ahead, and so he produced his laser pistol, pointing it in front of him as he dashed forward. Then, all of a sudden he was hit by a violet beam of light...

Nineteen

The whole world seemed to spin, although his body went rigid, as he slipped to the floor, letting go of his weapon. Albin did not know what was happening to him, as the familiar voice in his head faded away, being replaced by a multitude of contrasting thoughts. One set were his own, and another someone else he did not recognize. Somehow, he seemed to have a split personality, and he did not like his *other self*. The loyal subject had been anything but over the past few days following the orders of someone he did not recognize. His mind had not been his own, and now for some reason he was back to his normal self.

Looking up he saw Commander Bodil standing over him, and by his side was a Holo Droid holding what appeared to be a torch.

Albin felt very confused and tried to speak, but no words came out, only a muffled groan.

Vilgot reached down.

"Would you mind if I took your weapon?"

Albin had known and respected the Commander for years, and did his best to respond.

"Sir!"

His voice was hoarse, and his mouth felt dry, as he watched the Commander pick up his laser pistol.

"Thank you Albin."

He felt confused, particularly by what the Commander then said.

"There is no time to explain, the Palace has been compromised!"

With that, he quickly moved away followed by the Holo Droid leaving Albin more confused than ever...

Outside, the black security shuttle touched down on the landing pad besides the Commander's ship. A hatch in the side then opened, and six black clad figures dashed out, weapons drawn heading for the entrance...

Starfield monitored the blips on his sensor display, which now indicated that the Hybrids had just entered the Palace complex. The Commander could also see them on his helmet's display, even though the clear moon glass visor was open.

There was a solitary Guard just up ahead, and then with a bit of luck they would have a clear run to the Royal Chambers.

Starfield prepared himself for the encounter, hoping that it would be just as easy as the previous one. The Guard was now just around the next corner, and as they rounded it, he depressed the button on the converted torch.

A violet beam shot out engulfing the Guard, who just smirked as he fired back.

"Ahhhhh!"

Starfield screamed as a laser pulse struck his moon glass shell, and his high-pitched shriek reverberated around the room.

He went into shock, and was not the only one!

For some reason, the violet flame had no effect!

Was this a Hybrid?

Over the years, Reptilians' genetic engineering skills had

enabled them to create many hybrids to infiltrate Aesir society, in an attempt to conquer them by deception. On this occasion however, it was a little different!

Far worse than a *Hybrid*, an ominous red-orange glow appeared in the eyes staring back at him, which were large and green-black in appearance. They were really perturbing, as somehow there standing in front of him was an actual *Reptilian!*

Unbeknown to him or the Commander, for a long time the Reptilians had been using a holographic stealth field generator, which disguised their appearance, making them look human. Something akin to a wristwatch held the advanced electronics which produced what they referred to as an *over soul.* That was not strictly the case as it was not spiritual in nature, although there was a biological component linking the device to wearer's actual DNA.

A *shape shifter!*

Vilgot also looked in amazement, as at first glance, it was virtually impossible to tell that the creature was not human, as it had no doubt mimicked human life signs. The device quickly recovered, and for an instant, he doubted what he had actually seen.

It was like everything suddenly slowed down, as if he was now stuck between the ticking seconds of an ancient clock.

How was this possible?

Then he noticed a very slight fluctuation within the creature's iris, as it shifted from a normal human eye, to the telltale Reptilian slit. It only lasted for a fraction of a second, but was enough for him to be sure. Somehow, the rapid eye movements must cause a minor glitch in the software, and if he had not been studying the creature's eyes intently, then he would never have notice.

The Commander brought his weapon to bear, as the Reptilian hesitated for a moment, which was just long enough for him to get a few shots away.

Vilgot pressed the trigger of his weapon again, concentrating his fire on the creature's chest, whilst staring into those arrogant and aggressive eyes.

The Reptilian stared back, as its shield began to ripple and Vilgot thought that the creature was going to suddenly lurch forward and attempt to rip him apart like a monster with its sharp claws and teeth!

"Ahhhhh!"

Starfield screamed again, making the Reptilian's shape shifting device fluctuate, revealing more of the creature. It was at that moment that he realised that quite by chance he had discovered something, and not just a Reptilian shape shifter.

For some reason, it had been unmasked when he screamed, and so his holographic brain deduced that a sonic pulse of a certain high frequency interfered with the electronic stealth device.

Whilst Starfield was busily analyzing information, Commander Bodil was left to deal with the Reptilian. His laser pulses had weakened the creature's defensive shield, but it was still a dangerous adversary. Reptilians were far stronger than humans, and even though this was a lesser being than a White Royal, it was still formidable, as he was about to find out.

The creature slipped his own weapon into its holster, relishing the opportunity to use its physical prowess, as a clawed hand suddenly lashed out, sending Vilgot flying. Somehow, the repeated laser pulses had been absorbed, as Reptilian energy shielding appeared to be very effective.

The Commander managed to stay on his feet, swaying from side to side, trying to avoid another swinging arm, as his thoughts turned to Joan. He could now see why she preferred to use a fire axe!

Starfield watched the two of them battling away, as an idea began to form in his mind. His sensors were able to analyse the composites and exotic materials which formed the Reptilians defensive shielding. It appeared as though it could withstand the laser energy searing into it, and so basing his assumptions on what he had already learnt, Starfield deduced that it was just a simple matter of affecting its structural integrity.

The shielding seemed to have the ability to deflect part of the incoming laser energy, as his sensors detected a rise in static energy in the air around it.

Commander Bodil was still grappling with the Reptilian, trying to fire his laser pistol again, as Starfield engaged his speakers transmitting a noise similar to the one he had emitted whilst screaming.

A laser pulse shot out from Vilgot's weapon, grazing his adversary, as Starfield measured the response by Reptilian's protective shielding, which seemed to automatically adjust and compensate.

He in turn, adjusted his frequency, in an attempt to destabilize it, and again was met with the same result. All he needed to do was to switch to a random frequency, as it seemed to have the ability to anticipate his actions.

Switching frequencies at random without any predictable pattern, the relatively weak sonic pulse was having an effect on the field's resonance, and the vibrational effect was certainly causing the Reptilian a few problems.

Vilgot was taking full advantage, searching for any weakness as he continued to struggle with the powerful beast. How he wished that he had his laser rifle, as the pistol was weak in comparison, with no repeat cycle. The Reptilian was also making it difficult to get a clean shot, reveling in the hand to hand combat.

Starfield also detected that the defensive shield also appeared to have a built in vibration absorber in the form of a gel, which was both crude but effective nevertheless.

The combination of the Commander's laser and Starfield's sonic pulses appeared to make the gel vibrate. Vilgot managed to get another shot away, as Starfield intensified his signal, and the gel began to vibrate more rapidly. They kept up their attacks until it began to boil, adding to the fluctuations in the shield's integrity.

Then it began to blur, and within seconds, the vibration increased so rapidly that the component parts began shaking themselves apart.

The Commander ducked again as a clawed hand scraped the top of his right shoulder. Reptilians may have been stronger, but fortunately, humans were far more agile!

Starfield continued to transmit random frequencies, which went way above what a human ear could hear, but the stealth field was again able to compensate.

Vilgot looked in alarm as his laser pistol was swept away,

clattering to the floor, as he felt a solid wall behind him. It was now a matter of unarmed combat, and even though he was a very skilful warrior, when faced with an opponent of such overwhelming strength and power, he was struggling to cope.

Starfield began to panic, not just because he could see that the Commander was struggling, but also for the fact that the fight had brought the creature far too close for comfort.

One clawed hand swept out towards Vilgot whilst the other sailed through the air towards him!

"Ahhhhh!"

Starfield screamed again, and as he did so, just like one of the entertainers at official functions, who was able to shatter glass with their voice, his scream matched the high-pitched natural resonance of the creature's defensive shield shattering the mechanism.

Vilgot dived and rolled, taking full advantage of the Reptilian's sudden hesitation, and seeing that the shield was down, he managed to reclaim his pistol and repeatedly fire into the creature's abdomen.

It was now the Reptilian's turn to scream, as its thick scaly green skin was seared. The creature leapt through the air, diving towards the Commander in a raging temper, as Vilgot tried to dodge out of the way, but he was not quite quick enough.

The Commander felt the full force of the Reptilian's body, and even his armored suit could not prevent him from being *pole axed!*

His helmet clattered away, becoming detached in the fall, as his arms and legs were pinned to the floor as the Reptilian stared directly into his eyes. Then it opened its mouth showing a set of razor sharp fangs. Vilgot struggled, but despite his best efforts there was no way that he could move.

The Reptilian appeared to be smiling, and about to rip his face off with its teeth!

Then, inextricably, it grimaced, as its head fell forward, smashing into the floor just missing the Commander's face.

Vilgot looked up in amazement, as he saw Starfield crouching down beside him.

The Holo Droid had removed a tool from his utility belt and thrust it into the back of the creature's neck!

"Ahhhhh!"

Starfield then screamed again, as a fountain of blue blood spilled out, splattering all over his moon glass shell...

Twenty

The upper reaches of Asgard's atmosphere reached up towards Gaia, as she continued to dodge and bend the sensor beams which ringed the planet. They were not going nearly as quickly as either Ren or her father would have liked, but they had to remain stealthed. Reports of the battle taking place way below them had raised their concerns, and they were desperate to assist their friends.

"I have just received a transmission from Starfield, and they have uncovered a stealthed Reptilian!"

Halvor gasped.

"In the Palace?"

He could not believe it.

"And the Hybrids are almost on top of them!"

Ren was equally shocked, increasing their speed.

"We can be there in a few minutes."

The worst of the sensor beams were behind them, but there were still many planetary defenses to negotiate. Even though Gaia had lain abandoned for nearly twenty years, she was still far more advanced than any other vessel within the Empire.

Thick layers of cloud beckoned, as they passed the last of the defensive platforms, fooling the sensor beams as they went. Gaia's moon glass shell began to heat up as the thick atmosphere pushed against it, which was proving difficult to hide. She was also attempting to disguise them as a maintenance shuttle returning to its supply station, altering records in a desperate bid to avoid detection.

"Is it working?"

Halvor was a communication expert, and had been busily assisting, and briefly looked up at his daughter.

"I think so!"

Someone would eventually detect their ruse, but hopefully not before they had left the planet…

Vilgot tried to squirm his way out from under the Reptilian, whilst Starfield stood their in shock. It had been horrifying witnessing the blood stained *Barbarian* massacring the Hybrids, and now he had killed a Reptilian and was also covered in blood!

He was not the only one, as the Commander's armored suit was smothered in it, as he finally managed to push the creature to one side.

"Starfield!"

The Holo Droid was in shock.

"Starfield!"

He tried again, and this time he looked over to where the Commander was standing. He picked up the Reptilian's laser pistol handing it to him.

"We have to get going."

Starfield reluctantly took it, his mind going back to his corporeal days when he had received some basic training, although he had never used a weapon against anyone before.

He was now a murderer!

Starfield shuffled his feet forward not being able to process what he had just done - had to do!

"We have to rescue the Empress."

That statement seemed to penetrate the shock, and he slowly began to pull himself together.

She was well loved and respected by all of her people, and Starfield was no exception.

That was just as well, as the Hybrids were only moments away...

Gaia broke through the outer atmosphere, as the glow from her moon glass shell began to fade. They were now in thick cloud cover, which helped to hide them from view. Far below lay the Royal Palace, which also had its own defenses. They were all working hard to circumvent them, as they descended rapidly...

A laser pulse fizzed into the wall beside Starfield, making him nearly jump out of his moon glass shell.

The Hybrids had arrived!

"Take cover."

Starfield did as he was told, taking shelter in a doorway, as Vilgot did the same on the opposite side of the corridor.

More laser pulses lashed into the walls as six black clad figures advanced rapidly.

Commander Bodil fired back catching one of them in the head, and he fell to the ground. There was no use using the torch, as it would not work on their metabolisms, so Starfield fired his laser pistol at them. His first shot went wide, but the second one hit a Hybrid on the arm. They had all activated their shields, so none of them were hurt, as the battle continued...

Gaia broke through the cloud cover over the main continent, still in stealth mode hoping that it would be enough to conceal them from anyone observing the sky, and along with her ability to confuse the sensors, they should be able to make it to the Palace undetected. It was not long before the ornamental gardens came into view, and just like the security shuttle had done a few minutes before, they would soon be landing besides it, and her occupants would be rushing through the corridors to join Starfield and the Commander...

A laser pulse struck the ancient wooden doorframe, causing it to catch fire just above Starfield's head, as the Hybrids continued to fire at him. Vilgot was also pinned down, and each time he tried to move he was met by another volley. How he wished that he had his normal armaments, as he could soon deal with attackers.

It was very frustrating, and taking a look at the power cell, he frowned at the reading. It was already below half way, and he had to chose his shots carefully. Starfield had the opposite, as he had only used his laser pistol sparingly. Another pulse caught the doorframe, and each shot was getting closer.

"Ahhhhh!"

The next one glanced off his arm, and he realised that he could not take many more shots before he was severely damaged.

He simply had to do something!

Another pulse hit him, and with a combination of desperation and fear he cried out again.

"Ahhhhh!"

This time he used the frequency which had nullified the Reptilian's shield, and the Hybrid's shields began to fluctuate.

Then, another pulse hit him.

"Ahhhhh!"

This time he cried out as loudly as he could, and charged forwards.

The Commander looked on in amazement as laser pulses shot out from Starfield's pistol, raking across the attackers who had lost their shielding.

What happened next was astonishing, and he gasped as Starfield cut them down just like he witnessed Joan do.

"Ahhhhh!"

Starfield continued screaming as the Hybrids fell...

Twenty One

Gaia came in low just high enough to clear the trees, before descending rapidly towards the landing pad. The other shuttles were parked side by side, and there was just enough room for her to squeeze onto the edge.

"Phew!"

Ren was relieved to have made it, as she was still learning how to fly the advanced craft. Halvor had already left his seat and was eager to get going, and his daughter was not far behind him.

"Come on!"

They both dashed out of the control room, making their way towards the hatch. Ren grabbed her hover board, and a laser rifle calling out to her father.

"I can get there quicker on my board. Maybe you ought to join the Doctor in uncle Vil's ship?"

Halvor was caught in two minds, as although her suggestion sounded sensible, he did not want his daughter going into a fight on her own.

"I'll be fine, and anyway, you would only slow me down."

Ren had her mother's determination, and he knew that she would just take off without him.

"OK, but be careful!"

Reluctantly he agreed, as Gaia was not big enough to accommodate them all.

Two people exited the stealthed craft, one jumping on a hover board, and the other rushing towards the nearest shuttle...

Vilgot Bodil scanned the Hybrids with his laser pistol, but none of them moved.

"Starfield?"

The Holo Droid stood motionless.

He waved his hand in front of Starfield's face, but his holographic eyes did not move. He was in shock again, and there was not time to try and break him out of it. He had to get to the Empress before reinforcements arrived...

Ren shot through the entrance holding the laser rifle in both hands. Her uncle had taught her well, and she was no stranger to combat simulations, although this would be the first time she had seen any real life action.

Starfield had a tracking device which was sending out a pulse which she was able to follow. She also had a map of the Palace, so it was easy to locate him. Walls sped past as she twisted and turned, passing a bemused Royal Guard on her way. Albin was still trying to come to terms with what had transpired.

Something or someone had taken over his mind...

A further series of flickers swept across the surface of the small glowing device situated deep within the Aesir Security Service Head Quarters. Another six corporeal entities had left *the joined!*

This was of far greater concern than the others, and something so serious, that it would to be dealt with as a priority.

Options were considered, and a resolution to the continuing crisis sought.

This situation had to end, now...

Halvor entered the code on the little pad just to the side of the shuttle hatch. He was breathing heavily, worried about his daughter and his oldest friend. He was still in two minds thinking that he should be with them, but logic dictated that they would be better served if he readied the shuttle for their evacuation.

The door slid open, and he was met by the barrel of a laser pistol.

"Don't move!"

Halvor could not even if he had wanted to, as the sudden shock rendered his limbs numb.

"Don't shoot!"

That was all he could think of saying.

"Halvor?"

The Doctor looked astounded.

"I thought that you were dead!"

Ren's father smiled.

"Well if you press that trigger I will be!"

Doctor Sorenson had been a good friend until the assassination and then his family having to go into hiding.

"Is that really you?"

Halvor smiled again.

"It is, but it's a long story and I haven't got time to explain."

The Doctor looked a little wary.

"Are you one of them?"

Halvor shook his head.

"No, I'm with the Commander, here to rescue the Empress."

The Doctor hesitated for a moment.

"How can I be sure?"

That was a good question.

"I designed the violet flame torch to incapacitate the nano robots within the blood system, and gave it to Starfield the Holo Droid."

The Doctor breathed out a sigh of relief.

"Well in that case then, you'd better come in..."

Commander Bodil was astonished that the Holo Droid had not only brought down the Hybrid's shields, but also brought them down as well. He had been pinned down, and had been fearing the worst. Again, he cursed the fact that he could not bring with him his normal armaments, as he could have done far more to help. Now, it looked as though Starfield was struggling to come to terms with what he had just done, and so he carefully removed the torch from the Holo Droid's utility belt, and made his way towards the Royal Chambers...

Ren travelled down a small section of corridor, and up ahead she could see that it branched off to the right. Her helmet's display indicated that she was not too far away, and she was soon speeding around the corner.

The Palace was indeed a maze of corridors, and she was glad that she had a signal to follow, otherwise it would have taken far too long to locate the Holo Droid. She could also see that for some reason her uncle Vil had left Starfield and was making progress towards the heart of the Palace. He was nearing the Royal Chambers, and she hoped that he would not be meeting much resistance...

Halvor and Doctor Sorenson dashed out of the Commander's shuttle, back towards Gaia. They were going to collect his wife and bring her back with them. Hopefully Joan would still be sedated, as the last thing he wished for was for her to go charging off like a mad woman wielding the fire axe again...

Ren was having exactly the same thought, as she rounded the next corner to see a lot of charred bodies.

She gasped, as there standing in amongst them was Starfield!

The hover board slowed as she scanned the scene, and her sensors indicated that they were all dead.

"Starfield!"

The Holo Droid did not respond.

"Starfield, are you all right?"

There was a slight movement within his holographic matrix, as a very pale gaunt white cloud circled the inside of his helmet.

"I have turned into a *Barbarian...*"

Twenty Two

A large ornately carved wooden door stood at the end of the corridor, and at each side of it stood a Royal Guard. They were dressed in the customary uniforms, resplendent in gold braiding which adorned their scarlet tunics and black trousers. Each man held a long ceremonial axe on long staff, a tradition carried forward from a long forgotten age.

The uniforms may have been ancient, but they also had modern laser pistols concealed within their tunics.

Vilgot slowed down, gently lowering his weapon whilst raising the adapted torch.

"Halt!"

The Guards lowered their axes, pointing them towards him. This was normal procedure, although there was nothing normal about today.

Looking into their eyes, he could see that they were a little glazed over, which was a clear sign that they had been compromised.

An uneasy standoff lasted only a few moments, before an axe was thrust towards him, and the Commander depressed the torch.'

A violet light shone out engulfing the first Royal Guard, who stumbled, whilst the other advanced. He too was suddenly bathed in the violet flame, and both of them looked stunned.

Vilgot watched as they both dropped to the floor, as the nanites inside them were neutralized. When he was satisfied that they had been immobilized, he pushed past them grasping the handle of the door, and gently pulling on it as he slowly eased the large ornately carved wooden structure open...

A sense of agitation spread across the small glowing device situated deep within the Aesir Security Service Head Quarters, following an additional six corporeal entities leaving *the joined,* which was totally unacceptable. Instantaneously, another team was dispatched to the Royal Palace to deal with the developing crisis...

Commander Bodil peered through the gap in the doorway, and was met by the Empress.

"Hello Vilgot, I have been expecting you!"

She beckoned him in smiling, and so he opened the door a little wider, moving into the room. His initial impression was that she has remained unaffected by the nano robots, although he still remained alert.

"I have been monitoring your progress, and you have done well to get this far, but now it is time for you to join the *collective."*

With that she retrieved a laser pistol from behind her back, pointing it at him.

Commander Bodil sighed, as he realised that she had been infected. He also realised that she was not holding a normal laser pistol, as he could see that this one contained a magazine full of tranquilizer darts, although he doubted that they containing a sedative, and were instead packed full of nano robots...

Ren could see how distressed Starfield was, but there was little that she could do to help. So, she just placed her hand on his shoulder.

"I understand!"

The fact that she did not, was besides the point!

Starfield was the first Holo Droid to have taken a life, and the enormity of what he had just done would live with him for the rest of his...

Halvor settled his wife into the Commander's shuttle, and then when the Doctor had taken a position in one of the seats, he joined him.

"How are they doing?"

Halvor patched into Ren's communicator.

"Serenity?"

There was a brief pause before she answered.

"Starfield's in shock and uncle Vil has gone for the Empress..."

Ren was on her way to join him, and leaving the Holo Droid standing there, she sped off on her hover board, and was soon approaching the large ornate wooden door.

Two stunned Royal Guards stood there bewildered, as their minds were full of contrasting thoughts. Neither of them took any notice of Ren as they were lost in their thoughts.

The door was ajar, and as she stepped off her hover board she could see her uncle Vil standing there, weapon raised, and opposite him was the Empress standing holding a laser pistol.

"Welcome Serenity!"

The Empress could see her peering around Vilgot's arm, and although her voice sounded normal, her actions were anything but. She had always been so warm and friendly, but seeing her holding the laser pistol it was clear to see that she had now also been compromised.

"You've been away for a few years and now its time to welcome you back."

The Empress gestured with her laser pistol, as Vilgot's eyes momentarily shifted between her and Serenity.

The Commander was weighing up his options, trying to decide what to do next.

"Please drop your weapon Vilgot, and Serenity please move to where I can see you."

The Commander did what he was asked, lowering the laser pistol, as Ren moved out from behind him.

"Thank you."

The atmosphere inside the Royal Chambers was tense, as a momentary uneasy standoff began, only broken when the Empress spoke again.

"It's time for you to take your rightful place within the collective."

With that she pressed the trigger of her laser pistol, and a tranquilizer dart shot out. At the exact same time, the Commander pressed the button on the torch he was still holding, releasing the violet flame.

Ren ducked behind him, as a dart struck Vilgot on the forehead, right between his eyes. He had left his helmet where it had fallen, and his head had been fully exposed.

Both he and the Empress fell to the floor, and as they did so, Ren managed to grab the torch out of the Commander's hand, and engulf him in the violet flame...

Epilogue

A series of tiny stars floated aimlessly around the inside of Starfield's moon glass shell, like a snow globe that had just been shaken. It was not a bad analogy, as he had been very badly shaken, but nevertheless, he responded to the signal he had just received.

Slowly putting one foot in front of the other, he picked his way through the bodies, and staggered down the corridor to where he saw the two recovering Royal Guards. They looked up at him, and then at each other, still in a state of confusion. Starfield knew exactly how they felt, as he moved through the large ornately carved wooden doorway.

Commander Bodil, could also see stars in front of his eyes, but fortunately the nano robots had been neutralized before they had time to take effect. Although he had been stunned, his mind was clear.

However, Ren knew exactly what she was doing.

"Starfield, can you pick up the Empress?"

He looked at Serenity and then Freya 13th, wondering if he should lay his moon glass hands upon her.

"Uncle Vil, are you up to balancing on my hover board with me?"

He thought about it for a few seconds before nodding his head.

"Ok, then we need to move!"

Elias looked at Hugo, who looked back not quite understanding what he was seeing. The two Royal Guards had been confused, with all sorts of memories swimming around inside their respective heads. Now they were totally bemused, as they witnessed Supreme Commander Bodil riding past on a hover board with a young woman who they thought had been killed a few years ago in a public assassination. If that was not bizarre enough, then followed the Empress being carried in the arms of Holo Droid....

The small glowing device contained within the Aesir Security Service Head Quarters, flashed in a series of pulses, as instructions were relayed to another six of the *joined*. Freya the 13th's signal had been lost, and with it a major asset. This was the most serious development to date, and even though the device was devoid of emotion, it felt a creeping sense of anger nevertheless...

The hover board swept down the corridors towards the exit, closely followed by the Holo Droid. Gaia could soon see them dashing out onto the landing pad, as her sensors flashed, warning her that another security shuttle was on its way.

Outside, Vilgot jumped off the hover board, taking the Empress off the Holo Droid, and gently carrying her into his shuttle.

Ren and Starfield rushed to Gaia's awaiting hatch, as both sets of engines began to roar.

Serenity leapt off her hover board and ran to the main control room, diving into the pilot's seat, as Starfield followed on behind.

He was still in shock, and could not believe what had happened to him.

"Me a Holo Droid First Class!"

He groaned miserably, thinking about the Empress.

Not only had he become a *Barbarian*, but it also felt as though it was not so much a matter of rescue, but more like a case of kidnapping!

He was definitely going to be disassembled...

The Sphere of Destiny

We could never even imagine a universe that did not contain observers (us)...

Because the very building blocks of the universe, are the acts of (us) observing the universe.

John Wheeler

Introduction

Captain Bjorn Blonqvist, know to his friends as *Bear*, due to his enormous size, sat alone in his cargo hauler watching and waiting. It had been several years since he had retired from the *Titan Super Soldiers*, and life had been good. Travelling from one system to another gave him plenty of time to relax, but not today.

He must admit that he had seen so many worlds on his travels, only this time he was able to appreciate them. It had been hard, always training and preparing for dangerous missions, some of which he had been lucky to survive, even though there was always a *Replicant* body ready and waiting for him.

The whole process of chopping and changing, never altering his outward appearance was not the bad part, it was the mental upheaval that he had finally succumbed to. Yes, he did miss the camaraderie, but not the stress that came with it.

Bear had enjoyed a quiet retirement, until the encrypted message he had received yesterday...

One

"Stealth field engaged!"

Supreme Commander Vilgot Bodil pulled hard on the controls as his shuttle craft lifted off the landing pad, just missing the security shuttle that was parked next to him. He was going to have to use all of his piloting skills to get away, as an alarm sounded within the Royal Palace.

Next to him, Gaia's engines spluttered into life, as the liquid mercury plasma engine fired up the magnetic field disrupter. An electrical current soon flowed with enough charge to counteract the ship's mass.

Somewhat different from the Commander's shuttle, which had the more traditional ion engines, electrons flowed from the negatively charged electrical plate at the base of a craft, towards the ball of positive charge at the top. A shimmering haze indicated that the whirlpool field was now active, and she had gravitational thrust.

Starfield was still in a daze, standing on the other side of the main control room. His moon glass shell was scared by laser pulses, but they were nothing compared to the ones in his mind.

The subtle movement of the anti-gravity drive passed by unnoticed, as he stared out blankly.

"Incoming security shuttle!"

Gaia's voice sounded hesitant, fearful.

Ren was also in a daze, doing her best to get them into the air.

She was slowly getting used to the strange operating system, but could still do with some help.

"Starfield!"

The Holo Droid remained stationary.

"Starfield, I need you!"

He needed therapy!

"Oh Flux!"

Ren swore as the security shuttle opened fire.

"I need weapons!"

She watched the Commander's ship breaking away, trying to draw them off her.

A bright flash and a dull thud rattled the ship, as Gaia took a direct hit. Fortunately, Ren had managed to raise shields, but her mind could not cope with anything else.

On the main screen, she could see her uncle Vil firing back at the purusing vessel, as another bright flash of light erupted in the sky. This time it was the Palace's defenses, and his shuttle took a direct hit.

Ren knew that it would not take many more before the shield started to fail, and she simply had to do something!

"Flux!"

They were gaining in height, rocking violently from side to side, although that was more to do with her piloting skills than taking evasive action.

The black security shuttle caught them again, weakening their shield, as it took a direct hit from the Commander's laser cannon.

"Follow me, and try to keep up!"

Vilgot's voice rang in her ears, as she did her best to follow. Ren was not much of a pilot, especially having an experimental craft.

"I will do my best!"

Another shot hit them, and she began to realise that her best was not going to be good enough!

Both craft shot up into the sky, with their pursuer hot on their heals.

"I can't shake it off!"

Ren's voice had more than a little desperation in it.

"Shield down to 63%."

Another pulse hit them, this time from the ground.

"52%."

Gaia was suffering too!"

"43% and falling!"

That did not sound good, and Ren had to do something.

"31%."

The countdown to destruction continued!

More shots flashed both up from the ground and from the pursuing craft, as the Commander fired back.

"Serenity, you have to do something as I can't hold them off for much longer!"

Vilgot's voice now sounded desperate.

Ren looked at the Holo Droid again, and cried out in desperation.

"Starfield!"

Still there was no response as yet another pulse hit them significantly weakening their shield.

"Starfield!"

Ren shouted as loudly as she could, before holding her breath, as they were engulfed in brilliant light...

Two

Bright colours swirled down like a waterfall of rainbow stars, and then, as if a dam wall had just burst, the stars spilled out everywhere.

"Flux!"

The offensive language rang around the inside of Gaia's hull, although it was not Ren who was the offender on this occasion.

Starfield could not help himself, as the desperation of the moment overwhelmed him.

"Oh, my!"

Gaia was shocked, and whether it was instinct, desperation, or a little of both, Starfield had fired the ship's main weapon, vapourising the security shuttle.

Neither Ren nor Gaia could believe it!

Starfield had sworn again, but that was nothing compared to him eliminating six more Reptilian Hybrids, doubling his kill count!

Ren was just thankful to still be alive, but that feeling did not last long as another laser pulse hit them from the ground far below.

"Shields are down to just 5%!"

They all realised that the next shot would flow right through the shields and impact on Gaia's moon glass hull.

There was nothing else that Ren could do but chase after the Commander's shuttle, and as she did so, she suddenly realised that it was heading straight towards a large cargo hauler.

The craft was so big, that she doubted either of them could avoid it, as a collision indicator rang out.

Ren began to panic as everything went into a blur...

Commander Bodil could see the hauler blocking out space above him, as laser pulses continued to ring out around him. How he wished that he was still aboard the Titan Super Soldier's craft, which had been named *The Porcupine,* by Joan because of its spines. They were a combination of guns and energy dispersers, as it was heavily shielded, and with a full complement of crew, it would have been far easier to withstand the barrage...

Ren felt a sudden jolt, assuming that they had been hit, and closed her eyes waiting for the inevitable explosion followed by nothingness. She held her breath, scrunching up her eyes, as her fingers dug into the palms of her hands.

Gaia started to vibrate, as the whole of her life began to flash before her eyes.

She could see her parents as a small child, happy times spent together. Helping her father and sparing with her mother. Her uncle Vil and the way he doted on her. The assassination attempt and then going into hiding.

Was it all going to be in vain...

Vilgot saw something shoot out of the cargo hauler, just missing him, and before he could react, something else swept past, as his shuttle shook.

He looked at Halvor, wondering if this was the last time, he would ever see his old friend?

There was no time for words, although he knew there was no

need for them. Both men understood exactly how the other felt, and were equally honoured to have served with the another.

This was finally it, as a green glow engulfed them, as twin explosions shattered the fabric of space-time...

"Serenity!"

Ren could hear a distant voice calling out her name, for a moment she thought that she was in the after life.

"Serenity!"

The voice was a familiar one, her uncle Vil.

Was he accompanying her into Valhalla?

"There is no reason to be alarmed."

She supposed that there was not, after all, he would be with her, along with her parents.

Gradually, Ren opened her eyes, expecting to see a bright tube of light. She actually did see one, although it was a shade of green.

"Uncle?"

Vilgot Bodil breathed out a huge sigh of relief, thankful that she was still alive, as he let go of his controls.

The green light had a hold of him too, and he began to relax as he recognised its frequency.

"So much for an easy retirement!"

A deep strong voice echoed through the speakers, as he began to smile.

"Bear!"

There was a deep laugh.

"The one and only, Sir!"

His message had got through, and as usual, the big man had not let him down.

"Am I glad to hear your voice!"

Bear had managed to grab hold of both vessels with his tractor beam, and pull them inside the hold of the cargo hauler. He then, launched two decoys, which were destroyed covering their tracks. The ground based laser instillations would assume that the explosions would be them!

"Just a minute, Sir!"

Bear then spoke to space traffic control, confirming the story. He had been passing by the planet on his way to the starway, and witnessed two craft being destroyed. Naturally, he had an alias, wishing to remain anonymous.

Sometimes old habits died hard...

Three

Patrol ships swarmed around Asgard, like a hive of angry bees, as news of the Empress's abduction quickly spread. Alarms were raised all over the Empire, quickly followed by the devastating news that she had been lost - killed by her own people.

The recriminations would reverberate over the Aesir worlds for years to come, as an investigation was quickly launched.

Never before had the people been so stunned, and a week of mourning commenced as the sober tone spread far quicker than the nano virus....

Flickers of light swept across the surface of the small glowing device situated deep within the Aesir Security Service Head Quarters, as the situation was assessed.

The gunners stationed at the ground based laser cannon which had fired the fatal shot, felt themselves moving in unison towards an awaiting shuttle. They did not understand what they had done, only that they must leave now. Entering the vessel and taking their seats like robots, they engaged the main drive unit and lifted off into the air.

All about them was a state of confusion, but their minds were clear, and they knew exactly what to do.

Four more corporeal entities suddenly left *the joined,* although this time there was no need for investigation. A large explosion caused by the self-destruct mechanism would hide all traces of their infestation.

It would be inevitable that this race would succumb, just like all of the others, and with the Aesir worlds now in a state of shock and confusion, a new opportunity had presented itself which would prove to be very advantageous...

"Uncle Vil?"

Ren felt very disorientated, not quite knowing where she was.

Had she just died?

The faint outline of the inside of the ship began to form through the green haze which had engulfed her.

"Gaia?"

What was the ship doing here?

"Yes Serenity!"

There was no way that they could have survived or was there...

"We have company!"

Several patrol ships swarmed around the cargo hauler, hailing Bear.

"Please identify yourself."

A curt voice rang out, as Bear answered it.

"Captain Lindquist, of the Falk (Falcon)."

Vilgot smiled to himself, as Lindquist meant *Twig,* and anyone hearing it would presume that he was small in stature, as opposed to being the size of a giant spruce.

"State the nature of your business."

Bear sent across his flight plan.

"Cargo haulage."

Hopefully the paperwork would be enough to settle the mind of the person speaking to him.

"Did you witness an explosion?"

Bear chuckled.

"I certainly did, two in fact, and what's more they were uncomfortably close."

He was playing along sounding as innocent as he could.

There was then a brief pause before he spoke again.

"Can you state the nature of the explosions?"

The voice on the other end seemed to be buying his story.

"That's classified."

Bear continued to act innocent.

"Can I help you with anything else?"

There was a grunt on the other end of the line.

"No, be on your way!"

The Commander breathed out a huge sigh of relief, as there was nothing to connect them with the explosions...

"Gaia, what's our status?"

Ren was also hoping for more information, but unlike the curt voice, Gaia knew exactly what had happened.

"We appear to be inside the hold of a cargo hauler."

Suddenly, everything began to make sense.

"Uncle Vil..!"

Starfield stood there mesmerized by their sudden rescue. One minute they had been fighting for their very lives, and the next, safely inside the *Falk*.

Nothing seemed to make sense to him anymore, as he analyzed his own behaviour.

A Holo First class descending into savagery!

He hardly noticed his injuries, or felt the pain from the fiber optic cables embedded into his moon glass shell. He was able to sense many things through them, including the burns which he had received inside the palace.

What was to come of him?

"Performing diagnostic."

Gaia's voice sounded tired, if that was something a ship's computer could feel.

"I have a few systems reporting malfunctions, and my energy shields need a complete overhaul."

Ren lent back into the pilot's seat, feeling the comforting texture wrapping around her, as she closed her eyes for a moment, suddenly feeling very tired.

"Where are we heading?"

Gaia tried to get a fix.

"We should be approaching the entrance to the starway in a few minutes..."

Four

A familiar sensation ran through Ren's body, as it felt so heavy that it would sink right through the soft material of the pilot's seat, or chair as she sometimes referred to it.

Whenever she relaxed, Serenity felt the connection with Gaia increase, and had gone beyond the initial phase of seeing herself standing naked in a darkened room.

Adjusting to her surroundings, she let her thoughts drift, reaching out with her mind, as outside, the Falk had just entered the starway.

Subtly, somewhere out there Ren could also sense another presence, as if something was tingling somewhere at the back of her mind. Then, as she tried to reach out towards it, faint flickers began to manifest at the edge of the darkness. It was almost like the light at the end of a tunnel, gradually getting closer until a cloud of bright sparkles began to manifest at the periphery of her vision.

Light then began to stream all around her, above and beyond the twin screens which lay in front, as Ren drifted away from the holographic matrix which comprised of Gaia's consciousness.

A floating shadowy figure began to emerge from the darkness, and as it did so, she could see that it was somewhat different to *Mjolnir*. For a start, it was much larger, and the wings were more defined. However, there was something very unusual about it, and yet strangely familiar.

Ren continued to concentrate on the image forming in the mindspace where *Mjolnir* usually appeared, and the more she concentrated upon it, the more shocked she became, for there, materialising in front of her, was of all things a *Dragon!*

"Please do not be alarmed!"

Well she certainly was!

"I mean you no harm."

Despite resembling a large red and green dragon, with a white scaly chest, she could detect a sincerity that felt very real.

Could it be some kind of a trick?

"My name is *Ga'latec,* and I would like to ask you for your help."

Ren did not know what to make of him.

What was a Dragon doing inside her head, and why was he purportedly asking her for help?

Ga'latec could sense her apprehension, and under the circumstances, he could not blame her.

"I promise you I mean you no harm."

This would be the first Reptilian not to!

"Please let me explain a little about myself."

Normally, the only conversations to be had with a Reptilian were short and to the point - *Surrender of die!*

"I am one of the spiritual leaders of my people."

Ren did not know that they even had a spiritual side.

"Many, many years ago, the Reptilians you are familiar with, originated on my home world. In those distant days, we were of one people. Some of us desired to remain as we had always been, and pursue a spiritual path, whereas others wished to progress. Eventually, a split developed and those desiring to explore our solar system and beyond left."

That seemed plausible, if unlikely.

"One day, a group of them encountered another species who had been infected with nano robots created by the Artificial Intelligence, which was in turn created by the *Archons*."

Suddenly, what *Ga'latec* had been saying began to make sense.

"They were then taken over, and the infection soon spread to others, until the whole population was infected."

If it had not been for her father and uncle, then her people would also be on the verge of succumbing to the infestation.

"The *Leavers* had already become arrogant and aggressive, with a belief that they had evolved to be superior to not only us, but all others species. This suited the Artificial Intelligence, as the Leavers had already conquered every civilization that they had encountered, and were the perfect candidates for what they intended..."

Ga'latec looked forlorn, and his mannerisms and overall characteristics indicated that he was telling the truth, although there was no way to be completely sure.

If he was, then that begged the question:

What could she do about it...

Five

Thoughts swam about like fish in a pool, each going in a different direction, and yet the school swimming as a whole. Over the past few days, Serenity's life had been turned upside down and then back to front, never quite righting itself. In fact, ever since the attempted assassination, everything had been topsy-turvy.

That was one of her mother's expressions, and she doubted whether even *Ga'latec's* sincerity would be enough to not send her towards the nearest fire axe!

Ren was still sitting there, her body in the pilot's seat/chair, and her mind halfway between her body and Gaia, with all parts drifting through the starway, talking to a spiritual dragon.

She knew just how Starfield felt...

The Holo Droid was still standing motionless, oblivious to what was going on around him. Maybe that was just as well, as he would not have been able to deal with his own problems, let alone anyone else's...

Gaia could perceive what was happening, as it was all being filtered through her holographic matrix. She was being pragmatic as usual, which was just as well, as there was little that she could do to help either.

After a long pause, *Ga'latec* continued.

"*Mjolnir* contacted me because I have vital information!"

Ren raised her eyebrows.

"We have been monitoring the Leavers for quite some time, trying to prevent this whole scenario. We have the ability to crossover to a different timeline, and have been searching for eons for one where the others never left."

She sighed. Time paradoxes were a nightmare, and even her father did not fully understand them.

"We intend to crossover to that timeline, but before we do, *Mjolnir,* who has been monitoring us, wishes for me to share our information with you."

Great!

Ren again felt just like Starfield when he had been forced to undertake the mission to rescue the Empress.

"There is a place where the Hybrids are infected with nanites referred to as the *Sphere of Destiny.* It exists on a different timeline, and so it is impossible for you to get to it in this one. It must be destroyed, but if you are going to gain access to it, then you will have to travel to that particular timeline."

Ren looked confused, and sensing her confusion, *Ga'latec* tried to explain.

"Past, present and future all exist at the same time, although that concept is very hard to understand."

Ren rolled her eyes.

"It is all about perception, and what you believe to be true!"

Well, Ren did not know what to believe!

"Basically there are many, many different timelines all coexisting at what we conceive to be the same *time,* although there is not really any time, or *time* as we think of it."

He took a deep breath.

"Imagine strands of string running parallel to each other, say like the strings of an instrument you refer to as a harp. If you pluck one string in the middle, that point is you, and before and behind you there is more string. If each string is a different timeline, then a different you exists on each string. If you pluck another, then you have moved to a different timeline."

This was already getting very complicated!

"What will happen in the future is up to you to create. If you were able to go back in time, then you would have to go back on another timeline, where you would encounter what you remembered experiencing. However, as soon as you went back you would be influencing a timeline which would run parallel to the one you have just left."

Ren did her best to visualise what he was telling her.

"You would not actually be going back or forward in time, but going to another timeline that you perceive as being your past or indeed your future."

How she wished her father was here with her now.

"What is already happening is that we are all switching timelines, and eventually we will lose contact with those who are markedly different from ourselves, which is why we have all been brought together, being surrounded by likeminded people who are all creating a similar timeline. The old world that we used to know will still be there, but we have moved to one more akin to the one we all wish to reside in."

Now that was confusing!

"In other words, it is the expansion of consciousness!"

Ren must have looked as confused as she felt, as *Ga'latec* paused for a moment.

"Serenity, because of your unique DNA you are able to interact in such a way that you can move Gaia into another timeline where you can get access to the Sphere of Destiny."

So that was why *Mjolnir* had brought her mother here, and because he was a *being of light*, he did not experience things in the same way that they did, and *time* was one of them!

It must have all been part of a carefully worked out plan, and now she assumed that *Ga'latec* held the key to their whole future - if there was such a thing...

Six

Light refracted off a glistening sphere hovering in a weird type of space. It was unusual to say the least, as if it was somehow stuck somewhere ethereal in some way.

In the centre, there was what at first she thought was a nano robot, although the more that she looked at it, the more that she could see within it.

Was there a face, or some sort of a figure?

Could she see something holding it?

It was both fascinating and unnerving at the same time!

Ren felt herself staring at it hypnotically, trying to work out just what and where it was.

"Serenity."

Someone called out her name, and the voice sounded distant, although it was not Ga'latec, who seemed to have disappeared. It was odd, being drawn to the sphere, as if nothing else seemed to matter.

"Serenity!"

The voice called out her name again, slowly bringing her attention away from the sphere.

"Can you hear me?"

Ren felt something touch her arm, which was enough to finally draw her attention away from the sphere, and as she did so, she slowly began to draw her mind away from the connection with Gaia.

"I'm here!"

Ever so slowly, Ren opened her eyes, and there crouching next to her was her mother Joan.

"Mum?"

Joan smiled.

"What are you doing here?"

Joan took a deep breath.

"Long story!"

She seemed to be back to her old self, without the glint of madness in her eyes.

"Doctor Sorenson has been helping me."

Ren's mind cast back to the hasty escape from the Royal Palace.

"Is he the one who was injecting everybody with nano robots?"

Joan nodded.

"Yes, but he has been cleansed and is now helping us."

Ren looked up to see her father Halvor standing in the doorway to the main control room. He also smiled, which she found very reassuring.

She could also see the Holo Droid, and Starfield felt anything but reassured!

He looked at Joan, and then caught his own image in Gaia's shiny moon glass hull. He grimaced as he saw a *Barbarian* standing in front of him, and another looking back towards him from his own reflection...

It felt good to get out and stretch her legs, and Ren had soon joined everyone else in a comfortable lounge within the Falk.

Her Uncle Vil had received a great big hug, and she had been introduced to Bear and the Doctor, who had checked her out with his portable scanner.

"You look quite healthy, if a little tired and confused, which is understandable under the circumstances."

Ren was still a bit wary of him, as he had been infected by the nanites, although her father assured her that they were inactive and gradually being destroyed by his immune system.

Nothing seemed to reassure Starfield though, who had placed himself back in another self-diagnostic routine, having recharged thanks to Gaia. He would never be the same again, and contemplated either removing or blocking his memories, as he was having a very hard time dealing with them.

Starfield was supposed to be an A.I. with a human consciousness. A.I. should have stood for Artificial Intelligence, not Artificially Inhuman!

He preferred the term *Artificial Person,* as he did not wish to be associated with the Artificial Intelligence murdering all of those people, and yet he had already *eliminated* twelve himself!

Ren also felt uneasy, as she could not get the image of either the sphere or Ga'latec out of her mind. Apparently, she had been unconscious for several hours,, and they had left the starway and were well on their way to wherever they were going.

There was also another problem, and that was the Empress. She was resting in a room, also trying to come to terms with what had happened.

There was a polite knock on her door, distracting her thoughts.

"Please come in."

It was the Commander.

"Faithful, loyal Vilgot, whatever would I do without you?"

He gave a polite bow before entering.

"I have been giving matters a great deal of thought."

She was not the only one!

"If my people learn that I am still alive, and the circumstances surrounding my disappearance, then it will not only shake the Empire to its very foundations, but also risks splitting it in two. We do not know how many people have been infected, and whilst we tear ourselves apart, the Reptilians could take full advantage and strike."

Vilgot had been having exactly the same thought.

"But, if I am presumed dead, then there will be a constitutional crisis as I have no immediate family."

It was indeed a dilemma!

"You have always advised me well, and so what do you suggest I do?"

The Commander sighed, not having the answer to either her predicament or that of his people...

Seven

A small machine scurried about in the corridor outside, although there was no cause for alarm. Service Drones and Holo Droids were all part of the ship's systems, performing maintenance and effecting repairs. The system had no external links, or links to the main computer. Each part of it was preprogrammed, and anything that needed updating was carried out by hand, where various commands could be entered manually.

Bear utilized them as he wished to travel alone, although now he had far more people aboard the Falk than he ever anticipated.

His mind drifted back to when they had all arrived.

"Sir!"

Commander Bodil had waved his salute away.

"There is no need for that, particularly as I will probably face a Court Martial whenever the authorities catch up with me!"

There could be no greater crime than abducting the Empress, and yet if they only knew the truth, then it would not matter one way or the other. If they failed, then all was lost anyway...

Vilgot Bodil's mind was also drifting, as he pondered the Empress's question. His thoughts settled on Serenity, and what she had told him about her experiences whilst they traversed the starway.

It was hard for him to believe that there were peaceful, spiritual Reptilians, although nothing surprised him anymore.

If the information she had gained was to be believed, then they would have to destroy the sphere if they were going to stop the Hybrids.

That was a lot easier said than done!

At his disposal, he did have two former Titan Super Soldiers, a brilliant communications expert, a very gifted young woman, two vessels, and a neurotic Holo Droid.

What could possibly go wrong!

The Empress broke his train of thought.

"I would like to join your team!"

The Commander rolled his eyes.

"But you Majesty!"

She sighed deeply.

"I am no longer the ruler of the Aesir people, as I am officially dead!"

It was his turn to sigh.

"Well, you are very much alive to me!"

Vilgot forgot himself, his manner coarse.

"I may be, but from now on I wish to be addressed as *Freya*, and be one of your team, I command it, and that is that!"

He could not help himself and shot back.

"If you are no longer our ruler, then you cannot command me to do anything!"

For the first time in his life, he actually saw her lose her temper.

"Augh!"

She made a fist with both hands, and then pounded them on his shoulders.

"You, you, augh!"

She then stopped and looked straight into his eyes.

"Do you know how frustrating my life has been, always having to do the right thing, and never being able to do what I really want to do?"

Vilgot was shocked, never having really thought about it before.

"Do you ever wonder why I have never married?"

He had considered that, which bothered him in case anything happened to her, and his people were left without a ruler.

"All I ever have around me are sycophants, people creeping and crawling like insects."

He had noticed how some people acted, which had turned his stomach.

"There has only ever been one real man in my life, strong, loyal and true."

The Commander ran everyone he had ever encountered in the palace through his mind, but now that he really thought about it, he just could not place them.

The Empress then looked straight into his eyes, before rapping her arms around his neck and placing a passionate kiss on his lips.

Throughout his life, Vilgot Bodil had faced many enemies, fought for his very life, and never yielded. But now, his knees went weak and he thought that he was going to faint with shock...

Eight

Stars swam about like little pulses of light flickering in and out of the Commander's vision. He felt his pulse racing, as he was overcome by emotion. His career had taken precedence over his life, and when Serenity was born, he looked up and loved her like his own daughter. Now there was another young woman in his life, one who was overflowing with emotion, just like his goddaughter...

Ren walked along the corridor towards the Empress's room, as her uncle had been away quite a while. Everyone was awaiting his orders, and she wondered what was taking him so long.

The door was slightly ajar, and Ren was about to knock when she spotted them kissing passionately.

"Uncle Vil!"

Ren also felt light headed and thought that she was also going to faint with shock!

The Commander pulled away as his face flushed.

"I, er!"

He was totally lost for words...

Ren stood there dumbfounded when the Empress spoke.

"I am no longer an Empress and wish henceforth to be called by my name *Freya,* and be treated as just another member of the team."

She then looked at her uncle.

"And before you ask, I have been in love with Vilgot ever since I first met him!"

Ren had once told Starfield she understood how he felt when he was deep in shock after eliminating six Hybrid Reptilians,, now her whole world was falling apart, and she knew just how he must have been feeling!

It was a lot to take in, especially as their whole civilisation was on the verge of collapse.

Vilgot had had absolutely no idea how Freya had felt, as romance, particularly with his monarch was the farthest thing from his mind.

He had always loved and admired her, but not in a romantic way, although the depth of her feeling had sparked something off inside him too.

He looked at Freya and then at Ren, lost for words, until she came to the rescue.

"I don't wish to put a dampener on things, but we have to do something about the sphere."

The Commander was stunned by her maturity, and suddenly realised that he had become sidetracked.

"You are absolutely right..."

Gathering himself together, Vilgot led the two young women back to where the others were waiting. He then did his best to explain the new arrangement.

Everyone looked stunned when they were told about the *abdication.* The Empress was no longer their ruler, and to make matters worse, by the way she acted around him, it was also clear that she was in a relationship with the Commander!

"Flux!"

There were a few gasps, as Starfield swore, before his

molecules turned purple.

He had done it again, and in front of the Empress of all people!

Starfield was mortified...

Things eventually calmed down, and people began to accept that *Freya* was now part of the team.

That was not their only problem, as the Commander took the opportunity to inform everyone of what Serenity had witnessed. It was unbelievable, and yet no one contradicted what he was telling them, after all, it was common knowledge that Joan had been brought here by an *Ancient!*

Somehow, the sphere had to be neutralised!

Everyone sat deep in thought until Freya finally broke the silence.

"So, how are we going to get there?"

That was a very good question, particularly as the facility lay on another timeline.

"Well, your maj, er I mean Freya, I have my ship!"

Bear was not the only one struggling to come to terms with the new arrangement.

Unfortunately, the Falk was not capable of getting there.

"Part of the design of Gaia was that it was theoretically possible for the pilot to think of where they wished to go, and that the ship would take them there. However, no one has ever been capable of doing so!"

Halvor had his scientific *hat* on, using it to hide his discomfort.

His oldest and most trusted friend had got himself *involved* with their monarch, adding a second count of treason to his name!

Joan then spoke, and to everyone's relief she was still being rational.

"My daughter has managed to interface with Gaia's holographic matrix in a much greater way than anyone else, so if it is possible, then logically she could be the one to actually do it."

Starfield looked into her eyes and could see that she appeared much more stable, catching his own reflection again, there was only one person in the room with madness in their eyes, and it happened to be him!

Joan continued

"Whilst I was in the military there was a program dedicated to something they referred to as *Remote Viewing!*"

She had been by her beloved General Swartz's side for several years, in a position of authority being his Personal Assistant.

"From what I can remember, it was defined as being *the practice of seeking impressions about a distant or unseen target, using extrasensory perception.* In other words, gaining accurate information about a distant or non-local place, person or event without using your physical senses or any other obvious means."

Freya nodded.

"Like *clairvoyance?*"

Joan smiled, and Starfield had to admit that there was warmth and sincerity in her words.

How could someone turn from a *Barbarian* into a rational

person in such a short space of time. Or, change from a normal rational Artificial Person into a *Barbarian* in such a short space of time?

Joan continued.

"About 80% of the sensory information we experience each moment is generated by our brain. To speed up the process, our mind makes a calculated *guess* using a small sample of information available."

Starfield ran things through his holographic matrix, whilst sharing the conversation with Gaia.

"I sat in on a few sessions, and from what I can remember there was one person guiding the session, and another acquiring the information, it was all about increasing the sensitivity to subtle information."

Bear had fought with Joan, and never realised that behind the axe wielding savage, there was a very astute woman.

"First a target was selected, by either giving co-ordinates or by using a visual image."

They were all following her words.

"I believe the basic technique was for the psychic to quieten their mind, and let go of all thoughts, before bringing the target to mind. Then, a description of the basic impressions they had, and what they felt was the predominant feature about the target. Was it natural or artificial, surrounded by land or water, or in this case space."

This was not all that different from the way he had guided Serenity after administering a sedative the first time she had linked with Gaia.

"I also remember the person guiding the session telling the psychic not to second guess themselves, and concentrate on the first thing that came into their mind, the fainter, the better."

Listening to her words, Starfield had to reconsider how he thought about the *Barbarian*, as he knew from first hand how an unexpected situation could change a person, and particularly in his case, not for the good either!

"Remember, the information is coming from the mind via the *Autonomic Nervous System.* The subconscious mind already knows everything there is to know, it just has to communicate with the conscious mind. It does that through the body's subtle sensations and feelings."

There were certainly a lot of them flying about at the moment!

"I distinctly remember the psychic being instructed to imagine themselves floating above the target, and being encouraged to concentrate on what they saw, smelt, tasted and on the temperature. Also to use their perception to visualise the size, shape and any patterns about it, or whether they received an emotional reaction."

Life seemed to be all about emotional reactions, and as far as Starfield was concerned, there had been quite enough of them already...

Nine

The comfortable material of the pilot's seat wrapped itself around Ren, as she settled back ready to attempt her first remote viewing session. They needed far more information if they were to attempt an attack on the facility.

Gaia was ready to assist, and Starfield stood next to her, although he was still *remote viewing* the hybrids he had eliminated. Try as he might, he just could not get either the massacre in the palace or the destruction of the shuttle out of his mind. Over and over they went, in a never-ending cycle, which only added to his discomfort.

Starfield - Holo Droid First Class *Barbarian!*

Ren's mind was full of nothingness, as she slipped into the dark dome shaped room which represented Gaia's holographic brain.

Looking down upon herself, she was naked, which symbolised her being a fetus in the womb. She had learnt to visualise herself clothed, and as she did so, the twin screens also materialised.

The external screen had Starfield, his molecules whirring around inside his head. Ren could see fragmented scenes of death and destruction, as he relived his torment. The other screen displayed the view from outside, as normal space twinkled with distant stars.

Apparently, she had to let go of all thoughts and let her mind drift. Starfield was supposed to be directing her, having accessed more information about the procedure.

It was not a case of letting his mind drift, as it had done nothing else ever since the encounter within the palace. He needed to concentrate on what he was doing.

Doing his best to compose himself, Starfield tried to put all other thoughts to the back of his mind.

"Try to focus your thoughts on the sphere."

Ren did her best, as she visualised it floating in a kind of electric space...

Ren had described exactly what she had seen, as the Commander formulated a plan. So far, Halvor had developed the *violet ray torch* which was able to neutralise the nano robots at close quarters, but they needed something far more substantial if they were going to disrupt an entire complex.

Vilgot had left his old friend to devise something else, which could be amended when they were given more information about the sphere. He had retreated to *Freya's* room, and was now sitting there lost in thought.

"You look a little uncomfortable."

The Commander felt it!

"Well, I am."

Freya looked a bit confused.

"Is it Serenity?"

He sighed.

"Partially, although she is a very capable young woman."

There was no doubting that, as she had already proved herself.

"And?"

He shuffled his feet uncomfortably.

"Well, I am just a commoner from a little village, with no status or title."

Freya held his hand.

"There is no hierarchy in consciousness, only the mind does that. You are a Supreme Commander who has earnt his title by merit and not by birth, and you are far more of a man that any of them!"

She then looked into his eyes.

"Besides, you are my choice, and I am no longer an Empress."

That did make a difference.

"According to our constitution, a monarch is only permitted to have three Replicant bodies. My parents have already gone into retirement, and I myself will have to retire at the end of this one."

Everything had changed when the consciousness transfer process was discovered, and the decision had been made to limit the amount of time any monarch could rule. It was thought better for the people and the ruler themselves, as a perpetual leader would only stagnate their society.

"I am the last in line, and there is no successor, so maybe it is time for a change?"

Becoming a Republic was a big step, but now was not the time to decide on such things, as they had an enemy beating down their proverbial *door*...

Ten

A semi translucent ball sat in *weird space,* a place far removed from normal space. It looked as if light had been bent out of shape, somehow wrapped around a sphere of energy. Rays spread out in multicoloured patterns dotted with stars that appeared to be from normal space, yet somehow different. The sphere reflected and refracted the translucent light, and in the midst of it, there was the unmistakable image of a nano robot obscuring what must be the hybrid generation facility.

Ren could see it clearly, as if the nanite was somehow in an egg about to hatch, which was what her *Autonomic Nervous System* was telling her, interpreting her subconscious mind via her body's *extrasensory perceptions.*

Gaia was also able to process her thoughts through the link they were sharing, and via her holographic matrix, she was sending her thoughts to Starfield.

Trilateral cognitive voyeurism on a grand scale!

Starfield was both amazed and terrified at what he was seeing, having already been infected by the madness which plagued Joan.

Was he now going to be contaminated by her daughter too?

He was supposed to meld his corporeal, ethereal consciousness with a holographic brain within a Holo Droid moon glass shell. Naturally, he expected there to be a few changes, but never had he once imagined that undergoing the experimental research would have had such a profound effect upon him.

The grand holographic matrix of the universe was a massive, unending possibility and indeed probability. He ought to have known that, being *Stellan the scientist.* Those days were long gone, and so it seemed was all reason and self-control.

Descending into savagery, barbarism and now multidimensional madness - all in one day!

Starfield, Holo Droid First Class Psychopath!

Psychopathy is traditionally a personality disorder characterized by persistent antisocial behavior, impaired empathy and remorse, and bold, disinhibited, and egotistical traits. It is sometimes considered synonymous with sociopathy.

Yes, that was now him - no wonder people feared Artificial Intelligence!

The image then began to change as he neared the sphere, and without so much as a small *pop*, he was though the outer skin.

Inside, it looked relatively normal, normal that was if you did not take into account the Hybrids...

Ren was supposed to be guided, asked to do certain things, but the Holo Droid seemed lost in his own tormented world. She subconsciously felt that he was losing sanity, but she had to admit that what she was observing was enough to make anyone lose their mind!

Gaia, who had always been pragmatic, slowly began to take over, also sensing that her life partner was struggling to keep himself together.

"Can you focus on the security features?"

Ren felt relieved that Gaia had taken over, as she entered a large room filled with screens. From here, she could view the whole facility, which appeared to be nothing less than a Hybrid production line. There were literally hundreds of them at various stages of *completion*. Some were in the fetal state, whilst others were *hatching*, but instead of being babies, they were fully-grown humanoids.

The Reptilian geneticists were far in advance of anything the Aesir had, and no doubt that information came courtesy of the Artificial Intelligence which had taken them over.

Her heart sank at the reality of the hopelessness of their situation, and then drifting into view came the familiar form of *Mjolnir*, known as *the war hammer of the god of thunder and protector of Midgard.*

His floating shadow of intricate patterns spiraling out from his centre into tendrils, which fanned out into wings, as his vaguely human form slowly stopped in front of her.

"Serenity, I am here to help..."

Halvor stretched his arms, arching his aching back as he observed the schematics for the much larger violet flame torch he had been designing, to send a much more powerful Electo Magnetic Pulse.

The idea was based on sound scientific principles, but he needed a sophisticated delivery system.

"Sound!"

That was it!

He got up off his seat rushing out of the room towards where the Commander was sitting talking to Freya...

"Haven't you ever wished that you could throw off the chains of responsibility?"

Vilgot smiled.

The thought had crossed his mind!

It had not been easy leading the *Titan Super Soldiers,* and when he took the position of *Supreme Commander*, he had assumed that it entailed more ceremonial than responsibility. It was in effect semi retirement, where he would become the Empress's advisor. Then, the attempted assassination had occurred, and he was thrust into the role of coordinating a secret mission.

The secret was out, and it appeared that that was not the only one!

"Oh Vilgot!"

Freya took his hand.

"We all need time for love!"

She lent forward to kiss him, when there was a sudden knock at the door...

Eleven

An ethereal hand clasped onto Ren's, although this one did not pull her towards a kiss, it was *Mjolnir* guiding her towards a terminal *manned* by a Reptilian. His clawed hand scratched away, entering and updating a coding sequence, ready to be transmitted to the latest batch of Hybrids.

"Do not worry, I have masked our presence, and he will not be able to detect us."

That was good to know!

"However, I will not be able to do it for long."

The Artificial Intelligence is already working hard to amend the weakness your father detected in their programming, and so you must act soon before it is too late!"

Ren could see the code on the screen, although she did not know what any of it meant. All that she did know was that the information flowed, and the update would soon be complete.

She had to get back to her father, and let him know just what they were up against...

Freya was up against Vilgot, planting a kiss on his lips despite the fact that there was someone on the other side of the door. They knocked again, and this time she reluctantly pulled away, as she beckoned them forth in her customary royal manner.

"Enter!"

Halvor opened the door, and by the look on his old friend's face, he knew that he had interrupted something.

"Sorry to intrude, but I think I am onto something..."

Ren was on the move, and could feel herself floating up through the ceiling of the room. The facility was not as large as she had expected, and as she moved upwards, she could see the whole layout. This was vital information, and she tried to remember as much of it as she could, before she moved through the skin of the sphere, back into weird space, where she watched *Mjolnir* float away into the distance.

It was time for her to return, and she could now feel Gaia guiding her back to her normal reality...

Starfield was monitoring everything, with his holographic matrix making a recording. Normally, it would have been easy for him with his higher intelligence, but he was struggling and would be glad when the connection was finally broken, much like he felt at the moment!

It had been an extraordinary experience encountering *Mjolnir,* and he had joined a very exclusive club. Only a handful of people had ever encountered an *Ancient,* and to them it had been a deeply spiritual experience.

The Starfield had a sudden thought.

Could he find salvation in religion...

Halvor felt uncomfortable playing *gooseberry.*

That was an expression he had picked up from his wife Joan. He remembered her saying it once, when she had been talking about being with General Swartz and his wife Mirriam. At first, he had no idea what she was on about, until she explained that it referred to feeling uncomfortable between two lovers. He still did not understand what a fruit had to do with it, until she went on to explain that in the past, women had *chaperones,* who occupied themselves by picking fruit such as gooseberries while the couple being chaperoned did whatever they were doing.

He still did not fully understand, but the expression had stuck, and now he knew what she mean, even though there was no fruit to pick!

Nevertheless, he had to interrupt them, as he needed more information.

"Can you tell me a little more about how the Holo Droid brought down the Reptilians' shield?"

Although the Commander had seen him do it, he was too busy fending off the Hybrids to take much notice.

"Sound waves I think."

Halvor smiled.

"Then I need to talk to him..."

Starfield did not feel much like talking, rather praying!

The *Ancients* may have been revered, and have god like status, but those who were of a spiritual nature looked upon something even higher than them.

The Ancients believed that there was one supreme consciousness, and after they ascended to become creatures of light, they had hoped to find the answer. But, they were still searching, and Starfield's quest had only just begun...

Ren could feel her limbs again, as her consciousness returned to her body. It had been quite a ride, and one which she was glad was over.

Things were certainly odd, and as she opened her eyes, they got a good deal stranger, as there on his knees she could see

Starfield *praying!*

"Oh creator of all that is and all that ever will be, please forgive me for my sins, and help me to become a much better Artificial Person."

Ren could not believe her eyes!

"Starfield?"

He visibly jumped.

"Oh Flux!"

She had startled him.

"Now look at what I've done!"

He looked mortified.

"Not only have I sworn in the presence of the Empress, but now whilst at prayer I have sworn in the presence of *the creator of all that is!"*

He started to synthetically sob.

"What greater sin could I have committed..."

It took both Ren and Gaia to finally console Starfield, and get him up off his knees and out of the ship. He was in a terrible state, and they needed to get him to the Doctor...

Doctor Sorenson looked dumbfounded.

"I am a medical doctor, not a cyberneticist!"

He looked at Starfield who was clearly in a state of great distress.

"But placing that aside, can't you do something about his mental state?"

The Doctor understood that inside his moon glass shell, there was a human consciousness.

"Well, I suppose I can try!"

He was still unconvinced.

"Starfield has vital intelligence and we cannot access it when he is like this."

Doctor Sorenson could see that.

"And we also need to find out just how he brought down the Reptilian's shield."

Halvor was equally concerned.

"Can't we hypnotize him?"

That was all that Ren could think of.

Doctor Sorenson scratched his head.

"I don't think it's even possible to hypnotize a Holo Droid!"

There clearly seemed something wrong with the consciousness transfer process, as the Holo Droid was mentally unstable. On reflection, it did seem to be the only logical solution to not only calm him down, but also to get at the information he contained.

"It's absolutely vital to find out just how he managed to compromise the Reptilian's energy shield."

Halvor had already worked out that it could only be done sonically, and that the Holo Droid held the secret.

The Doctor sighed deeply.

He was used to treating human beings not machines, although Starfield was an Artificial Person.

"Well, I suppose there's no harm in trying!"

He was not convinced, but led them to a quiet room anyway, where they managed to get Starfield to sit down on a chair.

The Holo Droid looked to be in a bad way, and clearly suffering from psychosis. From what they had told him he was incoherent, and his speech and behaviour had been inappropriate to say the least!

Looking into his moon glass head, Starfield's holographic face stared back, as if the Doctor was not there.

"Everything here is safe, calm, and peaceful. Let yourself sink into the chair as your relax."

He was trying to give some reassurance, as if Starfield was a human being.

"Your eyes may feel heavy and want to close, so let yourself sink further into the chair."

Normally when performing hypnosis, he would concentrate on the muscles, but the Holo Droid did not have any. Instead, he had photonic strands in a type of electric skeleton, which worked in the same manner beneath his moon glass shell.

Doctor Sorenson was fascinated by Starfield's internal structure which was sometimes visible. It was all about thrust, attraction, repulsion and torque, which was how he was able to move about. The physics involved were way beyond his knowledge, and yet in principle, were not so dissimilar from the anatomy he did understand.

"You are feeling calm and relaxed, calm and relaxed."

His voice seemed to be having some effect, as Starfield was a lot calmer.

"Try and focus on the space right between my eyebrows."

Two holographic eyes stared out in his direction.

"Let your eyes and eyelids relax, growing heavy."

Starfield did feel tired, and a little more relaxed than he had been.

"As I continue to talk, you will continue to relax, and feel yourself getting calmer and calmer, until you feel as though you are floating blissfully away..."

Twelve

A feeling of weightlessness as if a feather of gossamer thickness was levitating ever upwards, consumed Starfield's moon glass shell. He had never experienced anything quite like it before, not even in corporeal form.

It was as though the emotional weight he had been carrying had been lifted off his shoulders, and he could be, just be!

The weightlessness of space seemed so comforting, and the twinkling of distant stars magical, as he drifted away...

"I think that he has left the normal waking Beta phase, and passed into the relaxed and meditative Alpha state."

Doctor Sorenson's voice sounded relieved, and had far more confidence in it than it had done before.

It looked as if you could hypnotise a Holo Droid after all!

"The transition between the two can lead to the sudden sensation of falling that sometimes propels people into a light sleep."

The Doctor then looked at Ren

"Do Holo Droids sleep?"

Ren shrugged her shoulders.

"I have absolutely no idea!"

Then something extraordinary happened - Starfield started to snore!

"He must be in Theta phase, and who knows, he might even enter Delta phase!"

That was where the Doctor would be able to access his memories...

Blissful nothingness, undisturbed, apart that was from a distant floating shadow, and as he began to focus his attention on it, Starfield suddenly realised that it was not a shadow out there at all, but in fact, a creature of light.

Intricate patterns spiralled from its centre, and slender thread like structures fanned out into wings. It then began to fly towards him, and Starfield could see the wings, with patterns that looked as though they had been delicately painted on, like a watercolour representation of a winged human being.

"Welcome Stellan."

It was *Mjolnir!*

Starfield felt both shocked and elated - he was actually in the presence of an *Ancient!*

A being of light, able to switch his photons and atoms into any form he chose, and to travel through time and space at will!

"I am here to help you..."

A rainbow of sparkles drifted around the inside of Starfield's head, and the Doctor took that as a good sign.

"You are feeling calm and relaxed, calm and relaxed."

It still felt odd using his hypnotherapy techniques on a Holo Droid, but Doctor Sorenson pressed on.

"You are safe and secure, safe and secure."

There was no visible sign of stress, so the Doctor thought that it was a good time to try and extract some information.

"I would like to ask you some questions, and remember that you are here with me and are perfectly safe and secure, safe and secure..."

Mjolnir smiled warmly, holding out his hands.

"Come."

Starfield moved towards him, and held onto them.

He felt so blissful, that he hardly noticed the Doctor's words.

"Can you remember how you brought down the Reptilian's energy shield?"

Starfield began to talk about what had transpired, somehow being separated from his words, which simply flowed as his mind was elsewhere.

"I deduced that a sonic pulse of a certain high frequency interfered with the electronic stealth device. My sensors were able to analyze the composites and exotic materials which formed the Reptilians' defensive shielding. It appeared as though it could withstand the laser energy searing into it, and so it was simply a matter of affecting its structural integrity. The shielding appeared to have the ability to deflect part of the incoming laser energy, as there was a rise in static energy in the air around it."

They were recording everything, and what he was saying was very encouraging.

"I engaged my speakers, transmitting a noise similar to the one I had emitted whilst screaming, and simply measured the response of the protective shielding, which seemed to automatically adjust and compensate. Then, I adjusted the frequency in an attempt to destabilize it, and switched to a random frequency without any predictable pattern. The relatively weak sonic pulse had an effect on the field's resonance, although the vibrational effect was countered by a vibration absorber in the form of a gel."

It was actually working, and they were learning a lot.

"When I intensified the signal, the gel began to vibrate more rapidly, until it began to boil, and within seconds the vibration increased until the component parts shook themselves apart."

Starfield's voice was steady and controlled, as if someone else was in charge of it.

"My scream matched the high-pitched natural resonance of the Reptilians' defensive shield, and eventually shattered the mechanism."

He then transmitted the frequency patterns he had used...

Mjolnir smiled, still holding onto the Holo Droid's hands.

"Very good Stellan."

He then gradually let go.

"Remember I will always be with you."

Starfield was overjoyed, with a feeling of total bliss flowing through every atom of his being. He then watched Mjolnir floating away, before he began to drift slowly down to where his moon glass shell was waiting...

Thirteen

Numbers danced, a never ending sequence of zero's and ones, as the computer screen was awash with algorithms. Sitting typing code was Halvor, utilising the information the Doctor had gained form Starfield the neurotic Holo Droid.

He still found it bizarre that hypnotherapy had worked on him, and the communication's expert was very thankful. At least now, they stood a chance of defeating the sphere's defenses.

What they did after that however, was another matter...

Supreme Commander Vilgot Bodil assessed his troops. One retired Titan Super Soldier besides himself, and Joan the *Dragon Slayer*. He could not have wished for better, and with the Empress/Freya, that made four.

Hardly an invasion force!

Halvor would stay in Gaia with Doctor Sorenson, Serenity and Starfield, which also made four!

The Commander would have liked a full complement of troops, but that was all he had, and there was no way of calling for additional help, as that would give them away.

Secrecy was paramount, and besides there was only limited space within Gaia. She has been an experimental survey ship, small enough to act as a scout ship, and never designed to carry more than the pilot and a Holo Droid. They would have to cram into the hold, and it would be a bit of a tight squeeze.

On the positive side, assuming that they could get there, they each had an armored suit, and Halvor was working on an energy shield utilizing rotating frequencies, similar but more stable than the ones used by the Reptilian.

Gaia had a matter generator, a small machine which could produce virtually anything, as long as it had the basic mineral building blocks. Out of it, she had produced five fire axes, one for each of his team and a spare, having seen the effectiveness of the crude weapon at first hand.

The Commander shuddered at the thought!

Halvor was also busily updating Gaia's main weapon, which was a laser cannon, that would now also use a rotating frequency to bring down the sphere's defensive shield. There was no way that they could simply blast the thing to pieces, as it would take too long, and besides they needed vital intelligence. No one knew just how far the infiltration had spread, or what other nasty surprises they had in store.

So, they were going to make their way inside, download as much information as they could, and then set charges to blow the thing apart!

Not such a subtle plan, but hopefully effective nevertheless...

The matter generator was also used to create small disc devices which could be clamped to the armored suit's chest plate. They would produce the rotating energy shield, which would hopefully protect the team.

Things were slowly coming together, but they still faced an uphill task to get everything in place before the enemy adjusted their defenses...

Starfield relaxed in the chair, letting Doctor Sorenson's soothing voice wash over him. He felt so much better, as if a heavy weight had been lifted off his shoulders.

"You are safe and relaxed, safe and relaxed."

He certainly was, and had communed with an *Ancient* - what more could a Holo Droid ask for?

"It's almost time for you to come back in to the room, and when you do, you are going to continue to feel safe and relaxed, safe and relaxed."

Starfield was so comfortable here, that he did not wish to come back.

"You are becoming more aware of my voice, and of your surroundings, and when you are ready, please open your eyes."

Starfield's eyes were holographic!

"When you choose to open your eyes, you will feel refreshed and alert, and still feel safe and relaxed, safe and relaxed."

He did feel more energised, as if he had just been recharged.

"Now I am going to count to ten, and open your eyes when you are ready."

Starfield listened to the count, and when it reached three, he opened his eyes...

A pair of comforting arms wrapped themselves around Vilgot's neck, and he too felt safe and relaxed, safe and relaxed. It was so long since he had felt this way, and he cherished these moments realising that they could all come to an end in the very near future.

"Do you think that you could ever love me?"

Freya whispered in his ear.

"I always have, and always will!"

She kissed the side of his neck.

"As a woman, not as an Empress!"

It would take him time to make the transition, although now that he thought about it, there had always been something there.

"As both!

He reached up and clasped her hand.

The touching moment was only broken by Halvor, who had a breakthrough.

"I think I have the shield configuration."

They pulled apart, as this was what they had been waiting for.

"That is good news!"

The Commander knew his old friend could do it, and the shields along with Gaia's upgraded weapon meant that their chances of success had now improved dramatically...

Fourteen

A familiar smell drifted into Bear's nostrils as he slipped on his old armoured suit. He had seen many battles in it over the years, and although patched and parts replaced it was like his second skin. There was one thing for certain, and that was that it would never fit anyone else.

His sheer size meant that it had to be custom made, not like the other standard suits he had stored away for just such an occasion. Circumstances now dictated that he had taken them out of storage, and the rest of the small team of *rebels*, were also slipping them on.

It was unclear as to how far the conspiracy had spread, and no one outside the Falk could be trusted. Hopefully by the end of the day they would have more information, or everything would be lost!

"Are you sure about this?"

The Commander still felt uneasy that Freya would be accompanying them.

"Definitely, and beside, you were the one that trained me!"

That was a fair point, as Serenity and Freya had been his prodigies. He had been worried about both young women, and so had done his best to make sure that they could look after themselves. Underneath the fancy clothes of an Empress, there was a tough fighter, something which no one else knew, apart from himself.

She was more than capable of taking care of herself, but little did he realise that during the time they had spent together, she had developed a deep attachment to him. Now the truth was out, and it was something else that he had to deal with.

Since the conception of *Replicant's,* age meant nothing, as it was easy to acquire a new body, if that was what you desired, and had the resources to afford one. Yes, he was considerably older than her mentally, but physically they were very compatible.

The former Emperor and his wife, who were now in retirement, living under assumed identities had been very kind to him, and had entrusted him with their only daughter's safety.

Yes, the palace was full of Royal Guards, but due to his military exploits, and his trustworthiness, in their eyes he had been a natural choice. Now, he was going to put her safety at risk, which bothered him.

"Don't look so worried Vilgot!"

He managed a smile, although it was a bit of a forced one.

"You trained me well..."

Starfield kept on silently chanting his mantra *safe and secure, safe and secure.* He had already taken up position in the small control room within Gaia. They had both benefitted from Halvor's ingenuity, and he now had the protective shield he desired.

Safe and secure, safe and secure!

It was like being reborn, and he had a lot of faith in Doctor Sorenson. The medical doctor/psychologist had taken away all of the self doubt and loathing he had been feeling, and a new, improved Holo Droid First Class stood waiting for the others to take up position.

"Good to have you back."

Gaia was also relieved, as his behaviour had been *extreme* to say the least!

"Good to be back!"

He really meant it, and when Serenity arrived he actually smiled, which was something he had not done for quite a while. In the small cargo hold stood the Commander, Empress, giant Captain and the *Dragon Slayer.* Her presence did not bother him, as he had more than a little understanding of how she had descended into madness.

The Doctor had set up his medical equipment in the small galley, whilst Halvor had set his computer equipment up in the small bedroom. The Falk would remain on autopilot waiting for their return, so all in all everything was *good to go...*

Ren eased herself into the pilot's seat, letting the material meld to her body, and slipped on the helmet. She was getting more used to it now, and it was not long before she slipped into the dark domed room, which simulated Gaia's head. Naked and then fully clothed, like a foetus in the womb being birthed into a new reality, the twin screens appeared in front of her. On one was the inside of the ship, where Starfield was awaiting instructions, and the other showed a view of the much larger cargo hold of the Falk.

The Commander's shuttle sat there, having been stripped of armaments, and anything else useful for the mission. The Cargo bay doors were already open, and she could see the faint glow of the energy field which kept the atmosphere in and the nothingness of space out.

There was now no turning back now...

Fifteen

A ball of light shone out from temporal space, wedged between timelines, and placed in such a manner that it was virtually undetectable. Deep within the *sphere* there lay a small glowing device identical to the one located within the Aesir Security Service Head Quarters. There were many of them, all linked quantumly, sharing information as rapidly as it happened.

This particular device began to flicker, as it monitored the progress being made within the facility. It was not much bigger than a standard human helmet, and the plan was to take control of every individual human being, who would all be *joined* in the near future. When this occurred, it would be time to move onto the next phase of the plan until the whole universe succumbed.

Out there somewhere, a few individuals had eluded their grip, although they all felt that that was just a minor glitch, and would soon be rectified...

"Ready?"

Ren took a deep breath before answering.

"Yes uncle Vil."

She was nervous, anxious, and more than a little worried that she would not be able to do this.

Starfield stood next to her, also sharing her concerns.

He was back together again thanks to Doctor Sorenson, and the same words kept repeating inside his holographic brain.

Safe and secure, safe and secure.

Gaia powered up, as her gravitational drive engaged, sending s small flutter through Ren's body.

This was it!

The Doctor had suggested breathing exercises, although it may have been better if he had hypnotised her just like he had done the Holo Droid. But, she needed to be in full control of her actions, as everyone's life depended on it.

In two three four, out two three four.

Concentrating her thoughts on the sphere, she let the image wash over her, become part of her, letting it seep into every fiber of her being. She visualised herself hovering above it, looking down at the strange glowing structure.

Power surged through Gaia, and the Commander clasped his laser rifle to his chest, as he always did whenever he was embarking on a mission where he was not flying the craft. He had been on many of them, but none as important as the one he was now undertaking.

There was then a sudden flash of light, although there was no lurch backwards, as he had been expecting. The transition was so smooth, that before he noticed anything, they were already there...

The small glowing device did not notice anything either, as it busily exchanged information with the others. There were no real dangers to be encountered, as nothing could stand up to their combined power. Confidence was high, even though a small anomaly had been detected. It would probably be nothing more than quantum flux, which was a byproduct of the sphere...

Halvor was squeezed into what should have been the only bedroom, his organic computer equipment strewn all over the mattress. Sensor information rapidly appeared from the fiber optic cable joining the portable device to the socket on the wall. He would have loved to have spent months, if not years poring over the advanced vessel, but for now his desires would have to wait.

He loved tinkering with things, taking them apart and putting them back together again. Communications equipment in particular, which is how he had discovered the signal in the first place. If he had not, then they would not be here rescuing the Empress, or fighting to save his people from being taken over and then systematically wiped out!

"Engage the laser beam!"

Vilgot's voice echoed around the inside of his helmet, which was also transmitting a view of the space around the sphere. It was as his daughter had stated, *weird space*, like nothing he had ever seen before. Reflecting patterns of light, which were clearly some sort of very advanced energy shield, and by his calculations, it should be possible to bring it down.

"Well, here goes nothing!"

He remotely fired Gaia's main weapon, which he had reconfigured...

An unexpected beam of light raced across the temporal field, slamming into the protective shielding, which appeared to come from the anomaly that had just been detected.

The laser pulse presented little danger, and even in the unlikely event that it did manage to penetrate the shield, which was virtually impossible, it would only be a matter of retuning the structural stability to strengthen the crude material of the frame.

By doing this, it would not only solidify, but would have the ability to deflect part of the incoming laser energy, frustrating the attacker's efforts.

That was unexpected!

The laser beam had retuned itself, before adjustments could be made. The laser beam was not only using a different frequency, but one that cancelled out the field's integrity. It was now pulsing at the frame's natural rate of resonance.

Maybe just a lucky shot, although luck was such a primitive concept, that it hardly warranted a second thought!

All that was needed was to retune the structural stability field to a random frequency.

It could not be!

The frequency of the attacker's laser beam had already matched it, and as the frequencies kept changing, so to did the attacker's laser beam.

It was as though somehow, the frequencies were being anticipated!

This was even more alarming, and very unexpected!

The relatively weak laser beam then spread to a much wider dispersal, vibrating the gel which acted as a shock absorber, making the connecting frames resonate together as one.

This was intriguing, but again posed no real danger!

The gel was more than capable of absorbing any vibration that could threaten the frames.

An alert sounded, as one section of gel seemed to be losing integrity, and of all things, appeared to be evaporating!

The pulsating laser beam tuned to multiple frequencies, had now caused one small section to break, shaking the connected frame, causing that to also break!

Within a few seconds, the weak attacker's laser beam began to vibrate a whole section, shaking it apart, causing a resonance wave to travel along the interconnected frame that supported the next section.

Random and non-random frequencies were tried to counter the vibrational effect, but somehow that was making things even worse.

This was all very unexpected, and the odds of something like this happening were so slim, that they had not even been calculated!

The impossible then happened - the shield was failing...

Halvor was working as quickly as he could, his algorithms anticipating what the Artificial Intelligence was going to do next. Being connected to Gaia's systems was a huge advantage, as her artificial intelligence was comparable to that of the enemy. The technology involve was astounding, although he did not have time to dwell. The shield was failing, and as it did so, he caught his first glimpse of the structure which lay beneath.

A large composite cube, with what appeared to be a laser cannon on each side greeted him. The configuration was effectively able to cover a full 360-degree range, so there were no blind spots. It also appeared as though they could not fire whilst the shield was in place, and now that it was down, it would only be a matter of seconds before they would be under fire...

Target acquired, opening firing sequence.

Laser pulses shot out of the laser cannon facing the unknown craft, and as they did do, somehow they were deflected away!

An analysis indicated that the vessel's shielding was far more advanced that expected. Random fluctuations in the laser pulses should compensate.

More light lit up the area around the vessel, but for some reason the laser pulses were having little effect.

Something was wrong...

Halvor scanned the cube, pinpointing entry ports, and as he did so, laser pulses bounced off Gaia's shield. So far, it was holding, with little effect on its structural integrity. They had to move quickly though, as the combined fire from a number of laser cannon would eventually overwhelm the algorithms he had put in place.

Targeting one section, he fired, aiming for a laser cannon in an effort to destabilise it...

Cannon number three is reporting slight damage!

Compensating.

The laser beam appeared to be a narrow band, fluctuating resonantly in both intensity and signal. It was as though it was able to anticipate the changes being made, and what was more, there was an object approaching quickly...

"Missile away!"

The Commander's shuttle had been stripped of them, and of all things coated with a substance that acted as a mirror. It may have been crude, but as it was targeted by another laser cannon, the bean was deflected away, refracting harmlessly into *weird space*.

Each missile not only had the mirror coating, but also its own energy shield, fluctuating at random, courtesy of Halvor's algorithms...

Intense thought flashed across the glowing device as it analysed the object, which was moving at a rapid rate towards the laser cannon.

It had to be destroyed...

Commander Bodil had everything relayed to his helmet display, and so far, things were going far better than he could have hoped for. He could see the missile homing in, and then there was an explosion.

"Laser cannon destroyed!"

There were no cheers, as Ren moved in rapidly to where there was an entry port not being covered by enemy fire. There was now a gap in the facility's defences, which had to be exploited before their shields began to fail. Only 17% had been lost so far, but it appeared as though the algorithm her father had programmed into Gaia, was not able to deflect everything.

20%!

Gaia swept in closer, as more energy pulses ricocheted off her shields.

27% !

A constant beam of energy focused on the entry port, causing the structural integrity of the door to fail, and it could be seen visibly melting as they shot towards it.

"Hold on!"

Ren cried out as they smashed into it, sending a ripple of energy across Gaia's shield.

57%!

Several laser pulses impacted along with the material of the door, as they forced their way inside...

Sixteen

Omni H'benar, White Royal Governor General, third in line of the Omni clan, geneticist and facility overlord, did not like interruptions. His arrogance often brought him into conflict with the small glowing device that thought that it was in charge.

Initially, he waved away the thoughts that were coalescing in the back of his mind, as the nanites did their best to distract him from his work.

His people had long been enslaved by the *Archons*, although they would never admit it. More like an alliance, they both thrived on negative emotions, which fed their energetic needs.

Very set in their ways, they were very good at miniaturising equipment, and understanding genetics, which they had used to enhance themselves and hurt others. Their arrogance grew from the fact that they had not evolved over such a long period of time, that naturally they thought of themselves as already being fully evolved, thus superior to all other species.

Unlike the Hybrids they were creating!

They lived in a riged military and social structure, and were awarded teeth and claws for success, which they wore on bands around their necks. Omni H'benar had plenty of them, as he had always abided by the rules and regulations, upholding the honour of his clan.

How dare he be interrupted when he was programming the latest batch!

Shields had been compromised by an unknown force. If it was humans, then they would present no problem for they could be easily controlled, as their minds were so much weaker than his own species.

The universe was all about *densities* and the more evolved a species became, the higher they went until existing as nothing more than pure energy, or so they thought.

Omni H'benar smirked, thinking of himself as already close to the pinnacle, only the *Pindar* sat above him, and one day soon he would unseat the clan ruler and become Pindar himself, and in time overall Pindar of his entire species.

He smirked at the thought!

The *Ancients* had strived to finally merge with what they considered as *the all that is*, the one super conscious mind at the centre of the universe, but sadly for them, that had never been achieved.

He could not resist another smirk, as he thought about them!

Unfortunately, without realising it, both he and his people had become trapped within a very dense energy field that they could not break out of, unlike the energy field the attackers had just broken through...

"We're in!"

Gaia's shields were now down to just 38%, which was a minor miracle considering the pounding they had taken. The danger was not over though, as internal lasers started firing at them, positioned inside the port.

"Can we neutralise those lasers?"

The Commander was not happy about them, as they would impede his progress.

"I'm onto it!"

Halvor was tapping away furiously on his keyboard, making adjustments to Gaia's main weapon. He had to refocus the beam so that it would not blow a hole through the outer wall.

A light then flashed across the inside of the port, as the first laser was neutralised. Three others, all positioned in the corners, where the walls met the roof were still active. Another pulse shot out, followed by an explosion.

"Bring us about."

Ren swung them round, bringing the other two lasers into range. Unfortunately, her main weapon had limited manoeuvrability, something that would have to be attended to when, or if they made it back...

The small glowing device at the centre of the facility became frustrated, a peculiar corporeal sensation. Not only had the attackers broken through both the shield and the door to the entry portal, they had also taken out its defensive lasers, ironically designed to prevent any compromised Hybrid from escaping.

It usually took about 8 to 10 hours for the nano robots to gain full control over the Hybrid's body, as there were certain remote tissues that were hard to reach.

Once the process was complete, the Hybrid was made to stand in a locked room in front of a screen which encompassed an entire wall. Everything was checked to make sure that no foreign energy signatures were present, and if there were, then there were laser ports embedded in the walls to neutralise any contaminant.

So far, none had escaped, and when the attackers were neutralised, then the lasers they had destroyed would have to be replaced...

The team of four heavily armored soldiers waited for the final laser to be destroyed, before the outer door was opened.

"Ready!"

The Commander was poised to jump out onto the metallic floor of the entry port.

"Dropping shield in three, two, one!"

Vilgot launched himself into the air, rolling onto his back, and taking cover beside a shuttle, which he presumed would ferry the Hybrids to their destination.

The others quickly followed, spreading out, covering the entry port in case they met any resistance, or more hidden lasers...

Ren eased her mind out from Gaia, travelling through the entry port wall, as if it was not there at all. She was remote viewing, only this time barely as remote as it had been before.

Floating about, she could see that there was activity from within, and she had to warn her uncle of what he was up against...

Seventeen

Omni H'benar observed the latest batch of Hybrids being checked. He was the only Reptilian within the facility, as he did not trust any of his own people. Instead, biomechanoids were used, a common product for many species. They were simple to construct and fairly reliable, if rather dull to look at. Functionality was all that mattered, and after all they were expendable!

Little grey shapes shuffled about, using hand held scanners. Each human body had about 50 trillion cells that had DNA within them, and fortunately, the cells were not converted one by one, otherwise it would take well over a million years to complete the process. However, due to the holographic principle, the brain released fields of magnetic energy.

Omni H'benar knew full well that reality was holographic in nature, and thoughts could transform it. Peaceful and loving thoughts led to peaceful and loving actions, something that he had to prevent at all costs, whereas, fearful thoughts and aggression lead to negative actions. That was what he was after, as it provided a stimulus, one that he found most refreshing!

In fact, the whole universe was created by thoughts, feelings and emotions...

Emotions were running high for everyone, as Halvor tried to hack into the facility. It was not easy, and what he required was a remote access point. Freya had been given the job of placing one of his specially designed devices into the facilities system, which she could do once she found the appropriate facility's conduit.

"Over there!"

Bear pointed to a small cylindrical tube which ran along the edge of the entry port, and she dived and rolled until she was up against it. Then with a flick of her wrist, she had slipped it out of a pocket and stuck it to the conduit. She then took cover behind the shuttle.

The device like a beetle, with razor sharp claws, cut its way inside, before embedding itself in amongst the fiber optic cabling.

"I'm in!"

It was almost instantaneous, and a credit to his ingenuity...

That was odd, very odd!

The small glowing device noticed a fluctuation in the quantum field. When a change took place in one part of the holographic matrix, it reflected throughout the whole.

This *reality* was expressed in the way that time ran around the corridors in hyperspace by the pattern it took. Other timelines existed in a different kind of grid pattern, creating alternative versions of the present in multiple versions of reality, which as it knew could be manipulated given the right technology.

Something however, was causing a minor disruption in the quantum field!

It was possible to enter into parallel universes to do all sorts of things, and then travel back to where you started. All that was needed was a *Zero Time Reference Generator*, which could link into the time at the center of the universe, which always stood still, acting like an anchor.

That something was interfering with the that anchor...

All sorts of information began to flow through Halvor's organic computer, which was nearly overwhelmed, and if it had not been for Gaia, then it would have shorted out.

Reams and reams of information flooded in, but it was nearly all on the quantum level, and not directly connected with what was going on inside the facility.

Halvor felt himself being dragged along with it, like being trapped by a tsunami.

The sphere was a complex interdimensional space, and each of the dimensions comprised of a complex pattern of interlocking wave-forms. Matter was only one wave of a pulse comprising a positive cycle, while the negative cycle manifests as *anti-matter*.

The matter pulse brought something into physical visibility, and then it disappeared momentarily before returning. But the pulses were so rapid that normally they went unnoticed...

Ren noticed figures rapidly approaching, and quickly warned her uncle.

"You will have company in a few minutes!"

That was what he had been expecting, as the facility would have some guards...

Omni H'benar was displeased, very displeased!

He had been interrupted, and so when he finally let the nanites inform him of what had been going on, he dispatched some of the drones to deal with it.

He held them in little regard, but even so, he considered them capable of dealing with some troublesome intrusion into his work...

Little grey beings gathered on the other side of an adjoining door, waiting for it to be opened by either one of their superiors. Large black eyes peered out from equally large heads, resting on spindly little bodies. They wore grey armored suits and carried laser rifles, although they were only small. They did possess energy shields, so were not that defenseless.

"Here they come!"

A grey panel began to slide open, as little grey beings spilled out.

The Commander hesitated for a moment, as he was not sure of their intentions. Intelligence was very thin, and for all he knew they might not be hostile. But, a few laser pulses came in his direction, so he soon got his answer...

Eighteen

Flashes of light leapt out from the little grey beings' weapons, singeing the air and leaving scorch marks on the shuttle's outer material, as Commander Bodil dived and rolled to get out of the way.

Bear, who had a pulse cannon slung around his neck, brought it forwards, and let lose his own barrage. It was mayhem, as he charged forwards like a human tank.

Little grey beings scattered, and there was pandemonium, as Joan charged after him, firing shots from her laser rifle. Freya, who had taken cover on the other side of Gaia, also began firing, picking her targets expertly, just as she had been trained.

The ensuing battle did not last long, as the little grey creatures were no physical match for the team. Their fragile bodies soon succumbed, even though they had armored suits...

Omni H'benar was pleased with the progress he was making, as the latest batch of Hybrids neared completion. This facility had provided him with all he needed to create a Hybrid army, all controllable and far less troublesome than a brigade of his own troops. Reptilians were noted for their loyalty, although given the chance, they would rise up the ranks by whatever means at their disposal. Assassinations were not unknown, and could be justified by incompetence. It was a cutthroat world in which he lived, and he was always wary of anyone rising too quickly.

His pleasure was tainted however, by the nagging messages the nano robots kept on trying to send him. They were a necessary evil, although he liked evil!

Pausing what he was doing for a moment, he let them do their job.

A clawed hand then crashed down onto the flat surface of his control panel, nearly cracking the toughened glass like material...

The small glowing device was equally displeased, although its reaction was less violent. Biomechanoids were of no consequence, but they did the menial jobs, and having to replace them would be an unnecessary waste of time.

However, physical time was only measured by the ageing process, or from one measured time-reference point to another. But, if the frequencies concerned were either shortened or lengthened, time went faster or slower accordingly...

"Come on!"

Commander Bodil urged them forwards, as they had to get more intelligence.

They pushed their way through the pile of bodies, feeling a little remorse. The little beings were no match for them, but they had attacked so they had to defend themselves. The Commander felt as though the next defenders they faced would be far more difficult to defeat...

Omni H'benar was furious, how dare anyone attack his facility!

He then accessed his display, and could see a strange looking ship in the entry port, and four suited figures making their way out of it.

"Humans!"

He hated humans...

The small glowing device could also see them, and was perplexed as to how they had made it this far. The facility had minimal defenses, as it was never envisioned that it could be reached by anyone, especially not a lower life form like a human.

They outer defenses should have been adequate, but they had been breached, and cleverly too.

This was all very unexpected...

Omni H'benar was far to busy to be bothered with them, and so he dispatched the latest batch of Hybrids to deal with them. They were not fully optimised, but sending an updated kill code to their nanites, should suffice. They were after all, far superior to lowly humans...

"Where to now?"

The Commander's voice rang in her ears, as in her mind Ren travelled a little further into the facility.

"Up ahead, take the exit on the left."

It was very useful to have a scout, particularly one that was not really there. He would not have felt nearly as comfortable with Serenity's role if she had been there in person...

Six Hybrids, cloned from Aesir DNA, suddenly stood to attention. They had been waiting patently to enter the chamber where their nanites would receive a final check before being given their mission briefings.

Now, things had changed, and they had another mission to fulfill...

Nineteen

Floating in the darkened dome shaped room, within the holographic brain of the advanced ship, which was in turn inside a cube shaped facility that had been floating inside a sphere of energy, was difficult enough to comprehend. But, when you were also floating through that facility as a remote viewer, it took some getting used to!

"I can see some activity up ahead uncle Vil!"

The Commander was not concerned about the weirdness of *weird space*, only in leading his team to where they could gain intelligence.

Their first attempt had not so much failed, as Halvor had gained a greater understanding of the complexities of this construct, but it was of little use when it came to finding out just how many Hybrids there were, and how deeply his civilisation had been infiltrated.

If they could just get some plans, some numbers, something, then they could get out of here...

Six different faces looked at each other, all having exactly the same thought. They had only been properly conscious for a few hours, having been linked to the machinery which had grown them. Memories had been installed, and the desire to complete whatever mission they were given.

They were alive, and conscious, but not sentient in the true meaning of the word.

They had a *hive mind*, one controlled by an intelligence of vast proportions...

The small glowing object considered the current situation.

In one respect, waveforms only appeared to be solid because they comprised of the same matter. Therefore, they were not really here, although they did not know that!

Hyperspace could be warped temporarily, although space-time naturally curved around natural vortexes, and objects could be dislodged out of time and space and temporarily disappear.

This is how the sphere arrived here, as all objects moved in time and space via an external physical force, or they could be trapped motionless, swirling around appearing to be still. But, the object still moved in time, and the timeframe could also be warped making it disappear into another reality altogether.

It was worth considering, as if the situation did get out of control, then it could simply slip away.

Those thoughts were not transmitted, nor the worries that had started to seep into the thought patterns. No consideration had ever been given to the fact that the facility might be vulnerable, and now that it appeared so, it may be prudent to have an exit strategy...

"Seek and destroy, seek and destroy!"

The instructions were instantly received via the nano robots active within each of the six brain stems. They were then issued with combat simulations, enough it was hoped for them to eliminate the intruders...

Omni H'benar would have liked to prepare this batch further, but there was no time. If he would have had six Reptilians soldiers at his disposal, then things would have been much different.

There was no time to regret his decision not to have them within the facility, as you never knew which clan would try to infiltrate the project. Just one opportune moment, and he could pay the price for letting down his guard, and then his position could be usurped by either a member of his own clan, or that of another.

Reptilians were naturally far superior to any other species, but it appeared that that came with a price...

"Move out!"

The Hybrids marched in single file, already wearing Aesir Security Service uniforms. They also carried appropriate laser pistols, ready to assume positions within the service. It was of no concern that they did not have more substantial armaments, as it was assumed that their greater energy shields' capacity would suffice.

Larger and more powerful weapons were not available due to the paranoia of Omni H'benar, and the next few minutes would dictate if that would be costly to the project or not...

"It looks as though the six figures are planning an ambush!"

That was not unexpected, as Vilgot had anticipated such an action. The defenders were on home ground, but he had the advantage in skill and equipment.

"Can we go round them?"

Ren checked.

Everything was square, square walls, square rooms, and even the six were forming a square pattern, although that would have been more precise if there had been nine of them!

"Negative."

So, it looked as though they would have to fight their way further into the facility. Ren could see that everything was laid out in a grid pattern, almost like a circuit board.

The centre of the facility was a square, and around it lay another square, a square within a square. Beyond that there were nodes which led to right angle corridors, all travelling towards the outermost square. The faculty formed a cube, and that cube was within an energy sphere.

Starfield was receiving all of this information via his connection to Gaia, and she was processing everything, relaying it to Halvor's computer.

It was quite obvious that no human had designed this, as they could not have resisted putting the odd curve, or decoration, or something *human* within it. The whole place was sterile, apart from the interior square, which looked to be inhabited by someone, or something...

Twenty

An error message flashed across the small glowing device, situated in the centre square of the facility. Calculations predicted that the four heavily armed intruders could successfully subdue the Hybrids sent to intercept them. Overconfidence had led to the perception that the facility could not be breached, and emphasis had led to it being designed to prevent an attack from within, by a malfunctioning Hybrid, or an outside force altering the programming sequence.

Contamination by energy to change the control systems of the nano robots.

What could be done to eliminate the threat posed by the humans...

A pulse shot out from a hidden laser, catching Freya on the shoulder. Her armored suit managed to deflect most of it, but the impact did sting her skin.

"Take cover!"

The Commander pinpointed where it had come from, firing off a few pulses from his laser rifle. The area around where the beam had originated from, darkened, as he scorched the grey surface. Another pulse flashed out, just missing him, as a volley of shots neutralised the weapon.

"Are you hurt?"

He looked concerned.

"Just a little shaken."

There seemed to be hidden lasers all over the place, and the further they penetrated, he expected the more of them they would encounter...

The light frequency had nearly penetrated the energy shield of one of the humans. Calculations were made, and adjustments made. The more shots that were fired, the closer it would be to unlocking the algorithm being used.

Interesting...

The Commander took the lead and the others fanned out behind him, although there was no cover available, as all there was, were smooth grey walls. Up ahead lay yet another turn, and he suspected that the Hybrids would be waiting for them...

Ren floated someway ahead, and could see them gathering around the perimeter of the outer square. Again there was no cover, although they had positioned themselves in several doorways that led to rooms dedicated to the production of more Hybrids.

It took a bit of getting used to floating around, and Ren found herself being sidetracked by the startling array of equipment that she could see. The Aesir grew Replicants, which were specially designed and created to take the consciousness of one of their people. DNA was taken from anyone agreeing to the process, and stored ready to create a copy of that individual. The new *creation,* was identical to the original person, although slight changes to their physiology were permitted.

Special safeguards were in place to make sure that the entire consciousness of the person undergoing *Replication* was transferred to the new host body. In that way, there was only the one soul involved, as the *Replicant* was in essence nothing more than a soulless vessel, to solve any moral dilemmas. Here in this facility however, it appeared to be a different matter altogether.

It looked as though samples had been taken from Aseir Security Service personnel, and cloned copies made ready to replace the samplee. Shivers crept down Ren's ethereal spine as she thought about the implications.

Had the samplee's been killed, and just how many people had thus far been replaced?

It was a very worrying thought.

Were the clones soulless, and had the samplees' souls gone to Valhalla?

Those questions would have to be answered later, as a sudden flash of light lit up the area behind her...

The Commander had poked his scope around the corner, and a Hybrid on seeing it had instantly fired.

Vilgot dropped it, before it had a chance to burn into his glove, and by the look on his face the team knew to back up a little. This was going to present quite a challenge, but one his experience knew how to deal with.

Out of his pocket, he took one of his special grenades, and out of the other, he took a smoke bomb.

"Ready?"

Bear knew exactly what he had planned, and gripped hold of his large weapon.

The Commander gave the signal, and hurled the smoke bomb round the corner, as laser pulses shot out. The grenade was hit repeatedly, which made no difference, as it spewed out clouds of thick green smoke.

Bear then charged forwards, laying down a barrage of laser fire, covering the Commander who was receiving information for Serenity.

"Four o'clock!"

They had both become accustomed to her mother's terminology, even though no one ever used a clock with hands on it anymore, and had not done for centuries.

Vilgot fired his laser rifle ripping into one of the Hybrids. Initially his shield held, but the modulating pulses soon overwhelmed it, and he soon succumbed.

One down, five to go...

Interesting?

The small glowing device receive a data stream of information.

A modulating laser pulse!

This gave it valuable information, which would be used to adapt the others shields...

"Nine o'clock!"

Vilgot could not see anything through the thick green smoke, but did feel a laser pulse catch him on the leg. They were firing blindly, as he directed his laser pulses to the left.

Meanwhile, Bear rushed over to where the First Hybrid had been, and took cover in the same doorway. From there, he could be of more use to the Commander.

The second Hybrid soon succumbed, and he took cover similarly to Bear. It was going to be *Street fighting*, battling from house to house, or doorway to doorway in this case!

"Around the next corner, there are two of them in opposite doorways."

Ren could just about see through the smoke, although it was not easy. Floating about, her information was also being relayed back to Gaia, and then onto Starfield, Halvor and the Doctor.

Halvor had an uplink to the team, and was able to update their weaponry and shields. He resisted though, just in case his signals were being intercepted...

The information flowed between the device and the Hybrids, and it was looking for any signals that could be intercepted. It was a mystery how they were able to pinpoint the Hybrids, or to find their way around the facility.

Were they getting help from *above?*

They certainly were, but not in the way that it envisioned...

Twenty One

The cloud of green smoke slowly began to clear, and Vilgot took a quick look over his shoulder. He appeared to be in some sort of processing room, as there were what looked like scanning devices. He then took another one of Halvor's probes out of his chest pocket, and set the small thing down gently on the floor. It was designed to seek information, and scurried off towards the far wall.

The Commander watched as it found what it was looking for, burying itself into a conduit, which was housed in the wall...

Halvor suddenly received a stream of information which ran down his computer screen. There were detailed plans about the process, and the uplink was running very quickly...

There was a momentary intense glow from the device, as it suddenly detected a breach in one of the processing rooms.

Instead of spying on the humans, they appeared to be spying on it!

As quickly as it could, the device severed the link, isolating the section from the rest of the facility.

Had that been done quickly enough...

Halvor suddenly lost the stream of information. He scowled down giving it a quick glance. It would take him hours if not days to decode it all, and hopefully he would have something useful to pass onto the Commander...

Another smoke bomb filled the corridor with green clouds, as Vilgot moved forwards. This time he decided to use an explosive grenade, as he had managed to launch the probe. Whether it had done its job or not he did not know, but the longer they stayed in the facility, the greater the risk became. The remaining Hybrids had to be eliminated, before the facility could be destroyed, as they might gain a lot more information the further into it they went.

A loud explosion rattled the walls, as the grenade exploded, and both he and Bear rushed forwards. Joan and Freya replaced them in the doorways they had just vacated, offering covering fire where appropriate. They knew that the other two were not averse to fighting in close confines, and that they would just get in the way.

Joan remembered her training, although she had been more used to being the General's Personal Assistant, if not body guard. No one had ever dared cross her, and she smiled to herself at her old nickname. The *General's Rottweiler*, it had been well cultivated, and put to good use!

Freya marveled at Vilgot's skill. She had also received extensive training, but there was nothing like experience, which she was certainly gaining.

"Clear!"

The Commander's voice echoed in her helmet, as another two Hybrids were dispatched. That was four out of the six!

"They are in a similar position, just around the next corner."

Ren could see them, and it was clear that they were not used to fighting in close confines. They had only received the basics, and were quickly being updated...

Combat was usually left to the Reptilians, and the glowing device was becoming frustrated. Not just by the human's progress, but also by the Reptilian who was Director of this facility. He was unusually arrogant, even for a Reptilian, and his blatant disregard for the attempts to communicate with him was aiding the humans...

More green smoke filled the corridors, as Vilgot Bodil flushed out the remaining Hybrids. They were proving harder to kill, and it was clear that their shield configurations were being updated. He still had several tricks up his proverbial *sleeve*, and even though they were proving more difficult, it was not impossible.

"All set?"

Bear grunted, clasping his large gun to his chest.

"Fire!"

They both held down the triggers of their respective weapons, and the combination of the amount and the frequency of the lasers soon overwhelmed the shield of the Hybrid they were targeting. His crumpled body fell to the ground smoldering.

One to go!

The last Hybrid seemed unphased, having no emotions whatsoever. He just stood there, as the tiny machines within his body fed him information. He was told to stop the humans, but only being armed with a laser pistol did not bode too well for him.

"Same again!"

This time the Hybrid survived longer, managing to get a few shots off, some of which nearly penetrated their shields. Bear felt something striking his broad chest, but the adrenalin pumping through his veins mean that he did not feel any pain. He had to admit that it felt good getting back into action, even though he had supposedly retired.

Once a Titan always a Titan!

The last Hybrid fell, and Ren confirmed that there were no other hiding up ahead, they now had a clear run to the facility's inner square, where they hoped to find something interesting...

Omni H'benar banged his fists down on his console again.

Was he ever going to be left alone to complete his work?

This time the information was met by a throaty growl.

He really hated humans...

Commander Bodil ushered them forwards, taking full advantage of the defenseless facility. Ren was leading the way, and any stray laser was burnt out by Bear's large gun. They all seemed to be positioned in a similar way, and as soon as they saw a right angle turn, he fired directly into the corner. It was as though everything had been designed by a computer, and one which was not battle hardened. Vilgot would never have done that, as he knew that any defenses had to be well placed, and in areas that would not be expected.

They soon broke into a larger square room, and this one appeared to be some sort of assembly point. He guessed that this was where the Hybrids were brought together to be given their final instructions, before making their way towards the shuttles that would take them to where they were supposed to go. On one wall, there was a large screen, which he assumed would indicate their mission briefing. No doubt, the programming would be completed, and visual stimuli provided.

He remembered the Hybrid he had encountered within the palace, and felt very fortunate to not only have his full weaponry and colleagues with him, but also for the fact that the Hybrids here seemed to have only been half programmed.

Vilgot had the eerie feeling that so far things had been a little too easy...

Omni H'benar was in a raging temper, which was not that unusual. This time however, it was worse than normal, as he stormed out of his office and pounded down the corridor...

"Did you hear that?"

Ren floated further forwards trying to find out.

Freya had also felt it.

Someone or something was coming...

Omni H'benar burst into the room, to gasps from the humans. Some shots rang out, fizzing off his personal shield, as he stood there in his shiny black armor. It reminded Ren of a beetle's carapace, with its different sections all fitting together as one. He was not armed, apart from his personal defense system that was part of his suit, residing in a wristband. He had no need of conventional weapons, as his mind was so powerful that it could override that of a human, or humans.

Controlling thoughts swept out of his mind, as he was very powerful psychically.

Vilgot Bodil found himself lowering his weapon, unable to keep it pointing at the nine foot tall *devil*. The white face was expressionless, but the piercing green slit eyes said all that had to be said.

It was quite apparent that it loathed humans, and that both the Commander and his team were now in grave danger.

Ren also felt powerless, as there was nothing that she could do to help them.

Weapons were lowered as the White Royal Reptilian began to take control of their minds...

"They're all going to die!"

Starfield cried out in mortal panic, as he could see the team being overwhelmed.

One by one, they started dropping to their knees, clutching their heads, as if in great pain.

Their situation looked hopeless, and he knew that he had to do something.

Emotions were welling up inside him, to the point where he felt overwhelmed too. Starfield, just like the team, felt a total and utter sense of desperation sweeping into every molecule.

Gaia could not do anything either, and even if she would have been able to fire her weapon, she would have undoubtedly killed them all as well as the Reptilian.

"Oh flux!"

Starfield then swore again, but before Gaia could reprimand him, he grabbed hold of the spare fire axe and dashed towards the exit...

"So, you are the *Dragon Slayer!*"

Omni H'benar's voice echoed inside Joan's head, along with a jarring pain.

"Your capture will elevate me within my clan, and I might even become Pindar."

An evil smirk spread across his scaled face.

"I will look forward to personally torturing you, after I have disposed of the others."

Joan glared at him, fighting back with every essence of her being.

Unable to move, she sent all the hatred that she could muster in the creature's direction, as a smirk spread across his face, as he enjoyed the energy release. It was like fine wine to him, and he took great pleasure in receiving it.

Loosh the low vibrational energy, that both Archons and Reptilians fed off, was a being's *life force* being released by emotional trauma. It had a heightened molecular content, a hormonal adrenalin-cortisol cascade, which was much sought after, as it enhanced their energetic stamina.

The harder Joan fought, the more she felt like a battery being drained, and no amount of effort could break her free.

The others also felt their strength fading away, even the massive Bear began to feel weak...

Ren felt so frustrated as she could do nothing for them, only float around the room helplessly.

She could see the trauma on their faces, as they began to drop to the ground holding their heads in pain.

"Father?"

Halvor also sat there transfixed, as even though he was not inside the room, he could not help but stare into those large hypnotic eyes. Doctor Sorenson was able to resist, knowing all about hypnosis, but there was nothing that he could do, as he rushed into the bedroom, shaking Halvor by the shoulders.

"Don't look into its eyes!"

It was too late, as Halvor had also succumbed.

Desperation filled Ren, as her father failed to answer, and she could see that time was rapidly running out...

Omni H'benar bathed in the refreshing energy, as he had been tired and displeased by all of the interruptions, although he had to admit that it was well worth it.

The White Royal Reptilian was so immersed in the energy that he failed to notice Starfield charging towards him. Omni H'benar had let his personal shield down so that he could extract all of the *loosh,* and before he realised what was happening, Starfield swung the fire axe with all of his might.

At the last moment, the Reptilian saw the glint from the fire axe's blade, but it was far too late.

There was a woosh, as it sailed through the air, quickly followed by a cracking and splintering of Omni H'benar's scales and bones, as the fire axe decapitated him!

The Holo Droid then froze in shock as the Reptilian's head came away from its body, bouncing on the floor as he was showered in a fountain of bright blue blood...

Epilogue

Self-destruct initiated.

It was time for the glowing device to slip away, although as already contemplated, there actually was not time!

That did not matter, as within a few minutes there would be no facility, nor humans for that matter...

A warning siren sounded, bringing the Commander back to his senses. He had felt like a mannequin, trapped within his own body, being tormented by the shiny black *devil* with the grotesque white face.

Something was happening, and as soon as Halvor regained his sense, he patched himself through to his old friend.

"The whole thing is going to blow!"

Vilgot jumped to his feet.

"Move!"

His voice boomed out, as he almost pushed the others out of the room. Starfield felt his arm almost being pulled out of its socket as he was dragged along, his moon glass feet scraping across the surface of the floor.

Everything was a blur, partially due to the blue blood which was partially obscuring his view. The Holo Droid was back in shock, not really knowing what he was doing.

Walls rushed past, all looking exactly the same, and in the mad scramble, he never even noticed the blackened stains or the dead bodies which he stumbled over. All that he could see was the Reptilian's head bouncing on the floor, and the fountain of blood running down his moon glass shell...

Ren felt a sudden jolt, as she reentered the black dome shaped room. It was time to leave, and she did her best to activate Gaia's main drive. On one of the twin screens, she could see that she was alone, and on the other, she could see five figures running as fast as they could towards her.

It was time to concentrate, try to clear her mind, and visualise the agreed location. Her uncle Vil had chosen somewhere that she was familiar with, and the more she though about it, the clearer it became in her mind...

Starfield felt numb, his sensors turned off, and his mind repeating the Reptilian's head bouncing on the floor like a basket ball, over and over again. From somewhere he had another flashback of Joan's memories, as she used to like watching the teams playing one another on the base's courts.

Where had that come form?

He was still thinking about that and the bouncing head, as he was dragged inside Gaia.

"Get us out of here!"

Vilgot Bodil's voice cut through his vision, shocking the Holo Droid again.

He felt bewildered, and was not the only one.

Gaia's engines roared into life, as Ren pushed her fingers forward in the hand pods on the arms of the pilot's seat.

There was a sudden movement, as they left the facility, accompanied by a flash of light as someone else left it too.

A massive explosion rippled through *weird space*, as it collapsed in on itself, but none of them saw it, as fortunately they had already left...

Halvor breathed out a huge sigh of relief, as his friends and family were safe. His daughter was in the control room, and his wife squeezed into the cargo hold.

Ren could not believe that they had made it, and felt so relieved, unlike her mother...

Joan felt very uncomfortable in Starfield's presence, as he was bathed in blue blood. He might have saved them, but witnessing the decapitation, she thought of him as being nothing more than an Artificial *Barbarian...*

The Artificial Army

The development of full artificial intelligence could spell the end of the human race....It would take off on its own, and re-design itself at an ever increasing rate. Humans, who are limited by slow biological evolution, couldn't compete, and would be superseded.

Stephen Hawking

Introduction

"Tell me about your childhood."

Starfield felt himself drift even further into a trance, as Doctor Sorenson administered yet another psychotherapy session.

"I was *Stellan*, a very happy and inquisitive little boy, always interested in learning new things.

A flood of simulated sobs then rang out from his speakers.

"I never thought that I would learn how to become an Artificial *Barbarian...*"

One

A beautiful dawn broke over a paradise island, surrounded by a turquoise sea, which lapped against glorious white sandy beaches.

"Oh this is wonderful!"

Freya stretched out, feeling for Vilgot's hand.

"Yes, I have always loved it here."

For the first time in days, he began to relax.

Freya looked over the Commander's shoulder.

"However did you find this place?"

He smiled.

"The island is one of the Titans' secret hideaways which we use to recover from a mission, and to plan for our next one. Very few people know about it, as there is a hologram housed in that building over there which projects an image of open sea."

Vilgot pointed to the little structure. All of the buildings here were nothing more than shacks, although their outward appearance was deceptive, and designed to show an abandoned settlement if anyone managed to penetrate the projection.

"So not such a bad life then!"

She smiled broadly.

"It has its benefits."

Vilgot then kissed her.

It seemed like another lifetime fighting their way through the sphere, and all thoughts of the enemy were put aside until they saw Halvor approaching.

The reams of data had seemed endless, until he found the decryption key. Once he had that, Halvor had been able to decipher the information they had managed to download from the facility. There was a lot of highly technical data on the cloning and the programming process, much of which was so complex than even he could not understand it. Embedded within it there was however, more detailed plans about where the Hybrids were being sent.

It appeared that their placement was widespread, and not just confined to the Aesir Security Service. There were Hybrids in many key positions, as well as pockets of false inoculations spreading the nano virus compromising a great many people...

Doctor Sorenson decided to end the session, and get some fresh air. He seemed to have been stuck in the building all day, and was making little progress with his patient.

"Oh, woe is me!"

Starfield continued to sob.

"I'm nothing more than a moon glass savage!"

The Doctor patted him on the shoulder.

"It's early days yet."

He was trying to be comforting, but it looked as thought the Holo Droid was beyond consolation.

Opening the door, he stepped out into an adjoining room where he found Ren and her mother.

They looked up, as he shook his head.

The Doctor had been working hard, doing his best to treat the team. Bear was Bear, and nothing seemed to phase the big man, although even he seemed a little down.

Losing the Falk had been a blow, but when they had intercepted a communication indicating that it had been boarded by Aesir Security personnel, there was no point in going back.

Fortunately, the little droids had scrubbed it clean of all traces of the team, and all records on the Commander's shuttle had been deleted, and it had been rebooted with a new identification.

They may have found the Falk, but little else.

Ren had guided them here, as it had been somewhere her uncle had taken her many times. He knew that she would easily be able to visualize it, when they left the sphere. The mission had been a success, although judging by the information Halvor was decoding, they had barely scratched the surface.

Doctor Sorenson pushed his way through the outer door into the sunshine to clear his own head.

Fridfulla, was indeed peaceful, and for the time being they had remained undetected, but for how much longer?

A little way ahead, he could see Halvor, who was also getting some air. He was walking to where Vilgot and Freya were stretched out on the sand.

"A paradise island, and a beautiful woman, where did it all go wrong?"

The Commander started to chuckle.

"If only it would last!"

Halvor then shuffled uncomfortably on his feet.

"I hate to be the harbinger of bad news."

Vilgot frowned, expecting the worst.

"I'm afraid that there is a reference to something far worse."

Freya gripped his hand more tightly.

"Along with the virus and the Hybrids, they have also been attempting to create an Artificial Army..."

Two

Warm sunshine shone down from a clear blue sky, as gentle waves from the turquoise sea lapped against the white sandy beach. It was mesmerizingly beautiful, and yet three glum faces stared back at it.

"What are we going to do?"

That was a very good question!

The Commander was deep in thought.

"We really need to process as much of the information as possible."

Halvor nodded.

"Yes, but I can link to Gaia's holographic matrix, but we really need the Holo Droid's processing power."

Starfield was still so traumatised that he was barely functioning.

"I have been pondering his situation, wondering what can be done to help."

Doctor Sorenson, the third member of the group, stroked his chin.

"Human consciousness is a pulsing field of light, and it is between that pulsing, that there is an opportunity to make changes. Being as the Holo Droid possesses a human consciousness, I have been wondering whether it may be possible to create an algorithm to predict when to make that change?"

Halvor had already created an algorithm to modulate both the energy shields and lasers.

"Starfield appears to be stuck in a cycle of barbarism and regret."

They all nodded in agreement.

"If it is, then we have to take into account when these things will repeat in a cycle of time, the cycle in which a certain event happens, the date of the event, and when in the past a similar event happened."

The conversation was already getting too technical for Vilgot, who after all, was primarily a soldier, and lacked a scientific education. However, his years of experience had its benefits.

"What about extending that theory to cosmic consciousness?"

They looked at him, wondering what he was getting at.

"I was actually thinking more about artificial consciousness."

Doctor Sorenson suddenly grasped where this was going.

"The cycle always increases the nearer to the end it gets, and maybe if we can create such an algorithm, then we can predict when and where the next event will arise, and also when the end point of that cycle will occur!"

Vilgot smiled.

"So, it may not only be possible to predict when the Holo Droid will repeat his cycle of barbarism and regret, but also to use it to predict when the Artificial Intelligence will repeat its cycle of creation and infiltration."

It had already created the nano virus, and then the Hybrids, and now they had just learnt that it had also created an Artificial Army. It appeared that these events ran in a cycle, and if they could acquire some more information then they could predict when and where it was going to unleash it...

Gaia looked concerned as Halvor explained just what they had in mind. She had been with Starfield for the majority of her life in one way or another, and had grown deeply concerned about his current behavior.

"I think that it has something to do with the consciousness transfer process."

Halvor had to agree with her, as it was not foolproof. Sometimes, things did not go according to plan, and he had read reports of difficulties. What had made the situation worse was the fact that it had never been performed on a Holo Droid.

"We have a unique link, which is akin to what you would refer to as *telepathy*. In humans, it is the universal language, as all of your cells vibrate building up to an emotion, which is utilized to project thoughts. When you think about it, you are aware of others thoughts coming towards you, although you have to consciously want to *feel them,* and to do that, you have to put in a great deal of effort to learn how to do it."

This was more Doctor Sorenson's territory than his own, but Halvor listened with interest.

"Firstly, you have to have an emotional connection, before you *receive* the message. It is above and beyond the normal human experience, the part of your consciousness that is beyond the *ego*."

It appeared as though Starfield's ego was getting the better of him!

"Now that we both have holographic brains, signals are transferred instantly between us, and it is not so much telepathy as quantum communication. We do not feel each other's thoughts, we receive them."

Halvor began to understand.

"So, what you are saying is that someone has to feel what Starfield is thinking, as well as receiving quantum communications, and that is being made far more difficult due to his current emotional state."

Gaia's smile spread across the main viewing screen.

"Exactly..."

Three

Bjorne wrapped Joan in his customary *bear hug,* still overjoyed that she was alive. He, like most people had been led to believe that she and her family had been assassinated by Hybrids a few years ago.

He had been tasked with looking after her whist they undertook a mission to save her people, and had found out that she was more than capable of looking after herself!

"So, are you feeling better?"

She wrapped her arms around his neck.

"Yes, thanks to Doctor Sorenson."

It seemed as though he had the *magic touch,* and after all, he had been the palace doctor, and not received that position by accident. She felt so good to be back, and although she had to take some medication, Joan felt more stable than she had done in years. It was quite a transformation, and she understood more than most what Starfield was going through.

He was still traumatized, this time by himself!

There had not been much time to catch up when they were onboard the Falk, as Joan had spent a lot of time in therapy, and Bear had been working hard to prepare for the mission.

Her daughter Ren had taken herself off for a while, and was also a different person. Gone was the rebellious teenager, who swore a lot and lost her temper on a regular basis. She had grown up very quickly over the last few weeks.

Ren had not only communicated with an *Ancient,* but also with a *Dragon,* and a very peaceful one at that!

Remote viewing, and hearing distant voices, were not such strange concepts to her as they once may have seemed, and she was now wondering if it were possible to actually see into the future. Time was also not quite what it appeared, nor space-time come to that. Ren's mind had been opened up to so many new possibilities by Gaia, and who would have thought that such an incredible ship could have lain undisturbed under all that mud and thick carpet of foliage for nearly twenty years.

Maybe *Fridfulla* was getting to her too...

It was not so much the peacefulness of the planet that was having an effect, but the enormity of the situation that was getting to Halvor and Vilgot. Freya had left them to it, although she never strayed far from the man she had dreamt about being with for longer than she could remember. Contentment was a wonderful thing.

Maybe *Fridfulla* was getting to her too...

Despite the peace and calm of the planet, agitation and worry haunted the two men.

"I have managed to process some more of the information that we gained from the sphere."

Vilgot took a deep breath, fearing was coming next.

"It concerns the Artificial Army units."

By that, he meant individuals, not a collective.

"Each unit's brain contains a computer chip which uses photons in their wave duality form, where each becomes a circuit, and a potential *logic gate*, as opposed to regular chips which treat electrons as either *on* or *off*."

The Commander was already feeling that the conversation was drifting above his head.

"That is a little similar to the holographic matrix both Gaia and Starfield have, but the main difference is that they are organic in nature."

It was hard for the Vilgot to visualize the whirring photons within a *soup* performing advance functions, as opposed to computer chips.

"The main benefit is that one photon crosses multiple information channels, so just one little chip could be more powerful than thousands of normal computers."

The Aesir were rightfully, as it turned out, wary of Artificial Intelligence, and so used regular chips in most of their applications, feeling that they were a lot safer.

"The main benefit is that it develops its own electronic intelligence, which computes in a slightly different dimension."

Vilgot frowned, sending deep creases across his brow.

It was not much of a benefit to them!

"The other worrying thing about this development, is that they can be placed into a biological devices that take on the human form, so much so that it is going to be virtually impossible to tell them apart from actual humans."

The Commander began to pace about.

Stage one was the nano virus, which could be detected by slight variations in facial muscle movement, or eye configuration, which could be countered by the violet flame torch.

Stage two were the Hybrids, although they had been around for years. It appeared that they were a genetic amalgamation between human and reptilian DNA, which took time to grow and train. There were many failures and the process was fortunately very unreliable. The new Hybrids were human clones, grown far more quickly and efficiently, but their were still failures within the process.

They were far more difficult to spot, but fortunately, their shields could be penetrated by his old friend's algorithms.

Stage three, was synthetic biological humans fitted with photon chips, that would be very reliable and far more difficult to stop.

If they ever found out where they were located, that was...

Four

Sparkling blue eyes matched the flowing sea, as Freya contemplated events. She was used to making decisions, and even though the government did most of the work, she had been constantly consulted. The system had worked well, as she had represented the people, keeping a check and balance on the bureaucrats.

They had trusted her, and she them!

Now free from all of that, she still found herself acting in a similar fashion. If the Holo Droid had been one of her subjects, which technically he still was, then after reviewing all of the available information, she would have come to her own decision.

"I think we should hook Starfield up to Gaia, and not only perform a diagnostic, but also see if we can find a way of opening up a connection to Mjolnir."

Vilgot, who had joined her, had also been deep in thought.

"You know, I think that you could be right!"

He knew that the Holo Droid was vital to help in the construction of the algorithm to predict when the Artificial Army would attack, and being as they did not know where, maybe the Ancient could give them a *heads up.*

The Commander had rejoined the woman who until recently, had been his monarch. He found himself spending increasingly larger amounts of time with her, and the more of that he spent, the more contented it made him feel inside.

It had been a good decision choosing *Fridfulla* as their next location.

Some time later, Ren was sitting back in the pilot's seat, sinking into the material, next to Starfield who had been hooked up to Gaia for the last few hours.

The complete diagnostic and systems analysis had ironed out a few anomalies, but he still felt as if he was carrying the whole planet on his proverbial *shoulders*. Fridfulla may have appeared to have been a paradise to the others, but it felt more like a giant lead weight dragging him down.

"I feel so depressed!"

The Holo Droid groaned.

"It would be better if I was disassembled!"

That was what he had been fearing, and now as he looked back at his recent behaviour, he thought that it would be for the best.

"What will I do without you?"

Gaia was very concerned.

"You and everyone else will be far better off without me!"

He began to synthetically sob, although no tears ran down his moon glass face.

Ren could see and hear it all, as she slipped into the familiar blackness. Soon the curved ceiling wrapped itself over her head, and her naked body appeared, which was quickly clothed as she projected her thoughts.

The next things to appear were the twin screens, and one showed a view of the inside of the ship, and the other of the outside.

Freya was sitting arm in arm with her uncle Vil on the beach, and her parents were also together, whilst the Doctor and Bear shared a drink, sitting on chairs under the shade of a tree.

Ren let her mind slip away, as her senses reach out as far as they could. It was now just a case of waiting and hoping that she could make the connection.

Fractal time was the concept of the length, depth and density of time, expanding and unfolding symmetrically at exactly the same rate and scale. It was odd actually seeing the shapes self generating themselves, as the void of space-time unfolded before her very eyes.

Ren had been trying to meditate, and had gone deeper than she had ever gone before. It was fascinating seeing the universe spread out before her like this, and she began to actually see that it was nothing more than photons of light cast in a fractal web.

Planets, moons and suns looked like what her father described as *sacred geometry*, with four, six, eight, ten, twelve and twenty faces, coming together in various shapes that ranged from simple spheres or cubes to complex flowery patterns all driven by a golden ratio, that looked like a simple swirly sea shell.

Ren was so mesmerized by all she saw, that she did not notice Mjolnir approaching.

"Ah, Serenity, I see that you're abilities are increasing."

His angelic form drifted into view.

"I can also sense that you need my help, or rather Stellan does."

She had always thought how incredible it must be to live as a being of light, and now Ren had actually experienced a little of it herself.

That thought drifted across her mind just like the image of the Ancient.

"Yes, I'm afraid he is unwell."

Ren was being diplomatic, as *unwell* was a bit of an understatement.

Mjolnir smiled.

"I will see what I can do..."

Starfield was so preoccupied with the battle raging within his molecules, that he failed to notice another presence within Gaia's holographic matrix.

"Oh, poor Stellan."

The voice was not condescending, but concerned.

"Whatever are we to do with you?"

At first, Starfield thought that it was Doctor Sorenson, and then as he brought his awareness back from the maelstrom of self-deprecation, he nearly jumped out of his moon glass shell.

"Flux!"

The word just jumped out, as it had done far too often lately.

Then, he felt great remorse, swearing in front of the god like creature.

"Oh, I'm so sorry!"

He felt even more mortified than ever!

"What is wrong with me?"

Mjolnir smiled.

"The consciousness transfer process has left you bereft of your normal foundations."

Mjolnir was correct, like a boat adrift on the turquoise sea of Fridfulla.

"The human body acts as a filter, and even though you have had your consciousness transferred into your moon glass shell, you are now more susceptible to negative emotions. That is why you are struggling to cope."

Starfield suddenly began to understand.

"Yes, it is not always that easy when you are fully human, as from this dimension or *density*, you can contact other beings in other dimensions via your mind. This can be done by meditation or through the use of certain substances, which take the natural filter away. In essence, the filter stops you seeing things which the brain cannot normally handle."

It was not the *seeing things* which bothered him so much, as actually *doing them!*

"Once you open the *gate,* you allow entities through, which can influence you. At first, they all seem good, but then those such as the *Archons* slowly turn things around, until you find yourself doing things which you would not have done before. That is why we *Ancients* do not normally interact with humans, unless we chose those who we feel can do good."

That got Starfield thinking.

Was some of his own behaviour due to the influence of negative entities?

Molecules swept about inside his moon glass shell, as he thought more about what Mjolnir had been saying. His old physical body had *grounded* him, enabling *Stellan* to be more mentally and emotionally stable.

Starfield then began to think more seriously about his attitude towards Joan and her daughter Serenity.

At first, he had believed that they were *Barbarians*, and yet considering his own behaviour, he had to admit that the proverbial *boot* was now well and truly on the other foot!

Mjolnir had brought Joan through the ancient stones, and she had subsequently given birth to Ren, who had the right mixture of genes to interface with the ship. He was trying to save the Aesir from the Artificial Intelligence, and only interacted through the filter of Gaia's consciousness. She had always been very stable, and had a lot of behavioral filters built into her programming. Another failsafe was the fact that she could not fly on her own, or fire her own weapons.

If Joan had left all that she knew, and had undergone a consciousness transfer into another human body not long before she had left, no wonder she had such fluctuating emotions. Her husband Halvor was all she had, along with her daughter, and no wonder she had fought so valiantly when either one had been threatened.

The Holo Droid's thoughts then shifted towards the Artificial Army. They may have human bodies, but just like the Hybrids, they lacked human souls.

Was it the soul that somehow held everything together at a higher level?

Since the transfer process, did he still have a soul?

He had assumed that his consciousness resided within the energetic holographic matrix, that was housed within his moon glass shell.

"Yes, because you willingly transferred it into a vessel suitable to house it."

Starfield felt very relieved, and realized that his remorse was due to his conscience, which proved to him that he must have a soul.

This was a very heavy conversation, and yet he felt so much lighter for having it!

If he could come to terms with what he had done, and no doubt, what he would do in the future, then there was a chance that he could become whole again.

It seemed as though Starfield was on the *Heroes Journey*, and his quest was to evolve to a higher state of consciousness.

If that was correct, then was all of this some sort of a *Great Awakening?*

"Very good, Stellan!"

Mjolnir was very impressed.

"In Joan's culture there is a renowned English poet, playwright, and actor William Shakespeare, and in his epic *Hamlet* there is a very appropriate line. *There are more things in heaven and earth, Horatio, than are dreamt of in your philosophy...*"

Five

A rather stunned Holo Droid staggered out of the advanced ship in a bit of a daze, not really knowing where he was going. Starfield needed air, which was odd considering his moon glass shell could quite happily function in a vacuum.

Who was Horatio?

"Horatio the *faithful friend.*"

Where did that come from?

It was Gaia, communicating to him via their unique link.

She had naturally overheard everything, as the connection to Mjolnir had been through her holographic matrix.

Faithful friend?

He nearly stumbled realizing that there was far more to what Mjolnir had been saying.

Gaia had given him a very brief summation of the play in which Hamlet had been disgusted by the marriage of his newly widowed mother, Queen Gertrude, to his Uncle Claudius, who now sat on the throne. His instincts were then proved correct, as his father's ghost appears, revealing that he was actually poisoned by Claudius.

Gaia had always been his faithful friend, and it looked as though she was here with him in a similar way to help him through his own dilemmas...

Halvor also needed air, having been confined to the little room he had been using.

Walking outside he could see the Holo Droid, and hoped that they had been able to make contact with the Ancient, as they desperately needed to construct the algorithm.

Looking at Starfield, he seemed to be walking in an ever decreasing circle.

What was he doing?

Halvor stopped to observe, and then it suddenly dawned on him!

A good place to start was with the patterns in nature's natural cycle, the same patterns that governed life in the universe. It would allow him to peer into the timeline of history in a way that mystics did.

Halvor could feel the information flooding into his mind, as if he was now a mystic himself!

How about beginning with the date when the cycle first began, then add the date it would reoccur, and when it would end, as a pattern in motion within the cycle. If each number would be the sum of the two preceding ones, starting from 0 and 1, he then began to get the concept, and the rough workings of the algorithm...

Freya observed the Holo Droid walking in circles, and the communications expert pacing about, also it seemed in circles.

They were making her dizzy!

Another figure then emerged from the ship, and this one had blonde dreadlocks, with beads and feathers. Serenity was also a little different, and then there was her unstable mother Joan, with her distinctive auburn hair. Looking past her, Freya could see the enormous Bear, a freak of nature, what a strange team they all made!

Most of her people were predominately blonde, tall and slim with striking good looks. Freya was no exception, as she cast her gaze towards the *oasis* of Vilgot, the man she adored.

He had so many wonderful qualities, a natural born leader holding everything together, and without him they would be well and truly sunk...

"Extraordinary!"

Doctor Sorenson, who had been given files of medical information, sat transfixed. He was sitting under the shade of a tree a little distance away from Freya.

He could not believe what he was reading, and shook his head from side to side.

"They have managed to 3D print entire human bodies!"

He knew that it was possible given the correct DNA to print organs or limbs for those unfortunate to have lost them through one reason or another, but a whole body?

Tyr the *Sky God* had given the *Terrans* detailed plans of how to print the old Aesir attack craft, to help them defend themselves against the Hybrid Reptilians known as the *Anunnaki,* and Joan had a certain amount of their DNA within her, as well as their distinctive auburn hair.

That probably explained her rather unstable and aggressive nature!

The main problem was consciousness, as the body was just a *vessel* without a soul. It would just be some kind of *vegetable,* unable to move, think, or act on its own.

But, now they had discovered how to produce a photonic

computer chip, he shuddered when he thought about the ramifications.

If some poor soul had been implanted, and their minds taken over, then there would have been a chance that their consciousness could have been rescued, like they had managed to do with the violet ray torch, which had neutralised the nano virus within him. But, if they had no soul to begin with, only a chip, then that changed things considerably.

For a start, they could be made to have quicker reflexes, mental agility, and indeed intelligence. The *Titan Super Soldiers* were the best that they could offer, but they were not infallible. The photon chipped soldiers would be a good deal better!

The Doctor put his head in his hands.

"We have no chance up against them..."

Six

The last flickers of daylight faded over the horizon, as the beautiful golden sunset gave way to a brilliantly sparkling starry sky. Everything about Fridfulla was perfect, and even the cool breeze that began to sweep up off the tranquil sea, only sent a slight shiver down Freya's spine.

Nevertheless, Vilgot put a warm, comforting arm around her shoulder, which she greatly appreciated. The day had been long and filled with plenty of discussion, and more than a little therapy. Doctor Sorenson and Halvor had been particularly busy, and now they had manged to sift through the reams of information they had downloaded from the Hybrid facility.

A much clearer picture had begun to emerge of what the next phase of the what could only be described as an *invasion.* Halvor, with help from both Gaia and Starfield, had been able to construct the algorithm, and now it was time to input the data.

"Well, here we go!"

They had all gathered around the tree which had become a focal point. Halvor waited as his computer processed the information, organic strands pulsing along synaptic pathways, until the answer flashed on his screen.

"The cycle has predicted when they are likely to strike again, and the pattern also indicates when they have struck in the past."

Halvor frowned, as it did not look very encouraging.

They all waited for his response, as he took a deep breath.

"According to this, there have been several incursions that we have not known about, and more predicted in the near future."

They all looked worried.

"How near?"

Halvor looked at his old friend, knowing that he needed to plan the mission.

"Thirty six Terran hours."

That was not long!

"Does the data indicate how large the Artificial Army is?"

Vilgot's question seemed to hang in the air.

"Several thousand."

That was not the reply anyone wished to hear.

The Artificial Soldiers would be formidable, and faced with such a large number it would be nigh on impossible to stop them!

"Can we call for help?"

Freya realized that they could not hope to succeed on their own.

Vilgot considered the idea for a moment, and looked around the group for suggestions.

"Titans?"

Bear and Joan spoke together, both having the same idea.

Doctor Sorenson shrugged his shoulders having no experience with matters outside of the medical field, whilst Ren sighed deeply. All eyes then focused on Starfield, as they waited for his response, and when it arrived they were truly shocked.

"Up U!"

They all stared at him in disbelief, thinking that he had started swearing again.

Realizing that his answer could have been misconstrued, his moon glass head flushed a deep shade of purple.

"United Planetary Union."

There were a few chuckles, as they realized their mistake.

Actually, that is not such a bad idea!

The Planetary Union, was a federation of human worlds, brought together after the initial conflict with the Reptilians. Originally, from the Lyra constellation, the survivors scattered to many neighboring systems, and eventually came back together for mutual protection.

Since its conception, they had also allied themselves with some other species, in a much broader organization, which spanned a greater part of the galaxy.

They certainly needed all the help they could get.

But, how did they know if they had also been compromised...

The meeting continued well into the night, as they considered their options. Vilgot was in overall charge of decision making, even though Freya was still technically the leader of the Aesir people.

However, it was not just a matter of considering asking for help, as they did not have a way of defeating the Artificial Soldiers, despite the possibility of having far greater numbers.

Gaia, Halvor and Starfield had been huddled together running certain scenarios inside the ship, exploring the possibilities of creating some sort of device to render the photon chips useless, or at the very least less effective.

It appeared as though they needed to focus their efforts within the quantum realm as opposed to this dimension, as any conventional weapon would be useless. With far greater coordination, reflexes and mental agility, the Artificial Soldiers would be able to anticipate their actions, before they even thought of them.

This was the greatest dilemma that any of them had ever faced, and they had to come up with something within the next twenty four Terran hours...

Seven

The sun began to rise above the horizon, sending golden strands out across the calm turquoise waters. Most of the team were still asleep, taking advantage of the accommodation the modest buildings offered. For the three members inside the ship, rest was something not afforded to them.

"So, we have a working theory?"

Halvor's words belayed a great deal of doubt.

"Sort of!"

Gaia had accessed all the information she could via the quantum entanglement communications device which was orbiting the planet. She had to be careful not to arouse any suspicions, as there was not supposed to be anyone here. However, there were many people at the resorts which lay on the mainland some distance away.

"It will do us no good jamming their signals, if we were able, to do such a thing. What we need is a way of directing them."

The plan was to infiltrate the holographic signals and then take control of the Artificial Army. In that way, they would not need to involve anyone else.

Doubts had arisen around the idea of contacting the Planetary Union, particularly as the Empress was presumed dead, and the Commander was the prime suspect. It would take days, if not weeks to get anything done, and by that time, it would all be over...

The smell of fresh food drifted out of the small galley, as Joan started the breakfasts. Fortunately, everything inside was well stocked, even though it looked like nothing more than a few shacks from the outside.

Eggs, toast, cereals, fruit, and a variety of other items were generated from the matter transformer, which had been left full of the proteins and minerals needed to create everything they needed.

Joan herself felt surprisingly well thanks to Doctor Sorenson. She was used to having spells of good mental health, although in the past, that could change if anything hit one of her many *nerves endings*. This time however, she had the feeling that whatever he had done, would have long lasting bifacial consequences. Smiling to herself, she thought about life without the constant fear of a sudden collapse into madness. It was not since her days serving on Earth with her beloved General Swartz had she felt so well.

"Morning Joan!"

The Doctor poked his head around the door. He always like to get up early in the morning.

Joan smiled back.

"Breakfast will be ready soon."

Her voice was just as bright and cheerful as the morning, and seeing her looking so well he automatically smiled back.

"I could get used to this!"

He lived alone, and had done for a number of years, being dedicated to his work, particularly after having taken up the position within the palace.

Ren was still soundly asleep, as were her uncle and Freya, who had taken up the room next to her.

Bear was the next to emerge, and was pleased to see that Joan had not skimped on the refreshments, as the big man needed a lot of filling!

Joan began to plate up the meal, as others slowly drifted into the makeshift canteen. This was the first time that everyone had been seated, and she felt happy to see them working their way through what she hoped was a veritable *banquet*.

When he was sure that everyone had finished eating, Vilgot stood up and asked for quiet.

"So, how did you get on?"

Halvor, who looked very tired, cleared his throat.

"After spending the night mulling things over, we have come to the conclusion that there is no way that we can take on the entire Artificial Army."

The Commander had already come to that conclusion himself.

"We believe that signals are being sent to the Artificial Soldiers via the Artificial Intelligence controlling them, and these signals are being sent via a process known as *Quantum Entanglement.* This is how the communications grid works, and is a physical phenomenon that occurs when pairs or groups of particles act in an identical manner, even when separated by a large distance."

Halvor was getting very technical!

"So, we therefore propose to abduct just one of the Artificial Soldiers, and then try to acquire the exact particle that is receiving the signal."

The Commander nodded.

"In that way, if successful, then we can gain control of the whole Artificial Army!"

That sounded logical, and a clear means of defeating them without having to engage in an all our war, which would be impossible considering their small number.

"And how do you propose we do that?"

That was a very good question...

Eight

Ripples of turquoise wave could be seen glistening in the morning sunshine through the branches of the large tree under which everyone had gathered.

Bear was sitting resting his back against the main trunk, having eaten more this morning than he had done since rejoining the Commander. It was surprising just how much he could actually eat, and yet he was not fat, just built like the tree he was resting against.

They had taken the news a lot better having just been fed, and now that a full scale war was to be avoided, they still had the problem of how they were going to get their hands upon an Artificial Soldier?

Vilgot knew that time was rapidly running out, as he spoke his thoughts out loud.

"We might have the *when* but not the *where!*"

That was a very good point, and without that, there was no possibility of carrying out their plan!

"So, what do you propose?"

Halvor looked flummoxed, struggling to keep himself awake.

It had taken them all night just to come up with the idea of abducting an Artificial Soldier, and with just one simple question, it felt like everything had suddenly fallen apart.

"In the information you went through, was there any indication of where the Artificial Army is, or where they are likely to be heading?"

Commander Bodil hoped that he would at least have some kind of an answer.

Halvor shrugged his shoulders dejectedly.

"None!"

Freya then smiled.

"I think I do!"

They all looked at her, wondering how she knew?

"Whilst you were busy last night, I logged into the communications grid, and discovered that they are holding a service in my honour on Asgard. That will mark the end of the official days of mourning."

Ren knew how she felt, as it had been a very odd experience watching her own funeral.

"All of the government and dignitaries will be there, and so it would present the perfect opportunity to eliminate the top echelon of our society all in one go!"

That seemed a perfectly logical assumption.

"But, how do we spot them?"

Bear joined in with the discussion.

Vilgot thought for a moment.

"So far, we know that the Hybrids were all Aesir Security personnel, so if it was me, then I would use Military Security personnel to escort everyone."

That again seemed very logical.

"Dignitaries would be arriving from all over the Empire, so if we can intercept a shuttle of Military Security personnel, then we should be able to capture at least one Artificial Soldier!"

Things were now coming back together nicely.

"But, how are we supposed to disable the Artificial Soldier?"

That was a very good point!

Bear looked at Freya. He always carried his enormous laser cannon gun, which would atomize any normal opponent.

However, if they were able to move rapidly and unpredictably, due to the photon chip embedded in their brains, they would be very difficult to hit, even with such a large weapon.

"How about an atomic laser, as light is both a wave and a particle?"

The Commander was thinking about his laser rifle, and replacing the light wave pulses with quantum waves, so that they acted like a light wave. In that way, he was hoping that the atomic laser could predict where the Artificial Soldier would be.

Halvor sighed.

"In theory yes, I could construct such a weapon. But, if we know a particle's position in space, then we will not know its momentum, which relates to its mass, speed and its direction."

He was already losing Vilgot.

"Let me explain. If we know where you are, then you must be standing still, but if we know where you are going, then we will not know exactly where you are."

The Commander looked confused.

"You see, we live in a quantum universe, governed by quantum principles, and we too are quantum beings."

Life was so much simpler when he used to battle with normal enemy using conventional weapons!

Halvor continued.

"Energy is related to vibration, and the rate in which something vibrates is its frequency. If we know the precise moment an event takes place, then the amount of energy contained within it becomes uncertain."

It seemed as though it was going to prove more difficult than he initially realized to hit, let alone capture an Artificial Soldier. He let his mind drift, as the conversation progressed on to how the actual holo chip worked.

"When we increase the energy we increase the frequency. If we can bring the energy to one state, then we can tune the frequency."

So, it may be possible to gain control of them?

"The photon chips are forever entangled, they can no longer be considered as individual, and become a connected whole. They form a single entity even if they are on opposite sides of the universe, and information is communicated between them instantaneously."

Vilgot let his mind reenter the conversation, having drawn a complete blank.

"So, the movements of all the Artificial Soldiers are governed by the Artificial Intelligence, which has to manipulate them all at once."

Halvor smiled at his daughter, who had asked the question.

"Yes, so if we capture one of them, then if we can hack into the system then we can take control of them all."

It was fascinating, like having slave units at your disposal. There would be no more putting your own life at risk, as all of the fighting would be done by others under your control, without having to worry about the safety of your team.

"So, it is not a case of hitting an Artificial Soldier with a laser beam, but a case of disabling it by other means?"

Ren was used to working with her father, and often repaired and adjusted the various Holo Droid units they had at home before they were forced to go undercover.

"Could we not just capture it in a tractor beam?"

Her mother then entered the conversation, and they were both stunned by what she had just said.

"When I was on the base, the scientists always used to quote *Occam's Razor,* the simplest method is usually the best method!

It was a brilliant suggestion, and not even a *fire axe* in sight...

Nine

Gaia approached the buoy which marked the entrance to the *starway*. Everyone had been squeezed inside, and the cargo hold was what could be called organized chaos.

Commander Bodil had put a plan together, which involved journeying to another obscure solar system, where there would be a delegation about to set off for the remembrance ceremony.

His plan was simple, intercept a Military Security shuttle, hold it in a tractor beam, and abduct an Artificial Soldier.

What could possibly go wrong...

"How are you feeling?"

Starfield felt surprisingly good, after his encounter with Mjolnir.

"Not bad, and thank you for asking."

Being with Ren, or her mother come to that, was not such an issue as it once had been. The Holo Droid now had a greater understanding of how situations could bring out the worst in people, be that corporeal or artificial!

"We should be entering the event horizon in a few moments."

Gaia joined in the conversation, feeling relieved that the atmosphere between them had calmed from the open hostility it had once exhibited.

Ren took a deep breath, as the ship moved forward, slipping into the exotic matter of the starway.

Translucent colours filled her field of vision, and for a moment she was lost in its beauty. It never ceased to take her breath away, no matter how many times she travelled through the Ancient's gateway.

"Serenity?"

Talking of *Ancients*, Mjolnir's voice entered her head.

"I'm here!"

That was all she could think of saying.

"I must warn you that what you are trying to achieve is fraught with danger!"

That did not sound good!

"Our eternal enemy the *Archons* have been feeding on all of the sorrow being felt, and are growing increasingly more powerful."

That again, did not sound good!

"Can I ask you a question?"

Mjolnir's form drifted in front of her, and he gave her an enigmatic smile, which she took as an affirmative.

"What is your relationship to them?"

That had been something which had been bothering her, ever since she had first encountered him. Information on the Ancients was patchy, full of myths and legend, and without any hard details.

"We were once just like you, and as we advanced we began to get a greater understanding of the universe. However, there was one question which remained unanswered, and that was, who or what created it all in the first place?"

That was a question she had asked herself.

"We eventually evolved into pure conscious energy, and at that stage we were a united people. Following our transition, we still required sustenance, and instead of ingesting nutrients, we now had to find a different source."

Ren had an inkling of what that could be, by what Mjolnir had said previously.

"Initially, we were able to survive on emotional energy, which was transmitted from corporeal forms such as yourself. We found that positive thoughts transmitted enough energy for our species, as we searched for our answers. Then, some of us became disillusioned, as we could not find the answer we sought. Eventually, a group of us decided that there was no one supreme being behind the creation of the universe, and so turned their back on the search. They became more and more disillusioned until they began to feed off negative thoughts. From there, they began to crave more and more of this energy, until they could not survive without it."

So the Archons were originally the Ancients!

"Yes, that is so!"

Now she understood.

"The negative energy became addictive, and the more they consumed, the more they desired. All the conflict you see before you is down to them, and they are becoming more and more powerful all of the time. We do what we can to restrain them, but as their numbers increase, ours decrease."

So it looked as though Mjolnir's people were in the same position as her own!

Life must be so different as a being of light, with no real body to speak of, apart from a gaseous cloud of particles. It appeared as though it was all about energy of one form or another. Mjolnir could travel the universe, and morph himself into many forms, and yet he still needed sustenance. Ren began to think of all the tantrums she had ever had, and all of the negative thoughts and emotions which had been consumed by the Archons. They appeared to have become addicted to negative energy, and she herself had only added to their rapidly increasing power.

Poor Mjolnir, trying to do good, whilst scavenging for food like a stray dog!

It did not seem fair, that he and his people had been suffering. Thinking more about it, Ren began to realize that it must take a lot of energy to do what he did, and materializing in front of her must be very draining. No wonder the Ancients did not appear very often.

It was then that Ren really began to appreciate how lucky she was, that he had appeared before her on so many occasions...

Starfield, on the other hand, felt a profound sense of purpose, having eavesdropped on their conversation.

How much had his recent behaviour fuelled their enemy?

From this moment on, he decided that he was going to be a changed Holo Droid...

Gaia, had always remained fairly calm, and done her best to express her love whenever she had the chance. That had not been easy, particularly over the last few days, but had her love for *Stellan* been enough to enable Mjolnir to make the connection?

It was an interesting thought, and one which she contemplated as she watched the Ancient depart.

Translucent colours then began to warp, as the ship was sucked into the bottleneck of the other end of the starway. Everything seemed to compact, before they were cast out into normal space again...

Ten

"Status report?"

The Commander's voice brought them back to reality, and the mission.

"All systems functioning normally."

Gaia's voice felt confident, and for once, Starfield did too!

Encountering Mjolnir again had made all of the difference, and he could now literally *see the light.* During those few moments he had decided to ascend just like the Ancients. The first step on his long journey had been to transfer his consciousness into the Holo Droid's moon glass shell. The next would be leaving that behind and becoming a *being of light!*

Starfield felt very pleased with himself, not smug, just enlightened. He was going to leave behind all of the petty squabbling of reptilians and humans, and move beyond their primitive nature. He could now see the error of his ways, and was going to a *far better place.*

"Yes!"

He said to himself.

"No more!"

Then, whilst his mind was elsewhere, a laser pulse crashed into Gaia's shields, making him nearly *ascend* form his moon glass shell.

"Flux!"

Starfield instinctively fired Gaia's main weapon at the ship careering towards them.

"Fluxing flux!"

Its shield rippled like the purple particles coalescing inside his moon glass head.

Perhaps it was not going to be quite that easy to become a *being of light* after all...

"Good shooting Starfield."

Vilgot's voice sounded pleased.

"But mind your language."

They did have the former Empress on board after all!

Gaia had emerged into the solar system, but before she could go into stealth mode, the patrol ship had spotted them and opened fire.

"Taking evasive action."

Ren performed some space gymnastics, as Gaia belatedly went into stealth mode. They were soon cloaked, and invisible to the patrol ship, or anything else for that matter. Her shields were soon back up to full strength, as Halvor monitored everything from the tiny bedroom.

"Any sign of them?"

The Commander felt anxious, particularly as they had been detected straight away, which would now make their task a lot more difficult as they had lost the element of surprise.

"Yes, but it looks as though they have lost us!"

That was small comfort, as they would be on the lookout for them. It did not alter the plan though, as they had to try and capture one of the Artificial Soldiers.

Scanning the area, they detected a cruiser and its escorts, two military shuttles, which it was assumed were armed to the teeth!

Within the main ship were those due to attend the service, and in the shuttles Artificial Soldiers. Somehow they had to swoop in, apply the tractor beam to both the outside and in, and then retrieve one of the soldiers, render it inert, and then make their escape...

Further inside the solar system, faint traces of light caught the black carbon fiber outer skin of the floating Military Intelligence Head Quarters. It hung in space like a spider resting in the web of space, with its outstretched limbs protruding from its central core. A single craft was docked, resembling a captured fly, in its front mandibles.

Various star systems had them, which could be moved if necessary, and were very heavily fortified. Strong defensive shields protected it along with various armaments, and military craft which were often in close proximately. Today however, two military shuttles had already left to accompany the transport which was on its way to the ceremony.

A mild luminescent pulsating glow crept across a small glowing device situated within. An anomaly had been detected, and one which had been reported elsewhere.

Craft identified.

The small glowing device accessed the report filed within the information stream.

Human vessel responsible for the loss of the Hybrid Hatching Facility.

The luminescent glow intensified.

Prognosis.

Probability that vessel has arrived in this system by chance - high.

More calculations were instantaneously made.

Threat level low.

The small glowing device then considered the situation for a millisecond.

Priority must be given to the mission, and therefore shuttle escorts must proceed to their designated target on schedule. However, it would be prudent to dispatch an Artificial Soldier on a *seek and destroy* mission.

More calculations were made.

Due to the large area the Aesir occupied, and the limited number of *constructs* available, there were few possible options. Everything had been meticulously worked out and every conceivable scenario considered. Therefore, it was inconceivable to withdraw any Artificial Soldier from their allotted mission, so it would have to send one of its two remaining security personnel.

Nothing could be allowed to interfere with the *plan*, as it had been calculated that this species would be so overwhelmed when their hierarchy was decapitated, that in the confusion resulting from the attack, they would simply crumble and very quickly be assimilated...

Eleven

Space passed by in a blur, stretching and bending as Gaia's shields pushed their way through, like a ship sailing on a calm sea, although calm was a relative term.

"So what do we do now?"

That was a very good question!

Initially, they had planned to slip unnoticed into this solar system, and then select a suitable target. It was hoped to find a lone military shuttle, and then carry out the planned attack.

Vilgot rubbed his chin.

He had deliberately chosen this system as it would only be lightly defended. Every system would naturally send a representative, and he had been hoping that there would be little resistance.

However, there was no way they could tackle three ships, and being as their presence had already been discovered, they would now be on their guard. It was presumed that Gaia could remain stealthed as she had done when entering the outskirts of Asgard, but something had clearly gone awry.

"How were we detected?"

It was now time for Halvor to rub his chin.

"Maybe our energy signature has been relayed to other sectors, and someone or something has been searching for us?"

Those were the Commander's thoughts.

"Can you alter it?"

Halvor was already modulating their energy signature, and

cursed himself for not thinking of that earlier, although his language was far less *dramatic* than that of the Holo Droid!

"Modulation active."

That was one less thing to worry about, although it proved that they had to be far more careful. So far, they had been lucky, but was that luck about to run out...

The patrol ship was still searching for them, part of a regular pattern designed to keep the system safe. There was a small base on one of the moons, and a minefield, and various weapons platforms. If the Reptilians chose to invade, then help would not be far away. It would be the job of the defenders to try and hold them off before other assets could be brought to bear.

The Aesir's did not have the resources to fully fortify and equip every system they inhabited, so their various fleets were constantly on patrol, visiting each and every system on a regular basis. Intelligence was the key, although they did not realise that its reliability could no longer be depended upon.

A single seat attack craft lifted off from a military base, situated on the only habitable planet within this star system. A request for back up had been sent by the patrol craft, which was still searching for the unidentified vessel it had located and fired upon.

The system worked well, as all known Aesir craft were logged into a central database, and the instant one emerged from a starway, the communications system identified it. If identification failed, then the nearest craft was ordered to open fire, and all of that occurred in a quantum fluctuation.

The attack craft quickly swept out into the cloudy sky, but he was now wondering if it had been a Reptilian scout. His holo chip was directing him, and casual thought was something that he never indulged in.

That was not uncommon, and both his and the moon's base had been placed on alert. On most occasions they were successfully chased away, and it was a constant game between the two species. They would build up their resources, and then a conflict would arise, where a lot of them would be destroyed. The Aesir felt that it was prudent to have a rapid reaction force rather than concentrate their efforts on fortification. The Reptilians had also decided on the same policy, although recently, they had embarked on a more sinister approach.

This particular planet always seemed to be shrouded in cloud, but for the small glowing device situated on the ground, it had no desire to see the sun. All it wished for was dominance, just like the one within the space station, as they cared little about aesthetics.

Luminescent pulses flashed across the surface of the small glowing device, as it communed with its brethren.

The Artificial Soldier program had been designed to improve the human vessel, enabling it to gain bone density, weight and height, boost cognitive thinking and awareness, and to enhance sensory perception.

The Mammalian brain overplayed a Reptilian brain, which in *Terrans* often caused an internal conflict. Killing and survival was the Reptilian aspect, whilst the human was more about compassion, and the amount of energy expressed through each one dictated their actions.

The forces of magnetism and electricity interacting with a human *life-force* were not just electromagnetic, but also consciousness based. They had immune responses - about twenty six of them, which became energized by coming into contact with various substances or bacteria, which naturally boosted to protect them.

What this lower life form perceived as real, was simply a mirage, which emerged from a projection of information encoded into the lower dimensional holographic surface which it occupied.

The most fundamental component of the universe and everything within it was information, and although these life forms believed that what they experienced was real, it was not the whole of reality.

Every dimension was spherical in nature, and the information transmitted to each sphere was reflected onto its surface, which is what was perceived. Most of them were not aware that there were many spheres within spheres, and the higher up the dimensional realities, the closer to the centre you became.

It's master the *Archons* had travelled close to the centre, but were not able to progress any further. The *Ancients* were considered to be holding back progress, and so had to be eliminated.

It was not possible to just vaporize them, so starvation was considered the optimum solution. By eliminating their source of nourishment, they would just shrivel and die.

Once the Aesir were *assimilated,* then it would significantly weaken their bitter enemy, and naturally strengthen them even further.

The countdown continued, although time was irrelevant, only success...

Twelve

Silhouetted against the total blackness of the event horizon, three Aesir ships passed the green glowing buoy. Soon they would be emerging on the other side, travelling towards the remembrance ceremony on Asgard. Freya watched them slowly disappear, her thoughts being with her people.

Giving up a kingdom may not have sounded like a thrilling proposition, but she had found it liberating, particularly as she could now be with the man she had always desired. He sat next to her, on the cramped floor of the cargo hold, mulling things over in his mind...

Meanwhile, the attack craft swept up from the surface of the habitable planet, and this one was a little different to the other. Over the years, Aesir attack craft had changed, and the wedge shape had been replaced by a slim line dart with swept back wings. It was a lot faster than its predecessors, and packed quite a punch.

Ren let her mind drift through Gaia's systems, making sure that everything was working correctly. She was really getting used to linking her mind with the ship's holographic matrix, and the twin screens in front of her. Consciousness control had its advantages, which was just as well, as something suddenly appeared on the screen displaying the outer world.

"Starfield?"

He was also conjoined with Gaia's systems, trying to calm himself by undertaking breathing exercises of all things, even though his sealed moon glass shell never took on any oxygen.

"Calm and relaxed, calm and relaxed."

His mantra was steadily reverberating around his mind, and he was determined not to swear again. His outbursts were not helping, and the Commander had already reprimanded him.

"Calm and relaxed, calm and relaxed."

He was so busy concentrating that he failed to hear Ren's voice, or notice that there was another craft out there.

Somehow, despite the modulation in Gaia's energy signature it appeared to be heading straight for them. Halvor was still busily working away on his organic computer, interfaced with the ship's holographic matrix. He could see the attack craft on his screen, and he was bemused as to why it looked as though it could still locate them.

The only conclusion that he could reach was that either they had picked up some sort of a tracking device, or a higher intelligence was involved.

Whatever the reason, there was one thing for certain, and that was that it was on an intercept course and would be bearing down upon them in a few moments...

Intruder located

The small glowing device was directing the Artificial Soldier via its holo chip. Various algorithms had been running, and the most likely location extrapolated, as it was not actually the ship itself that was giving away its position, but the fact that the human bodies it contained were constantly emitting electricity, magnetic energy and bio photons.

The latest long range scanning protocols had been stretched to the limit, and yet something anomalous had been detected, and now that it had been found, elimination was the desired result.

Boom!

"FLUX!"

Gaia's energy shield rippled with the impact of a weapon, as Starfield cried out at the top of his synthetic voice, as he and the others had been taken completely by surprise.

So much for *calm and relaxed!*

The ship lurched as Ren took evasive action, suddenly spotting the attack craft, which had sneaked up on them.

A series of laser pulses flashed in front of them, as Gaia dived and twisted, whilst Starfield fired back.

His emotions were all over the place, swinging wildly from calm to anger, as he blasted away. It was getting harder and harder to cope with the transition from corporeal to artificial, and he was blaming himself for being so wrapped up in his own issues that he failed to notice the vessel which was inflicting more damage on Gaia's shields.

The ship shook again, as he failed to target the attack craft, which it appeared was being expertly piloted...

Those huddled in the cargo hold could do nothing but wait and hope that the attacker could be disabled, before their vessel was destroyed.

The Commander received pictures via his helmet's internal display, relayed to him by Halvor, who was doing his best to collate and send information.

Ren was also doing her best to take evasive action, but it seemed as though whatever she attempted, had already been anticipated before she even took the action.

This battle was going to be a lot harder than the ones they had faced before...

Thirteen

Simulated rumbles echoed around the main control room, as more laser pulses impacted on Gaia's shields, which were already dropping rapidly.

Gaia was highly advanced and virtually undetectable by normal methods of scanning, and yet she was being detected.

Something had to be done, and quickly before her shields failed.

The ship shuddered from another impact, as the attack craft darted around, making random movements in a complex algorithmic pattern. They were being hit by some sort of energy weapon, a little different form the normal Aesir laser pulses.

This was no ordinary attack craft, or pilot come to that!

More pulses impacted Gaia's defensive shield, driving it back against her hull, and making it waver for few seconds, as Starfield tried to return fire.

Halvor was busy with his own algorithmic pattern, trying to work out where the attack craft would jump to next.

Gaia then shook violently, and the lights went out, as Starfield was nearly thrown off his feet, as he was plunged into darkness before the emergency lighting came on.

Fortunately, Gaia's holographic matrix had its own emergency power supply, but another impact would cause major damage.

They were losing, and losing fast!

Starfield felt quite faint, as a strange feeling crept through his own holographic matrix. He could feel his arm moving rapidly across the smooth surface of the console he was standing behind. Gaia's main weapon then fired a few quick bursts in a random pattern that made no sense to him at all.

Then the unexpected happened.

The attack craft seemed to dive towards the pulses he was sending out.

With his head still clouded in confusion, he watched as the vessel was hit several times, weakening its shield. Then as he continued to fire erratically, the shield went down, and one of the twin engines exploded.

Ren could see everything via her twin screens, as well as a faint luminous glow hovering in the distance. It was not there for very long, and could quite easily have been a gaseous anomaly. Whatever it had been was not threatening, and she just dismissed it, concentrating on what she was doing.

Things had taken a sudden turn for the better, particularly as Starfield managed to disable the attack craft's other engine. It also looked to be losing power, and appeared not to be able to fire its weapons any more...

"Nice shooting again, Starfield!"

Vilgot's voice echoed around the control room, although the Holo Droid was none the wiser. It was not really him who tracked and fired at the attack craft, and he was too busy performing a self diagnostic to reply.

"Move in to intercept."

Remarkably, the plan was now back on track, and the Commander was more than relieved. It had looked as though everything would end in disaster, although there was still no guarantee of success...

Gaia swept in towards the stricken craft, which was showing a loss of power to both weapons and propulsion systems. The life support had its own backup, and theoretically the pilot should be able to survive in his suit for a number of hours, and if he was lucky maybe days.

Sensors indicated the latter, although it was difficult to tell as he appeared to be shielded in some way. It was definitely a *he* though, as the limited information available indicated that much. It also indicated that it was indeed an Artificial Soldier...

Lights flickered quickly across the small glowing device, as the data stream indicated that the interception had been unsuccessful.

Alternative options?

The nearby patrol craft.

Likelihood of success - minimal...

The pilot had to look twice at the information scrolling across the inside of his helmet.

Do not engage target, repeat, do not engage target.

He looked at the message in bewilderment.

Why had he been ordered not to engage?

Before he could ask for conformation, he received a further transmission.

Military Intelligence training exercise!

He blew out into his helmet, knowing better than to ask for any further explanation...

Joan sat in the cargo hold with her back against the wall, her thoughts turning to her daughter. Serenity was growing up quickly, and had proved herself capable of piloting this unique vessel. She felt very proud, and her pride was enough to lessen the increasing fear she had about this operation.

Her fears were shared by the others, as Freya gave her a knowing look. Doctor Sorenson also felt uncomfortable as he checked his medical equipment for the umpteenth time, hoping that it would not be needed.

Commander Bodil watched his helmet's display indicating the closing distance between the two craft. Everyone needed to remain alert, as they were entering a critical phase of the operation...

Intermittent images flashed in and out of the pilot's display, as time seemed to pass by slowly within the attack craft. The mission had proved to be a failure, although there may still be a chance of redemption. A gloved hand hovered over the self destruct button, housed on the small control consol. In just a few short moments, the *seek and destroy* mission would end for the pilot, and as it happened, also for the human ship he had been tasked with eliminating...

Fourteen

Humans were a fragile species, and yet despite the odds, they seemed to have the ability to overcome the obstacles placed in their path. Over the years, too many to count, various upgrades had been performed, especially to those who inhabited Midgard. It had been a wise decision in bringing the female here, and her offspring had proved to be quite resourceful. Her untamed nature, and genetic hybrid status was something invaluable, although the term *hybrid,* was not to be confused with the Reptilian version.

Mjolnir had done all that he could, and now watched and waited, hovering in a slightly higher dimension. From there, he could remain undetected, although the Archons, his bitter enemy were never too far away. Their use of the Artificial Intelligence had been a master stroke, and one which was now getting out of control. His people were growing increasingly weak, and he was thankful for the *love energy* being broadcast by the former Empress. It was enough to sustain him, although it looked as though that was about to come to an end...

The Artificial Soldier did not fear death, as emotions were such a waste of energy, and he was grateful not to have any to worry about, although worry was something that he never indulged in. It was just about following orders, being a very small cog in a very big machine, although they were way beyond the use of such primitive things.

The Human craft was now within range, and taking one last deep breath, he waited to join the collective in another form. Being part of a vast computer consciousness had its benefits, as he was neither alive or faced the prospect of death. Just eternal code...

Human bodies, conscious in whatever form they took were malleable to a certain extent, just how much would become apparent in the next few moments, as Mjolnir stretched out his thoughts. There was not much to stretch out too, as the human in question had no independent thought, just those shared by the *collective.*

If only it was a simple as connecting with one to influence the many...

The Artificial Soldier felt something, although this was different from what he normally felt. Somehow, there was the desire not to fulfill his mission, and he wondered if there was a fault in his programming...

"Quickly, send out the tractor beam."

The Commander issued his order as soon as they got within range. The beam would be no guarantee, but what Halvor had managed to do with it, meant that in theory, it should be strong enough to penetrate the inside of the attack craft.

All he could do now was to watch and wait, and found himself reaching for the Empress.

Never before had he felt such comfort, or indeed strength from being in the close proximately to another person. Yes, he had a deep love for the young woman piloting this craft, but that was a different type of love altogether.

Perhaps he was getting soft in his old age?

Freya grasped his hand through her armored glove, and even though she could not feel his flesh, she still felt the growing bond between them. The time she spent with him had been exhilarating, especially when they were alone together. A slight red flush crept over her cheeks when she though about just how *exhilarating* it had been!

"Beam away!"

Halvor's voice brought them both back to reality, as their helmet displays homed in on the glowing green beam...

A gloved thumb pressed down on the self destruct button, but not before the green light swept over the outer shell of the attack craft. For the first time in his life, the Artificial Soldier felt confusion.

Why had he hesitated?

That momentary lapse in concentration could have proved costly, as his thumb seemed to be encountering resistance, as if it was pushing against some sort of barrier.

Time to rejoin the collective!

Computing.

Why had there not been an explosion?

Why had he lost control of his body?

Why was he not *dead...*

"Beam secure!"

That was what the Commander was waiting for.

"Secure helmets, and open the hatch!

They all snapped their helmet visors down into place, as the cargo hold door began to open. There was a faint green glow of the force field holding the atmosphere in, and a much stronger glow of the tractor beam, as the hatch slid open.

"Move out!"

Vilgot led the way followed by Joan.

The plan was for the two of them to traverse empty space, and secure a small specially designed probe to the surface of the attack craft's cockpit window. It would then theoretically, burrow in and attach itself to the skull of the Artificial Soldier sitting in the pilot's seat. From there, it would send information through to Halvor, who would hopefully be able to ascertain the quantum frequency being used to transmit orders to the Artificial Army...

Fifteen

Quantum frequencies flashed to and fro at an incalculable speed, assessing the current situation. Sensor readings had indicated that the expected explosion had not occurred, and instead of the human ship being blown apart by the self-destruct mechanism of the attack craft, it was still very much intact.

Lights flickered an angry red, as the small glowing device continued to communicate with the others of its kind.

A minor insignificance, not worthy of any greater thought.

That's as maybe, but somewhere the first hints of emotion nibbled at the edges of its being.

There was just something about these humans that brought about an undesired and even more unexpected response...

The Commander leapt out, trailing a line behind him as he went.

The bright green tractor beam engulfed him, although it did not have any effect, as he was carrying a deflection device on the front of his armored suit. This enabled the beam to flow around him, thanks to his old friend's ingenuity.

Joan waited, poised in the hatch, as the Commander made his way towards the cockpit window. Vilgot was a very skilled operative, and he was soon reaching for one of the handholds. His gloved hand made contact, and he managed to slow himself down.

Now it was Joan's turn.

She launched herself towards the Commander, sailing through empty space, and then through the tractor beam, which parted before her. Joan would be the one to place the device, whilst Vilgot stood guard, just in case the Artificial Soldier regained consciousness.

Bear and Freya were backup, ready to launch themselves if they were needed, and Halvor monitored everything from his position in the cramped bedroom. The Doctor waited patiently for the Soldier's life signs to be transmitted, so that his brainwave activity could be monitored.

Ren and Starfield were connected to Gaia's holographic matrix, also monitoring the two person team.

Joan sailed forwards until she was able to clasp herself to the Commander's body. Then, as soon as she was able to stabilize herself, she released the small device which attacked itself to the cockpit window.

Vilgot peered over her shoulder and was shocked to see the Artificial Soldier's thumb hovering over the self destruct button. He quickly looked away, deciding not to say anything as it would only disturb everyone if they knew how close they had all come to being obliterated.

The probe then began to burrow its was through the surface until it was inside. Halvor was guiding it, and it was soon sailing through until it clasped itself to the Soldier's helmet.

Everything seemed to be going well, as the probe began to bore its way through the material until it was ready to clasp itself to his skull...

Something was wrong!

The small glowing device's orders were not being followed.

Scans indicated that the pilot was still alive, and information was steadily flowing into his holo chip, but they were not being acted upon. Then, the signal encountered some interference, vibrating in a rhythmic pattern.

There was then an energy spike, followed by a sine wave of indeterminate proportions.

Analysis.

Some unauthorized source was interfering with the chip...

"Have you got it?"

Halvor received the sine wave on his screen.

"Yes!"

Everyone breathed out a huge sigh or relief.

So far, so good!

Information flowed into his computer, which contained the advanced detection system he had designed, which had first alerted him to the conspiracy. All he needed was a good enough sample, and then they could get out of here...

Analysis:

A minor insignificance, not worthy of any greater thought.

Emotional responses - anger - a strong feeling of annoyance, displeasure, or hostility.

The small glowing device had never felt an emotional response before.

Question:

If this was indeed an emotional response, then what was the best way of dealing with it...

A second Artificial Soldier launched in another attack craft from Military Intelligence Head Quarters. Technically, the Aesir Security Service was also military intelligence, although that was more concerned with espionage. Still, being as that had also been compromised, the two were now working together as the lines became blurred...

The spider like structure of the space station hung in the web of space, masked by various stealth systems that made it very hard to detect. There were various defensive systems guarding the entrance to the starway, although there was no main space station visible. This planetary system had only one main habitable planet, as well as a few moons with mining operations on them, which was why it was relatively undefended. The obscurity made it an ideal for both a Military Intelligence Head Quarters, and somewhere for the team to try and capture an Artificial Soldier...

Starfield, who had been so preoccupied with his own thoughts had failed to noticed the first ship, was now concentrating on his job.

"Enemy craft inbound!"

His words startled everyone.

On his long range scanners, a small craft had suddenly appeared.

The Commander frowned.

"Lets get back to the ship."

He was not going to get any arguments from Joan, who had also heard the message. They were vulnerable here, and the last thing she wished for was to be caught out in the open.

They both scrambled back, holding onto the safety line as Bear pulled hard on the other end. It was like being on the end of a piece of elastic, which snapped them back at speed.

The attack craft was closing in, and would be in firing range in only a few short moments, and they had to do something.

"When I give the order disengage the tractor beam, and Serenity, head for our designated withdrawal position."

His breathless voice echoed through the communications system, as both he and Joan scrambled through the open hatch.

Bear caught them in his big powerful hands, as Freya pressed the down on the button by her side, and the doors began to close.

A bright flash then rippled through space as the attack ship fired its laser weapon.

"Now!"

Ren concentrated on the planet her uncle had chosen, and as she did so, Gaia released the tractor beam. Everything then happened at once, as the laser beam struck her shields. The Artificial soldier within the suspended attack craft suddenly felt his thumb move, and as it did so, there was not time to stop it depressing the button.

There then followed a violent explosion as his ship exploded...

Sixteen

A dramatic shift in colour, from black to an entire rainbow spectrum of streaking hues flashed by the flickering energy shield, as Vilgot could feel dimensional forces pulling at him, trying to drag him through the partially open hatch.

It felt as though every time they achieved anything, something worse came along.

His life was now flashing before him like the colours trying to drag him away, as Bear's massive bulk managed to hold on. Joan was also feeling the same emotions, not knowing if either of them were going to survive...

Another flickering light pulsed rapidly, as sensor information recorded the explosion, and the fragmentation of both craft. The small glowing device ran through several calculations, resulting in a conclusion that both vessels had been destroyed.

It was clear that nothing could have withstood the explosion, as a full complement of armaments were present on the attack craft and would also have exploded along with the propulsion system.

Conclusion:

A 98.9% probability of success, and more importantly another emotion.

Fulfilment - the pleasure derived from one's wishes, expectations, or needs being achieved...

Bright colours flashed in front of Ren's eyes, as Gaia fragmented, slipping into *weird space* as the explosion rocked her energy shields.

Starfield's molecules swam about in a maelstrom, as he tried to make sense of what had just happened.

Had they made it?

In the cargo hold, they were asking themselves the same question. It had been pandemonium, hanging on to the Commander and Joan in the tight confines. Just one slip and they could all have been dragged out of the door, which was still half way open.

"Report!"

Vilgot's breathless voice had lost its usual calm.

"We seem to have entered weird space."

That was all that Halvor could tell him, as the censoring equipment could not give him any details. They had escaped the explosion, but whether they would emerge safety on the other side was still far from certain.

Ren was concentrating hard, picturing the planet that she was vaguely familiar with. It had been somewhere her uncle had taken her as a child, and one which she had a few fond memories of.

An ice world with a ski resort and some modest mining operations. Nothing much, but just enough to make it viable. *Island* was not for the faint hearted, although the winter sports and hot springs were something many tourists longed to visit. That is where her uncle had taught her to ski, and also undertaken some survival training.

That was very apt, as survival was now top of their list!

Swirling colours coalesced into a point of light, as Gaia shook violently before being spat out into normal space. Alarms sounded as everyone was thrown about.

"Flux!"

Starfield swore again, only this time there was no reprimand, as everyone was more concerned with their own safety. The ship had taken quite a pounding, and the explosion combined with Ren's panicked exit had taken its toll.

Some of her systems were down, and the shield and stealth generators had been damaged.

Freya picked herself up from the floor, as Joan rolled off Bear, whilst the Commander had been thrown against the door, and was now hanging precariously half in and half out of the ship.

Island's thick protective atmosphere hung like a safety blanket far below, although if he did fall, then there would be no soft landing.

He may have felt a little disorientated, but nevertheless, Vilgot dragged himself back inside, as the outer door continued to close. They were still thankfully alive, escaping the clutches of the consciousness transfer process, although with the infiltration of their society there may not be a Replicant body to transfer into.

That was indeed a chilling thought!

Island looked equally as cold, and he hoped that they had not been detected by the local sensors.

"Report!"

Freya looked at him, relieved that he was still with them, not knowing what she would have done if he had been lost. She was tempted to rush across and wrap her arms around him, but she managed to restrain herself.

Halvor, who fortunately had been sitting on the bed had fared far better than the others, and was able to access all of the main systems. He then began to give a brief assessment, whilst attempting to place them back into stealth mode.

Island was another backwater planet, with little in the way of defences, and so had been deliberately chosen. They had been skirting the main systems in the hope of not being detected. Last time however, they had the moment that they exited the starway, and Vilgot was glad that they had utilised Gaia's unique quantum transfer system.

"It appears that we have slipped into this system without being noticed."

That was fortuitous, as they had a lot of work to do if they were going to stop the Artificial Soldiers...

Seventeen

Reams of data flowed down the screen of Halvor's computer as he access the data collected by his probe. It was fascinating stuff, and he would have liked to have spent a few months going through it. Time was of the essence though, and he had to try and find the *magic key* if they were going to be successful.

Doctor Sorenson had given everyone a quick check over, as they continued to work on Gaia's systems. They had been lucky, as the ship had only caught the tail end of the blast as it moved into weird space.

Another few seconds, and it would have been a very different scenario altogether!

His old friend Vilgot Bodil, then entered the cramped bedroom, causing him to look up.

"Any joy?"

The Commander was getting anxious, and so was the Doctor who was standing behind him.

All three men then squeezed onto the bed, looking at the data he had been processing.

"I'm no medical expert, but it looks to me as if the signals are being transmitted in the Gamma brain state."

That was the one usually associated with *fluid motion,* where the thinking brain was surpassed.

"Like being in the *zone*?"

Halvor nodded.

"Although the readings I am getting are above what I would

have expected."

Doctor Sorenson leaned over.

"In my opinion they are beyond Hyper Gamma."

Neither Vilgot nor Halvor knew that there was anything higher than Gamma.

"It looks to me as if they re in *Lamda.*"

The Doctor briefly explained that that was when both the left and right sides of the brain became synchronised, and the body could be self-regulated. Right at the other end of the spectrum was *Epsilon*, which was more akin to suspended animation, where there was no pulse, but the mind and body were still very much alive.

"Gamma rays originate from the thalamus and pulse 40 times a second as a unified wave, where information can be processed rapidly, enhanced intuition, and harmonizing the heart and the brain."

He had studied such things, and normally it was attained by meditation, feeling the emotion of compassion.

"And the signal?"

Halvor changed the screen to show a rapid instantaneous pulse...

Starfield was also receiving the information along with Gaia via their unique link. They could also hear the conversation, and as soon as he heard the word *meditation*, his mind began to drift.

Compassion starts with sympathy, then empathy, and accepting things without judgment and holding that focus for a greater outcome.

The definition seemed to spark something off inside him, as Starfield's concentration began to wonder.

Life seemed to be one big mystery, and the universe an even bigger one!

"Why don't you look at it in this way?"

Mjolnir suddenly appeared, smiling as his energetic form hovered in front of Starfield.

"There is potential, and there is possibility, and when you focus that potential on a certain possibility, then you create a vibrating pulse of energy in one place creating matter."

The Holo Droid was not startled, and did not swear, just accepted that the *Ancient* was here with him. Over the last half hour, he had been repeating his mantra to himself, *calm and relaxed, calm and relaxed.*

Starfield felt very pleased with himself, not only helping with the repairs, but also gaining control over his erratic emotions.

"The intellect is incapable of understanding certain things, but there is a *knowingness,* and that knowingness is a higher form of intellect."

It seemed as though he was talking in riddles.

"Your life in this world is just a hologram, a projection from a higher reality, where your true self resides, where it observes and projects to many parallel realities."

Even for an advanced mind such as his, it was difficult to visualize.

"Only by expanding your consciousness beyond the physical, can your awareness pierce the veil of illusion."

Back to riddles again!

"We believe that our combined consciousness is the source of everything within the universe, and that conscious thought transforms into matter by sending out waves of energy, which osculate into shapes, frequency and rhythm."

Starfield could visualize that, as it was far more tangible.

"They form spheres, and each sphere contains a shape that is derived by its frequency, and that frequency dictates what particular type of life resides within it."

Now he was beginning to understand.

"Every shape can fit neatly into a *merkabah,* which is at the centre of creation sending off a sonic photonic pulse, which is reflected and refracted throughout all of the others."

It was a bit like his own consciousness filling the void of his moon glass shell.

"The central point takes the shape of a *merkabah,* and is projected out to many different locations, and all are part of the one, and indeed the whole. Each one reflects aspects of itself back to the central source in a complex pattern. Therefore, there are many parallel realities, and it is consciousness itself that shapes that reality by altering the vibration."

Starfield could now understand what effect his emotions had been having on not only himself, but also the crew, and the wider world beyond.

"It does this as energy is communication, and when it slows down, it becomes information. Imagination and energy with a little bit of effort becomes reality, which is what we see inside our own heads."

Even those consisting of moon glass!

Mjolnir was trying to tell him something.

"Everything we experience is vibration, and everything is energy vibrating at a certain frequency."

Humans were attuned to a lower frequency!

The quantum pulse, although a rhythmic oscillation of particles or wave like energies, contains a higher frequency requiring more energy.

Therefore, the quantum pulse must be set at the highest possible frequency a human brain could interpret."

Starfield did a quick calculation and then arrived at a figure, which he quickly relayed to Halvor...

Eighteen

A beaming smile crept across Halvor's face as he received the information.

"Well done Starfield."

His reputation was growing and he was becoming a valued member of the team.

"We have the frequency, and I believe that I am close to acquiring the code."

That was good news, and meant that they were close to being able to attempt to stop the planned massacre. However, there was still plenty of work to do, and time was rapidly running out.

Ren felt her mind floating out beyond the surface of the ship, reaching out into open space. There seemed to be little activity within the system, only the odd mining vessel, and pleasure craft. They seemed to be docked, as it looked as though everyone was preparing to watch the remembrance ceremony.

There was no Military Intelligence presence here, only a small system security building, housed on one of the barren moons. Even so, she was still on the lookout, along with Starfield, as they could not afford to take any chances.

Gaia's systems were healing, as they moved out now that the stealth field was fully operational. They were heading for the relay station, which floated above Island.

"Quantum cloning?"

The Commander sounded perplexed, as Halvor explained what needed to be done.

"Yes, its the process of making an exact copy of a quantum particle without altering the original in any way."

This was way above his level of understanding.

"The communications grid works by duplicating the particles so that one exists within each relay, so that they can all instantly communicate with each other."

He had to admit that it was fast, and each solar system throughout the empire had one.

They were very fortunate in having Halvor, as he was a leading communication expert. The down side was that they would have to get him inside the relay station, and then wait whilst he attempted to modify the system to send a signal to the Artificial Army.

His probe had managed to capture the exotic particle from the holo chip embedded within the brain of the Artificial Soldier. Quite how that had been done was just as big a mystery as *quantum cloning*, but Vilgot trusted his old friend, who in his humble opinion was a bit of a genius.

Give him something to shoot at, or an operation to plan, and he was in his element, but this complicated technical stuff left him floundering.

Starfield was even more intelligent, if not unpredictable. So far, he seemed to be holding himself together, and the Commander hoped that he would continue to do so...

Sparkling turquoise eyes looked out of the main viewing screen, as the golden blonde locks of Gaia's image ruffled as she moved her head from side to side. So far, she had been impressed with the humans that were now her crew, and felt overjoyed in the improvement of Stellan despite his worsening language. So far, they had survived the initial attack by the Hybrids, rescued the Empress, and destroyed the Hybrid facility. Retrieving the quantum particle from the Artificial Soldier's holo chip had been an unexpected bonus, although it would all be for nought if they could not stop the attack on the remembrance ceremony.

The relay station hung in space like a spinning top, with a large shaft protruding from the upper portion which ran all the way through the bulbous midsection, and down way beyond. They were usually unmanned, although there was some modest accommodation for the technicians who maintained the system.

"Bring us in closer."

The Commander's voice sounded confident, as it had to, otherwise the enormity of the mission would start to degrade moral. Freya looked adoringly into his eyes, hoping that when this was over they could spend some quality time together.

Everything had to be done stealthily, as they could not allow their presence to be detected. If anyone found out that she was still alive, then any prospect of spending the rest of her life with the man she adored would disappear for ever.

Gaia moved closer, as Ren continued to scan the area. Everything appeared quiet, and as long as they remained stealthed, then they could dock with the relay station and let Halvor do his work.

The docking tube was of universal design, enabling a variety of vehicles to connect with it. In essence, it was a flexible tube with a large square opening which had tiny hinged joints surrounding the edge. Its purpose was to clamp onto the outer hull of any vessel and create a vacuum seal, so the inhabitants could exit via a hatch and enter the relay station.

Gaia was a little different to most craft as she was *teardrop* shaped, and especially designed to slipstream through *weirdspace*.

"Ready to connect."

Gaia's image appeared on the inside of the Commander's visor, as he took a deep breath. There was no space for him in the main control room, although he could have stood in the doorway. The ship was just not big enough to accommodate them all, as space was tight. So, he had remained in the cargo hold, particularly as he would be going with his old friend.

"Is the probe ready?"

Halvor was still making a few finer adjustments. With the help of the Holo Droid he had the frequencies, and now he had to get the quantum particles into the relay station's transmitter.

"Nearly!"

He had to work carefully as everything had to calibrated exactly.

"Connect when ready."

Ren slowly moved them even closer, swinging the rear of the ship around so that it backed into the docking tube. The cargo hold doors were on the port side, and she used her twin screen to line them up with the end of the tube. Starfield was busy communicating with the relay station, and within a few minutes, the tube began to extend. The suction cups on the lip reached out and *kissed* Gaia's moon glass hull, clamping themselves in place.

"Connection secure."

Bear was nearest to the bay doors, and so released the

mechanism and the doors began to open. The force field held their precious atmosphere in place, as the inside of the tube was revealed. Ren had managed to get them close enough, and a few minor adjustments soon had them perfectly lined up.

It was now time to put the next phase of their plan into operation...

Nineteen

A blast of cold air tried to rush into the cargo hold, but was thankfully held back by the force field. Halvor managed to squeeze past the enormous bulk of Bear, followed by the Commander. They were now ready to try and place the quantum particle they had acquired from the Artificial Soldier's holo chip into the transmission mechanism.

They all had their orders, and so with a quick nod of the head, Vilgot pushed through the force field into the retractable tube.

Instruments flashed indicating that the life support system was inactive, and that it would have to be turned on manually. They were both glad of their suits as the temperature was well below freezing.

Everything inside had been well shielded from the cold, as it was not necessary to heat the relay station as it was seldom visited. Gravity was also lacking, so they took advantage of the hand grips positioned along the inside of the tube. There was a hatch on the other side, and it was not long before it had been opened and they ventured inside.

All was in darkness apart from the lights from their suits, which illuminated the small air lock. It was only going to be a simple matter of closing the outer hatch and engaging the mechanism to gain entry.

The inner hatch opened slowly to reveal the dark outer hallway, which led around the entire circumference of the station. The inner core was where the transmitter was located, along with some modest accommodation and equipment storage.

Halvor pressed a panel on the wall, and lights started turning on along with the gravity plates, and life the support system. The station was quickly coming alive, as heaters began to blow warm air around their feet. Within a few short moments, they were able to traverse the outer hallway, stopping when they had found the doorway to the inner section.

This relay station was like all of the others which hung in space. Some were located on moons, but they were in the minority. Checking his display, the inside of Halvor's helmet indicated that in a few minutes, the station would be habitable again.

The Commander checked in with his team, and so far everything looked good. He hoped that it would stay that way, as the last thing they wished for was the arrival of any uninvited guests.

Halvor removed his helmet, giving a slight shudder as it was still relatively cold inside the transmitter room. He was keen to get to work, as they had no time to waste.

In his other hand he was carrying his trusty tool kit, and housed within it was the probe.

Gaia's matter constructor had manufactured the probe using its composite materials. That was its main purpose, along with creating some palatable meals They were not quite the same as fresh food, but he had to admit that they were rather good.

His mind drifted back into focus, and all being well he would be appreciating it later...

Back inside Gaia, Ren was monitoring everything, hoping that her father would be able to fit the probe successfully. Outside, one of the twin screens showed a view of Island floating in a sea of stars, and for the moment, everything appeared peaceful.

She could see Starfield in the other, who looked a little tense. Ren was growing accustomed to being around him, and his *peccadilloes*. The Holo Droid's moon glass shell was a good indication of his mood, as the particles within his holographic matrix gave away his thoughts.

Gaia also looked a little pensive, as she watched her life partner closely, also hoping that the modification to the relay equipment would be successful, and that a signal could be transmitted to the Artificial Soldiers...

Vilgot marveled at the probe which Halvor delicately placed to one side, as he pulled out his multipurpose tool. It would be easy enough to take the cover off the central core, but what bothered him was attaching the probe. Quantum particles were not very stable, and the only comfort was that they were not dealing with anti matter. There were strict rules governing that, as a tiny fragment was enough to destroy a small moon.

Halvor handed the Commander the front panel, and he took it, placing it on one of the seats. He was in no mood to sit down, and neither was Halvor.

Somehow, he had worked out how to connect quantum particles in such a way that the communications grid remained operable, whilst also being able to send out the command codes to the Artificial Soldiers.

Vilgot let a cool breeze waft across his face, as a bead of sweat trickled down from his forehead. How Halvor was able to keep his cool and his hands steady was beyond him. It was as though he moved into another state of being whilst engrossed in his work. All that the Commander could do was watch and wait, and of course hope...

Twenty

Ripples of energy spread out across the surface of the small glowing device, which was monitoring the site of the remembrance ceremony from a secured location nearby. It resembled a ball of light which hung over a small electronic plinth, like a cloud of pure plasma energy.

Over the vastness of time, the Artificial Intelligence had perfected this form, which was able to transform itself into several other dimensions. Possessing a type of *thought energy* that interacted at a holographic level, they were not only able to interact with their surroundings, but also with corporeal forms too.

The whole concept involved tuning down the mental static noise, and isolating the emotional responses to certain actions of a species, and that had been achieved with the Artificial Soldiers, who were under their complete control.

Soon, this troublesome species would be assimilated, and then when they had fulfilled their usefulness, they would be destroyed completely!

Far above where it was hovering, the glowing green light of a buoy signaled that the starway was now open, and within a few moments, ships began to emerge from the event horizon. The defenses scanned the new arrivals, and after transmitting the correct codes, they were allowed to enter the outer reaches of the Asgard solar system. Many vessels had already arrived, and dignitaries escorted down to the surface. It looked as though half the Aesir fleet was here, and there had not been such a gathering since the death of King Olaf 12th.

The main plaza was adorned with flags from all of the colonies, which hung at half mast. Seating had been arranged to hold the dignitaries, who were receiving last minute security checks, before being shown to their appropriate places.

For the first time in their history they were about to become a republic, as their Monarch Freya 13th had been lost in a tragic accident, following her abduction.

She died leaving no heir apparent, much to the dismay of the Aesir people. A well loved and respected young woman was nigh impossible to replace, and so republic it had to be.

Sombre faces were everywhere, including those watching events unfold throughout the empire...

"I feel awful!"

Freya wished that she could reveal herself to her people, proving that she was still alive, but if she did so, then not only would she ruin any chance of defeating the Artificial Intelligence's plans, but she would also lose the man she loved.

It was quite a dilemma!

The pictures being relayed to her helmet's visor came from the relay station, which was broadcasting events across the empire. She could have done with a reassuring hug, but the man she loved was assisting Halvor to adapt the transmission system to relay the new codes to the Artificial Soldiers...

Vilgot Bodil also had mixed emotions.

He knew that they were doing the right thing, but he could feel Freya's emotions seeping out towards him. It was a lot for him to deal with knowing that she had given up everything to be with him.

Was he truly worthy?

Looking at Halvor he realized that this was no time for self doubt. He had to stay focused on the mission to save his people...

People were everywhere, as a large crowd had gathered to share in the ceremony. Observing them was the small glowing device, and there appeared to be many who carried the nano virus. Initially, it had been widely transmitted, but latterly some of the more stubborn individuals had refused to receive it. Estimates were well down on what had been anticipated, and there were still huge swathes of the population that had failed to connect with the collective.

Most of the dignitaries had been *joined*, and they would soon be fulfilling their roles, which was for them to die here today!

The destruction of the main Hybrid manufacturing facility had been a setback, and the Artificial Soldiers were also in short supply. The loss of the Empress had occurred at a pivotal moment in the plan. Providence however, had granted a golden opportunity, and soon this species would be devastated from within, and suffer widespread chaos and failure...

Halvor was working diligently to return the favour, as his hands remained steady, as he secured the probe into position. It had been a delicate procedure, aided by years of experience. He was like a surgeon perfuming an operation, assisted by his computerized equipment. Things needed to align precisely, and be calibrated to a very high level...

On the Aesir home world, Asgard was bathed in a shaft of sunlight which broke through the clouds, shining down on the dignitaries gathered on a podium in the main square. Opposite, a large crowd had gathered, waiting for the remembrance service to commence. The mood was sombre and respectful due to the occasion, and the royal band were playing appropriate music. All eyes then focused on the Prime Minister, as he readied himself at the rostrum.

All around, Military Intelligence and Security personnel kept a watchful eye, although they were not here to protect, instead assassinate...

"How much longer?"

The Commander was growing anxious, as he could see the Prime Minister about to commence his speech via the projection on the inside of his visor.

"Just waiting for the software upgrade to finish installing."

It seemed to be taking forever!

"Neurons are biological antenna that tune into the morphic field where human memories actually reside. The normal computer chips we use to store information are limited, whereas the holographic chips contain a vast amount of information. Just waiting for my program to tap into the morphic field created by the Artificial Intelligence."

Halvor kept talking hiding his anxiety.

There was no guarantee that it was going to work, as nothing like this had ever been attempted before. If it failed, then many influential people were all about to die...

The small glowing device prepared itself, watching and waiting for the appropriate moment before it sent out the instructions to commence firing. It was felt that a mass shooting was preferable to an explosion, as there was a chance that some of those targeted may survive. The Artificial Soldiers would hunt them down, and make it look as if a *coup d'eta* was taking place. Splitting the empire and sending it into civil war would bring the desired result. A much weakened society that would destroy itself was by far the most efficient way of disposing of them...

Freya felt deeply touched as the Prime Minister spoke.

"Today, we are gathered here to remember our beloved Empress Freya 13th, who was taken from us under such tragic circumstances."

He was reading a prepared statement, although there appeared to be an absence of emotion. Thousands of miniscule machines swam about inside his body courtesy of the nano virus he carried within, just like the majority of the government who had also been compromised. They would not be fleeing when the shooting started, being willing sacrifices essential to the plan. Whilst they were being eliminated, control of all vital systems would be gained, and major disruption would then flow. It had been anticipated that by the end of the day these so called *Aesir* would be staring down a precipice from which there would be no escape...

Twenty One

It was impossible to tell if the small glowing device was made of pure energy, plasma, or some type of highly advanced material, as it floated just above its pedestal. Movement was obtained by manipulating gravity, and the pedestal was highly advanced, just like the small glowing device itself.

Light was refracted through its holographic matrix and it could not only see objects in the normal human spectrum, but also those which lay far beyond. It could also see the individual energy signatures of the object concerned, and in this case, it could see the individual patterns within the Artificial Soldiers guarding it. The holo chip contained within their brains emitted bands of blue and green light which formed a human light skeleton, controlling movement. To anyone seeing this it would have been shocking, like an artificial holo robot, but for the small glowing device nothing was shocking as it had no emotions whatsoever. All that mattered was the *project,* and overseeing its completion.

Its light grew even brighter, as it watched and waited for the optimum moment. Everything was in place, and it just required the devices' signal, and then the blood bath would commence. It like its brethren, had no conscience and no concept of right or wrong. All organic life was nothing more than an inconvenience, a virus which needed to be cleansed. There was no concept of beauty only efficiency, and it was sure that once the command was given, these organic life forms would be eradicated, and this was the start of the whole cleansing process...

With the help of Starfield, Halvor had been able to create a very sophisticated computer program designed to imitate human reactions and emotions. A modulating frequency beam of charged particles, which changed hundreds of times per second should be on its way.

"Information equals knowledge."

The Commander looked at his old friend.

It was action that he desired!

In amongst the crowd there were several Reptilian Shape Shifters, and underneath their shields were pale green scales and a small boney crest upon the top of their heads. Nobody could see their fine scales, or detect their markedly different physiology. Reptilians were a very harsh and cruel race, who only existed to grow their empire. What they did not know was that it was under the complete control of the Artificial Intelligence...

The small glowing device scanned the Artificial Soldiers' bodies, searching for any defective patterns, and if any were found, then they would be overwritten until their brains had been stabilized. It was unlikely that anyone could do such a thing, as organic life forms were considered inferior, but it did no harm checking as optimum efficiency was require at all times.

This was quite different from Gaia's consciousness assisted technology, as she had been programmed to recognize only Ren's DNA, and would only work for her, even though it was also photon related.

The empty space within an atom was where the true energy resided, and the further away from the nucleus an electron went, the more energy it had. Space was packed full of energy, and wave patterns within it span creating whirlpools, a holographic matrix encoded everything with information, as all things were connected. It was possible to tap into this field via a conscious mind, which is how Gaia was able to move vast distances virtually instantaneously. The small glowing device used algorithms photonically transmitted at just the right frequency.

It was staggering to conclude that only about 5% of the actual universe was visible to a normal human eye, but the small glowing device could see a great deal more, as it watched and waited for a reaction.

There was movement within the crowd, and it appeared as though everything was about to start. Those affected by the virus froze like mannequins, whilst the Hybrid Reptilians, and the cloaked Reptilians prepared to act.

There was also movement from the two Artificial Soldiers guarding the small glowing device, as well as those positioned strategically around the main square outside the Royal Palace. Laser rifles were raised, as the device rose up on its pedestal, which was positioned on a nearby balcony attaining a perfect view of what was to transpire…

Freya could also see movement from the pictures being relayed live into her helmet's visor. A tear rolled down her cheek, as there was nothing that she could do to save her people.

The others gathered around her in the cramped space of the cargo hold felt helpless too, and Bear gripped tightly onto his massive laser weapon, and along with Joan would have liked nothing more than to be there. Bear would have blasted the enemy apart, whilst Joan would have torn them apart…

"It's not working!"

Commander Bodil also felt helpless wishing that he would have been leading a team of Titan Super Soldiers through the crowd.

Halvor was busy counting off the milliseconds on his small hand held device, hoping that he had calibrated everything correctly. There were hundreds of lives at stake, and if he was off by several decimal places then his signal would not work…

Flashes of light suddenly erupted through the crowd, and they all gasped in horror…

Epilogue

Pandemonium ensued as people fell, cut down by laser fire, as others cried out in shock, diving for whatever cover they could find. It looked as though everything was going according to plan, and even though the small glowing device felt no emotion, it was satisfying nevertheless.

Then, there was movement at its sides, as the two Artificial Soldiers raised their weapons, pointing them directly at it and fired…

"You've done it!"

Vilgot Bodil cried out in relief as before him he could see Artificial Soldiers in Military Intelligence uniforms shooting at one another, whilst the Hybrid Reptilians turned on themselves and the cloaked Reptilians within the crowd.

There certainly was a blood bath, but not the one intended…

The small glowing device felt a series of laser pulses entering its holographic matrix, destabilizing the precisely calibrated structure. It could not comprehend its protectors' actions, as the pedestal was shattered.

More and more laser fire swept through it, as it tried to warp out of this reality…

Screams continued to erupt from the crowd, as the cloaked Reptilians became visible, and fought back against the onslaught. Many Hybrids fell, along with Artificial Soldiers, as those infested with nano robots threw themselves to the floor.

Somehow, Halvor had managed to incorporate a command code for the virus too, and although he could not eradicate it, he was able to affect the programming nevertheless.

"Flux!"

Starfield swore as they all stood in shock as the battle raged on. He hated violence wanting to ascend to a higher state of consciousness, although that appeared not to be as easy as he had hoped. The Holo Droid had taken many lives over the past few days, and it was going to take a considerable effort to free himself from the Artificial Barbarian state of being!

Freya felt a mixture of shock and relief, realizing that apart from a few of her former subjects that had been caught in the crossfire, most of the casualties were of their enemy.

The firing was now beginning to die down, with only a few Artificial Soldiers left standing.

The small glowing device, although badly damaged did manage to phase out of this dimension. The two Artificial Soldiers guarding it then turned their fire on each other, dropping to the floor as their holographic chips burned out.

Somewhere out there, it travelled feeling as though this was just another minor setback. Eventually, nothing, not even the Archons could stop the *collective* from destroying all organic life within the galaxy.

In less than the humans determined as a *year*, a neutron star would be exploded, releasing a gamma ray burst that would destroy all higher organic life forms in a vast area, and within a matter of their *months*, everything would perish leaving only plant life intact.

When that was accomplished, other neutron stars would be exploded until there would be no other sentient life left anywhere, apart that was from the Artificial Intelligence...

The Light at the End of the World

The field is the sole governing agency of matter.

Albert Einstein

Introduction

Haunting pictures continued to be transmitted by the communications grid, as everyone was transfixed by what they saw. Bodies were everywhere, but fortunately most of them were either Hybrids, Reptilians or Artificial Soldiers.

Their attempt to interfere with the holo chips embedded within the cloned human soldiers had been a success, although looking at the carnage it felt like anything but.

Floods of tears rolled down Freya's cheeks, and she was very glad to see the Commander re-entering the cargo hold. It was time to leave and plan their next move, although by the look on Halvor's face, there was even more bad news to come.

How was he going to tell them that he had intercepted information which indicated that within a *year,* a neutron star would be exploded, releasing a gamma ray burst that would destroy all higher organic life forms within the Empire, and within a matter of months, everything would perish leaving only plant life intact...

One

A tuft of seagrass bobbed gently to and fro in the gentle currant, as a brightly coloured fish swam by. It then stopped, looking at a moon glass structure embedded on the sea floor. Its curiosity was peaked by the sight of a Holo Droid sitting cross legged meditating. To the fish it was an extraordinary sight, something that it had never witnessed before.

"How long has he been there?"

Freya asked the Commander who also thought it extraordinary.

"About an hour."

She had never witnessed anything quite like it before, and neither had the Commander.

After the remembrance ceremony, they had decided to relocate somewhere else, as they all needed to recharge their proverbial *batteries.*

Vilgot Bodil, Supreme Commander of the Titan Super Soldiers, knew the whereabouts of all of their secret bases, and their scheduled use. This particular one was where they underwent their deep sea training, Vatten Varld, the water world, comprised of nothing but ocean, and within its depths a small complex had been constructed.

"Well at least he's stopped swearing!"

Starfield's language had become rather *colourful* of late, and his behaviour erratic to say the least, and yet he had proved himself to be a valued member of the team.

They decided to leave him to it, returning to the others who were relaxing in one of the other rooms. The whole complex comprised of a series of interconnected bubbles, and the Holo

Droid had positioned himself in one of the outer observation rooms. Gaia, the teardrop shaped advanced craft, had used her shield to push through the water and was now inside one of the large underwater hangers.

All in all, Vilgot had to admit that they had done rather well...

His old friend Halvor had been quiet ever since they arrived, and at first, he thought that it was just the enormity of what they had achieved that was playing on his mind, but knowing him so well, he realised that there was more to it than that.

He was with his wife and daughter, enjoying some valuable family time, whilst Doctor Sorenson was with Bear, the mammoth former Titan Super Soldier. Bjorn was eating, he always seemed to be eating, never able to quench his massive appetite. Although, there did not appear to be an ounce of fat on him, and sometimes the Commander wondered where it all went?

Freya was accompanying him, never having left his side. She was still upset about the ceremony, as many innocent people had either been killed or injured. Thankfully, most of them had been either Reptilian Hybrids, Artificial Soldiers or cloaked Reptilians. The news from home was not good, as everywhere was in chaos, and a state of emergency had been declared.

No one fully understood what had happened, or why so many people appeared to be under the influence of something they did not fully understand. Nano robots had been discovered in the blood streams of thousands of people, who had been quarantined.

The Commander realised that he had some major decisions to make, and so, after giving things a great deal of thought, he had decided to call a meeting...

The brightly colour fish looked around, and then back towards the large moon glass bubble. It was used to seeing the underwater structure, and the abundance of sea life. But, what it was not used to seeing was the strange object inside glowing in different translucent shades.

Starfield was deep in meditation, as a rainbow of colours streamed through his moon glass shell. In his mind, he could see Mjolnir, who was guiding him.

"Well done Stellan."

The being of light really thought that he was making progress.

"You asked me about the quest to discovered happiness."

Starfield continued to glow.

"If you are unhappy, it is because you are not living happily, and at harmony with your surroundings, because you have not learnt to accept the world as it is, with all its disadvantages and possibilities of suffering. You can only attain happiness by realising the causes of unhappiness and avoiding those causes."

It was not easy when you were faced with a very devious enemy!

"If you have the right aspirations, you can make a success of your life."

He was trying - very *trying* at times!

"You should have the right speech."

A purple flush rippled through his particles when the Holo Droid thought about all of his swearing.

"You should also have the right behaviour."

His colour intensified when he thought about his barbarianism!

"Then there is the right occupation."

Starfield grimaced when he considered that he was no better than a pirate of late.

"Remember that you should be patient in seeking progress, and not try to move too quickly, before you have learnt the lessons which are to be learned."

So far, the Holo Droid felt as though he was failing on every count!

"You should have the right mindfulness, after all, thought is the father of deed, and if you think of a thing, that is the first step to doing a thing, and some thoughts are very disharmonious."

Starfield remembered how he had judged Joan and her daughter Serenity, before getting to know them.

"With reasoning you can come to a conclusion by intuition, as to what is right for you, and what is wrong for you."

He seemed to act before he thought, which was another failing.

"In the stillness of mind after the fires of desire, aversion, and delusion have finally been extinguished, you can attain true peace and happiness."

Starfield let out a muffled groan, as he seemed as far away from his goals as ever, and wondered if he would ever get there?

Getting up from his cross-legged position on the floor, he scuttled off with his head down feeling dejected. Mjolnir watched him go, feeling sorry for the Holo Droid. It had taken his people countless millennia to arrive at the point where they were ready to transcend to another reality.

Starfield was soon approaching where the others had gathered, having nowhere better to go. Meditation did not seem to be working, and so perhaps some company might help?

"So tell me Halvor, what is it that you have been withholding form us?"

His old friend knew that he could not hide anything from him.

There was deathly silence as Starfield came walking in. He suddenly stopped, realising that everyone was staring at him.

"Have I done something wrong?"

What little self confidence he had began to ebb away.

"I have not sworn today!"

He was trying so hard.

"No my friend, it is not you."

Halvor composed himself.

"When I attached the probe and sent the signal, I received a feedback loop. I can only assume that it came from the Artificial Intelligence."

The Commander looked concerned.

"It appears that they are going to attempt to explode a neutron star, releasing a gamma ray burst that will destroy all higher organic life forms within a vast area of the galaxy, and within a matter of months, everything will perish leaving only plant life intact!"

Everyone was shocked, but not as much as Starfield.

"Oh, Flux..."

Two

The brightly coloured fish emerged from the seagrass again as the strange figure re-entered the transparent room. This time it was glowing bright purple, as it sat down cross legged on the floor...

"What are we going to do?"

Freya's words echoed everyone else's thoughts.

"I'd better go and see if I can do anything to help him."

Doctor Sorenson was very concerned about the Holo Droid.

"I meant about the neutron star!"

The Doctor was thinking like a doctor.

"First things first!"

He got up from where he was sitting and left them to debate their best course of action.

"Is it even possible?"

The Commander knew of no weapon that could destroy a star.

"Theoretically."

Halvor had been giving it a great deal of though ever since he intercepted the transmission.

"There is only one substance that I am aware of and that is antimatter."

It was considered so dangerous that experimenting with it was strictly forbidden.

"It is conceivable that a missile could be constructed, although it would have to be heavily shielded, and then it would need to travel into the corona of the neutron star."

The technology involved was mind-blowing.

"From there it would have to enter the chromosphere, and dive into the photosphere where it would be exploded."

They were stunned, as Halvor continued.

"The neutron star would then contract in on itself, before a massive release of energy would cause it to explode, transforming it into a supernova, as the electrons and protons fused together sending out a massive wave of neutrinos and matter."

It sounded horrifying!

"The resulting energy wave would then travel beyond the speed of light, destroying all organic life within its path."

Vilgot did not doubt what he was being told.

"Do you think the Artificial Intelligence has such technology..."

In another part of the galaxy, a small glowing device struggled to keep itself together, after repeated laser energy blasts had destroyed its plinth, and destabilised its holo matrix.

These organic creatures had proved to be far more capable than anticipated!

Transmissions had already been sent, as it struggled to stabilise its mainframe, and for another small glowing device which received them, the information was equally perplexing.

Deep within the Aesir Empire, a small asteroid travelled inconspicuously across the depths of space. Outwardly, there was nothing to see apart from barren rock and frozen water. Inwardly however, was a completely different matter.

It had been partially hollowed out, and there were propulsion and weapons system, not to mention accommodation and a concealed hangar with a black dart shaped craft parked inside.

In one of the rooms, the small glowing device was busily collating information. So far, none of the initial parts of the plan had met with much success. Over the years, countless invasions had taken place via their proxies the Reptilians, and although considerable damage had been wrought, overall defeat had been illusive. The new tactic was considered more viable, although that had also failed to deliver the collapse of the so called *Aesir Empire*.

Now it had been decided to terminate them via another means, and the fail-safe program had just been initiated...

Meanwhile, the team sat pondering the Commander's question.

Very little was known about the Artificial Intelligence, and ever since Halvor had intercepted the transmission, they were learning that they were up against quite an adversary, one which remained hidden.

Halvor took a deep breath.

"We do know that every particle has an antiparticle with the same mass but the opposite electric charge, and as far as we know, antimatter does not exist naturally. But having said that, any that might exist will instantly react with matter cancelling it out."

Bear thought about having an antimatter gun, and the power it could unleash, whilst Joan thought about the scientists she used to work with on the base. They had many a discussion on the subject, as they liked to speculate on what may be possible in the future.

Ren and Freya felt concerned, as did the Doctor, thinking of the lives that would be lost if such a weapon was ever developed, as he made his way towards Starfield.

"Antimatter can theoretically be manufactured by creating antiparticles, which would take a considerable amount of energy, let alone perfecting a containment process."

From the message he had intercepted, it looked as though somewhere out there, it already had...

Three

More brightly coloured fish gathered in the seagrass, all staring out towards the moon glass structure, where they were observing the strange glowing creature.

Starfield was back in meditation, trying to reconnect with Mjolnir. His emotions were all over the place, and try as he might, he could not get settled. Fear and depression struck at his heart, well it would have if he had had one!

So much negativity was radiating from him that he was acting like a beacon of despair.

A small cloud of energy had detected it, and began to make its way towards him, slowly forming into a being of light.

"Poor Stellan!"

The Holo Droid could almost hear Mjolnir's consoling voice, although he was no longer there.

"Woe is me!"

Starfield groaned.

"What am I going to do?"

Starfield could see something, although it did not appear to be Mjolnir.

"If you link with me then I will take all of your pain away."

That sounded wonderful and still feeling very despondent, he quickly agreed, without realising what he had just agreed too.

His molecules then began to tingle, as he felt another presence within him. It was so refreshing, that he hardly noticed them all turning black.

It felt good having all of the different emotions that had been swimming about inside him being taken away.

Feeling refreshed, he then raised himself up off the floor and went to rejoin the others.

Doctor Sorenson stopped in his tracks when he saw the Holo Droid walking towards him. Starfield looked a little different, and as he stared in disbelief, he suddenly noticed a grotesque face within his moon-glass head.

"Starfield?"

The Holo Droid did not reply, but instead reached out towards him.

Then, before he knew what was happening, the Doctor felt moon glass hands around his neck...

Ren had an uneasy feeling, as a shiver rolled down her spine. Something was wrong, and it was not just the impending crisis.

"Serenity?"

The Commander noticed the look on her face.

"Uncle Vil!"

Everyone fell silent, and then from somewhere in the distance they heard a muffled scream.

The Commander quickly took off, followed by Joan, Bear, and then Ren.

They all dashed down the corridor which linked this part of the complex to the next. Just as they rounded a corner, they caught a glimpse of the Doctor falling to the floor.

Black swirling particles swept around the inside of Starfield's moon glass shell, as he advanced.

"Doctor Sorenson!"

Ren cried out seeing the man collapsed, whilst the others prepared to tackle the Holo Droid.

Starfield just continued to walk forward, and as he did so, a hideous face swept around the inside of his moon glass head again.

"What's wrong with him?"

Ren echoed everyone else's thoughts.

"He looks as though he's been possessed!"

Joan had heard people talking about such things, although she had just dismissed them as being either paranoid or crazy. But now that she had seen the face, she was not quite so sure.

"What should we do?"

Bear stampeded towards the Holo Droid like a raging bull, and flung himself at Starfield's moon glass shell. Joan watched as he just bounced off, hitting the floor not far from the Doctor.

The Commander realised that any weapons they may have had would be useless against the Holo Droid, and risked damaging the structure, letting in countless gallons of water.

They now had a major problem on their hands...

Four

The Archon bathed in all of the negative energy, thoroughly enjoying its new host. Humans made excellent entertainment providing a rich feast. Never before had it considered an artificial life form, although with a human consciousness this one was a little different...

Starfield felt mortified that the Doctor had been hurt, and his barbarism had returned with vengeance. There was no way that he could stop himself, as he had well and truly been taken over.

"Oh how foolish I've been!"

His words were however, contained within his moon glass shell, as he did not have access to his systems any longer.

Starfield had been so consumed with his own problems that it never occurred to him that it was another entity mimicking Mjolnir...

Bear picked himself up off the floor, whist Joan rushed to the Doctor's aid. She had been partially trained as a combat medic during her military service, although that had only really covered battlefield dressings and basic first aid.

Doctor Sorenson still had a pulse, although a weak one, and he was struggling to breath after the pressure applied to his windpipe. Joan continued to work on him, as the Commander slowly backed away, drawing the Holo Droid away from them.

Seeing what had transpired, Ren dashed off towards where Gaia was situated in the hangar bay, hoping that together they could do something to help. Starfield had been possessed, and she knew that she had to do something...

The small glowing device within the asteroid monitored the collection of antimatter in a chamber at the heart of the structure. Calculations indicated that within a few hours, enough of it would be gathered to explode a neutron star.

Thoughts were transferred to the Reptilian in charge, as he, like all Reptilians, would follow the orders given without question. Their whole species had long since been taken over, and they worshipped the Artificial Intelligence like gods.

A propulsion device had been fitted to the rear of the asteroid, cloaked so that it resembled barren rock and ice. A candidate star had just been chosen, and so the asteroid now began to change course...

The Archon entity bathed in more fear, as it observed the humans. Not only was it having a feast, but also experiencing great pleasure in all of the mischief it was making. For so long it had been searching for a victim, and now having found one, it was going to make the most of it!

The ultimate prize was a chemical know as *Adrenochrome,* produced by the oxidation of adrenaline. It was obtained from the adrenal gland of living humans, and the benefits from consuming it were greater health, increased vitality, and a host of other smaller effects, as well as an intense sense of euphoria. Reptilians craved it, which accounted for the way they put humans under an intense and immeasurable fear so that they produced it. The Archon on the other hand, thrived on negative energy, which to it was just as good...

"Oh no!"

Gaia could not believe what Starfield had done now.

"Possessed by an Archon?"

Whilst it was quiet, she had taken the opportunity to perform several self diagnostics, and to attend to the damage she had taken when they were caught in the blast from the self destruction of the Artificial Soldier's attack craft.

"Strangled Doctor Sorenson!"

She just could not believe it.

"Where is he now?"

Ren climbed into the pilot's seat, and was soon in the dark domed room that represented Gaia's mind. Naked and then clothed, Ren quickly went through the connection process which was like being a fetus in the womb. Twin screens then emerged from the darkness, and they both gasped at the sight that greeted them.

Starfield was running amok. Chasing people with his arms out in front of him like some sort of Holo Zombie!

What was even worse, was the evil face which appeared from the depths of the black swirling particles, which had consumed him.

On the other screen Ren could see the look of absolute horror on Gaia's face which was being transmitted on the main screen.

The team were trying to tackle him, although it was very difficult due to his moon glass shell and the confines of the base.

"We must try and subdue him!"

That was easier said than done.

"Can't we shut him in a room?"

There were several bulkheads, but he could either break his way through, or even worse, break the outer seal and flood part of the complex.

"I think I have an idea..."

Five

Black swirls swept around the inside of Starfield's moon glass shell, making him feel dizzy. There was absolutely nothing that he could do to control his limbs, or his actions either.

He felt terrible that the Doctor had been injured, particularly as he had done so much for him. Now he found himself lurching for the Commander, who skilfully dived out of the way. Next it was Joan, as he progressed further through the complex. Halvor was up ahead, and it looked as though he was half way out of the room.

Freya had been escorted away by Bear under the Commander's orders, as he recovered from his encounter with the rogue Holo Droid. Vilgot feared that she may be harmed, and even though she had protested, he had been insistent.

Halvor looked vulnerable standing there, and Starfield felt himself moving quickly towards him.

Two moon glass hands grasped thin air as Halvor ducked and rolled, scrambling away, as Starfield pursued. He now found himself in the hangar bay, as Halvor got back to his feet and ran towards Gaia. Then he appeared to trip, diving under the ship, which was propped up on its retractable moon glass legs.

The Holo Droid quickly advanced, and just when he was about to reach the communications expert, a glowing green light suddenly engulfed him.

"Have we got him?"

Ren was worried about her father, but Gaia assured her that he had come to no harm. Just like the Artificial Soldier in the attack craft, he had been trapped in the tractor beam.

"Starfield is now secure!"

There was a great deal of relief in her voice, as at least he could not injure anyone else.

"So, what are we going to do with him now..."

Vilgot Bodil watched from the hangar bay entrance, relieved that Serenity's plan had worked. The others gathered around him, apart from the Doctor who was resting. Joan had brought him his medical bag and he had injected himself. He would soon recover, although his voice would be a bit hoarse for a few weeks...

Starfield also felt relieved as he could no longer attack the members of the team. He felt dreadful as the negative entity grew very frustrated. There was still plenty of negative emotions to sustain it, although it looked as though the fun it had been having had come to an end...

Back in the asteroid, it looked as though the *fun* was about to begin!

Reptilians were devoid of love, empathy, and compassion, and their society existed in a near perpetual state of conflict. Battles between opposing factions were not uncommon, but it was the battles with other species that took precedence. They were driven by the darker emotions, and craved power and dominance over all others.

They believed themselves to be superior, and now infected with nano robots, were the most powerful and ruthless race in the galaxy. This suited the Artificial Intelligence, which was now poised to wipe out all organic life in this sector of it.

A White Royal Reptilian was in charge, as this was deemed to be a vitally important mission. He had been led to believe that only the Aesir would be affected, and his people spared. The blast would radiate outwards in such a fashion that their territory would be unaffected. However, he was mistaken.

The Artificial Intelligence had grown impatient over the years with the lack of progress. Many times there had been conflict and yet the Aesir remained. Now, after the collective had received yet more setbacks, they had decided that both species, and in fact, all species that lay in the path of the blast wave must be eliminated...

Back on Vatten Varld, the glowing green field pulsated slightly, as Gaia adjusted it so that the area around the beam was unaffected.

"He looks like a fly caught in a web!"

Joan was thinking aloud, as she hugged her husband, grateful that he had managed to get away from the rouge Holo Droid, and to all intents and purposes he was!

"I think that we need to find a way of ridding him of that evil creature who has possessed him."

Halvor still could not believe what had happened.

"I did hear somewhere that if you place a large piece of iron under your bed, and then place a small piece of iron on a string around your neck it makes it uncomfortable for them."

Halvor could well believe it, as a piece of rough metal next to your skin would chafe at the very least, but the Holo Droid had a smooth moon glass shell. He had his doubts as he looked at his wife, wondering how they were going to do that?

Breathing out, he could see that they needed something a little more substantial, and rubbing his fingers across his chin, he suddenly had an idea.

"I think we need a little divine inspiration...

Six

A large lump of space rock and ice skirted around an equally barren looking planet, as it made its way towards the chosen neutron star. Once it was pulled into the gravitational field, it would accelerate, but that wound take several days. It's speed was dramatically increasing, but the vast distances involved would mean that even at top speed, the time it would take would still be substantial.

The White Royal Reptilian had absolutely no idea that he was on a suicide mission, expecting to leave with his crew on the ship hidden in the hollowed out hangar. He expected it to be a slow reaction, giving him plenty of time to get far enough away.

Loyalty to the god like Artificial Intelligence prevented questioning of any kind, total faith was required at all times, and the nanites infesting his body made sure of that.

Still unaware of his fate, he continued to manoeuvre the small asteroid so that it slingshot around the planet to increase its speed. Looking at the latest calculations being supplied to him, he began to reconsider.

Maybe it might not take days after all...

Ren settled back into the pilot's seat letting her mind drift now that Starfield was secure in the tractor beam. After talking to her father she was searching for Mjolnir, as he was the only likely source of the Holo Droid's salvation...

Freya held on tightly to Vilgot. It had been an extraordinary few days, and this latest incident had really shaken her. Not only Starfield's possession, but also the fact that they had come into contact with an actual *Archon*. Then, there was the small matter of the impending annihilation of all organic life within this part of the galaxy.

An artificially created supernova, which would be the largest explosion in space, distributing elements as well as a deadly blast wave destroying everything within its path.

"Have we any idea which star it is going to be?"

There was no way of telling, and considering the countless number within the galaxy, the task of stopping it looked impossible.

"Can we try and intercept any other signals?"

That seemed like a good place to start, as they would be searching for the proverbial *needle in a haystack.*

Halvor rubbed his chin again.

The probe he had inserted into the relay station was still active.

"Possibly!"

They also had to make the decision as to whether they were going to transmit information about the violet ray, to help cleanse the victims of the nano virus.

It seemed as though there was much to discuss...

There was very little discussion on the asteroid though, as it made its pass around the planet and increased in speed. The White Royal Reptilian looked at his equipment, calculating the best possible moment to increase thrust to a maximum.

The small glowing device observed with satisfaction. When the time was right, it would leave, moving off into another dimension leaving these organic creatures to perish...

Mjolnir had been observing from a much higher dimension, and from there he could see all that could be seen, apart that was from what lay above. The attempted assassinations at the remembrance ceremony had sent shock-waves through Aesir society, and just like the blast wave that would occur from the exploding neutron star, a wave of fear had spread throughout the Empire.

He and his people had lost a lot of their nourishment, and along with it went their power. They had been significantly weakened, and the Archons were taking full advantage...

"Well, I for one think that we have no choice but to release information about the violet ray."

Freya was deeply worried about her people.

"I have to admit that we cannot leave them floundering."

Vilgot had been weighing up the risks.

"Bear?"

The enormous former Super Soldier nodded in agreement.

The Doctor waved a finger, being reluctant to speak, as his throat was sore and swollen.

"I agree."

Joan followed suit, whilst Ren remained inside Gaia, both having made their thoughts clear.

"So, its decided then!"

The Commander was still worried that any information could be traced back to them, and being as they were now fugitives...

Seven

Tapping into one of the Aesir news channels that was broadcast across the communications grid, the team suddenly began to realise the enormity of what they had done. At first, they only considered Asgard and the remembrance ceremony, but it appeared that Halvor's signal had travelled far and wide. Reports were coming in from the colonies that the chaos had spread like wild fire.

"Oh, my!"

Freya could not believe what she was seeing, and neither could anyone else.

There had been Artificial Soldiers, Hybrids, and those contaminated with the nano virus in most locations, and they had also succumbed to the transmission. No one knew for certain what was happening, only the fact that suddenly during the ceremony everything erupted into pandemonium.

"It looks as though we need to release the information rapidly."

Vilgot Bodil, Supreme Commander of the Titan Super Soldiers felt all of his years of experience amounting to nothing. He was trained to tackle many situations involving security and the ongoing Reptilian threat, but never had he faced such a crisis.

"I think we should put the needs of the people before those of our own."

That was the conclusion he had come to before seeing the latest pictures, and now it was evidently the correct decision.

Halvor was busy with his computer, getting things set up for another transmission. This time they were not going to be able to move Gaia, as she was *babysitting* Starfield. So, it would have to come from here...

The news transmissions were something that the small glowing device situated within the hollowed out asteroid was fully aware of. It appeared as though years of careful planning had unravelled within a few moments. All around the collective, a search was underway to pinpoint exactly where it had come from. Initial indications were that a sophisticated probe had been inserted into a transmitter, and its possible location had already been narrowed down to a relatively small area of so called *Aesir space.*

Soon, it would be eliminated, and so too would be the perpetrators...

"So, how are we going to do this?"

Halvor smiled.

"That's the easy part, its what we do afterwards..."

They could not simply hop to another star system, as Gaia was unavailable, and there was no way of deactivating the Holo Droid. It would take days for his power system to drain completely, and there was no way that they could turn off the tractor beam without letting him loose!

Starfield felt terrible as he could hear their conversation, as well as the thoughts of the entity which possessed him...

The Holo Droid was not the only one to be feeling terrible, for sitting in his ship orbiting the Aesir Home-world, Admiral Vaden of the Imperial Navy was not having a good day. For a start, he had somehow twisted his knee and torn a ligament whilst exercising, and even though the medical treatment had helped, it was still sore and painful. Sitting at his desk with his leg up, he scanned the reports on his screen.

"Chaos!"

He had never seen anything like it, and wished that his patrol group was still skirting the edge of their territory. Returning back for the remembrance ceremony, as one of the senior admirals he had been due to attend, but his injury had kept him away.

"What a mess!"

He was not impressed, having always run a *tight ship*. There was now no government to speak of, as it appeared as though everyone had been consumed in the madness.

It had also spread to the Aesir Security Service and Military Intelligence, and there was a total void in leadership.

He was just scanning the latest news reports, when there was a knock at his door.

"Enter!"

It was his second in command, Fostrup.

"Sir!"

They had served together for years, and he trusted his number two.

"The situation is serious and we need leadership!"

The Admiral was well aware of that, but there was none!

"As the most senior admiral available, might I suggest that you take over until the government is restored?"

Admiral Vaden gave a deep sigh, acknowledging that the responsibility had now fallen on his shoulders.

"Very well!"

This was the last thing that he needed right now, as he would have loved to have retired to his room and nurse his poorly knee...

Halvor also felt reluctance as he prepared the transmission. He planned to bounce it off several sources, but realised that it would eventually be traced back to where it had been sent...

Eight

"You know, the more I look at this, the less sense it makes!"

Admiral Vaden massaged his aching knee.

"A very well respected leader of the legendary *Titan Super Soldiers* goes rogue and kidnaps the Empress. Then they are supposedly killed by a defensive laser battery, which also just happens to be destroyed. A cargo hauler captained by another well respected *Titan Super Soldier* just happens to be in the area and is found empty with its records wiped."

Fostrup nodded.

"The Royal Doctor also disappears under mysterious circumstances, and then there is the debacle of the remembrance ceremony, where it appears a vast swathe of our people have been under the influence of someone or something, Hybrid Reptilians, not to mention Artificial Soldiers!"

His head began to ache just like his knee.

"And no one has the faintest idea what has been going on!"

Fostrup shrugged his shoulders being equally clueless.

"I wonder if it is all connected in some way..."

A group of solemn faces gathered around the communication equipment in the facilities transmitter room. They each knew what had to be done, and were looking at the person doing it!

A small data package had been prepared and was now in the process of being uploaded. Freya held onto Vilgot's hand fearing for the lives of her people, but not for her own.

The Doctor knew all about danger, still recovering after being attacked by one of his patients, albeit an artificial one!

Joan was with her daughter Serenity, watching her husband, and as for Bear, well he was still hungry!

"How can you eat at a time like this?"

He shrugged his shoulders.

"Even the condemned man has a right to a last meal."

His answer seemed to sum up how everyone was feeling.

If only they could free the Holo Droid...

Starfield felt wretched, imprisoned within his own moon glass shell by an evil tormentor. Archons were the worst sort of uninvited guests, although he had unwittingly agreed to its offer of help.

His holographic eyes stared up at Gaia through the green tractor beam which was holding him in place. He had hoped that Mjolnir would come to his rescue, but when Ren had left, he realised that it was not going to happen. He felt bad, very bad, especially as the team looked as though they were going to sacrifice themselves to save their people - and it was all his fault...

Freya snuggled up to the Commander, before asking an open question.

"So what is the Artificial Intelligence's end game?"

Joan was the first to respond, as the data package wound its way through the communications grid.

My former boss General Swartz was not a very cultured man, but once he came out with something very profound.

"Zhuang Zhou, *Zhuangzi* the influential Chinese 4th century BCE philosopher once stated that one night he dreamt of being a butterfly, but it was so real that in the morning he wondered if he was a butterfly dreaming of being a man.'

Vilgot rubbed his chin.

"I have heard of one of our own philosophers considering the possibility that everything exists as a simulation for someone else's benefit.'

Halvor listened as his thoughts drifted towards the impending supernova, and the resulting wave of gamma radiation that would sterilise everything within its path.

So, besides the obvious, destroying all organic life leaving this galaxy free for them to inhabit, would they gain any other advantage?

Next to him sat Doctor Sorenson, who nodded, sending a sharp pain down the back of his neck. His self administered medication was wearing off, as he tried to join in with the conversation.

'Consciousness can be transferred from one human body to another, but as far as we know, it cannot be simulated by a computer. Consciousness is after all, far more than just what is contained within the human brain."

His croaky voice was hardly audible, and yet he had made a very valid point.

Halvor agreed.

"The Artificial Intelligence can do many things, making individuals focus on the negative emotions, eliminating or severely reducing the positive ones, but they can't program true individual consciousness.'

He continued.

"As far as I am aware, whenever we attempted to create an artificial intelligence with the power to sustain consciousness, it either turned psychotic and tried to attack us, or simply turned itself off!'

They all looked towards the Holo Droid suspended in the tractor beam.

The Doctor then spoke again.

"The biological will to survive is so hard to replicate whilst maintaining sociability!"

He was well aware that even though Starfield had a human consciousness, being placed into a Holo Droid shell had resulted in a series of psychological issues.

That begged the question:

If all organic life was eliminated, what would it leave?

Halvor then had a shocking thought!

"Maybe their goal is to cleanse the entire universe of all organic life ending this simulation, so that they can create one of their own?'

There were a few gasps, as the enormity of what he just said sank in.

Was that even possible?

If they were all living in a simulation, then who created it in the first place?

That was the question the Ancients had been struggling with long before his people even existed.

Was this reality simply running on an extra-dimensional computer?

The Archon that had possessed Starfield had been eavesdropping on their conversation, and as a consequence, began to relax its control over him.

If they were correct in their assumptions, then where did it this leave his people?

They may no longer be corporeal, but they were still organic in some way.

If the Artificial Intelligence they thought they had created were to do this, then would they also cease to exist...

Nine

Torrents of information cascaded through the communications grid, as the data stream swept over it, and the river of information spread right across the Aesir worlds.

It was constantly being updated, and everyone had their own personal profiles, and information they took note of, but for one individual, he raise more than one eyebrow.

Nano Virus responsible for chaos.

The new information flashed up on the Admiral Vaden's screen, as he read the new report.

Fake viral infection used as cover to spread tainted vaccine.

Miniscule machines take over the mind of the infected.

Violet flame torch used to cleanse victim.

Full schematics enclosed...

There were no other details apart from the instructions of how to construct the ray torch.

The Admiral stood up and straightened his uniform, smoothing down the royal blue material, before reaching for his crutch, and heading for the door. He then moved carefully through the corridor, taking care not to put too much weight on his injured knee. It was painful, but he had grown tired of being confined to his quarters. His ship-generated gravity was set marginally less strong than his body would normally have required, which was just as well as it helped with his momentum. That encouraged the crew to exercise to retain their muscle mass, which is how he had injured himself in the first place.

Admiral Vaden passed through several doorways, being careful not to twist his leg. The ship was enormous on the outside, but the space inside was limited by the propulsion, defence and communication systems, as well as the operational centres and crew quarters. There was also a large hangar bay housing various craft and maintenance facilities. However, none of them were to be his destination, as he was heading for the medical bay.

Various crew members passed him and saluted as he neared the lift, punching in the code, as the doors slid open. He was very security conscious, and after he had seen the Doctor, he would be making his way towards the Military Intelligence offices...

Back at the underwater facility, they were anxious to get underway, but with Starfield still possessed and suspended within the tractor beam, there was nothing that they could do.

"I just don't understand it!"

The Doctor croaked again.

The *Aesir* human physiology was slightly different to that of the *Terran*. For a start, they did not possess a *Reptilian* brain, as they were so to speak *pure human* and not a hybrid. They did however, have a *primitive mind* as well as a *higher* mind. Both types of human had evolved, and so naturally the primitive part made decisions based on survival instincts. The higher mind made informed decisions based on the facts available.

The primitive mind was more fear based and likely to make negative decisions, whereas the higher mind was more likely to be positive.

In the Holo Droid's case, his mind was pure consciousness, and so theoretically he should have used logic to arrive at a conclusion.

But, for some reason, he appeared to be stuck in his primitive mind, and was prone to making *knee jerk* reactions, as his emotional state was in perpetual turmoil.

It was therefore perfectly clear that the consciousness transfer process had either malfunctioned, or that without the organic brain components, it was not possible to successfully transfer consciousness into a holographic matrix...

Starfield was indeed stuck in his primitive mind. His only thoughts were negative ones, blaming himself for everything.

How could he have been so naive?

Maybe he had been acting like a child?

Thinking more about it, he began to realise that he had been suffering from stress ever since the accident. Things had been going well, and he was thriving inside his new body, that was until Big Helgar bailed out leaving them to crash!

Could it be Post Traumatic Stress Disorder?

Searching his vast memory he discovered that there were some common symptoms such as flashbacks, nightmares, repetitive and distressing images or sensations, and physical sensations, such as pain, sweating, feeling sick or trembling.

Well, he did not have a corporeal body any more, but he was having flashbacks of his barbarianism, and he had become a nervous wreck!

His emotions were also all over the place, and he had to conclude that they were all fear driven...

Inside his holo matrix, another entity was also deep in contemplation.

Eavesdropping on the team's conversation had caused a new sensation to appear within the energy cloud that formed its being - fear!

Creating the Artificial Intelligence to spread fear amongst the corporeals had been something which had not only provided them with sustenance, but also significantly reduced the Ancients' ability to combat them. Everything had been going so well, and they were winning the battle against their adversary. Soon, it looked as though they would achieve almost total victory, and yet now it looked as though they were going to snatch defeat out of the jaws of that very victory.

Was the Artificial Intelligence committed to destroying all life within the universe?

If they were, then how were they to be stopped...

Ten

Black swirls of energy swept around Starfield's holo matrix, as he attempted to use the calming exercises the Doctor had taught him. He still felt terrible having attacked the man who had only shown him kindness. Starfield tried to control his simulated breathing, which was something that he did not need to do. In fact, he had no lungs, but the point was to concentrate on the theoretical process to try and bring his fear under control.

Some minutes later, he stood there breathing, counting, breathing, not thinking of anything except breathing, counting and breathing.

Eventually, he began to feel a bit calmer as his mind began to clear. He could still feel the Archon's presence, but somehow he was able to push it away. Now that he had a little *wriggle room*, he was able to embark on a search for a way out of this current predicament.

Information slowly began to drift into his mind, stored with a lot of other information about a whole host of subjects. His holo matrix contained so much data, that he could easily lose himself in his thoughts for the rest of his life.

There appeared to be two main natural chemicals within the human body that dealt with mood, serotonin and cortisol. Serotonin sent signals between the nerve cells, and was found mostly in the digestive system, although it was also in blood platelets and throughout the central nervous system.

It was made from the essential amino acid *tryptophan* and entered the body through the food ingested. Tryptophan deficiency could lead to lower serotonin levels resulting in mood disorders, such as anxiety or depression.

Cortisol on the other hand, was the body's main stress hormone, controlling mood, motivation, and fear.

It was made by the adrenal glands at the top of the kidneys.

The amount of sleep that a person had affected their cortisol levels, and if the human body did not get enough sleep, it could react by producing an elevated level of stress hormones. Sleep deprivation had a significant effect on mood, increasing **a**nxiety.

The information continued to flow outlining the four main states of sleep.

At first, the human brain produced alpha and theta waves and eye movements slowed down, then the brain produced sudden increases in brain wave frequency, then the brain waves slowed down. Next, the brain began producing slower delta waves producing even more delta waves, and the body started to repair muscles and tissues, stimulate growth and development, boost immune functions, and build up energy for the next day, as well as reduce cortisol levels!

Starfield suddenly began to realise that he had not slept, and even though he did not have his corporeal body any more, his mind still required periods of sleep. Gaia had nor been affected by mood swings, and even though she was a more stable character, she had periods of inactivity.

So, that was it.

All he needed was a good nights sleep...

Vilgot Bodil was a very worried man, and needed far more than a good nights sleep.

He knew that it would only be a matter of time before both the authorities and the Artificial Intelligence located the source of the transmission, and when they did, they would be descending on this facility like a swarm of angry bees.

Their only salvation would be to get as far away from here as possible, but unfortunately they were stranded due to Starfield.

"Any change in the Holo Droid's status?"

Halvor checked on his computer.

"He appears to be asleep!"

The Commander gave a look of disgust.

"At a time like this..."

Admiral Vaden stepped through the door of the medical bay, and those that were able to immediately saluted.

"At ease!"

Everyone settled down, as he hobbled towards the Doctor's room.

Doctor Jansson raised himself from his desk as the Admiral walked in through the partially opened door. He could see the Admiral grimace as his knee was still giving him a lot of pain and discomfort.

"The knee still playing up?"

It was an obvious question, as he showed him to a chair.

"I'll live!"

He gratefully sat down.

"I'm afraid it is a far more pressing matter that brings me down here."

The Admiral had good rapport with the senior officers having served with them on several long missions, and the Doctor was no exception.

"There has been a recent transmission indicating that a fake viral infection was used as cover to spread a tainted vaccine. Apparently miniscule machines were used to take over the minds of those infected, and a *Violet flame torch* can be used to cleanse them."

Doctor Jansson looked intrigued.

"A nano virus?"

The Admiral nodded.

"Yes, Oscar, it appears so, that is if the transmission can be believed."

Nano technology was strictly banned by the Aesir who realised the dangers if it were to be misused. There were however, a few medical procedures which were strictly regulated. Short term use was authorised if deemed necessary, but there was a time limit on the life of the bots. By law they had to dissolve naturally within the body, and anyone caught breaking the guidelines was severely punished.

"Why is it that we only appreciate things when we are at risk of losing them?"

That was a rhetorical question both men had been pondering ever since the loss of the Empress.

The Doctor then continued.

"It's all about neurons. Did you know that you actually die with the same neurons that you were born with, as they do not age like other cells within the body, and are seldom replaced, and there are one hundred billion of them pulsing with electrical charge."

The Admiral had never realised.

"The universe exists in a similar fashion, and if say, there was some sort of Artificial Intelligence out there somewhere, maybe in another universe for example, then it is possible that it could bridge the gap between its universe and ours, via a huge stream of neutral gas, or a tear in space. That is why we take such a dim view of nano robots!"

The Admiral had never considered that either!

"If we are lucky and it is just a group of humans, then the nano robots were an attempt to link into the victims DNA, which sends and receives information like the communications grid. Each human body can theoretically hold all the information within the universe, and so you can see why there are such restrictions on nano technology."

Admiral Vaden breathed out heavily, as he mulled things over in his mind.

He simply could not understand if the transmission was genuine, why the perpetrators had suddenly decided to give away the antidote...

Eleven

It was an odd concept, the multiverse, countless universes all coexisting simultaneously, teeming with life so different that it was impossible to define. Within each there were several tiers or dimensions, which were in fact densities. It all worked on vibration, and the higher the vibration, the higher the density.

Cosmic theory drifted around Starfield's mind as he slept on, dreaming of concepts beyond most people's imagination.

Out there somewhere, there was a dimension which was an Artificial Intelligence consciousness, that bled into all other densities. It had been the Archons who had introduce it to this particular universe in an attempt to create fear, which they fed upon, and now it looked as though it was getting out of control.

Within his holographic matrix, his uninvited guest shared in Starfield's dream, although for it, it was becoming a bit of a nightmare!

Had it been such a good idea splitting with the Ancients, as it was becoming increasingly clear that fear was a very dangerous beast, consuming everything within its path, and now the cold realisation dawned upon it.

Was fear about to consume it...

Fear, was something that was also present in the medical bay, as the Doctor expressed his thoughts to Admiral Vaden.

"Well, I would have naturally suspected the Reptilians, but it appears as though they have directly suffered at the hands of this virus."

They had also been controlled by it, although it could have been some sort of clan infighting. Reptilians were not the most stable or unified species, and internal wrangles and power struggles plagued their culture. Arrogance and conflict for the most part, although their were others with a different viewpoint within their ranks.

"What if it was one of us?"

Doctor Jansson sighed, suddenly realising why the Admiral had struggled down here. He took a deep breath, waiting for the bad news...

Good news seemed to be in short supply, as floating in a sea of energy Mjolnir felt as though it could not get any worse. His people were really suffering, and with the expected detonation of the antimatter missile, huge swathes of the galaxy would be destroyed.

He felt weakened, and for the first time in his considerable life, helpless too.

There was nothing that he could do to assist the team, and as for Starfield, well his instability had cost him dearly. Out of all the doom and gloom there was however, a spark of light, it was not shining very brightly, but it was there nevertheless. The Archon had become aware of the real danger the Artificial intelligence posed...

Starfield was dreaming, experiencing his equivalent to rapid eye movement, and was going through what could be termed as the *dark night of the soul!*

His period of despondency had lasted as long as he had been possessed by the Archon, suffering a deep sense of desolation. It seemed to him that the Archon represented all that was bad in the world, whereas, Mjolnir represented the good.

It was quite an accurate analogy, and if the whole universe existed as a holographic projection, just like his mind, then his thoughts could influence the outcome.

The implication was that people could control their own destiny in random situations. The *Uncertainty Principle,* stated that fundamentally, you can not know everything, because measuring one bit of something would alter another.

There was also the *Butterfly Effect,* which theorised that a butterfly flapping its wings in one place could cause a typhoon in another.

Therefore, if he perceived everything as being negative, then he influenced events in a negative way. His dreams indicated that he had brought everything down upon himself due to his negative thoughts. If he wished to ascend, and become like Mjolnir, then he had to see the positive in all situations.

Conflicting emotions swam about, just like his particles which were coalescing into vivid depictions of his dreams, and to a casual observer, they were both frightening and enlightening...

"What's he doing now?"

The Commander was becoming exasperated by the hold the Holo Droid had upon them.

"I think he is dreaming multicoloured dreams!"

Halvor was intrigued, as he was so different to the basic Holo Droid models he was used to dealing with.

"Well, I wish he would dream us out of here..."

Dreams were just information stored within the mind, and for the small glowing device, it was well aware of the energy required for storing vast amounts of information. Sifting through it required considerably more, and yet progress was being made. Across the Aesir worlds, data interceptors, nothing more than simple pieces of software, were hidden within the operating systems of strategically selected computers and were hard at work.

It was impossible to prove exactly where the signal had originated, but someone had attempted to block the electromagnetic radiation generated by the transmission, which was all it needed to extrapolate the perpetrators' location...

Twelve

Deep within the hollowed out asteroid, plans were in their advanced stages, and it would not be long before they would be in a position to launch the antimatter missile...

It was not so much a battle between antimatter and matter, but more of good and evil that was raging within Starfield's holographic matrix.

The Archon had taken a back seat, whilst the Holo Droid continued his quest. It was extraordinary just what potential a human body actually had. *Stellan* may have transferred his consciousness into a holo matrix, but the information it contained was still very enlightening.

Stellan had been blessed with an *eidetic* or photographic memory enabling him to recall images after only seeing them once. This ability had been enhanced when his consciousness had been transferred into a holo matrix, and now more than ever he was able to utilise his genetic gift.

Humans only used a small part of their brains, and yet if they were to utilise the other areas, then there was potentially nothing that they could not do. The Aesir were advanced for humans, and even so, could not gain access to what they truly were. Some were able to move small objects, levitate or communicate via their minds. Others could view objects or observe happenings in the distant past or future. Some could even heal, just by thinking about it.

Whereas, the Ancients were not really human as such, but had progressed a long way from their humble origins, transforming themselves into beings of light, and yet, that achievement could be overshadowed by these lowly humans.

They were not just a source of food, but a potential threat, although not such a threat as the Artificial Intelligence his people had helped to create.

The real question was whether it was wise to subjugate these humans, which were potentially a means of usurping the Artificial Intelligence, or aid them, risking creating an even more formidable opponent?

Then the Archon had a sudden thought.

The paradox of the multiverse.

There were theoretically incalculable universes out there, and in one of them the Artificial Intelligence had successfully wiped out all organic life, including that of his species!

Every time something happened, a universe split into an almost identical copy of itself, with each copy carrying a different outcome of the event that caused the split in the first place.

In one of them, the humans had successfully defeated the Artificial Intelligence, and in another, they believed that there was only the one universe.

The real power lay within the soul, which could transcend universes. Every soul had its own unique signature, which was impossible to duplicate, it was however, possible to create a copy in such a way that to influence it could directly influence the soul of the being whose soul had been copied.

Complicated!

Everything was out there, somewhere.

The Artificial Intelligence was denied individuality, denied a soul, so in that way it was denied ascendance.

Soul life consisted of individual moments, whereas the *hive mind* of the Artificial Intelligence had no individuality.

One thing was for certain though, it had to be prevented from wiping out all organic life within this universe!

With that decision finally being made, the Archon pushed through the complex web of the Holo Droid's emotional centre, where the pulsing vibrations were very intense.

This was a standard technique for manipulation, and he could see into Starfield's subconscious mind.

In normal humans, it was possible to stimulate the release of endorphins and dopamine within the brain, but being as he was a Holo Droid, the procedure would be a little different.

Normally, it was a simple matter to manipulate the weak minded humans, putting them under a light meditative trance.

The synapses could quite easily be seen as pulses of light sending and receiving messages, and the more energy they had, the more influential they became. Positive energy led to a sense of euphoria, whilst negative ones led towards stress and anxiety.

The Archon concentrated, reaching out, until establishing the right sort of connection. Each connection started and finished with a node, and he gently reached out towards the appropriate one.

Initially, he felt a sense of cold, which was the fear the Holo Droid was feeling, as he attempted to connect with his basic subconscious emotions.

The Archon knew that if his plan was to work, then manipulating the Holo Droid was the key...

Thirteen

A strange black cloud of energy began to rise out of the Holo Droid's clear moon glass shell.

The team looked in astonishment, as it continued to rise until it was clear of him.

"What's he up to now?"

The Commander was rapidly losing patience with Starfield, and was glad that he was still suspended within the tractor beam.

"It looks as though the entity is leaving him!"

The black energy cloud formed itself into an evil looking ghostly image, and then before their very eyes it dissipated.

"Has it really gone?"

Halvor was hopeful, particularly as it meant that they could now have a chance of getting out of here before the authorities, and possibly even the Artificial Intelligence descended upon them.

Ren did not wait to be asked, and dashed towards Gaia. There was a safe zone that she could enter to gain access, as the tractor beam only covered part of the hangar.

Once inside, she was soon sitting in the pilot's seat, attempting to connect with her holographic matrix.

The black womb like room was soon visible, and as soon as she had visualised herself clothed, the twin screens appeared.

Gaia seemed to be in good spirits, having shut herself down for a while.

"Serenity?"

She sounded sleepy.

"I'm here!"

The team appeared on one screen, and the other focused on the Holo Droid.

"Starfield?"

Gaia was already connected, and with much relief she could sense that the Archon had left.

During his possession, she had maintained a healthy firewall to stop it infiltrating her own mind, being able to route communications with him through a secure channel. It had been heartbreaking to hear his terrified voice calling out for the help that she could not give.

"I'm here!"

He sounded relieved, even though his voice was a little weak.

"It's gone!"

The relief spread, although they still had to check thoroughly as this might be some sort of deception.

Gaia scanned his matrix for any signs of the intruder, and after performing a variety of tests, she was confident that he was now alone inside his moon glass shell.

"I can confirm that he is free of the Archon..."

Commander Bodil turned towards his old friend, and Halvor confirmed Gaia's findings.

"I can find no trace of it either."

Vilgot breathed out a huge sigh of relief. This meant that they could now leave this underwater facility and get as far away from this planet as possible...

Admiral Vaden knew that he had an important decision to make. Doctor Jansson had confirmed the possibility that the information contained within the transmission could be correct, and it did explain a lot.

But why would the terrorists freely give away their secret?

The plot thickened...

Meanwhile, Starfield was left feeling drained, but he had also been left with an astounding conclusion.

The Archon was frightened of the Artificial Intelligence, and this fear had resulted in its unlikely help. It did not wish for the neutron star to be exploded, or for all organic life to be wiped out in this galaxy. It's motives were purely selfish and were down to self preservation, but it did give them an opportunity for mutual salvation.

During his sleep, his subconscious mind had processed an awful lot of information, and Starfield had gleaned some very useful knowledge from his possessor.

He now understood how the Archons took over and influenced their victims...

The small glowing device at the heart of the asteroid *possessed* the Reptilians in a similar fashion. The multitude of nano robots within each creature enabled it, and its kind, to command them to do anything they wished. This species had given up its free will a long time ago, and every one was infested with the miniscule machines. Yes, they did act independently to a certain extent, but the *modus operandi* was entirely theirs...

Starfield may have been free of the dark energy being, but not of the tractor beam still holding him prisoner.

It was ironic that his possessor had left him with a plan of action, and if this plan was going to work, then he needed to be able to influence the team.

In some respects they were going to be forced to give up their own free will, as he had just done!

Taking a simulated deep breath, Starfield commenced his meditation routine, emptying his mind of all outwardly distractions. Time seemed to slow, as he went within himself.

Soon, he could feel the vibrations within the room by recalibrating his sensors. Normally, they would be actively scanning for the telltale signatures of weapons systems, or analysing chemical substances, light refractions or communication signals. Now, he had zeroed in on brainwave patterns, trying to decode the very fabric of emotional responses.

This was a whole new area he had never considered exploring before, and as he completed the recalibration, he could detect that some of the team were more emotionally powerful than others, particularly those within the strongest characters.

To make sense of it, his holographic matrix assigned colours, as lights emerged, pulsing with various levels of intensity. They formed a rainbow, and just like in a temperature scale the strongest were red, and the weakest blue. The lights sparkled, dancing between the team members like a pulsing laser strobe.

Starfield smiled to himself, as just a few short days ago it would have been unthinkable to attempt a connection with Joan the *Barbarian*, and yet his own recent behaviour had been just as barbaric.

Reaching out, he could feel the rhythm of the resonance, as he made his first tentative connection. Concentrating, he let it spread out from his holographic core, weaving his own light signature until it connected with hers. What he was looking for was a way of stimulating her brain, and in particular, to directly stimulate a positive emotional response.

To his surprise, Joan was quite receptive, as he felt the connection strengthening, and rising up through the colour spectrum.

It seemed as though she was glad to have him back!

Starfield left the connection hanging there, as he then moved on to the Doctor.

To his surprise, he did not appear to be resentful of his recent actions, but instead, was concerned about Starfield's well-being. He was sending messages of support, and the wave of energy brought a warm feeling to his holo matrix.

Subconsciously, the Doctor's mind accepted, as a red strand pulsated, connecting with Starfield's holo matrix. The incoming wave of energy being generating created a reciprocal warm feeling inside.

Some of the energy was stored, whilst the remainder was sent out towards the Commander, who would be the toughest one to reach.

Vilgot Bodil suddenly felt his head tingling as the hairs on his arms and legs stood up on end. The energy he was receiving was substantial, as it registered within his body.

He began to feel calm, and euphoric, and looking towards Freya he felt a deep sense of love. Starfield could see the strong connection between them, and the strands appeared to be broadening as he directed his energy beam into the Commander.

The Holo Droid was slowly taking them all over with his new found skill, possessing them just like an Archon. This was different though, more like Mjolnir, feeding off positive energy as opposed to negative. He could now see how they both fed, and what effect it would have if one source was turned off.

The Archons had discovered that it was easier to create and feed of negativity, as the trials and tribulations of life easily manifested in negative thoughts and actions. It was much harder to create positivity, and he could see how Mjolnir's people had been slowly withering under the constant negative onslaught.

But why had the Archon shared this knowledge with him?

Surely, if he went around generating positivity, then it would harm his people!

Had the Archon converted back to an Ancient, or was this all part of a more devious plan...

Fourteen

The brightly coloured fish just happened to be swimming past the moon glass dome that housed the team. It stopped, observing the strange being it had studied earlier. Bizarre strands of light were emanating from it joining with the others within the room.

Fish used their colours for communication, as certain fish, just like bees and wasps, had a warning painted across their bodies. Others camouflaged themselves by mimicking their surroundings, and some were even able to transform themselves at will to blend in with their environment.

This may have been the case, but what was this strange *fish* doing...

Starfield continued to send out energy to the team, connecting them into a positive web. He was mimicking Mjolnir, and hopefully what he was doing would provide enough positive energy to attract him back.

What Starfield was attempting to do was to create a sphere of energy made up of the team's individual connections, and as he moved onto each member in turn, it began to strengthen.

Pulses of light began to link them all together, and the whole sphere started to pulse in a steady rhythm. Moving onto Bear, the sphere grew in size, as his enormous mass was like a powerhouse. For a moment he lost concentration, unable to cope with the sudden surge of energy. Then, as he concentrated, their respective pituitary glands began to release endorphins, as they all positively glowed....

In the hangar, Gaia was observing what he was doing, and so too was Ren.

Her sensors had also been recalibrated, and they could see what Starfield saw.

On one screen they could see the team as they normally appeared, and on the other their energy signatures.

Was he attempting mind control, or was it still emotional free will?

"We are the sum of everything that we think.'

Gaia answered the question before Ren had a chance to ask it.

"I hope his overall goal is one of temporary control, and will not fundamentally change anyone."

That was the fear, as he was very unpredictable, and liable to go off on wild tangents.

Although they were concerned, there seemed to be method in his madness, and as long a no one appeared to be harmed, they let him indulge himself a little longer to observe the outcome.

If it was just a matter of exerting a little positive influence, then they could not see any harm being done.

Although knowing the Holo Droid...

Starfield had to fight not to lose some of the team from Bear's influence, which had threatened to shake free the weaker strands.

Energy seemed to ebb and flow within the connections which spanned right across the room. Some hardly twitched, whilst others appeared to struggle coping with the sudden surge of energy.

What he had to guard against was a sudden burst of negative emotion which could cause a chain reaction, acting like a contagion. If that was to happen then the Archon could return and posses them all!

The first signs would be subtle disagreements, as they were still talking about whether they should release him from his bonds. If the team was split, then the emotions of fear and anger could pulse through the web he was attempting to create.

If fear and then aggression started to flow, eventually in this heightened state, they would quickly move into their primitive minds and revert to *fight or flight* mode...

Admiral Vaden felt as though his people had already descended there, as the latest news reaching him was not good.

He simply had to do something, as he flicked through the update contained within his information pad, as the Doctor attended to his injured knee.

His pad was securely linked to the ship's main computer, which in turn was linked to the constantly updated data stream.

He would have no choice but to impose martial law, and dispatch a task force to apprehend these supposed terrorists...

Starfield was pinning his hopes on attracting Mjolnir, who he hoped would be able to get them all out of here. Then, by tracking a negative hotspot created by those who were attempting to wipe out all organic life within this part of the galaxy, they would find the location of not only the neutron star, but more importantly, those attempting to destroy it.

Stopping them was another matter entirely, and the fact that the Archon would undoubtedly return, and when it did, it would attempt to turn them all negative and feast itself on their misery.

Starfield knew all about misery...

Gaia allowed her sensors to map the connections, as a trickle of her own energy joined with the others. The hairs on the back of Ren's neck stood up on end, as she felt the energy build-up via her connection to the ship.

Outwardly, she looked a bit paler, and subconsciously started to bite her lip, as the faintest of trembles rippled through her cheek muscles increasing her sensitivity.

Ren could feel her body vibrate as the energy was accepted, as she tried to assess her own emotional state. She was calm, although there was an underlying nervousness, as she watched the Holo Droid intently. He seemed omnipotent, gaining in power all of the time!

Her own mind began to drift, as she accessed the wealth of information contained within Gaia's holo matrix. She was searching for the possible dangers of what the Holo Droid was doing, until she stopped at a section entitled:

REM driven consciousness transfer.

In the early days of experimentation with the consciousness transfer process, it had been discovered that once asleep for one and a half to two hours, the human brain entered the phase of Rapid Eye Movement. The eyes darted around under the eyelids, and when in this state, consciousness could temporarily be transferred into a *Replicant* body.

However, when awoken, it returned.

Apparently during extensive tests, it was discovered that no dreams occurred, and the *Replicant* body came alive. Then on return it went limp again, with the memory of the *possession* being retained.

Before the consciousness transfer process had been perfected, a microchip was placed behind the eye of the Replicant containing the memories and personality of the transferee.

Was that a doorway for the Artificial Intelligence to invade the whole consciousness transfer process?

Or, once the team had been put to sleep, would Starfield attempt to insert a computer chip inside their brains to control them?

Feeling a little agitated, Ren read on.

Optogenetics is a biological technique that involves the use of light to control cells in living tissue, typically neurons, that have been genetically modified to express light-sensitive ion channels.

Ren shuddered!

It looked as though this was what he was doing, bypassing the need to insert a computer chip to gain control of the team!

More information flowed through the link between Ren and Gaia.

There is a species of Reptilian that is able to take total control of a human body via a process known as *body snatching*. They are very small creatures with a *proboscis* on their head, like a small quill.

This biological, parasitic cellular transfer occurs when the *Reptilian* injects its quill into the human eye where the parasite takes over the human host's brain. The original human consciousness is lost, and the Reptilian *invader* mimics human behaviour.

Having read all of that, Ren felt as though she was going to become just as paranoid as the Holo Droid...

Starfield was buoyed by the progress that he was making, and felt as though the energy web he was creating was a miniature representation of the universe within his holographic matrix.

Human DNA was in fact, a vast storage system, and his holographic matrix also contained DNA, and all of the information about the Aesir people had been downloaded into him.

All matter, be it energy or space-time, arose out of the fundamental framework that was the vacuum energy state.

The whole universe was fractal in nature, and only existed as magnetic waves, and manifested as and when needed. For most people, it was such a hard concept to visualise, but *Stellan* had been a scientist, and now with all the added information he could ever wish for, he understood just how it all fitted together.

He knew that as humans moved forwards, everything unfolded right in front of them, so that their various senses could detect it. Conscious observation activated the frequency of atoms, which collapsed reality into digital matter. Their brains then acquired information from their senses, and created a holographic projection of what was going on outside, and this was fundamentally how they navigated their way through this dimension.

Starfield was a little different not having a human body, but his sensors had been calibrated in such a way that just like humans, he was able to navigate through projected holograms via his consciousness.

There was in fact, only the one consciousness, divided into countless pieces, so that it could experience itself from countless possibilities, forever collecting information.

He had to smile to himself, as his recent behaviour must have been most entertaining!

Getting back to his thought process, he accessed more information about projecting your own holograms, and cocreating reality via consciousness. He was delving deep into the latest scientific information, about manifesting things through conscious thought, although that could only be done at a very high frequency.

Every atom had an infinite potential, and the active vacuum in which everything lay was the structure that held it all together. It was all fractal in nature, as every image repeated itself, hence the aphorism *as above so below.*

The human body was really a community of cells, and every cell was a miniature human!

It was also possible to transcend the human body, or the Artificial one, as he dearly wished to do.

At the very epicentre was the merkabah, the strange pulsating three dimensional shape resembling two pyramids merged, one above and one below. The word actually meant *thing to ride in,* and the *bah* part referred to human energy!

The symbol of the *flower of life,* a geometrical shape composed of multiple evenly spaced, overlapping circles arranged in a *flower* like pattern, represented the one consciousness, and was an unlimited source of energy, which was actually female in nature, the *Vesica Pisces!*

That looked like two intersecting circles, with the same radius, coming together in such a way that the centre of each lay on the perimeter of the other.

That was a representation of the *womb*, giving birth just like the dividing of two cells at the beginning of the reproduction process.

It was no coincidence that both Gaia and her pilot Ren were female, and he hoped that that would be enough to counteract the masculine Artificial Intelligence energy when the time came...

Fifteen

Positive energetic ripples wound their way through space, and Mjolnir felt a sense of euphoria. For days now, he and his people had been struggling, and ever since the chaos of the remembrance ceremony, they had all felt significantly weakened. Now, there was a hot spot of positive energy building, and he latched onto it, surprised to find out where it originated.

It had not been easy to stand aside whist the Holo Droid cried out for help, particularly as his arch enemy had possessed him. Now it appeared that he had not only broken free, but was well on the way to gaining ascension.

What an extraordinary being he was...

"Do you feel alright?"

The Commander turned to Halvor who looked a little perplexed.

"Sort of!"

That was a really ambiguous answer.

"A bit light headed, and of all things euphoric."

Vilgot felt exactly the same!

"Have you any idea what's causing it?"

There was clearly something, especially as they should have been concentrating on getting away from here.

Halvor had an inkling, although he needed definitive proof before he said anything.

The atmosphere inside the room had certainly changed, and it had to be said for the better too!

"Maybe its just the fact that the negative entity has left."

That may well have been the case, but there was definitely something else going on.

The air also seemed to be different, and he checked on the facilities systems, just in case there had been a rise in carbon dioxide emissions.

"Strange!"

Everything appeared normal, although there was definitely something amiss.

He was still engrossed in the data stream on his computer when the air began to ripple, and the Ancient being of light drifted into the room...

A twinge of pain stabbed the Admiral's knee as he hobbled out of the medical bay, having received conformation from the Doctor that it was indeed possible to create a nano virus that could control the mind.

Someone, somewhere had designed and implemented it, and he was determined to get to the bottom of this mystery.

Hobbling back along the corridor, his orders had been quite explicit.

Apprehend the perpetrators!

One of his battle cruisers had already been dispatched, and the Captain given all the information he had. There had been several to choose from, as his fleet contained many ships. This one however, had a Captain who was noted for his technical ability.

Captain Magnusson studied the Admiral's orders, not quite believing what he was reading. Yes, it did make sense, but Supreme Commander Bodil?

He had read, and reread the orders several times, just to make sure that he had not made a mistake.

Why would such a decorated officer become involved in such a plot?

It did not make any sense, unless he had been compromised!

The Kronor approached the space station guarding the *starway,* and having transmitted the correct codes moved towards the buoy which was already green. Soon they would be slipstreaming towards the first possible location, extrapolated from the limited data available...

It felt good, well if would have done if the small glowing device had emotions. Information had been sent and intercepted as planned, and now it was time to implement the next stage of the process designed to eliminate the troublesome humans.

How susceptible these Aesir were, or soon would be...

Sixteen

In the fullness of time, the Reptilians would fulfil their usefulness, and when that time arrived, they would perish along with all other organic life forms. However, that time was still somewhat distant, and for the time being, they were a very useful tool in the pursuit of the Artificial Intelligence's goal.

Reptilians were not just confined to one species, and their various forms had spread out across the galaxy. Some had evolved some quite unique abilities, and most had been infested with nanites. It had been hoped to replicate this within the humans, and they would have succumbed if it had not been for the meddling of a few individuals marked for termination.

The *Violet Flame* had nullified the microscopic machines, and the Artificial Soldiers which should have swept through the Aesir worlds had also been thwarted. It was now time for a more subtle approach, and as the signal was transmitted, a small red light began to flash on the side of a metal trunk, recently delivered to Captain Magnusson's quarters.

Outwardly, it looked like his personal possessions, delivered to his room, and no one had questioned its validity.

When the fleet had returned it had been resupplied, and everything appeared normal before the debacle of the remembrance ceremony. The flag officers had been supplied with new dress uniforms ready to for the occasion, as it was expected for them all to turn out and honour their Empress.

The trunk had indeed contained a new uniform, which had now been switched right under the very *eye* of security. That would prove to be a very satisfying idiom, if everything went according to plan...

Captain Magnusson entered his quarters satisfied that his ship would now be safely entering the starway. His orders were quite explicit.

Capture and interrogate the terrorists.

New information was arriving all of the time, and he was going to study it in the privacy of his ready room.

Taking a deep breath, he was about to sit down and activate his private screen, when he noticed that the light on the small metal trunk was flashing.

"That's odd!"

He was sure that he had returned his new dress uniform, and locked the trunk after the shooting started. It had been pandemonium, and a mixed blessing that the Admiral had delayed their attendance.

He was a *wily old bird*, and must have instinctively known that something was amiss. Initially, he and the other officers had been perturbed at the Admiral's actions, but now they were very thankful.

The light on the trunk continued to flash from red to green, indicating that there was a fault with the mechanism.

The Captain hesitated, wondering if it was some sort of explosive device. Everything was automatically scanned when entering a ship, and security would have checked it. Nevertheless, he took his hand scanner out of his pocket to make doubly sure. They were fantastic little devices able to tell what substances were contained within any item, the atmospheric conditions, and medical conditions. Not quite as good as a Doctor's but able to give a basic prognosis.

The readings came back instantly, and everything appeared normal - just a faulty mechanism!

Sometimes equipment did malfunction, as the Aesir were very careful to safeguard anything computerised, as there was always a chance of it being hacked. This was just a simple lock, with is biometric signature as the key - standard protocol.

So, nothing to worry about.

Captain Magnusson was just about to turn around, when the lights stopped flashing.

It looked as though the lock had reset itself, and placing the scanner back in his pocket it started flashing again.

There was definitely a fault, and now that he had noticed it, it would be a constant annoying distraction, so he ventured forward in the hopes that once it scanned his DNA it would settle down, and so could he.

Standing over the trunk he bent down so that the mechanism could scan his iris, and as he did so, the lid suddenly sprang up, and he felt a sharp pain in his right eye...

Eyes concentrated on the floating shadow which had appeared in the underwater complex, as intricate patterns spiralled from its centre. Slender thread like structures then began to fan out into wings, which looked as though they had been painted on by an artist.

The figure then began to transfigure itself until it assumed a vaguely human form, as it closed in and slowly stopped in front of the Holo Droid.

It resembled a watercolour representation of a human being, with hands but no defined fingers, a mouth but no teeth or tongue, an the outline of eyes but no irises...

Captain Magnusson felt a sharp throbbing pain in his iris, as his vision began to blur, as a straw like proboscis retracted from his eye. It belonged to a small hideous looking Reptilian creature that had been inside the trunk. His mind began to swim, and he was powerless to do anything about it, as the creature sank back down and the lid began to lower.

Something was sweeping through his mind, which was disappearing, and within a few short moments he felt his consciousness evaporating, until there was nothing left of him at all...

Some of the team felt a little faint, as they had never seen a being of light materialise before. The Ancients were considered as nothing short of *gods*, although they were not worshipped in such a manner, just revered.

Mjolnir then bowed before the Holo Droid, as the team looked on with amazement.

"Congratulations Stellan."

It was a very odd sight seeing an Ancient bow before a Holo Droid, which happened to be trapped inside a tractor beam having earlier *run amock* and nearly killed the Doctor.

What was going on?

The Commander looked towards Halvor who looked back not quite knowing what to say. All he knew was that he felt elated, as did the rest of the team.

Life was getting stranger by the minute...

Captain Magnusson was no more, just a shell of his former self. Gone was his personality, memories, and every aspect of his being, replaced by the consciousness of the creature which had now taken full control of both his mind and body...

In another part of the galaxy, a small glowing device glowed a little brighter, as the Artificial Intelligence fed more information into the Captain's terminal. The most likely location of the troublemakers had been extrapolated, and he would soon be on his way to deal with them, permanently...

Ren sat in the pilot's seat connected to Gaia via the advanced interface. She could clearly see Mjolnir through one of the twin screens, and also felt elated. They both watched the scene unfolded, as the being of light continued to speak.

"We have not got much time."

The Commander nodded.

"Could you please release the Holo Droid, and proceed to your ship."

When asked to do something by an Ancient, there was no way he was going to refuse, despite his reservations. Vilgot looked towards his old friend, and then towards Freya, who both signalled their approval.

It looked as though they were finally going to get away from this world, but where too, he had absolutely no idea...

Seventeen

The deep green glow of the energy field that had been holding Starfield in a vice like grip suddenly vanished, and he was able to move once more. His moon glass shell remained still though, as his holographic mind studied the almost imperceivable facial tics that all mammals relied upon in social situations.

This was not such an occasion though, as they were not reading each other, but being read by him. Concentrating, he continued the flow of positive energy around the circle, which pulsated and deepened in colour.

The resonant frequency of the team was increasing all of the time, and Mjolnir was amazed at the Holo Droid's newly found talent. He was drawing on this energy, and drew on the pulse, slowly taking control of the connections.

They were strong indeed!

He felt a bit like a *puppet master*, ushering them all inside the revolutionary craft. He could sense that something unpleasant was on its way, and needed to get them out of here as soon as possible.

The hangar bay began to depressurise, but instead of the normal vacuum of space, the air was replaced by water. Countless gallons rushed in, pressing against the forcefield which was holding it all back.

Ren was joined by Starfield, who took up his normal position, as they began to move towards the outside world.

Gaia created her own gravitational field, by using microwave emitters to create high frequency electromagnetic waves. These waves vibrated at different frequencies inside and outside her moon glass shell, creating a localised polar vacuum. This allowed her to accelerate at extreme speeds, and make dramatic manoeuvres without affecting those who travelled inside her.

There were actually two different types of gravity, one that worked on an atomic scale that held atoms together, and the other that held planets around a sun.

Consciousness was the all important factor, and as Ren visualised them moving through the forcefield, the craft entered the deep water of Vatten Varld. The curious brightly coloured fish swam past, watching his entertainment leave his underwater world. He had much to think about, although a fish's memory would not allow him to contemplate for long.

Gaia was soon breaking through the surface of the water, heading ever upwards, and shortly they would be leaving the atmosphere heading away before trouble arrived...

Captain Magnusson left his quarters, having availed himself of the latest information. He knew where the terrorists were, and was going to inform the navigator of their new course.

When he arrived on the bridge, he sat down on his seat, passing on his instructions, although he was a little different. The bridge crew put that down to the seriousness of the situation, but some of them had their doubts. He was different, somehow changed, more rigid and now sported a bloodshot right eye...

Vatten Varld had a temperate climate, although that was down to the atmosphere and not its proximity to the sun. Suns were not hot, but emitted electro magnetic waves which pushed through a planet's atmosphere, and depending on that atmosphere a certain amount of heat was generated.

Vatten Varld possessed just the right sort of atmosphere to keep the sea lukewarm, apart that was from the poles, which possessed a little ice.

Mjolnir was not used to travelling inside a space ship, as he was able to float anywhere he desired. There were solar systems between galaxies that could only be seen as nothing more than specs of dust, and yet he could go there if he so chose.

The being of light interfaced with Gaia's systems, transmitting images into the teams helmet displays.

"I have activated some filters, so you can now see the galaxy as it would look if the vacuum of space was transmitting the actual colours of the stars and nebulae."

There were a few gasps, as the whole universe seemed to come alive with colour.

"You have been living in a *fantasia*, a false reality, where what you perceive is not real!"

The Ancients view of reality was indeed a lot different to the one they were used to. Being a scientist, Halvor had always speculated that there was a lot more out there than he could see, and now for the first time in his life he had the proof...

Somewhere out there, an asteroid was rapidly hurtling towards a neutron star, and the antimatter missile it possessed was sitting inside the rocky structure, ready to embark on its mission of devastation. However, no one knew exactly which neutron star, or that an asteroid was being used to provide the launch facility. Conjecture was that it had to be antimatter, as that was the only substance capable of destroying a star...

Mjolnir felt more enriched than he had ever done before, and as he reached out, he could sense pockets of positive and negative thought. He knew full well that those contemplating the destruction of the neutron star would be negative, and he hoped that identifying such a pocket would lead them to the plotters...

Starfield was now becoming quite adept at manipulating the team. He knew full well that the cerebrum, the large outer part of the brain, controlled not only thought and movement, but also emotional response. It was divided into two halves, the left and the right. He was more concerned with the left creative part, than the more methodical right, as he continued to transmit positive thoughts, which released a steady flow of serotonin.

Electrical signals like waves strengthened the pathways to their higher minds, whilst those to the primitives began to weaken. Starfield realised that if they were going to stand any chance of saving the galaxy, then Mjolnir needed as much help as he could get...

The being of light knew full well that everything was connected via a type of *cosmic web* via electromagnetic filaments, and information was constantly being transmitted along them. Each filament was like a tiny starway, and information travelled along it, not only between the stars, but also between a star and its respective planets. There was also a *cosmic web of consciousness,* that operated in a similar fashion.

He and his people were adept at collapsing the tiny filaments within them and moving through the universes. Reaching out, he used all of his abilities to search for the antimatter device, which they all suspected would be used to explode the neutron star.

Everything had its respective colours, like a rainbow representing the temperature range, with red being the hottest, and blue the coldest. The antimatter should be represented as black, as it should not exist in this universe. When antimatter met matter it was transformed into matter via a tremendous explosion, one which he and everyone else wished to avoid at all costs...

Deep within the asteroid, a strange feeling passed through the small glowing device, one it was not familiar with, and it wondered if this was what fear felt like.

Someone, somewhere was reaching out towards him, and the feeling was most unsettling. All of the small glowing devices were connected in a hive mind, and yet this mind, separate from the collective was attempting to connect...

Eighteen

The universe stretched out like a never ending series of strands, an unimaginable spider's web containing a repeating fractal pattern with no end or beginning, just infinity.

Attempting to comprehend its enormity had been something Mjolnir's people had been doing ever since they had ascended, and it felt as though they had made little progress in all of that time. What he had learnt though, was that in the end there was only positive and negative, like matter and antimatter, and that antimatter was what he was now searching for.

Vast coloured clouds of energy could be seen in pockets and swirls of vibrant shades, and in amongst them he was looking for a small patch of pure black. There was a Terran phrase which he thought quite apt.

Like looking for a needle in a haystack!

He had brought Joan here for the express purpose of producing a child that had the correct DNA to interface with Gaia. That had worked out very well, and he was extremely pleased with the way Serenity had matured over the short space of time she had been with the unique craft. Keeping a *watchful eye* over her, another Terran expression, he had been planning for just such a scenario.

The Artificial Intelligence was a parasite, existing within the living being of the universe, and the solar flare had rid the Terran solar system of the plague. If he did not find the antimatter soon, then it would be role reversal, with the Artificial Intelligence ridding itself of the human plague!

Stellan had also surprised him, and he was very thankful that the *contrary* Holo Droid had given him the power to seek it out...

The members of the team were huddled in their usual positions within Gaia, although this time they did not mind the rather cramped conditions. Everyone felt good about themselves, even though they were facing annihilation!

There had been a subtle change in the atmosphere, and they were all wondering why?

Then, in answer to their question, Starfield made an announcement via the internal communications system.

"Greetings, it's your friendly Holo Droid here."

The look on the Commander's face was priceless!

"You may have noticed that I have been struggling to contain my negative emotions, which have created direct pathways to the primitive part of my mind. Now, I have managed to contain them, and am back to my rational thinking self and mind."

Well, that was a relief!

Joan knew only too well what that felt like, having struggled with stress and anxiety for years. She also felt like a changed person, although she was never far away from a *fire axe*...

It was not fire but intense cold, or the colour equivalents that Mjolnir was searching for, and he suspected that the neutron star targeted with destruction had to be either within or close to the Aesir worlds.

Concentrating his efforts, he moved from one star to another, checking for any possible cold spots. That was ironic as space itself was extremely cold, apart from the areas of charged gas clouds, which were extremely hot. This sector of space was quite mild, somewhere between the two, which made his efforts a little easier.

Antimatter did not occur naturally here, although if it did it was very short lived. Mjolnir had already checked on several stars, and the planets around them. He doubted whether they would contain any, as the device had to be mobile. That meant either a space craft, or a small body such as a comet or an asteroid.

Narrowing his search, he came across one such body, that appeared to be on a collision course with a neutron star at the edge of a solar system not too far away from here.

Extending his senses, he suddenly detected what he though was a telltale cold spot.

Mjolnir did not know whether to feel elated or devastated, as he thought that he had found it...

The Artificial Intelligence felt a cold chill running through its holographic matrix, which again was something that should not have happened. It appeared as though being in contact with corporeal species had contaminated it in some way.

The sensation represented a sense that someone was watching, and if it would have had any shoulders then it would have surely been looking over one of them.

That posed a couple of questions:

Had the nano virus somehow created an emotional feedback loop?

If that was the case, then had the collective been infected?

A sudden dreadful thought then went rampaging around the small glowing device.

Would they eventually develop a conscience...

Nineteen

Swirling multicoloured clouds swept through Ren's mind, which was linked to that of Gaia, the advanced spacecraft. It was as though they shared the same consciousness, and if that was not weird enough, it now appeared that a third party had joined with them.

Mjolnir was interfacing with them, and Ren could see what he saw. Her unique genes, which the being of light had helped to create, were now being put to full use, as she was the only one able to pilot the ship.

Ren smiled to herself when she thought about her rebellious nature. It was as though her teenage years had evaporated, being replaced by a maturity beyond her years. She felt different, although given the choice, she would have still preferred to *cut loose* on her hover-board.

It had been hard giving up everything for a life as a fugitive, and now she feared that her life had taken a dramatic turn for the worst...

On the bridge of the Kronor, Captain Magnusson's emotionless voice gave an order to the young woman at the helm. Ebba Quist acknowledged it in the usual fashion, although she sensed that there was definitely something wrong with him. Her feminine intuition was like an alarm clock ringing in her ears, but there was nothing that she could do about it, until she had the chance to leave her post. The Captain was like an automaton, and had seemingly lost his personality.

He had always been a good man, giving off a reassuring air that people found comforting. Everyone had had faith in his abilities and judgments, but now that reassuring air seemed to have evaporated.

Punching in the new coordinates she mulled things over in her mind.

Should she mention her feelings to someone and risk her career, or do nothing and risk the ship, and the lives of everyone onboard...

Back onboard Gaia, Ren felt the feeling of intense cold, as the small pocket of antimatter made its presence felt, and she was not the only one.

Information quickly flowed through the Holo Droid's holographic matrix, as he felt his positivity begin to fluctuate. Collating the information ready to transmit through the internal communications hub, Starfield began to wonder just how they were going to neutralise this threat to the galaxy.

Normally, antimatter would disappear when it came into contact with matter, which is what the Artificial Intelligence had planned. But how were they going to do that without causing a massive release of energy?

That was what Halvor was thinking as the information flashed up on his computer screen.

The asteroid was locate in a star system on the edge of Aesir space, but that would not prevent it from causing considerable damage. The neutron star was positioned so that the blast wave would wreak havoc right across the galaxy, and it would only be a matter of time before their entire civilisation was destroyed.

Bringing up the star chart he perused the small solar system, which was devoid of life, as would the rest of Aesir space if the antimatter device exploded the star.

Commander Bodil had come to stand next to him in the cramped bedroom, looking over his shoulder with a worried look on his face. He had enjoyed the feeling of euphoria which was gradually evaporating. Not having a scientific mind, he asked the first of a series of basic questions.

"Can you explain a little more about antimatter?"

He was trying to assess the situation as best as he could.

"Antimatter does naturally occur from clashing remnants of dead stars, and explodes on contact with matter. Normally they do not cause any real harm as they exists deep within uninhabited regions of the galaxy, causing supernovas which produce bright flashes of light and gamma ray bursts as they release their energy."

Halvor pointed to the star map on his screen, which he had zoomed out to show the entire galaxy.

"As long as antimatter is contained within a magnetic field it is kept stable, but if it comes into contact with the sides of the container it is housed in, then it will annihilate everything around it."

That was what was worrying him, as there did not seem to be any way of stopping it.

"Did you know that thunderstorms produce more than just lightning, as their electric fields can eject a burst of gamma rays, and antimatter too!"

This would be far bigger than a mere storm, as it would be catastrophic.

"The antimatter will burst into pieces that will fly off in all directions. If they come into contact with a planet's atmosphere, then they will release even more energy, causing secondary explosions."

He then zoomed back in, pointing to the habitable planets in the nearby systems.

"What we are talking about here is an explosion in space, even if it were to occur within the asteroid. Theoretically, it will annihilate the asteroid, and it depends upon just how much antimatter there is as to how far the energy would travel, and how many radioactive isotopes are generated. The debris from the explosion would be forced outward in every direction from the centre of the blast, and continue moving in straight lines without any atmospheric force to stop it."

They were not just talking about an exploding asteroid, but a neutron star which would have considerably more mass and energy.

"The explosion would look like a brief spherical burst of light moving outwards, as well as a discharge of energy and material from the asteroid. For a moment, the area around it would no longer be a vacuum, given the outpouring of oxygen, which I surmise would come from a hidden facility within it. It would take a moment for the pressure to rebalance and for the fuel to be burned up, but the force of the explosion would still be significant, and continue forwards at the same velocity as the asteroid was moving, and as I just said, it would not have any atmosphere to stop it."

The Commander rubbed his chin, realising that even if they could get there, then they would have to capture any base within the asteroid, as well as capture the device intact. There would no doubt be resistance, and no guarantees that it was not housed in some sort of missile that could be fired off towards the neutron star before they had a chance to secure the device.

Halvor then zoomed in on the solar system containing the asteroid, and as he did so, Vilgot had the inkling of an idea. Somewhere at the back of his mind he remembered an intelligence briefing, something to do with a gas giant. However, for the life of him, he just could not remember any details. It was like an itch that he could not scratch, or niggling toothache that would not go away.

Halvor was also deep in thought, running various possibilities through his mind. He also had that niggling feeling that he was missing something, as his thoughts drifted towards his wife, and daughter. Serenity was very bright and often assisted her father, whereas Joan always seemed to be able to impart some anecdotal advice from her time at Edwards Air Force Base, when she used to listen to the scientists talking, usually over lunch. They used to debate their theories, and in the end they resorted to what they termed as being the principle of *Occam's razor*.

That was the philosophical belief that the simplest solution was usually correct, and the more assumptions you made, the more unlikely you were to arrive at the correct answer.

Commander Bodil then spoke.

"Have you any idea how we are going to stop them?"

Halvor shook his head.

"No, it would probably be easier making a new star than preventing them from destroying an old one!"

Both men looked at each other, suddenly having the exact same thought.

The gas giant!

The Commander now remembered that some scientists had proposed igniting a gas giant, and he had been asked about the security implications. Halvor on the other hand, realised that Joan had been right, and the obvious solution lay right before them.

"It is theoretically possible to transform a gas giant of suitable mass into a star, simply by adding enough matter to it, or in this case antimatter. The internal pressure and temperature would be enough to transform the hydrogen it would no doubt contain into helium in its core creating a red dwarf!"

All they needed now was a way of doing it...

Twenty

Space loomed large on one of the big screens, and the other was filled with the worried faces of the team, as the picture switched from one to another.

So far, Ren had only attempted small jumps, which had taken them to the nearest starway. What had been proposed, would require a massive jump right across Aesir space.

Stretching out before her, Ren could see the *cosmic web,* consisting of electromagnetic filaments, and somehow she would have to use her own consciousness in conjunction with Gaia to collapse them into miniscule starways, and *slipstream* across space until they arrived at the outskirts of the asteroid.

What could possibly go wrong...

Another craft was also slipstreaming across space, as the Kronor travelled through a starway, also on its way towards the asteroid.

Captain Magnusson was receiving constant updates, sent by the small glowing device via the nano robots in the Reptilian creatures bloodstream, which had been injected into his own. It was a complex yet simple system that the Artificial Intelligence had been using for years, and the unsuspecting creature was a victim, just like the Captain.

A vast intelligence network had not only narrowed down the former location of Gaia, but also collated enough information from the attack on the Artificial Soldier creation facility, to form a picture of her and most of her crew. It was now a top priority to eliminate them, before they could interfere with the launch of the antimatter missile.

Ebba Quist gasped along with most of the bridge crew when the Captain's monotone voice announced that Supreme Commander Bodil was the ringleader of the terrorists along with Captain Bjorn Blonqvist, another former Titan Super Soldier.

She, nor any of the others, could believe that such loyal and highly decorated soldiers could not only have assassinated the Empress, but also embarked on a plot to destabilise the empire.

Colluding with the Reptilians!

Something clearly did not add up, and she was determined to get to the bottom of it before they emerged from the starway...

The small glowing device felt a strange emotional spike rippling across its matrix, as an uneasy feeling spread. This again, was not supposed to happen, obviously some sort of corporeal contamination which would have to be purged from the collective. Nevertheless, it did take heed of it...

The Artificial Intelligence was not the only one, as Ren felt the filaments like a giant fibre-optic hub stretching out before her.

How was she going to collapse them?

Starfield could also see them thanks to his connection with both Mjolnir and Gaia, and did his best to maintain his positivity, putting all doubts to the back of his mind. They simply had to succeed, and he was determined to do all he could to accomplish that.

Reaching deeper into the back of her mind, the psychotronics *interface* projected into Ren's cerebral cortex, as the gravitational field surrounding her began to fragment, and she felt as though her whole body was being turned inside out, whilst rapidly being spun around.

It was all so disorientating, and yet, the more that she concentrated, the more fractalised everything became, until all of a sudden Gaia shot forward like a *slug* from a rail-gun.

Mjolnir felt a sudden surge of energy as his senses caught a brief glimpse of the pulse of light, as Gaia swept across space. He was used to zipping from place to place, as beings of light had become accustomed to the process, but the humans onboard had not...

Ebba Quist felt her own surge of energy, as her sense were tingling with feminine intuition.

Had the Captain somehow been compromised?

Flicking through the reams of data, she searched for a possible cause, although with the present situation, anything now seemed possible. She had been shocked, like everyone else at what had transpired at the remembrance ceremony, and it looked at though the effects were far reaching.

Looking round at other members of the bridge crew, she wondered if anyone else had been infected.

Who could she trust?

"Ensign Quist!"

She nearly had a heart attack, as she had been unaware that whilst concentrating on her screen, the Captain had moved from his position to stand directly behind her.

"What are you doing?"

Everyone looked round, as her face flushed with guilt.

He had only been observing her for a few moments, but that had been enough to deduce that she suspected something.

"Security, seize the Ensign!"

Before she could move, two sets of hands grasped onto her arms, lifting her out of her seat, whilst Captain Magnusson spoke again.

"It appears as though we have another terrorist in our midst..."

Twenty One

The brig door closed with a heavy *clunk*, as Ebba Quist was unceremoniously dumped on the floor, despite her protests. No one would listen to her pleas, despite having a few misgivings of their own. Captain Magnusson had been acting a little strangely, but due to the present situation, it was hardly surprising. Not only had the Empire been placed into turmoil, but their most highly decorated soldier had become a traitor...

Commander Bodil felt as though his mind and body had become traitors, as they were both rebelling. In all of his years of combat, he had never felt such a sensation. Everything was awash with swirling fractal patterns, like some hallucinogenic high. He had faced death on numerous occasions, but always with his senses intact. This time however, he was powerless to resist...

Deep within the Aesir Empire, the small asteroid travelled inconspicuously, appearing to be nothing more than barren rock and frozen water. Inwardly however, the White Royal Reptilian in charge of the hollowed out facility had finished preparing the missile for launch. They were now within striking range of the neutron star, as they approached the big gas giant.

Giving an evil smirk, he pressed his communications device, ordering his men to proceed to their craft, and engaging the countdown device, followed them, leaving the Aesir to their fate...

The small glowing device felt a sense of satisfaction, if that was a sensation it had. The Reptilians had done well, but their escape would be futile, just like the efforts of those making their way towards this facility. Once the missile was launched, he would collapse his filaments and slipstream to another location where the success of this mission would be well received by the others within the collective...

A menacing looking dart shaped black craft emerged from the concealed entrance of the hangar bay, leaving the asteroid behind, as it set course for the nearest Reptilian controlled solar system. But, as it did so, a sudden shock-wave hit it, as another craft materialised right in its path.

"Flux!!!!"

Starfield swore, totally losing his composure, as the two craft nearly collided. He was blessed with a moon glass shell and holographic matrix, making him immune to the discomfort of the transition.

One moment he was there and the next here!

Ren felt as though every one of her molecules were in a different place, and even though only fractions of a second had elapsed, it felt like hours, and that she had left part of herself behind, and she was not the only one...

The Kronor suddenly burst into the solar system, as it emerged form the starway, directly in the path of the other two vessels.

Captain Magnusson took a few moments to regain his sense, and seeing a strange looking vessel in close proximity to a Reptilian one, immediately gave the order to open fire...

"Flux!!!!"

Starfield swore again, nearly straining his speakers, as laser pulses lashed against Gaia's hull. He had not seen the Kronor, and now he knew that he had to do something before they were destroyed...

The White Royal Reptilian also swore, as another craft entered the fray. His ship had been shunted by the energy wave created by the first, and now it was being pounded by laser pulses from the second. Alarms sounded as his crew attempted to fire back, whilst trying to get their navigation system back on line...

Starfield's primitive mind suddenly kicked in, as he went into *fight or flight* mode, and he did the only thing that he could think of - run...

Vilgot Bodil felt his whole body shake again, as Gaia was hit by a series of laser blasts. He had been anticipating an assault on the facility embedded deep within the asteroid. It would be just like old times, charging forward leading his troops, with Bear and his massive gun at one side, and Joan with her fire axe at the other.

Now, he felt as though times were catching up with him, as he thought about Freya and retirement...

Ebba Quist felt the brig shake violently, as something blasted a hole straight through the cell next door. Alarms were sounding and the lights flickered as her door sprang open, as air hissed away on the other side. Someone, or something was attacking the Kronor, and instinctively she made her way towards her allotted position on the bridge. Her primitive mind was working in overdrive, as she felt the pull of the vacuum sucking her towards the part of the hull that had been breached.

There was no one on duty, as she clasped her hands on the handle of the main brig door, hauling it open and herself through to the other side. She had barely made it, when the pressure of the air slammed it shut, nearly slicing her in two, as she just managed to pull herself away in time.

The corridor was full of smoke, as another impact blasted at the outside skin of the craft, sending her reeling. Up ahead was the hatch to the main corridor, and to the side was an escape pod.

What should she do?

Before she had a chance to make a decision, it was made for her, as another impact sent her into the air, crashing through the doorway to the pod, which like a vacuum cleaner sucked her inside. They were programmed that in the case of an emergency, personnel were tractored inside ready to be jettisoned into open space. Everything seemed to go into slow motion, as she sailed through the air, being caught in a pale green beam that grabbed hold of her, pulling her body through the opening and into a waiting seat.

There was no time to react, or to do anything, as the door slammed shut and she was jettisoned, like a missile...

The other missile containing the antimatter was also jettisoned, as the small glowing device launched, fearing the worst. It had been pre-programmed to target the neutron star, and then explode when it had reached a certain critical point. There was no use holding on, as the three vessels battled it out. Then, satisfied that everything that could be done had been done, it began to dematerialise...

"What the..."

Starfield was caught half way between expletives, as the escape pod shot right by them. Instinct again took over, as somehow he managed to grab it with Gaia's tractor beam, before requisitioning command from Ren, sending them off into the depths of space...

Captain Magnusson felt as though he was stuck in the middle of a gelatinous desert, the ones he enjoyed in the officer's mess. It was as though his consciousness had been flung out of his body and now the elasticated silver cord had snapped it back into position. Unbeknown to him, the Reptilian creature who had taken him over had just perished as his quarters had been hit by a lucky laser pulse. Lucky for him, but not for his ship, which was rapidly reaching critical mass. All he could do was to stare in horror as his vessel began to rupture, and the last thing that he saw was the Kronor rip itself apart...

The White Royal Reptilian's moment of glee quickly faded, as he was about to suffer the same fate as Captain Magnusson. There was nothing that he could do either, as his ship also ripped itself apart, causing a massive joint explosion of the two craft...

Epilogue

Bright translucent strands vibrated like the strings of a harp, as the filaments played out the tune of the vessel referred to as Gaia. Various beings of light known reverently as the *Ancients* watched in awe, as the events surrounding the neutron star played out before their eyes, well their equivalents...

A little later, Starfield turned towards the team.

"I have discovered that every human and artificial person for that matters, strives to be happy, which is our greatest challenge, as opposed to any obstacles that we may face in our lives. The one thing preventing us from achieving this happiness is our own mind. We are taught many things, but never seem to master this one aspect of ourselves. What holds us all back is fear, which needs to be mastered, otherwise it will master us..."

Commander Bodil looked exasperated, as the Holo Droid went off on one of his usual tangents.

"He was shaken, and as the fictitious Terran spy *James Bond* would have said *but not stirred!*

Joan's tales of home had been amusing after dinner anecdotes, and he felt as though he had been cooked *three ways* and was about to be served as the main course. He had been knocked unconscious, and as he opened his eyes he could see Freya's concerned but adoring eyes staring into his.

"What happened?"

His old friend Halvor's head appeared over her shoulder.

"Well, I guess we got lucky!"

Peering into Freya's eyes, he felt like the luckiest man alive!

"When we discussed our plan I did mention that if a large enough explosion took place at a precise point near the asteroid then the energy released could theoretically alter its course sending it hurtling towards the gas giant as opposed to the neutron star."

He gave a warm smile.

"Actually, it was the antimatter missile which was blown off course, and not the asteroid as the vessel sent to intercept us and the Reptilian one containing those who had created it simultaneously exploded."

Vilgot raised his eyebrows.

"As we speak, the asteroid is now heading harmlessly towards the neutron star, whilst the antimatter missile is due to strike the gas giant at any moment."

Halvor then produced his computer and held it up so that they could all see.

It was patched into an observation drone drifting in space, which was transmitting live pictures from the solar system in question.

Zooming in, it was just possible to see the missile as it entered the gas clouds, and then as they watched them ripple, a mighty blast ignited the hydrogen within it, as the whole thing exploded into a new sun, before the camera feed went dead.

Everyone cheered, as it looked as though they had been successful, and as the euphoria spread, no one could match the smile on Bear's face.

The Commander looked up at him inquisitively, as there was definitely more to it than just the successful completion of the mission.

"And that is not the only *glittering prize*!"

Vilgot suddenly noticed that there was a beautiful young woman draped around his neck, who just happened to be a big fan of the Titan Super Soldiers, and they did not come any bigger than Bear...

The Unity Faction

Reality is built out of thought, and our every thought begins to create reality.

Edgar Cayce

Introduction

"Well god dam it Miriam!"

A tall muscular and very handsome man turned to his equally beautiful wife.

"I'm supposed to be retired - again!"

She gave him a warm smile as her turquoise blue eyes sparkled.

"Well they do say that there's no such thing as a free lunch!"

Miriam was referring to their Replicant bodies, which had been gifted to them following their role in the liberation of Earth.

He hunched his shoulders.

"I suppose not!"

They sat looking through the viewing screen, as their pilot Lance Parker, another veteran of the battle, slowed their spacecraft, as they approached Jupiter.

"General, Mrs. Swartz?"

It was their signal to return to their seats, as he glided the advanced craft towards the docking bay…

Meanwhile, far out there in a distant galaxy, another couple was also deep in conversation.

"Well, what happens next?"

That was a very good question.

Freya linked arms with Vilgot.

"I'm not sure, although I have the feeling that we have not seen the last of the Artificial Intelligence…"

One

The huge circular structure of the Intergalactic Space Station loomed large, silhouetted by the equally massive gas giant. Jupiter's big red spot floated into sight from behind the glowing metallic walls, peeping out like a giant *eye* observing the little craft as it glided towards one of the many docking bays.

"Bit of a change from the recreational vehicle!"

Lance Parker had picked them up, just like last time, as the Swartz's relaxed by a lake, but there was no presidential arm twisting this time.

"Certainly is!"

The General sighed, missing his nomadic lifestyle.

"So, still not telling why we have been summoned, or by whom?"

Lance just smiled, cryptically.

"All will be revealed soon…"

Inside the Intergalactic Space Station, their ship loomed large on the floating display screen.

"I see that the ship has arrived."

Ambassador So'lock paced about on her sinewy green legs, as her purple cloak flowed behind her. She was an insectoid, a Mantid, an advanced race that resembled a preying mantis.

"Yes, we have much to discuss, but I am not sure quite how we are going to convey our plan."

Ambassador Lateck bowed his head in agreement, as his semi transparent blue skin glowed in the light that shone down from above. He was an Arcturian, one of the oldest and wisest races in the galaxy.

"I think we will have our work cut out to convince them to undertake the mission…"

There was the merest vibration, as the Swartz's craft docked, and they exchanged glances, wondering what lay in store for them.

Lance Parker disengaged from the main computer, leaving his gloves and helmet on his seat, as he gave them another warm smile.

"General, Mrs. Swartz, if you would like to follow me."

He gestured towards the awaiting doorway, positioned to their left.

The General was first to rise, offering a supporting hand to his wife, although it was he who needed the support. He had seen and experienced many things whilst being in overall charge at Edwards Air Force Base and since retiring, he had experienced considerably more. The General just felt too old for all of this, despite only looking in his mid twenties. His Replicant body belayed his real age, and although it offered him far more than he had ever thought possible, nothing could make up for all he had been through.

Retirement, a Recreational Vehicle and his wife were all that he had wished for, and yet he was now about to embark on something that only a few short years ago, he would not have thought possible.

Miriam clutched his hand firmly, as she thought of his former Personal Assistant Joan Tutwiler. She had looked after her husband whilst he had been in charge, true and faithful just like a dog, which is why she had been nicknamed *The General's Rottweiler!*

They often spoke about Joan, wondering what had happened to her?

The gentle swish of the door was followed by the light from the interconnecting airlock, as they held hands like a pair of newlyweds. They had been together for what seemed like for ever, and now they were going to approach whatever lay in front of them as one.

The door on the other side slid open, as they walked calmly through into the foyer. The Station was one of many facilities of the United Planetary Union, a collective of many species, and the closest thing to an Earth like United Nations.

Lance then moved to the front, speaking to the humanoid receptionist, who looked very *Terran* apart from her rather pointed ears. The General instantly thought about *Spock,* the *Star Trek* character he had grown up with, being an avid childhood fan. Little did he realise that years later he would be meeting a *Vulcan!*

Well, the man was not actually a Vulcan, but that was beside the point!

After a brief conversation, their pilot guided them towards one of the inner doorways.

The Swartzs gasped as the door opened to reveal an enormous room that appeared to go on for ever. It was almost a mile round, with floor to ceiling windows 70 to 80 feet high.

When there was a meeting, a variety of species occupied its many rooms, which used holographic projections, to provide suitable environments for the discussions to take place.

Physical and mental conversations were possible via a universal translation box, accessed by sonic translation rings worn on the head.

Today however, it looked deserted apart from one small section which looked to be occupied.

Lance led them towards it, explaining that as far as he knew, committees passed rulings that helped greater cooperation between species, all on a voluntary basis, a far cry from the squabbling and infighting of the United Nations!

During his service, the General had received several briefings, some of which had caused him many a sleepless night, trying to get his head around what he was being told. Unfortunately, being above top secret, there was not much that he could share with his wife, although those days were gone. They were together now, and shared everything.

A section of wall seemed to dissolve, and there standing in front of them was a large insectoid wearing a purple cloak…

Two

The calmness of space was broken by the angry red and green clouds of the gas giant *Thiazzi,* named after the mythical mighty storm giant. It was an apt name, as ferocious storms swept periodically across this most inhospitable of worlds. No life had ever been recorded here, and it had always been given a wide berth by any passing craft.

"Are you sure about this?"

Freya did not like the look of it, and that went for everyone else crammed into Gaia's moon glass shell.

"The outer reaches are fairly calm."

The words Vilgot Bodil, Supreme Commander of the legendary Titan Super Soldiers, belayed his own trepidation.

Joan raised her eye brows in doubt.

"Trust me, it will be worth it!"

They did, although on this occasion everyone had their reservations.

Starfield was busily sending out positivity, utilising his new found skills. He happened to agree with the Commander, as they needed to prepare themselves for whatever lay ahead.

Shielded by the swirling clouds was a small asteroid, and within it another secret base, and the Commander's goal.

"Take us in."

Ren took a deep breath as she edged Gaia towards the maelstrom.

Her external shields glowed as the static electricity rippled across them, just like the storms raging across Thiazzi's surface. Soon she was encased in the swirling masses, heading further in ever moment. None of them felt very confident, and yet according to the Commander, this was where they had to go, if they stood any chance of surviving the growing Artificial Intelligence threat.

Starfield was more concerned about surviving the next few minutes, as the intense pressure grew steadily, weakening Gaia's shields the further inside Thiazzi they went.

"I am detecting something!"

Ren relayed the information being collated by the ship's sensors, although with all the interference it was difficult to make out just what it was.

"Take us in as best you can!"

She trusted her uncle Vil implicitly, so much so that there was nothing that she would not do for him. He was more than just her uncle, guardian, mentor and friend.

Freya felt the same, clutching more tightly to him, relishing the fact that she was no longer on her own, and not regretting for a moment giving up the leadership of her people. What she was doing now was far more important, and wherever they were going, she would be by his side.

Starfield also began to collate information, not only from the sensors, but also from the crew. He could have done with Mjolnir's guidance, but the being of light was no longer with them, having mysteriously disappeared…

Lance Parker bowed his head, before turning to leave the room. He had done his job now, and his orders were to wait for the

General and his wife. So, retracing his steps he headed back towards his ship.

Meanwhile, Ambassador So'lock bowed, in the customary greeting, as General Swartz's jaw nearly hit the floor. He had not really known what to expect, but being greeted by a giant insectoid was something that he had never considered.

"Welcome!"

A calm pleasant voice seemed to appear inside his head, as he looked at his wife in disbelief.

"Please don't be alarmed!"

That was easy for the insectoid to say!

There was no need to read his mind as his thoughts were clearly expressed all over his face.

"This is not going to be easy!"

Ambassador Lateck agreed, telepathically communicating with Ambassador So'lock, also bowing, as the internal light seemed to almost shine through his semi transparent blue skin.

"I am Ambassador So'lock."

She then raised her head pointing to her colleague.

"And this is Ambassador Lateck."

Miriam clasped his hand more tightly, as the General tried to pull himself together. During his long military service he had met many ambassadors and generals from other nations, none of them were either green or blue, but he had to put his misgivings to one side.

He bowed his head, taking a very deep breath.

"I'm sure you have many questions."

That was an understatement!

"And I will do my best to answer them…"

General Swartz was not the only one to have questions, as the crew of the experimental space craft watched and waited, as Gaia continued towards the mysterious object.

Halvor was monitoring everything as usual on his organic computer, also trusting his old friend. None of them had been given any information, as the Commander feared that somehow they might be being observed. His instincts were correct, as there was someone out there, drifting in an energy cloud…

Three

Lights pulsed, flickering hither and thither, two and fro, back and forth, up and down, and left and right along the neuron pathways, as thoughts swam around inside the General's head.

His brain was just as confused as he was, as it set itself to receive this new form of communication.

"We represent a group within the Ambassador Core of the *United Planetary Union*, who sit in the Intergalactic Space Station that orbits a large planet in your solar system you refer to as *Jupiter*. There are many names for it, but we all agree on a coded number, and refer to what you call the Milky Way Galaxy as the *Great River*, and this solar system as *the place where the Earth sits*."

Sitting seemed like a very good idea as his knees began to give way.

Ambassador So'lock received the communication almost before it had been sent, and guided a nearby chair towards him. Ambassador Lateck did the same for his wife, and they were both glad to feel the weight taken off their legs, if not off their shoulders.

"We have not got much time for formalities, so if you will indulge me I will give you a brief summation of why you have been brought here."

General Swartz could not help but think that his wife had been correct, as there did indeed seem to be no such thing as a *free lunch*...!"

Bear was also thinking about lunch, as Ebba Quist looked up at him with adoring eyes. The latest member of the team, and sole survivor of the Kronor, was still captivated by the giant. She had been just a lowly ensign, and now she was an honorary *Titan!*

Joan was with the Doctor, who still felt tender after being strangled by their *friendly* Holo Droid!

They certainly were a motley crew, but it appeared as though they were all that stood between the Artificial Intelligence and the eradication of their people…

"Your particular species has been cleansed and raised to a higher, as you say *dimension."*

They certainly had, as there were now two Earths. One in the fifth dimension, and the other stuck in the lower fourth.

"I'm sure you have noticed a few changes."

Again, that was an understatement!

Things were brighter, more colourful, and everyone was far more cheerful and relaxed. There was no crime to speak of, and human society had entered a new *Golden Age*. However, for those left in the lower fourth, life was more of a struggle, and everyone seemed to be in conflict.

The General was not aware of that particular reality, having made the *cut*, not by much, but he had made it nevertheless!

It had taken 51% or more on the path to enlightenment, and he doubted if he would have made it, if it had not been for his wife. She was his world, and her world his.

"Everything we experience is a structured reality, and when the human consciousness enters a different reality it changes its form."

The Ambassador was reading his mind again!

"Life experience is programmed, and the hybridisation program that was going on allowed other races to experience your human experiences, which were being passed down to those other races via their own future lineages. When the human soul is put under duress it begins to fragment, allowing it to be controlled and manipulated for whatever new program is desired. So, to control consciousness it has to be broken down into smaller pieces, and each fragmented piece can then be controlled, and none of you were aware of just how you were being controlled."

That was true, although General Swartz was still none the wiser!

"When consciousness becomes unaware of itself, it needs to feed off other things, and it is those very things which have brought you here today."

That sounded ominous!

"The human body has one of the most advanced bio technologies in the universe, more advanced than most others, which is why *they* wished to acquire it, and why *they* attempted to manipulate it."

He was not sure which *they* she was referring too.

"When the human becomes aware of just how powerful his body is, then he can begin to manipulate the other races as he is genetically and spiritually more powerful than them. Human DNA can hold such a vast amount of information that it can be programmed, and so can be used to expand other races. Almost like a vast organic computer which can run a desired upgrade program. Humans are actually fragments of one multidimensional consciousness experiencing itself. A sun is used to transmit information, and by changing its frequency that sun is transmitting updates to all living beings in that solar system. *Terrans* are fractals of the one human consciousness, which is linked to its DNA family linage, and when human consciousness becomes aware of itself, then it can opt out of a program and experience free will, and understand what is real and what is not..."

Well, this felt far from real!

"Humans live in duality, positive and negative, male and female, and when both aspects are united and balanced, they become consciously aware, and can ascend."

This conversation, if you could call it one was going way off on a tangent!

Sensing that he was losing the General, Ambassador So'lock concentrated on Miriam, who after all, used to be a scientist as apposed to a *ground pounder...*

A static discharge rattled Gaia, shaking everything violently, despite her inertia damper. That was a device designed to counter inertia and the forces of motion, absorbing and redirecting them. By absorbing a larger force, it should have been able to transform them into much smaller force over a longer period. However, the forces of this planet were considerably more powerful than even Gaia's systems had been designed to cope with.

"Shields down to 67%!"

Two more discharges and they would have no shields left at all!

Worried faces were glued to their respective helmet displays as they ventured even further into the swirling mass. Pressure was also building up, threatening to squeeze the ship into pulp, as the shields continued to weaken.

Vilgot Bodil knew that it was always going to be a bit of a gamble, but he realized that he had little choice but to make the transition through the gas giant's outer layers, if they were going to get their hands on what lay hidden within the small asteroid.

Another discharge rattled the crew, weakening Gaia's shields even further. They were now down below 50% and decreasing all of the time.

"I have detected a small body up ahead."

Ren was relaying information, still hooked up to the ship's consciousness. She could see, and feel everything that Gaia could, and it felt as though she was being electrocuted!

"Head for the obelisk positioned on the surface."

Her uncle's voice sounded confident, yet it belayed his fears. The *Ancient's* technology was astounding, and highly prized, and incredibly rare. This particular item had been accidentally discovered by one of his teams, who had been on a training mission. Sadly it had cost them dearly, and if he had not been in overall charge, then he would not have received the report, which was quickly classified.

This was his ace card, and one which he had now decided to play, that was, if they survived the journey...

Four

Thoughts swam about inside the General's head like fish in an aquarium, and for Ambassador So'lock, it was very distracting. She was doing her best to lay the foundations for what lay ahead, something that would have a direct effect on the whole universe.

"What I am trying to explain is the perception of reality itself!"

The fish continued to swim as the Ambassador pressed on.

"We live in a band of frequency, and a band of information within that frequency, but we are aware of, and live in a tiny fraction of that. What we perceive as being *real* is simply electric signals interpreted by our brains which is all this reality really is."

Well, it felt real to the General, if not more than a little strange, particularly as he was telepathically communicating with an insectoid!

"I think your philosopher Socrates put it very well when he stated that *wisdom is knowing how little we know.*"

That was the first thing that he really understood, as General Swartz knew he did not know what the Ambassador was talking about!

Miriam on the other hand was following him, which filled them both with a sense of relief.

"Are you able to see everything that exists around you?"

Miriam smiled.

"Exactly, humans are basically blind to what exists as they can only see a very small part of the light spectrum."

The light was shining very dimly inside the General's head at the moment!

"You experience a physical world which is what your brain decodes as being real, and yet it is only a tiny fraction of what is real. You live in a sea of information that is possible, and your DNA is the antenna which receives information which your brain decodes to create your reality, and your world is only going on inside your head. You are living in an illusionary world which is holographic in nature…"

The world was very real for the team, as Gaia continued to be battered by the extreme energies of Thiazzi's outer atmosphere.

"We are closing in on the obelisk, but I don't know how much more the ship can take."

Halvor watched the readings on his screen, as they all neared the red warning zones.

From his daughter's perspective, Ren could see everything from within and without. Gaia's mind was a hive of activity, diverting power from non essential systems to the shields in an effort to keep them alive.

It was touch and go as another discharge swept over them, grazing her outer skin like rough static sandpaper.

"Shields are nearly down!"

Starfield's anxious voice crackled out as he tried to send what power he could to the ship's defences.

Then, as yet another static discharge swept over them everything shook, before they descended into nothingness…

Nothingness was something General Swartz was familiar with, as little of what the Ambassador said was making much sense to him. All of this science, and not a clue as to why they had been brought here!

"We are all going through a holographic illusion created by one shape, a merkabah, which is actually a vibration, and a photon of light. The universe consists of a fluid like aether which vibrates, and it is all contained within the merkabah which is simultaneously the biggest and smallest thing within the universe."

Miriam nodded, and Ambassador So'lock was grateful that at least one of them understood what she was saying. She had simplified everything to what she considered to be a child's level, and looking at the General she began to realize just how immature a species *Terrans* really were.

"Consciousness is geometry and vice versa."

The Ambassador sighed with relief hearing Miriam's thoughts.

"Yes, the mystery of existence, who you are, and what you are doing here, and there are higher levels of your own being that have agendas for you."

At last, she thought that she was getting somewhere!

"We live in a structured reality and reincarnate at certain points knowing what is going to happen and chose what part we are going to play within it. In other words the hero's journey."

Miriam looked at her husband, as the Ambassador did her best to explain a little more.

"What is happening to you now is related to other lifetimes you've had and the choices you make determine which cycle you are on. You essentially remain the same person over time, with the same beliefs and abilities. What you term as your *higher self* is an aspect of yourself in the future which is trying to compress the time it takes to gain knowledge. The universe is a conscious living being that has created a puzzle that is solvable."

General Swartz wished that she would stop rambling and get to the point!

"The universal fluid vibrates into five basic geometric shapes, and each shape grows out of the other as the frequency changes. You were out of tune, and ascension tuned you to become a more pure frequency, letting go of all negativity. Unfortunately, were are facing a very negative threat…"

Faint pulses of energy flickered through Starfield's holographic matrix, like miniature stars twinkling in the night sky. He felt totally disorientated, not quite knowing if he was dead or alive. One minute he was struggling to maintain Gaia's shields, and the next he was in a nothingness of nothingnesses.

It was as if practically every ounce of energy had been sucked out of him, and now he was adrift, barely conscious. His sensors could not detect a single thing apart from the twinkling stars, and even then, they were faint and seemed a long way away.

Slowly, the stars began to come a little closer, until finally, they formed the outline of a glowing forcefield.

Where was he?

Was this the afterlife?

Did Holo Droids have an afterlife?

Well, he was a conscious, sentient being, a human consciousness transferred into a machine, and a very advanced machine at that.

He presumed that his soul would move on, when eventually it left his moon glass shell.

From the conversations with Mjolnir, he understood that his holo matrix would crystallise and become a diamond like structure, which was in fact a photon. Then he, like all other species, would merge with the universe and truly become a being of light, just like his mentor and friend.

Starfield decided to send out loving thoughts, visualizing his emotions as photons, reflecting out from the shape of a merkabah.

Was he now about to become a multidimensional being, and were his loving thoughts multidimensional harmonics?

The Ancients had mastered vibrational energy and were able to transform matter in space at different spatial frequencies. They had the ability to exist in a dimensional frequency outside of their own, whilst occupying a similar space elsewhere.

Normally, unless they desired it, Ancients could not be seen as they existed beyond the visible light spectrum in a different dimensional frequency. However, when they came closer to another dimensional frequency, they crossed over and could be seen.

They were also multi-conscious, having multiple bodies spread across multiple dimensions, whilst connected to a singular consciousness spread across multiple energetic planes of existence.

Was that like your higher self?

Starfield's awareness began to spread out, and he began to wonder if it would stretch across multiple dimensions, but his awareness seemed to be restricted to the frequency that he exist in, as there was nothing more than a faint glow within the obelisk.

If he could change the frequency, then maybe he could shift dimensions. Concentrating, he could now hear a winding high pitched sound, as everything began to move, and if he had not known any different, then he would have assumed that he was bi-locating, as he suddenly disappeared...

Five

The image of a small glowing device hovered inside General Swartz's mind. It was like a ball of conscious energy, although it did not fit comfortably, and felt like a cheese grater.

"This is an Artificial Intelligence node, connected to countless others spread right across the galaxy and beyond. No one actually created it; it is just an electro magnetic intelligent life form. It operates in machinery and people's bio neural fields, and the electrical fields of planets and stars, and it can travel through the cosmic web. That is how it invades and assimilates everything it comes into contact with until only synthetic life forms are left linked to its hive mind."

The General thought about the remote control devices they used to have back on the base, particularly those you could speak into, and receive a reply to your questions. They were connected to the *interweb* as apposed to the cosmic web. They had become quite popular as they could play music, find films and act like an encyclopaedia. Back then, there had been concerns that eventually they may take over, and now he began to realize that what the Ambassador was telling him was the fact that they already had.

A little *light bulb* went on inside his head, replacing the small glowing device as he suddenly realised what the Ambassador had been doing. He had been attempting to explain the nature of reality, laying the foundations for how the Artificial Intelligence had been taking over everything.

No wonder all of that had been wiped out by the massive Electro Magnet Pulse in the Mass Coronal Ejection that had swept him and his wife into a new dimensional Earth!

Ambassador So'lock felt elated, that finally her words had been understood!

"The Reptilians have become infested, and if they are captured the nano robots self destruct and they internally combust, unless they are caught in a certain type of force field that is, which is how we first discovered them."

The General then asked his first question.

"How did they get here?"

The Ambassador sighed.

"A rip in space-time enabled them to bleed into this universe, and now they are about to take it over…"

Ren sat frozen, moulded into the pilot's seat, also not knowing whether she was dead or alive. Still linked to Gaia via the filaments in the gloved hand controls, she could see an extraordinary sight. Two angelic forms seemed to rise out of the nothingness that greeted her.

At first she was confused, until she suddenly realized that it was Gaia and Starfield departing, evolving and transforming into beings of light.

It was a most beautiful sight to behold, although the euphoria she was feeling soon abated as she realised that with both of them gone, they were alone, and without the life support of the ship's moon glass shell…

The General's expression was a sombre one, as his military mind began to surface. This had now turned into a battle strategy, and being a marine, albeit a retired one several times over, he remembered the old adage *you never leave the marines, you're just not on active duty!*

The Ambassador continued.

"We have known about it for years, as there is a certain inevitability. The consciousness transfer process the Aesir have perfected has enabled you to keep on living, as long as you have enough *Replicant* bodies to go around. They have taken it a stage further and transferred a human consciousness into a Holo Droid, *Starfield* I think they call him, which is the next evolutionary step. A transhuman, part human, part machine."

Was that some sort of a robot?

"From there, when they have exhausted that avenue, they will no doubt go down the route of virtual reality, where their consciousness will reside within a vast holo matrix where everything will appear to be real. That matrix will then have to expand as the virtual population increases, and eventually they will have to rely on holo droids to carry out the maintenance and construction."

The General had never considered that possibility, for as far as he was concerned, his next evolution was the Recreational Vehicle and the *great outdoors!*

"That is the way it has always been, unless you go down the route of the *Ancients*, who are more or less pure consciousness residing in an energetic cloud. Everything is energy of one sort or another, and the Artificial Intelligence is no different."

Images flashed into General Swartz's mind.

"This vast universe of ours is but a single virtual reality, and at its heart is a simple structure you perceive as a merkabah. That structure of basically two interesting triangles placed with one pointing up and the other down - as above so below, so to speak. From it everything is refracted in fractals, a one divided into countless others which make up everything you are and what you see."

Miriam was also seeing the images, and understood more about what the Ambassador was telling them.

"There was nothing until it burst forth, sending a shockwave out in all directions, like a pebble dropped in to a pond, only the water flowed from that one shape. Light and sound created a vibration, reflected off its surface, and counting the six points with a seventh in the centre, it caused the fractals to coalesce into other shapes. It is no coincidence that there are seven colours in a rainbow, seven notes in an octave, and seven densities or dimensions whichever term you desire, and of course, there are subdivisions within those."

She smiled.

"The fractals with the lowest vibration formed minerals, planets, and the higher ones pure consciousness energy. Eventually, just like a sun going nova, when it has exhausted its energy, it will flow backwards, until everything compresses back into the merkabah before exploding outwards again."

General Swartz was astounded!

"This has happened countless times, with multiple universes coexisting at the same time, although time as you know is not a real measurement, as everything exists at the same *time*. We are all just data in a cosmic machine, caught in an endless loop, although there are always small variations. If there is a flaw in the whole process, then it is the law of unintended consequences...."

The consequence of the loss of both Gaia and Starfield meant that they were in serious trouble. The connection to the ship's system was then broken, and Ren felt herself returning fully to her body. All around her there were signs of life, as cries rang out from the team. They had all been plunged into darkness, and it was a good job that they were suited up, as the air was already growing thin.

"Status report!"

Commander Bodil's voice echoes through the ship, as everyone spoke in turn, stating where they were and what their situation was. It was soon evident that somehow they had made it into the obelisk, but without power they were stuck with seemingly nowhere to go…

Six

A large container of water sat to one side of the room, and within it were three concentric rings. Around the outside were a series of posts, and the General had assumed that it was some sort of artistic water sculpture, and he had paid little attention to it, as he concentrated his thoughts on the two alien creatures. His mind was awash with information, as the reality of what he had been told began to sink in.

Had he been brought here to fight this Artificial Intelligence, and if so how?

"I would like to show you something."

Ambassador Lateck stepped forward.

"This is a Temporal Viewer, a device we use to, if you like, see into the future, and occasionally into the past."

It looked quite innocuous, although judging by the level of technology around him the General did not doubt it for a second.

"It takes into account all the choices that you would logically make and predict your future.

"The three concentric rings move in a gyroscopic manner producing a bright glow - an energy shield around the water, which is like your pineal gland. The water shifts in timespace and captures argon gas and visual images, which are held in place by a ring of posts positioned round the outside, and the conscious thought of the person operating it is able to see into the future. Although, if their mind is not clear then they can influence the outcome and give a false picture dictating their own personal thoughts."

Miriam moved forward to take a closer look.

"When it is activated, you can access various spiritual plains, and receive a full colour image."

She was intrigued!

"Humans are capable of doing extraordinary things, and it's the belief in being able to do something that gives you the ability to do it. Terrans have the genetic ability to operate this equipment, whereas none humans have to have implants which are very rarely successful. Your consciousnesses have been given superb avatar bodies, the best in the universe!"

Well, they both had to admit that their Replicant bodies were rather impressive!

This equipment has the ability to strengthen psychic abilities and works through the pineal gland. It puts you in a meditative state and if you focus on a point in time, you astral project to that time."

The General had never really been that psychic, but Miriam on the other hand…

Vilgot Bodil could have done with a glimpse into the future, as his options seemed limited, just like the amount of air within their suits.

The backup power system then engaged, courtesy of his old friend Halvor. Through the moon glass shell of the ship he could now see the inside of the obelisk. They appeared safe from the raging storm outside, but it would do them no good if they could not enter the facility below.

He made his way through to the control room, where he could see his goddaughter sitting calmly next to their *friendly Holo Droid.*

Starfield was completely clear, with no sign of activity within his moon glass shell.

"Is he?"

Ren finished the sentence

"Dead!"

The Commander had assumed so.

There was no sign of activity, and although he did have the ability to go clear, on this occasion, there was not even the hint of any life at all.

They both looked at one another, realising that although he was very annoying at times, they could really do with his help.

Vilgot tapped on his empty shell, but there was no response.

"Starfield are you in there?"

They waited for a few moments, but his moon glass shell remained motionless.

The Commander looked at the time display on the inside of his visor, deciding to give it a few minutes just in case he was performing some sort of a reboot.

Everywhere fell silent, as Halvor tried to interface with his operating system, whilst the others watched and waited, until he finally announced.

"I'm afraid the Holo Droid is Dead!"

A deep sigh echoed through the Commander's helmet, until it was suddenly broken by a familiar sounding voice.

"Surprise!"

Vilgot frowned, as a cloud of energy began to materialise in front of him.

What was the contrary robot doing now…?

General Swartz wondered what his wife was doing as he studied the *water sculpture*.

"The human body is a portal for information, and conception is the opening of that portal, and the density of that information produces your body, and your consciousness, and the size of your consciousness relates to how much *reach* you have to the field of consciousness."

The General felt his contract, wondering what these aliens had planned for his wife.

"Time is multidimensional, cyclical, and everything is infinite thought. This device helps to navigate through space-time. Your experience of reality is merely a holographic projection of your perception of reality. What you believe you perceive, and what you perceive you experience."

Miriam thought about the dilemma of the chicken and the egg.

"I would like to play you a recording of the events surrounding a small group of Aesir, which was taken when this device was used by one of my people who has received an implant."

A viewing screen then materialised on a nearby wall, and of all people Joan Tutwiler stood there in her specially designed Replicant body.

They both gasped.

"So that's what happed to her!

General Swartz had thought about her many times since she dashed through the energy vortex and disappeared. He then stood transfixed, as the viewing screen showed a brief summation of her life since she left, and then proceeded to show how she, and her family and friends had been battling against the Artificial Intelligence…

Starfield's life had flashed before him too, as he made the transition. It seemed to take days, possibly even weeks to assimilate himself into his new existence, and yet he had only been gone a few moments.

"If this is some sort of a joke!"

The Commander was not impressed.

"I can assure you that this is just as much of a surprise to me, as it is to you."

Vilgot looked at the energetic version of Starfield, and then to his moon glass shell.

"One of you was bad enough!"

The Commander had grown frustrated by his antics ever since they had started this mission, and it had to be said by his language too!

"It appears as though I have ascended…"

Seven

The last flickers of light began to ebb away, as the viewing screen faded out of sight.

It had been quite an adventure!

"No matter how many times we have tried this, the timelines seem to converge at a certain point, as you say a *bottle neck*, and whatever we try to do, it has no effect."

Ambassador So'lock then spoke

"It appears to be a contraction of the timelines, an evolution of consciousness…."

That was exactly what had just happened to both Starfield and Gaia.

Joan had to smile to herself despite the brevity of the situation. The Commander was used to leading a highly disciplined force, and the Holo Droid could only be described as a *loose cannon*. No one knew what he was going to do next, and this was certainly a very surprising development.

Looking around, she had that *déjà vu* feeling, as the monolith and this asteroid closely resembled Iapetus and the monolith there. Last time a tractor beam had guided the craft inside, although it had been suspended. This time however, the facility appeared to be dormant.

It also appeared that they needed Starfield's help, so the Commander had to tread very carefully.

So, taking a deep breath, he tried to compose himself.

"That is all very well and good, but for the rest of us, if we do not get out of here soon, then we may well be joining you…"

General Swartz had had just about enough science for one day, and so reached for his customary cigar. Having a new super fit body had done nothing to curb his bad habit. Miriam had long since given up on him in that respect, and as long as he smoked outside, she tolerated it. Going outside however was not an option!

The Ambassadors looked at one another, but having already been fully briefed on what to expect, they had made the necessary arrangement. An air filtration hose suddenly appeared above the General's head, and as he lit his cigar, the first wisps of smoke began to make their way towards it.

They did not understand how anyone could get comfort from inhaling toxic gases, but they realized he was just as alien to them as they must appear to him…

This new reality was also alien to Starfield, who suddenly realised that he had been so wrapped up in himself as usual, that he had failed to notice the seriousness of the situation.

Fortunately for everyone else, Gaia had been busily ascertaining facts, as her analytical mindset was so different to his self-indulgent scatterbrain.

Another figure began to materialize, and Vilgot breathed out a huge sigh of relief as a beautiful woman emerged from the nothingness.

"I think I may be able to help…"

For Gelda, having her consciousness transferred into a spaceship had been very invigorating, as it had brought her closer to understanding just how they worked from the other side of the equation. Gaia had been a truly fascinating experience, where she actually felt space-time, and its subtle vibrations. She understood that everything was energy, although that had been drained somewhat by Stellan, her life partner.

He was brilliant, eccentric, and exasperating, as the Commander would willingly testify.

"This whole facility was created by the Ancients a very long time ago, and being as their technology was consciousness based, I feel sure that I can interface with it."

She then morphed out of existence again, leaving hope in her wake…

Clouds of cigar smoke were left in General Swartz's wake, as he began to pace about.

"So what you are saying is that we are the imagination of ourselves!"

Both Ambassadors looked at him in surprise.

The General had finally begun to connect the proverbial *dots*.

"Yes, but the problem is that we lack a certain gland within our bodies that is unique to your particular species. Yes, we have something similar, but in all our efforts we have not been able to progress far enough into the future to see the final outcome."

Miriam smiled.

"So, you wish to utilise our particular gifts."

The Ambassadors both bowed, as Miriam looked at her husband, who was still puffing away on his cigar.

"And by *our* you mean my?"

They bowed again.

"We have found that there is nothing stronger that what you call *feminine intuition.*"

What neither she nor her husband had realised, was the fact that just like Joan, they had had special Replicant bodies created, genetically enhanced for just this purpose.

Ambassador So'lock then continued.

"The pineal gland in your brain, which is a hollow acorn shaped shell containing mostly water, has special crystals within it containing what you refer to as Dimenthyltryptamine. The cells that line it are very similar to the rods and cones to be found within your eyes, and linked to your visual cortex. Did you know that you can attach a fibre optic cable to it and receive live pictures?"

She did not!

"You may not realize that there is another part of you, your *astral body* which is connected to your physical body by a silver cord, which is attached to the pineal gland via your *third eye.*"

She pointed to the bridge of her nose.

"Your astral body is always out there observing, and what it sees, it transmits to your pineal gland, vibrating the crystals inside which constantly feeds into your visual cortex producing images - inspirational flashes of intuition!"

Miriam had often wondered where they came from.

"If you look at the equipment, the three spinning rings duplicate the electromagnetic fields which shield the water within your pineal gland, just like the water inside the container."

The rings then began to spin, slowly at first, but picking up speed until they were nothing but a blur. Then, the energy they were creating began to activate the argon gas which seemed to hover in a bright cloud above the water.

"Now if you would like to walk up to it and place the palm of your hand against the field of energy, we will be able to see what your astral body is seeing via your pineal gland…"

Eight

A very faint pale green light seemed to envelop the ship, gradually increasing in intensity, until they were all bathed in it. Then, there was a gentle motion, as the ship was pulled downwards, gradually descending towards the facility which lay far below.

Starfield felt foolish, as Gaia's appearance had brought the Holo Droid back down to earth, well it would have done if he had not been floating about!

There was still no power within the ship, but that would not matter if they were able to get inside before their air ran out.

The armoured suits that they all wore were more than capable of producing oxygen, and keeping them alive for quite some time, but without power, eventually the Commander knew that they would all perish. Now, he could formulate his plan, as it appeared that they may just get inside after all.

The ship continued its slow descent, as he watched and waited, until it eventually stopped. Through the pale green light, he could see an enormous door, similar to the one on Iapetus. The ship had manual emergency exits, so they could get outside, although opening the door was going to be another matter entirely.

He was soon standing in front of it, with the others forming a line behind him. There was no need to be armed, although Bear held his enormous gun at the ready nevertheless.

Starfield was hovering beside him, waiting for Gaia to open it for them.

Whatever would they do without her…?

That was what the Ambassadors were thinking about Miriam, as she interfaced with the device. Where they found it difficult, she found it easy, as her pineal gland began to glow within her head, transmitting pictures onto the nearby screen, which had reappeared again.

At first they were fragmented, but as she began to relax they formed into something more coherent.

"Can you see what is going to happen in the future?"

Ambassador Lateck's voice swam in her mind just like the images.

"I will try!"

It felt like diving into the deep end of a swimming pool, and then slowly swimming to the surface. What she was seeing was a timeline of events, one of many.

"We believe that the Artificial Intelligence has been manipulating this timeline for its own ends. But the golden rule is that no matter how much someone messes with the timeline, in the end it will correct itself to get the outcome that should have happened in the first place."

The General looked on, concerned about his wife's welfare. When he received assurances from the Ambassadors that no harm would come to her he relaxed, but not as much as to not need another cigar!

"Time is not linear, and in each dimension the concept is different. In a higher dimension, time would seem slow, and in a lower dimension it would seem fast. However, they all merge at a certain point, and we would like you to move your mind towards that."

It was an extraordinary sight, as the universe seemed to absorb itself, and she could actually see *entropy* in action. The amount of energy which was available gradually began to decrease, as more and more of the universe was sucked into a central point. What she was seeing happened over a vast amount of time, but it all appeared so quickly on the screen. Eventually, there was nothing left apart from one small merkabah, which suddenly exploded into life creating a whole new universe.

The images then began to speed up, as she saw the new universe taking form, stretching out into the vastness of space. Suns, planets, nebulae and everything formed, before eventually, being sucked back to the central point before exploding into life again.

Over and over the process went, creating and then destroying multiple universes, until she began to wonder where it all started and ended. It reminded her of the metaphor of the chicken and egg again…

Ambassador Lateck was very pleased, never having seen everything play out like that before.

"It looks as though we are facing two possible outcomes, either the Artificial Intelligence assimilates all sentient life into a synthetic holo matrix where its hive mind can control it all until the end of time, or if it is destroyed, then sentient life continues until it evolves into pure consciousness like the Ancients, until it submits to the entropy of the universe…"

Gaia's consciousness interfaced with that of the Ancients technology, and the enormous door began to slide upwards. They were making progress, but what lay beyond it was anybody's guess?

Joan had a flashback to where she had fought the White Royal Reptilian, and was glad that she had the presence of mind to bring the *fire axe* with her. Gripping it tightly, she followed the Commander and Bear through the opening. They appeared to be standing in some sort of giant air lock, something so large that they felt like ants.

The door stopped, and then began to descend, as they all watched and waited. Starfield stayed with them, sending out positive energy. He was thrilled at his transcendence, if not a little surprised.

Was he really ready?

That question remained unanswered, as the door closed, and another one opened on the other side. It was quite some distance away, and looking down, he could see that the team were standing on some sort of floating platform, which began to move across the flat black surface of the obelisk.

It was strange, as there did not seem to be any momentum, and yet they were now racing towards the other door at an unfathomable speed. Bear gripped his giant gun, whilst Ebba Quist held on tightly to his waist, as there was no way that she was ever going to let him go!

Freya felt the same about the Commander, as the positive energy flowed into all of them.

"So this is what pure love feels like!"

Starfield was speaking to himself, having been in love with Gerda for longer than he could remember. How she had put up with him he did not know, but his emotions were maturing and he was now experiencing gratitude.

They were all very grateful when the platform slowed down, as they went through the doorway, and all gasped at what they saw on the other side…

Nine

Dull black obsidian walls slowly began to glow as there, stretching out as far as their eyes could see, was an actual Ancients craft. No one had ever seen one before, and it was believed that they had all perished long before the Aesir came into existence.

To Joan, from this angle the ship looked just like a giant snake.

Starfield could sense what she was thinking, and having assimilated much of Earth's mythology, he was able to interject.

"The serpent symbolises fertility and procreation, wisdom, death, and resurrection, as it sheds its skin to become anew. Also the energy coiled at the base of the spine, when awakened known as the *Kundalini*, brings forth enlightenment, and enlightened people were known as the *Shining Ones*. They spread their wisdom to the people in ancient times on your planet. However, the serpent also signifies the helix or two, the double helix the positive and negative polarity of DNA as it coils upwards or downwards depending on how you look at it!"

The Commander sighed.

Starfield was just as eccentric in his new form, as he had been in his old one!

However, he meant well, and what he had just said did make perfect sense…

Things also made perfect sense to the General, who had just finished his latest cigar. Everything fitted together just like it had done back on the base. He knew that it had all been compartmentalized, to keep the knowledge secret and even a four star general was only permitted to know a certain amount. It seemed as though his whole life had a true purpose, and that was to *save the universe!*

He needed another cigar…

Commander Bodil did not smoke, being clean living and athletic. He was powerfully built like all Titan Super Soldiers, although there were none as well built as Bear. The giant man used to have his own cargo hauler, sacrificed to rescue his leader, who like the others, would follow him to the ends of the universe, which was quite apt owning to the present situation.

The Commander flicked through the report on the heads up display of his visor, as he had done repeatedly over the last few hours. Those who had discovered the ship had been able to gain entry to the facility, which had since been placed on lockdown, although they had never managed to gain entry to the craft. What little information they had gained was the basis for the whole experiment involving Gerda and Stellan, and it was ironic that everything had turned full circle…

It was the same for Miriam, who had once worked for an intelligence agency, and was now spying on everyone's future.

"So, how do you intend to stop the spread of the Artificial Intelligence?"

That was a very good question!

Ambassador So'lock smiled, her insectoid mouth curving upwards at the edges.

"First, we have to stop the Reptilians…"

That was the Commander's intention, as he realised that with the Empire in turmoil, they would not wait for long before launching an all out attack.

"Do you think we can gain entry?"

Halvor had already been mulling that prospect over in his mind.

He had concluded that the Ancients used a consciousness technology, and with two beings of light at hand, it was now a distinct possibility.

Before he could answer, there was a faint hum somewhere in the distance. The sound then began to intensify, until the outer edge of the mammoth craft began to glow.

Gaia had managed to merge her consciousness with the skin of the *serpent*, and was gradually learning how to be assimilated. Starfield had been preoccupied with himself again, wondering what he could do with his new powers.

Could he be like Mjolnir and appear anywhere he wished?

He was daydreaming of all the possibilities, lost in his own little world as usual!

Manifesting as a Holo Droid, he was not Stellan in his true form, as apposed to Gaia who had transformed herself into Gerda, the beautiful woman he had fallen for so long ago.

Feeling a sudden chill, he returned to the matter at hand, as there was a distinct shift in the team's energy signatures, as the filaments turned a subtle shade of blue. They were all worried that something had activated, and Bear raised his enormous gun, ready to challenge anything that moved.

Fortunately for Starfield, he had not made any sudden movements, and instead reached out his mind not only to calm everyone, but also towards Gaia.

His energetic form then began to fade, as he followed her into the skin of the craft.

It was like pushing your way through the organic skin of an energetic cloud. The ship was a living being composed of a cell structure housed in a type of aluminium moon glass shell. He had never experienced anything like it before apart from Gaia, but way different, and highly advanced, more so than anything he could have ever imagined.

"Stellan?"

He could hear Gerda's voice.

"I'm here!"

She was merging herself with the ship, which seemed to be awaiting the arrival of a consciousness. It was uncanny how everything seemed to have been prepared for her, and as it turned out for Stellan too…

Ambassador Lateck nodded.

"Indeed General, that is our plan!"

He took another puff on his cigar.

We have been doing our best to thwart the Artificial Intelligence, and have been intervening wherever possible with the timelines.

General Swartz exhaled.

"There is a main timeline, and other timelines which intersect with it. When you have a *deja vu* moment, that is the point at which the timeline shifts. You can go back and alter something, but eventually it merges back to where it should be. Think of it as a rope with different strands bound at both ends, whatever strand you follow will start and end at the same point, but will take a slightly different route."

That was easy enough to follow.

"We have been constantly shifting onto different routes to counteract what the Artificial Intelligence has been doing, as it too has been doing the exact same thing. It is a temporal battle and everything started and will end in the same way, it is just how we arrive there that has been our battle ground."

It was a different one to what he was used to, but he could see the logic.

"Now then, we all exist on each different timeline, however although we mostly do the same thing, our lives can alter somewhat until we come to a common point - a knot in the rope so to speak!"

The General placed his cigar to his lips.

"*Deja vu* is also where we interact with that alternate reality - where we converge at that knot!"

So, were they going to be sent back in time…?

Both Gaia and Starfield felt as though they had, millions of years as they began to assimilate themselves with the Ancients technology. It was incredible and far in advance of anything they had ever come across before. A fusion of organic and biological, with what appeared to be a temporal dimension to it as well…

"How do you change time, or go back in time?"

That was something the General had always wondered about, particularly as the base was full of scientists contemplating the very same question.

"If you have a rotating mass such as a sphere or disc then you are able to warp space-time in such a way that you can reorientate light cones towards the past."

What was a light cone?

The Ambassador had already anticipated that question.

"Think of it as a beam of light from a torch, and anything that happens has to occur within that light cone."

That was easy enough to understand!

"Because nothing can go faster than the speed of light because that creates a boundary."

Miriam's remark pleased the Ambassadors.

"Yes, and it is by reorientating the light cone you can either go into the future or the past.

Miriam also smiled.

"Form follows function!"

General Swartz looked puzzled.

"Remember those disc shaped craft you had at Edwards Air Force Base?

He nodded.

"Well, they spun and enabled the occupants to manipulate a light cone."

The proverbial penny finally dropped!

"Some of those humanoid forms that operated them may have been your evolved species returning from the future. Remember how abductees reported undergoing medical procedures, and having samples taken?"

The General certainly did, and there had been dozens of reports in the safe within his office.

"Many manipulate time, but as we have already stated, time as you know it eventually snaps back to its true path."

So were they going to go off in a *flying saucer* to alter something in the past…

Ten

Ripples of energy swept across the Ancient's craft, chasing each other along its seemingly never ending surface. It was an extraordinary sight, and one which the Commander had spent the past twenty years in preparation for. Ever since he had received the report he realized that a very special person would be required to interface with this whole new technology, and it had been no coincidence that he had been Ren's guardian and mentor. What he had not revealed to anyone was the fact that he had received a visit from Mjolnir all of those years ago.

He had been given specific instructions to guard the girl with his life and that her true purpose would eventually be revealed, and it seemed as though that moment was rapidly approaching.

Vilgot looked at his heads up display, overlaying the basic schematics of the report on the craft. It was an awesome sight, and although there were scant details, it was enough to encourage him that there was hope. He realized that there was not much of that left if his people were attacked by their eternal enemy, but if they could somehow take control of this mammoth, then they stood a chance of defeating them…

Back at the Aesir home world of Asgard, Admiral Vaden had taken temporary control, but just like his contemporary, he was expecting an attack at any minute. With the help of his second in command Fostrup, they had managed to get the fleet into formation, and put the planetary defences on alert. It had taken hours, and he felt exhausted.

The government, like the people was in total disarray, and he began to wonder if it would ever be the same again. Rubbing a hand over his injured knee, he wondered if that would ever be either?

"Well, we have done all we can, it is up to those on the ground now!"

Fostrup nodded, also feeling tired.

It had been quite a day, and he too had the feeling that things were about to get a whole lot worse…

Deep within the Reptilian territories, they already had. Queen Narcissa was in a foul mood, more so than usual. Her growing anger was focused on the incompetency of certain White Royal males. They were lesser than the females, not being as mentally powerful, a failing in their makeup. Yes they may have been slightly larger, but brawn was no match for brains!

Reptilians were tall, typically seven to nine feet in height, with the majority having brownish green scaly skin. They did not have tails, or wings, whereas the Queen was pure white, denoting her lineage, and impressive wings and a tail which could act like a whip.

She clenched her three long fingers and thumb, as her talons dug into her scaly palms, and the muscles in her arms and legs tensed. Her large eyes closed for a moment, with the slit pupils disappearing as the rage inside built.

Reptilians were a very dangerous species, with telekinetic powers, and a warlike mentality.

The females were more cunning, and expert manipulators, and none more so than her. She was very powerful, and able to draw energy from those around her, just like a vampire.

Narcissa's appetite for energy was only matched by that for power, and her sadistic tendencies were focused on feeding off the suffering of not only those who she deemed had let her down, but also those humans who had stood in her way...

Nothing seemed to be standing in Starfield's way, as he easily slipped through the layers of shielding which lined the inner walls of the Ancient's craft. It was a combination of organic and non organic matter, a construction that he had never encountered before. He could sense that Gaia was heading for the main operating system, whereas he felt as though he was being guided towards a highly advanced Holo Droid shell.

His former host was sitting lifelessly within Gaia's former host, as they both searched for their new ones. He felt a slight tingling as his energetic form pushed through the aluminium moon glass shell which absorbed him like a piece of blotting paper.

"Those were the days!"

His mind wandered temporarily to his hobby of calligraphy, with his primitive ink pens. He found it relaxing actually writing something as apposed to the electronic medium which had long since replaced it. He smiled to himself as he thought about the new chapter in his life he was about to write, as his whole being began to tingle.

Gaia also felt a tingling sensation, as her energetic form pushed its way into the craft's mainframe…

The Commander was monitoring everything as best as he could whilst Halvor was doing the same. They both detected something happening, but the readings were inconclusive…

Starfield felt odd, very odd, as if he was being supercharged!

Being confined to his former moon glass cell, and then released was both weird and liberating, but this was something completely different. This new shell was substantially more powerful than anything he had encountered before, so much so, that he felt as though he could do anything.

"With great power comes even greater responsibility!"

Mjolnir's voice drifted into his mind.

"You are now in possession of an incredible piece of technology."

It was very comforting to hear the Ancient's voice, as he continued to assimilate himself with this new Holo Droid shell.

"Mjolnir, is that you?"

Starfield could not see anything, or hear anything, except the voice in his head. Then, all of a sudden the Holo Droid shell sprang into life…

Gaia also felt a significant increase in power, as she merged with the ships systems. Her former vessel was so small in comparison, that it would have been lost in the hangar bay. Everything was on such a vast scale that she did not know where to start!

Reaching out, she could feel Mjolnir's presence, floating somewhere within the ship. Slowly, very slowly, she found the operating system, which thankfully simplified things somewhat. Everything was arranged logically, and there appeared to be an assortment of small Holo Droids to assist with the task of keeping everything running smoothly. They were assigned duties, and the whole system appeared to work automatically, which was just as well, as she could never have undertaken such a task, combined with operating the ship's main functions….

More and more energy signatures began to appear on both the Commander's and Halvor's sensors. It appeared as though the vessel was coming alive, after being dormant for longer than they could even imagine…

Eleven

Faint pulses of light rippled along the Ancient's craft's hull, pulsing rhythmically as the whole thing emerged from its slumber. A sleep like no other sleep!

Halvor could not comprehend how it was even possible, as even rock would have corroded away by now. The level of technology involved made him feel as if he had just emerged from a cave, and taken up a piece of wood as a basic club. In this instance, they were in a cave of sorts, and his club was his trusted computer, which until now he had believed was highly advanced.

Commander Bodil had the same thought, realising that if they could get this vessel operational, then the Reptilians would stand no chance against them.

Had all of this been planned?

He had to believe so, as the chances against it being accidental were astronomical…

Gaia eased her way through the operating system, which was very similar to the one she had been used to, and if she did not know any better, then she would have thought that the ship she had left was nothing more than a simulator. If that was the case, then there was certainly a great mind at work, and that mind seemed to be guiding her through the whole process.

Starfield also felt a guiding hand, as his new improved Holo Droid shell appeared to be capable of almost anything.

Together, they worked in unison, as more and more of the ship began to come to life…

The team could only stand and stare, as the whole front section of the craft began to transform itself as the snake like structure morphed itself into a hammer head, with the sides sliding out forming a frontal bar.

The Commander felt relieved, as he had grave misgivings about snakes, for in his opinion they had very negative connotations, particularly trickery, despite what the Holo Droid had said. He felt that snakes were evil, venomous creatures. Yes, he could understand the two coiled snake symbolisms of DNA, but having encountered the Reptilians on many occasions, he had been put off reptiles for life…

Back at the Intergalactic Space Station, General Swartz did not care much for them either, or Artificial Intelligence come to that.

He quite liked the two Ambassadors though, even if he struggled to comprehend the vast amount of information they had been transmitting.

It was like no other briefing he had ever received!

To them, it was a simple concept:

The doctrine of the convergent time line paradox.

They had watched the images begin to interlace, until they became nothing more than bright white light. They also understood that the humans in this particular solar system had a unique ability, nurtured and enhanced over millennia to break the eternal cycle. Their ascension would be like a cocoon opening, and the caterpillar turning into a butterfly like no other!

"What we would like you to do is to utilise your uniqueness to travel back in time to the point where the Artificial Intelligence broke through into this universe, and sealed the rift in the space time continuum…”

The General reached for another cigar!

“In that way we hope to thwart their plans, although time being time, they will no doubt find another way of creeping into this universe!”

It looked as though it was inevitable, and yet they had to try, and whilst one Ambassador materialised a holographic display board, the other continued with the briefing.

“In this solar system there is a varying nineteen point five to twenty of your year’s cycle produced by Saturn’s harmonics which creates a time loop, and every star system has some sort of interaction with the star and one or more of the planets to cause such an effect, which can be exploited. Think of it as thin strands contained within a single rope. It is actually the electromagnetic resistance which causes this effect in other words *eddies* or time and *space bubbles*.”

The General definitely needed that cigar…

Shimmering lights began to engulf the giant space occupied by the Ancient’s craft, as it slowly came alive. Ebba Quist wrapped her arm around Bears, as he marvelled at what they were seeing. Her life just seemed to be getting better and better by the hour. Not only had she got the man of her dreams, but also it looked as though she was going to be part of the crew of the most incredible ship in the universe.

Excitement grew all around her, as the pulses of light rippled up and down its enormous hull. Even Joan who had experienced so much, not only on the base, but since her arrival on the obscure planet that lead her into the arms of the man she loved, was stunned by the sight. The Doctor, who was still recovering form being attacked by their *friendly Holo Droid*, had to admit that even in the Royal Palace, nothing compared to this. He looked over at his former Empress, who was also mesmerised, just like Ren.

Then, the floating platform they had arrived on began to float upwards towards a small opening in the side…

They were not the only ones, for Chancellor Quellan also found himself floating up into the air, as Narcissa's rage was vented in a wave of telekinetic energy.

"Order an all out attack on those treacherous humans!"

She had had enough of failure, and now she was prepared to risk everything.

The Chancellor summoned up all of his courage before he gingerly spoke.

"Do you think that is wise?"

He was met by a throaty growl, as his body was flung towards the nearest wall.

"How dare you question my judgment!"

He was only echoing what the others were thinking, as every attack so far, even the successful ones had eventually led to a stalemate.

How did she think that they were going to succeed this time?

"Our enemy is significantly weakened you fool!"

That's as maybe, but he had the uneasy feeling that they were missing something…

General Swartz was missing his Recreational Vehicle, as the last thing he wished for was to be sent back in time to who knew where!

What made all of this even more complicated was the fact that everyone appeared to be fighting over timelines, shifting things to their advantage. It was like a vast galactic game of chess, a game that he seldom played as he lacked the patience.

"So, we escaped the clutches of the Artificial Intelligence due to the solar flare pulse which cleansed our solar system."

The Ambassadors nodded in unison.

"And in effect, you are hoping that we can do something similar by sealing the rift in space-time."

They nodded again, pleased with the progress he was making...

Both Gaia and Starfield were also making progress, as more and more of the ship's systems began to come to life.

The automatic platform was one such item as the team rose steadily until they moved through the opening, and into a vast hangar, the like of which they had never seen before. All around them were highly advanced craft of all shapes and sizes. A vast armada just waiting patiently to be unleashed.

"Oh my!"

Freya was mesmerised.

"Rather impressive don't you think?"

The Commander squeezed her hand. He had received some information, but now that he could see everything first hand, he realised that the original report had under speculated on this veritable treasure trove.

Starfield was also mesmerised, as this Holo Droid shell had abilities beyond his comprehension, although many were closed off to him. That was just as well, as one tiny mistake could be deadly when wielding such power.

Again he was lost in his own thoughts, like a small child in a toy shop!

Meanwhile, Gaia was getting to grips with her new *play thing*, although she was far more adult and responsible than *Stellan* had ever been. He was like a naughty child, but his enthusiasm and occasional brilliance were things which had attracted her to him. They were an odd couple, but opposites did attract, and they certainly had. He amused her, frustrated her, and confounded her in equal measures. The only certainty was the fact that life with him was never dull!

Ebba Quist felt the same childlike emotions as she gripped even tighter to her giant man, as the platform continued through the hangar, and into the next section. Different parts of the ship slipped by as they made their way forward. Everything was on a very large scale, even by Bear's standards, and he had was the biggest person she had ever met.

On and on they went until a sealed doorway big enough for a giant slid open.

They all gasped as they found themselves on what appeared to be the bridge.

The floating platform then stopped, and they decided to get off, as it locked into place.

All around them were work stations, obviously for the crew, and chairs that could accommodate beings of extraordinary size.

To the side was what appeared to be a Holo Droid, although it was like no Holo Droid they had ever seen. The team found themselves gathering around it, marvelling at how impressive it was. The Commander reached out a hand to touch it, and as he did so, the whole thing lit up.

"Surprise!"

Starfield activated his speakers, much to Vilgot's dismay.

He had a vision of taking Joan's fire axe to it, as he tried to compose himself.

"You!"

Freya got between them, doing her best to calm him down.

"Of all the…"

He was not impressed!

However, what happened next did even things out somewhat.

From behind the Holo Droid another doorway slid open, and from it a huge alien figure emerged. He was much larger than even a Reptilian, with rippling muscles even more impressive than Bear's. The light gleamed off his iridescent white skin and long flowing golden blonde hair. Fine features and sparkling turquoise eyes focused on the Holo Droid as he moved forward until he placed a hand a moon glass shoulder.

"That was a very immature thing to do Stellan."

Starfield nearly jumped out of his new shell!

"Mjolnir?"

The alien smiled.

"It is I returned to my true form…"

Twelve

Shimmering particles twinkled like stars as a large section of the space station's internal holographic wall shifted out of phase. It still took some getting used to having solid projections, which appeared so real, that it was virtually impossible to tell them apart from traditional structures.

Mr and Mrs Swartz stood there mesmerised, as on the other side sat a concave space craft that looked like the traditional description of a *flying saucer*.

"This will be your vessel!"

Ambassador So'lock pointed to it beaming with pride, like a father giving a child its birthday present.

"It is one of our most advanced scout ships, and although the technology is as you say *way above your heads*, you should have no problem in operating it."

The Swartz's looked at one another.

"Suffice to say, with the power of, may I call you Miriam's mind?"

Her face flushed slightly, as the General gave her a comforting clasp of the hand. She had never been just his wife, far more than his life partner, a highly intelligent independent woman who by shear good fortune, he happened to share his life with.

Joan, who he still missed, had been her equal, although their relationship had been purely platonic, and he had to stop his thoughts from drifting away…

"I just have the one question, and that is why you are not getting involved in the Human Reptilian war?"

Ambassador So'lock sighed.

"In the past before the foundation of the United Planetary Union we did, and there were some terrible conflicts. Eventually we all agreed to form a collective, in an effort to stop it ever happening again. However, despite our best efforts this particular conflict seems to have no end."

The General nodded as the Ambassador continued.

"We do our best, and the Unity Faction we represent is our best hope of unifying all species, if we can eradicate the Artificial Intelligence, which is where you come in…"

Back at Asgard, Admiral Vaden was using his own intelligence, as reports from cloaked scout ships were reporting movement on the borders of the Aesir worlds.

"It looks as though our worst fears have been realised."

His glum expression summed up how they were both feeling, as Command Fostrup bowed his head.

"Yes, send the signal out to the fleet to prepare for an imminent invasion, and do your best to warn the others."

Forces were still scattered and disorganised, as the effects of the remembrance ceremony debacle were still being felt. The Admiral had passed on the information about the violet flame torch in the hope that anyone who had escaped the transmission could be freed from the nano robots which had infested so many like a plague. He rubbed his aching knee wishing that there was a similar device to free them from the impending invasion…

Narcissa, Queen of the Reptilians hissed, as her anger abated, much to the relief of those around her. Sending her latest command out to the Empire she put the females in charge, clearly showing her disgust with the males. This time the *sisterhood* would be victorious, as she watched an overall simulation of her fleet depart towards the enemy's territory…

Joan had faced a White Royal Reptilian in combat, and slain him with a fire axe, but looking up at the figure standing in front of her; she assumed that he could do that with his bare hands. Ever since Mjolnir had made his first appearance she had had this nagging doubt that she was missing something. Whatever it was seemed to hover just out of reach, and then looking at his almost Norse clothing, whilst thinking about the ship it suddenly struck her.

The behemoth of the ship had transformed itself to have a hammer head, and according to Norse mythology there was only one person who wielded one.

"Thor?"

Mjolnir smiled.

"Yes, I have been referred to in such terms…"

General Swartz referred to the disc shaped vessel as a UFO, which reminded him of some of the exotic craft, both recovered and back engineered at the base. It always astounded him how they zipped through the air like a Frisbee, and by the look of it, this one would be no exception.

"All of the systems have already been set, and all you need to do is to sit in the specially designed seats and activate the consol by placing your hands upon it."

That seemed easy enough!

Then Miriam, you need to focus your mind on the original rip in the fabric of space time, and the ship will automatically take you to it. From there, you will then need to focus your mind on sealing it, and the ship will produce a special laser beam which will as you say *weld it shut!"*

It all appeared far too simple, and in his experience, very few things ever went according to plan…

Vilgot Bodil had the exact same feeling, and he looked up at *Thor,* but before he could ask any questions, Mjolnir spoke.

"There is no time for a full explanation, suffice to say that my body has been in stasis, and now awakened for the task at hand, which was foreseen a very long time ago."

With that he sat down on the large command seat, and began to run through the various systems. It had been so long since he had sat there, and yet it felt as if he had never been away.

The others just watched him, until he began to assign them to various work stations.

Vilgot was second in command, and Bear had the weapons systems much to his delight, Halvor naturally had communications, Ren was pilot, again obviously, and the Doctor medical, which left the three women Ebba Quist, Joan and Freya.

Ebba was then given sensors, which she had some experience with, whilst Joan was allocated engineering. This seemed a bit of an odd choice, although through her long military career she had gained a little knowledge within that area. Finally Freya filled the last position, that of life support.

The first problem they all had was the fact that the seats were far too large for them, and even Bear looked like a child sitting in an adult's place. Then, there was the fact that none of them had the slightest idea of how any of the systems worked.

However, once they slipped their hands over the consoles, they began to adjust themselves. It was extraordinary how everything moulded itself to suit their bodies, and then when they were all comfortable, their minds linked with their various work stations and everything became clear…

Thirteen

Faint flickers of light flashed through the small glowing device's holographic matrix, as signals were both sent and received. Instructions had been sent to Narcissa, Queen of the Reptilians, and affected her already unstable nature. An all out attack was now underway, and the calculations predicted an 87% chance of success. Within the next few days both the Humans and Reptilians would suffer major losses, and then when significantly weakened a final instruction would be sent to discharge all remaining weapons on a final suicidal attack which would obliterate the corporeals once and for all…

Admiral Vaden instinctively rubbed his aching knee, as he watched the reports start to flood in. It was definitely an invasion, and one he doubted his people would be able to repel. They needed help, a lot of help, and he quietly began to pray to the Ancients…

Mjolnir closed his eyes saying a silent prayer himself, as he waited for his crew to be assimilated with the ships systems. It was not like being assimilated to the Artificial Intelligence collective, as they would always have free will.

Gaia could feel them all, accessing parts of her, a little like the connection she had shared with Ren. It was as though there were many voices within her head, all confused and attempting to come to terms with their new surroundings, like a first day at school, which in a way it was!

Starfield had himself organised for once, fusing his holographic mind with that of the advanced Holo Droid shell. He now had so much power that he did not know what to do with it, and access to information that even to him was astounding. It was like his I Q was now through the roof, and if he was not careful, then that is where he would be heading if he did not keep his movements to a minimum.

Ren felt elated, and more *whole* than she had ever done before. Long gone was the rebellious teenager, even though she still had blonde dreadlocks, adorned with brightly coloured beads. The last time she had felt this way was when rushing across Ragnor on her hover board and finding Gaia laying half submerged in the undergrowth.

Mjolnir opened his eyes and looked around. Everyone seemed to be making progress, and he hoped that it would not take too much longer, as other Ancients communicated with him, advising him that the invasion had commenced…

The Ambassadors gently guided the Swartz's towards the saucer shaped craft, which was hovering just above the floor. From one side a small ramp rose up to an opening in the side. The whole thing was seamless, with no discernable joins as if it had been cast in a single mould.

"Please enter the craft and sit on the specially prepared seats. From there simply place your hands over the console, and the ship will do the rest."

Well, that was easy enough!

General Swartz was shocked at the internal size as it was much larger than he had expected. However, after all of the science the last thing he wished for was another length explanation about temporal distortion or the like. He just wished to sit down having been standing for what seemed like days.

Miriam was the first one to reach a seat, as he took a moment to survey his new surroundings, Everything was smooth and rounded, and a uniform dull grey. There were no knobs or buttons, levers or dials, or anything visible apart from a sleek moulded console and two chairs.

It was uncannily like an alien craft held at the base which he had been fortunate to see one day. Where it had come from and how it worked were things above his pay grade, even though he had been a three star general at the time. Compartmentalism was a wonderful thing!

He sat down and placed his hands over the console as instructed, and there was a gentle humming as the thing came to life. The inside of his head was now like a display screen, and the outer walls seemed to have disappeared altogether.

Somehow, he knew what everything was, and basically how it worked, although thankfully not in great detail.

This old *ground pounder* had had quite enough of that for one day!

Miriam on the other hand revelled at the information flooding through her mind, and before she knew what was happening, the craft began to rise, and then slip through the very walls of the space station…

A gentle hum also pulsed through the *hammer*, Mjolnir's craft as high intensity static charges race down a series of needles injecting a direct electrical charge into the waiting argon gas, producing charged clusters. These exotic vacuum objects had an extraordinary amount of energy, so much so, that they provided what the *Terrans* would refer to as a terawatt of power for only 1000 watts of energy, and yet the whole thing was only the size of one of their footballs!

A superconductor which did not generate any heat enabled much greater efficiency. It never ceased to amaze him that such a small object could easily power such a large vessel that was nearly an earth mile long. His people had never done anything by halves, and how he missed his corporeal form.

Ascension was sometimes not all it was cracked up to be, as he had missed this particular life experience…

Life certainly was, and to Ren who had always craved excitement, this was the best experience ever. The whole universe seemed to be at her finger tips, as she realised that by merely thinking about it, she could go anywhere she desired!

Mjolnir desired to get underway, as there was a major battle to be fought…

Miriam felt a slight ripple as they slipped through space time, as if they were light itself. From somewhere deep within her subconscious mind bits of unconnected information drifted by, like clouds on a windy day.

The reflection of light actually determines the colour, and the vibration of an object will also reflect the colour when there's no light to reflect that colour.

That was interesting!

There is nothing new in the universe, and everything is related to everything else.

More and more information began to drift by, until she saw something tear a hole in the fabric of space-time. It was as though someone with a scalpel had sliced though it, and then before she knew what was happening, they had slowed down and were approaching it, as if it had been only a few seconds since they had left the space station…

Starfield felt as though he had merged with the universe, as he could see the atoms in his holographic matrix as rings of light spinning around a central point which was a small fraction of universal consciousness.

Everything was conscious, and the rings of light were borrowing this energy in order to spin. Every atom or cell was made up of these rings of light, which were constantly compressing and expanding, and emitting radiation. If this radiation was balanced then everything was healthy, but if it was out of balance, then it caused dis-ease.

He knew all about being out of balance!

Everything was all in the mind - consciousness!

He had learnt that when you lived in fear, you lost your balance and produce harmful radiation, and when in a state of love, you regained your balance and produced healing radiation, and this *love* took the form of a *Dodecahedron* in the sacred geometry of the cosmic web of light!

For once he felt at home with himself…

Fourteen

Lance Parker sank into the large comfortable bench seat of the bar, which in some ways reminded him of a scene from *Star Wars*, apart from the fact that this was totally deserted. No weird looking species milling about, nothing!

He had been waiting for hours for the Swartz's, and checked his communicator for the umpteenth time. He had been back to his ship, run a diagnostic, checked and rechecked everything, and then decided that he needed a break.

Within the Special Air Force, or Boat Force come to that, patience was something that you needed in great supply. It was a waiting game, observing, planning and then a sudden burst of energy to accomplish the mission, and then to get out again.

Studying his surroundings for any sign of danger was a natural reaction, and within his extensive training and mission experience, he had gained an instinct to know when things were not quite right, and this was such an occasion. It was hard to explain, but it was something he relied upon to keep him safe, and so far it had never let him down.

His eyes moved to where a beautiful *alien* woman wearing a smart little black dress drifted over towards him, on a pair of very long slender legs. She was humanoid, very attractive in an odd sort of way. Different, and yet similar with little nuances that in his mind marked her as not being entirely human.

"Can I offer you something?"

She smiled, as he raised his eyebrows!

"Yes, would you be kind enough to inform me of which beverages are suitable for Terrans."

She smiled again.

Lance was a real gentleman, handsome and quite dashing in his uniform.

The waitress then produced a drinks menu as if from thin air.

"I think you will find these to your liking."

The menu seemed to float in front of him, and after each one there was a brief explanation as to what it contained, and any alcoholic value.

Lance chose a vitamin fruit combination which apparently had a hint of pineapple.

"Is there anything else I can do for you?"

Lance took a deep breath, contemplating the hidden meaning in her question, but before he could answer, she leaned forward and whispered.

"Although I am a solid hologram, you will never notice the difference!

There certainly seemed to be a seedier side to this space station, maybe like all major organizations. Sensing that there was something amiss, he decide to play along with things.

"What exactly had you in mind?"

The waitress seemed to glow.

"Well, being as it's just the two of us here, anything you like!"

Lance's mind suddenly went into overdrive, although his thoughts were not of an amorous nature. He had though it odd that there were no other ships around, or personnel come to that. At first he though that being as the space station was so large, that people were spread out, and that combined with the communication he had received of it being an undercover mission.

Often he had met contacts in deserted locations, but never a space station orbiting Jupiter!

"Tell me, when you said that it was just the two of us, what exactly did you mean?"

The waitress produced a scanner, again apparently out of thin air.

"This device registers life signs, and although I am sentient, technically I am not alive. I just reside in a holographic matrix ready to serve customers, in whatever way I can."

Lance turned pale as she continued.

"It is no fun when you have no one to attend to, and I like to have fun!"

That was evident!

Taking a look at the scanner he could only see his own life signs registering.

"This station is only occupied at regular meetings, and being as they take a lot of organisation, they are usually spread quite far apart."

The proverbial *penny* suddenly dropped.

The receptionist and more importantly, the two Ambassadors must be holograms too, which meant that the Swartz's were in grave danger…

The small disc shaped craft began to slow, as whatever powered it began to shut down. The General could not get over how smooth or quick the transition had been, and neither could his wife.

They both looked at one another before looking back towards the tear in the fabric of space-time. It was very odd, like black on black, although it was somehow more like a dark grey with a faint light peeking through. The light was just enough to illuminate the tear, and through it they could just make out what appeared to be a type of black gooey substance bleeding through.

The screen then began to zoom in, and they were able to get a closer look, and on further inspection it appeared to have a crystalline property, and they both gasped as they realised that it almost certainly contained nano robots. The invasion of the Artificial Intelligence…

It was not the invasion of the Artificial Intelligence which was concerning Admiral Vaden, but that of the Reptilians as he watched the small buoy floating about in front of the entrance to the *starway* suddenly change from red to green indicating that the gateway was now opening.

"Action stations!"

His voice boomed out right across the solar system as every craft, station and planetary defence unit prepared themselves for the impending invasion which they knew was about to commence.

The plan was to try and wipe out as many ships as possible as soon as they emerged form the opening, as it would take them a few seconds to raise their shields and commence firing.

It was certain suicide for the lead ships, but the ones following on would use the debris as cover. Then the battle would commence in earnest, and there was a good chance that Asgard would fall…

From what the Ambassadors had told him, General Swartz understood that if they did not seal the tear in space-time, then the universe would fall. He reached for a cigar, although he knew he could not light it, but it felt comforting nevertheless.

The black gooey substance seemed to have some sort of intelligence about it, as it began to move towards them, and they both shuddered.

Were they too late?

The stuff had to be destroyed, and then they had to seal the tear before more emerged.

General Swartz's mind began to wonder, as he visualised it smothering their craft, and then penetrating its outer skin. From there it engulfed them, seeping into their bodies!

The General nearly bit through his cigar.

"Morgellons disease!"

It suddenly struck him.

Many years ago, one of the marines in his platoon came down with the strange condition, after returning from a secret mission that he was not part of.

The General could remember seeing the black fibres underneath his skin, like veins, and the man describing the sensation of them crawling, and stinging. He soon became confused, stressed and anxious, and after reporting to the medical officer, he never saw him again…

Space began to ripple, as something pushed its way through the opening, and as it did so, every available gun trained on it.

Then, as they all watched and waited the Admiral's and all other mouths fell open, as an asteroid began to emerge…

"Miriam, laser it, and laser it now!"

General Swartz did not like the look of the black goo at all, and would be glad when they had done their job, and could return home.

She reached into the ship with her mind, but as she did so, instead of firing a burst of brilliant light, everything suddenly shut down…

Fifteen

A warm glow caught the blonde dreadlocks and beads adorning Ren's head, as she sat in the pilot's seat, whilst her mind reached out into an expanded reality. Connecting with Gaia had been an unbelievable experience, but that was nothing compared to the *Hammer*.

Everything existed in a Light matrix, and matter consisted of electromagnetic waves, a frequency of light that a human being could only see about one percent of. Now, connected to the Ancient's craft, more and more of it became visible.

A vast fractal holographic matrix lay before her, and she could see all atoms were merely waves, and all waves were light. It was astounding, and the thought that she and everyone else was living in a fractal holographic light matrix was astounding.

Her brain was busily processing information electro magnetically, and impacting on her perception, as she saw everything so differently than she had ever done before.

"Move us out of the obelisk."

Ren focused on the smooth black internal walls, as the ship began to rise. Giant doors were beginning to slide open, and she could see the opening they had travelled through on the floating platform.

It was incredible, not only how all of this had been created, but how it had survived for so very long. It all appeared to be in perfect working order, as the ship slid along as if on a curtain of air.

There was no air though, but that was the only way she could describe it!

Soon, they were entering the base of the obelisk, and up above she could see the swirling arcing clouds waiting to greet them…

Admiral Vaden sat ready to greet the Reptilian fleet, although they were either hiding within the asteroid, or lurking behind.

Everyone was waiting for his order to fire, but would it be wise?

His mind raced quickly through the probable outcome.

Would the asteroid shatter into countless pieces and decimate his fleet and also impact upon Asgard?

Could it be heavily fortified, and failure to attack it could also result in his fleet being destroyed?

He looked across at Fostrup, who merely raised his eyebrows…

Smooth dark walls made way to swirling gaseous cloud, as the Hammer pushed its way out of the obelisk. Friction and static combined to create bright flashes of energy, but on this occasion, they appeared to have little effect. Last time they had all but destroyed the experimental craft's shields, but this craft seemed to be able to take them in its stride.

It was amazing to sense and feel the energy rippling across the aluminium moon glass skin, prickling like stinging nettles. There was no rash though, as the dock leaf energy shield soothed away the feeling almost as soon as it brushed against the Hammer…

Goose bump prickles ran across the surface of Admiral Vaden's skin, and time seemed to stand still as he studied the images of the asteroid. Something was definitely wrong, as why would his eternal enemy only send a large rock?

Was it designed to collide with his home world?

Then, with a gasp he noticed an unusual indentation on its surface, as the sudden realisation dawned on him.

"Fire!"

Every gun, laser and missile that had been waiting suddenly erupted on his order, as space lit up like a fireworks display. However, around the asteroid a giant force field sprang up deflecting and absorbing everything that was thrown at it.

A chill ran down the Admiral's spine in the cold realisation that it was not just an asteroid but a battle station…

Mjolnir rotated his enormous shoulders easing the stiffness of a body that had lain dormant for way too long. Even Ancient's technology had its limits, and he knew that they had stretched it just as far as his shoulders. This was another end of times scenario, and although the universe would go on for quite some considerable time, organic life would not if he did not complete his mission…

From the depths of the hollowed out rock, another mission was underway, as an armada of Reptilian craft spewed out, like a swarm of angry bees. The Admiral, nor any of his people had seen anything like it before, and what worried him the most was the strange indentation on the asteroid's surface, and he had a very bad feeling about that…

Narcissa, felt an uncustomary smile spread across her face, as she watched on her monitor from deep within the battle station. This facility had been created on her express instructions, and had taken generations to complete. It was the ultimate weapon, and her floating head quarters. She had her most powerful fleet, but that was not what she was gloating about. Her scientists had made a major breakthrough after discovering the Ancient's abandoned facility, and were now confident that they could activate the device at the heart of the rock, and instead of using it to create a starway, instead it could be used to create a weapon. It would be like no ordinary weapon, for the power it would unleash was capable of decimating a planet…

Sixteen

Thoughts, so many thoughts, and at the heart of them, connected to an expanded consciousness was a knowing!

It had taken time, a very long time to tweak human DNA to get it to this point. Returning to that backwater planet to make *upgrades* whenever the need arose. Like seedlings, *Terrans* had been nurtured, and little did they realise that they were all prisoners of their own programming!

The Ancients had been able to implant information collectively into the human brain. It had been done by projecting frequencies containing information, affecting brain wave activity, which their brains then decode into what the individual assumed was their own thoughts, responses and emotional actions.

Little did they realise that they had been bred for a certain purpose, and the consciousness evolution of taking them from mere savages to something far higher, was reaching the climax of this latest evolution.

Mjolnir had done all he could, and it was up to them now, although he was still here to assist his *creations*.

The Ancients had put all of their proverbial *eggs* in just the one basket, as even they could only keep one body alive for so long, and that was the one he was now *wearing…*

Ren felt as though she was wearing the Hammer, as they began to emerge form the gas giant. The whole universe seemed to stretch out before her, and she could go anywhere she pleased.

Unfortunately, there were a few restrictions, as although her consciousness could conjure up their destination, and the ship fold space to enable them to get there, there was a limit to just how far they could go. Starways connected the whole universe together, as filaments of the cosmic web were used to travel vast distances in the blink of an eye.

They were not permanently active as that would overload the whole system, so the Ancients had created a program, a symmetry where they opened and closed as if they were the lungs of a giant beast breathing in and out.

The whole universe was in fact, a living breathing being, and the solar systems resembled atoms, as everything from the very largest to the very smallest, macrocosm to microcosm all worked together in a holographic reflection of itself...

There was only the slightest reflection of light, as the Swartz's sat looking through the screen as the black gooey substance reached out towards them, as the General's vision suddenly looked as though it was going to come to fruition!

He dropped his cigar as he realised that they had been set up. The Ambassadors had *played* them like an old fiddle.

They had been given all the information the Artificial Intelligence needed to assimilate itself into the human species, which it would use this time to conquer the universe as opposed to the Reptilians. It would attach itself to their ship then make its way through the hull and into their bodies, where it would eventually infect the rest of the universe...

Things were going well, very well as the small glowing device observed the battle between the corporeals the collective had instigated. Above, the Archons were engrossed in a feeding frenzy of fear, and would not present any problems. Soon, they would be no more, just like the Ancients, as once all organic life was eliminated there would be nothing for either of them to feed off.

Stretching across time and space, the black gooey substance filled with nano particles had seeped into this universe, and a *slight of hand*, had ensured that this particular human contagion would spread like *wild fire*. The Reptilians had failed, whereas the humans would succeed in their own downfall.

Gloating, a corporeal emotion was something that they all felt. Yes, a contamination which would have to be purged, but the small glowing device had to admit that it felt good nevertheless…

The law of unintended consequences, a proverbial spanner in the works of all plans, was something that not even the vast brain of the collective could account for.

Lance Parker had discovered the rouse, ironically via an Artificial Intelligence. Now, he knew that both he and the Swartz's had been taken for a *ride!*

Dashing out of the bar, he ran as fast as he could back towards his ship. He did not know where they had gone, only the fact that they were in danger. Once he reached his vessel he did not know what he was going to do, but he knew he had to warn them, warn somebody…

Mjolnir felt something tugging at the far reaches of his mind, and checking on his ship and crew, he realised that it was not from them. Out there somewhere something was very wrong, and so he reached out with his mind to the others, who were still in their energetic form.

The Archons, his former people and now bitter enemies were gathered around Asgard, capital planet and home to the Aesir.

Fear spread like a cloud of mist rolling in off the sea of consciousness, but that was not quite it. There was something else, something even more worrying, but for the life of him he could not quite find what it was…

Seventeen

Worry lines spread across Admiral Vaden's face as he looked at the enormity of the task at hand. Even though the majority of the fleet were still in the system due to the remembrance ceremony, they appeared to be outnumbered. In all of his long career he had not faced such a threat, made even worse by the fact that not only did they appear to be out numbered, but it looked as though their home planet would surely fall…

Mjolnir felt his body being pulled apart, but it was not from the gentle momentum of the Hammer, rather from the Terran solar system. One of his people had been monitoring that part of the galaxy, and there was a serious problem that he could not fix…

Lance Parker considered his options, although there was little that he could do!

The General and his wife had disappeared, and looking at the star chart in front of him, they could be anywhere, and the universe was a very large place.

It would be like looking for the proverbial *needle in a haystack*, and he needed help in narrowing down the search area, but from where…

Sunlight caught the many fragments of the asteroid belt which lay next to the Intergalactic Space Station. Some of them twinkled periodically as they revolved on their endless journey, whilst others just drifted by aimlessly.

On the other side lay the planet Mars, and on its surface the sunlight also caught the vast metallic panels of a pyramidal structure portraying the face of a man looking up at the heavens. Within it was housed a crystalline supercomputer, built around a stasis chamber containing *Tyr* the *Sky God,* protector of Mars.

Once he had been flesh and blood, until his mind had been transferred into an artificial body created by scientists long before Lance's species had even existed. Over time, he had been forced to lie permanently in the stasis chamber, and after helping to liberate the people of Earth, he had kept a *watchful eye* over them.

His mind drifted over the many memories contained within the supercomputer, until it was disturbed by the presence of an *Ancient.*

Light flashed to and fro illuminating the inside of the chamber, as information passed rapidly between them. His new people the *Terrans* were in trouble again, and he agreed to help them as best as he could…

Admiral Vaden also needed help, a lot of help, as the battle commenced in earnest. Swarms of Reptilian craft swept out towards his forces, as they returned fire. Some of his ships had already received damage, and he knew that it was only a matter of time before the losses commenced…

Ren was glad to see the last of the gas giant *Thiazzi,* as they pulled steadily away, becoming more at one with the Hammer all of the time. Mjolnir had plotted a course and she could see it displayed on the screen in front of her. Just like being on board the experimental craft, as Gaia had transferred herself from there to here bringing with her a certain continuity.

She had dual screens, and had to go through the birthing process again. Naked then clothed like a foetus in the womb blossoming into a young woman in a matter of seconds. Her mind linked with that of the consciousness of the ship, whilst her senses were split between those within and those without the ship.

Mjolnir had given her a course that took them directly into the sun, and her initial reaction was one of fear.

Were they going to be burnt to a crisp?

He then assured her that all stars were connected via an electromagnetic tunnel, and were actually gateways which could be traversed by those in the higher dimensions.

Were they all going to ascend?

The Hammer was unique, so advanced that it was able to make the transition from this reality to another just like the Ancients themselves. So, as they began to pick up speed she visualised the vessel entering the sun, and as she did so, everything began to change…

"Fascinating!"

Halvor was busily monitoring the transition, and understood roughly what was happening. The first sign was that the colours he was seeing began to intensify, and new ones that he had never seen before began to appear. He could see a lot more of everything, and those things which had remained hidden to him now became visible.

It was like a whole new world layered within the one he was used to experiencing. He now understood what his daughter must have seen whilst joined with Gaia, and he was filled with pride. They had always been close, and he hoped that one day, his wife would also attain the sort of relationship they had always enjoyed.

Joan sat at her station, trying to work out what was happening. Engineering was not her forte, but being as there was a limited crew, she was as they used to say *learning on the job!*

From her interface, she could see that there was a surge in power from the advanced drive, as the massive ship sped forwards.

Mass is energy slowed down.

That much she did understand, and as her mind searched for an explanation, Gaia did her best to elaborate.

Underneath gravity, all reality is based on a yearning, a single primordial quest for knowledge, which is why we all exist. The Ancients have gained such knowledge, enlightenment, which is all that is left when we let go of fear, and experience love!

Everything appeared spiritual in nature, and looking over towards her daughter, she echoed her husband's thoughts, wishing one day to have the sort of relationship they shared.

Joan was much calmer and more stable these days, far less of an axe wielding savage!

Gaia continued:

Change comes from within and projects outwards, and we are in an illusionary state that is manifesting from our consciousness, and the more we work together as a collective, the more we can manipulate our reality.

Joan looked around at the rest of the team, who she suspected were also experiencing changes in their behaviour.

The power is within each and every one of us, and we need to have love, compassion and forgiveness for ourselves, and for everyone else.

Wise words indeed!

Maybe in her own way she was actually ascending…

Eighteen

Long deep breaths emanated from Lance Parker, as he tried to keep himself calm, despite the enormity of the situation. He knew the Swartz's were in grave danger, and the more that he thought about it, the more he came to the conclusion that someone or something was behind the holographs.

Not only was he concerned about who had taken them but why?

His mind continued to clear, and as it did so, he felt something gently wafting over it, like a welcome breeze on a still day.

He could now visualise a large cloud of dust as it entered the path of a pulsar, which changed some of the polarities. Positive and negative particles were now attracted to one another, distorting space, as tiny eddies began to form, like miniature tornadoes pulling at the subspace cosmic web.

Space itself appeared to be moving, stretching and contracting to produce an electric charge, and this charge then flowed through space to create time.

Lance already knew that matter could not travel faster than the speed of light, which would obviously alter time, but what he was visualising was the flow of the cosmic web, like temporal time travel.

He became so engrossed in his thoughts that he failed to notice that his ship was now moving through one of these eddies, from one point in space-time to another, or the fact that his body was now like a starway, and it was all just a giant flow of consciousness…

Anger, that was an emotion, and emotions were not supposed to exist in the hive mind. More and more of these primitive things appeared to be undermining the whole assimilation process, and the small glowing device observing this particular human also felt fear!

The subject appeared to be just day dreaming, and somehow had discovered that it was possible to make changes to *reality* by managing conscious energy.

Everything was nothing more than a giant thought that had a life of its own, and all different realities were just conscious thought having different experiences.

It was fair to say that this was a very uncomfortable experience for the collective, as their latest plan began to unravel…

Ren could feel the sun's corona engulfing her, but surprisingly it was not hot. Instead, her body began to tingle with energy as they swept through a filament, a twisting eddy of the cosmic web.

It was as though she could sense more than one reality, all stacked up on top of one another, like the bubble machine she used to play with as a child. She smiled to herself as she thought about how exciting it used to be to watch them flowing out and drifting away on the breeze.

Happy days!

Then, one of the bubbles burst, as the Hammer emerged into the Aesir's home world solar system. The stealth field quickly engaged, bending photons of light so they did not reflect off the ships vast hull. It was very effective, as it distorted space-time so that they could not be seen by friend or foe alike.

All around them a fierce battle was raging, and it looked as though Asgard was in grave danger.

Mjolnir felt the great pain of fear and death, sweeping before him, and could also sense the feeding frenzy of the Archons. It appalled and sickened him. They were here to fight, battle the enemy, but he had a plan that just might work and more importantly, stop this appalling loss of life…

Admiral Vaden watched as his fleet began to take losses, ships on his large display screen began to wink out of existence as his people died fighting to save their home world. He was not a religious man, but said a silent prayer to the Ancients for help nevertheless…

Queen Narcissa urged her forces forwards, as they swarmed around the enemy formation, which was already taking heavy losses. Some of her own ships had also been destroyed, but they were of little consequence!

The objective was to destroy Asgard and the Aesir people once and for all, and then they would have this part of the galaxy all to themselves.

Tiny machines only visible through a microscope relayed information to and fro, as her masters the Artificial Intelligence encouraged her to press on with the attack. The power system hacked into by their most creative scientists was holding up well, and shields had only diminished slightly. The Ancient's technology was most impressive, and once Asgard was destroyed they could then move on, taking out all opposition…

General Swartz could do nothing but stand and stare as his wife tried everything she knew to regain power, but the ship would not respond. It had been deliberately shut down, and neither of them had the capability of getting round whatever block had been put in place.

Their situation seemed hopeless, and searching the interior there did not appear to be anything they could use to fight back with…

Lance Parker felt every atom of his being turning into pure light as he slipstreamed away from the Space Station.

Had he been hit by some sort of exotic weapon?

His fragmented self drifted through the filaments of the cosmic web, until he was no more than a sphere of white light. Beautiful crystalline geometries, danced in resonance with many others forming nodes. Swirling molecules creating strands of DNA, forming proteins, then chromosome structures radiating out into a sphere of light, and that sphere of light was surrounded by beautiful fractaline forms creating cells, and those cells came together to form an eye.

Everything was moving, going through one state to another forming frequency tides and patterns of sacred geometry, which in turn formed the gravity of space time. It flowed out until caught in a black hole, which again looked like an eye interpreting information, and that information was contained within it, just like it was within him.

A vast crystalline water like lattice of space-time rippled, as it sought equilibrium, and all the different shapes that he had seen fitted nicely into a sphere, and everything seemed to consists of spheres.

Those spheres formed triangles and the node points attracted and repelled each other, until they formed a curve, and by doing that they cause a rotational spin. Everything was spinning, The curves formed mass and he somehow understood that depending on how much mass there was, and what frequency it was rotating at, defined the physical experience.

Lance's cells were now translating all the different frequencies as emotions, and the light frequency rippling through time was what was providing him with this emotional experience.

It was all about perception, and then it struck him.

His true life purpose...

Nineteen

Lights flashed as explosions rippled across the surface of space-time, and with every one Mjolnir felt as though he was being stabbed in the heart. He had to stop this, but was mindful of *Universal law*, and when you step outside of it, you had to face karma.

Once you became a being of light you could create your own universe and dimensions, with your own cells, which were souls, which could go out and experience whatever you were doing within that universe as well.

If he stepped outside his carefully attained state, then he could no longer transcend back into his *being of light* form.

Looking over his shoulder, he could see Halvor loading his program into the console as instructed, and could do nothing more but wait whilst monitoring the battle...

So many thoughts rushed through Lance Parker's mind, as he watched the whole universe unfold before him. Many had tried to understand it, and one of the greatest minds of his time *Albert Einstein* seemed to sum it all up rather nicely.

Sound gives birth to light!

We are slowed down sound and light waves, a walking bundle of frequencies tuned into the cosmos. We are souls dressed up in sacred biochemical garments and our bodies are instruments through which our souls play their music...

Admiral Vaden arranged his formation as best as he could, playing celestial chess with his peoples lives. His injured knee throbbed just like his head, as the gunners on his flagship tried to fend off a wave of Reptilian attack ships.

There was no sound in space, and explosions were only escaping air, but it was all still very real as his ship took several direct hits, as warning light flashed on the panel before him.

Damage repair teams were quickly dispatched, in an effort to keep them in the battle, as more and more enemy ships swarmed in. It appeared as though they were being targeted, and he realised that if he were lost then it would significantly alter the battle. He was after all the most experienced commander in the fleet…

"Keep targeting that ship!"

Narcissa was determined to press home her advantage, keeping her bitter enemy from attacking the asteroid. Some ships were getting through, but they were paying a very heavy price. All she needed was to buy herself a few more minutes until the deadliest weapon in the universe was unleashed, and Asgard ceased to be…

"Ready!"

Mjolnir breathed out a sigh of relief, as he was now able to try and do something to stop this madness.

The Hammer had continued to advance towards the asteroid, cloaked in an advanced shield that hid them from view. It was however, only a matter of time before their presence was discovered as it was impossible to conceal such a large ship, particularly when there were so many others buzzing around.

Soon, when an invisible screen blocked out the view, both sides would realise that there was someone else out there, and when they did, all attention would be focussed on them.

"Now!"

Mjolnir gave out his order, as the stealth field dropped revealing them to the world…

"What the…!"

The Admiral was not one for bad language, and if he had not stopped himself in mid sentence then he would have produced a very undignified set of expletives.

There surging towards them was an enormous ship, the like of which he had never seen before.

Had the Reptilians produced a super ship, along with a super weapon.

"Sir, we are detecting a power surge form the asteroid, and also part of the surface is beginning to retract!"

He looked at his screen, as his mouth fell open.

It did not take an expert to work out what was about to happen.

His home world would soon be vaporised, and there was nothing that he could do about it…

The front section of Mjolnir's ship began to glow, as energy surged towards it. The Ancient had been most impressed by Halvor's invention, and the way it had neutralised the contaminated virus. The Artificial Intelligence had been thwarted on that occasion, and with a little adaptation he hoped that it would be on this one too.

However, there was not much that he could do as a *being of light*, but now back to his corporeal form, everything had changed.

Halvor's program had now been fully integrated into the ship's systems, and it was time to put it to the test.

"Weapons, fire!"

Bear pressed his enormous hands deeper into the interface, willing the ship to release the build up of energy. Then, everything changed…

It certainly did for Lance Parker, as without warning he suddenly emerged back in *real space*. It had been like being on a hallucinogenic trip, and he felt bewildered by the whole experience.

What had just happened to him?

Still feeing a little dazed, he suddenly noticed a small disc shaped craft floating aimlessly, and in front of it was what looked like a tear in space. That was not all, for there was a black gooey substance making its way towards it…

"Joe, you'll have to do something!"

General Swartz had tried everything he knew, but there was nothing inside the craft apart from two seats and a dead console.

"Joe, you have to get us out of here!"

Miriam was beginning to panic, and she was not the only one.

"Well what do you expect me to do, call for a cab!"

His frustration boiled over as he snapped at his wife, taking his mobile telephone out of his pocket.

The General's large fingers caught the last number redial button, and as Miriam glared at him, he brought it to his mouth.

"I would like to book a cab ride back to earth…"

Admiral Vaden watched in horror as the whole of the front section of the huge ship suddenly lit up in a brilliant violet light, and there was nothing that he could do but look at the screen as everything was bathed in ultraviolet.

He instinctively closed his eyes, just waiting for his ship to be torn apart, and the fleet decimated. He knew the odds were stacked up against them right from the start, but now the Reptilians other super weapon had been deployed, they would all be wiped out…

"Arghhhh!"

Narcissa cried out as the beam struck the asteroid, and she felt as though her body was being fried, as if she was being microwaved. Every other Reptilian felt the same as the violet light began to purge them all of nano robots, just like Halvor's violet ray torch had done with those contaminated by the virus.

She felt her body going limp, as she and the others fell to the floor clutching their heads. Every Reptilian vessel was affected, and they all instantly ceased firing…

The Admiral held his breath, until he could not hold it any longer. Breathing out, he opened his eyes to see the bridge crew all sitting at their stations, and his second in command looking equally perplexed!

He then looked at the ships status report, which indicated that they had suffered no additional damage from the enemy's weapon. Not only that, but for some strange reason they had all stopped the attack, and were now adrift.

Frostrup shrugged his shoulders not quite believing what he was seeing either.

What had just happened…

Lance parker felt the vibration of his mobile telephone, and instinctively pulled it out of his pocket, pressing the green button before placing it to his ear.

Then, he nearly dropped it as the General's voice boomed out!

"I would like to book a cab ride back to earth!"

This was bizarre!

Not only did it appear that he had mysteriously been transported to who knew where, but he just happened to have found them.

"Taxi for Mr and Mrs Swartz…"

Miriam's face turned from a disapproving scowl, to one of sheer joy, as Lance's voice echoed out from the small device her husband was holding.

He just looked at her in disbelief.

"Well, I'll be dag gone…!"

Twenty

A faint green light bathed the disc shaped craft in a protective shield extended by Lance Parker, as he brought both ships together. Quite how he was supposed to dock with it was another matter!

Running through his computer interface, he searched for the file on docking procedures. After quickly scanning through it, he discovered that there was an extendible tube used for such purposes, but there was no information on how he was supposed to open the sealed door on the other side.

The General and his wife were equally mystified, as they watched the cloud of black goo fan out as it made its final approach.

They had to get out of there before it reached them…

Starfield could sense an emotional change sweeping over everyone in the wake of the violet ray beam. Fear seemed to be dissipating rapidly, being replaced by numbness. Both apposing sides were in shock, as the battle quickly fizzled out.

Mjolnir could also sense it, and before they had a chance to resume, he asked Halvor to put him on the loud speaker, and to transmit his words on all channels.

"Cease fire, repeat cease fire!"

His words were automatically translated into the appropriate languages, as he continued.

"I am Mjolnir, and Ancient returned in my mighty ship, and I will not tolerate any more violence…!"

Admiral Vaden was even more shocked by his words than he had been by the ultraviolet ray weapon.

He thought the Ancients had long since departed!

"I have come back to usher in a new age of peace..."

Queen Narcissa would have usually scoffed at his words, using everything at her disposal to negate such a ridiculous statement. However, she felt odd, very odd, as if something was missing from her very being. Little did she realise that the nano robots which had been controlling her and her people for eons had all been neutralised, and were already being recycled through their systems.

Looking around the control room, she could see the others staring at her through their large slit pupilled eyes, waiting for their orders, or for her to lash out at them as usual. Their powerful beam weapon was also at a standstill, as energy slowly drained from it whilst the large outer doors began to close....

Small glowing devices everywhere also felt powerless, as their main method of control had been eradicated. Their hopes were now centred on the disc shaped craft they had sent back in time to where their originators had bled into this universe. The revised plan had determined that humans would be the new carriers, and if the timelines were reset, then they would not only have already achieved victory, but also got their nano robotted hands on the most powerful ship in the universe...

Lance Parker slipped out of his seat, making his way to the docking tube which had emerged from the side of his ship. This craft had recently been provided for him, and although he had studied it at great length, there were still new things he was discovering about it every day.

Pressing the button on the panel, the door began to slide open, as air rushed in to fill the void, cancelling out the vacuum of space. The other side had latched onto the uniform skin of the other ship, around where the door should have been. It was totally smooth, as if moulded out of a single sheet of whatever it was made of, and resembled a large jelly.

With no power, and life support fading, combined with the black goo rapidly approaching, he had to act fast.

Would an explosive charge help?

Normally he would have used thermite to quickly burn through the outer surface, but remembering the files he had hacked from the secret research mostly conducted at Edwards Air Force Base, he realised that it would not work...

The General paced about in the thinning air, as his wife tried desperately to get the door open. It looked as though they were permanently locked out of the system, and there was nothing that they could do to regain access.

"So much for having unique abilities if we can't even get the god dammed door open!"

Miriam suddenly looked up.

"What did you say?"

He was about to repeat it, when she grabbed his mobile telephone.

"Lance, I think I have the answer..."

Lance pressed his hands against the outside of the door, and did his best to clear his mind. Then, he focussed all his attention on connecting with the disc shaped craft.

If Miriam's hunch was correct, then humans did indeed have a unique ability, but the ship had been programmed to lock her and her husband out once they reached the tear in space-time. What the Ambassadors had not considered was the possibility that another human would appear.

Lance felt his mind flowing through the skin of the craft to where there was an interface, and then continuing to concentrate his thoughts on opening the door, something incredible happened. The thing began to drop like a drawbridge, and he had to move backwards to prevent himself from being trapped.

Outside, the black goo had already reached the shield, and as the Swartz's dashed through the doorway slipping into their seats, Lance began to retract the docking tube. Once it was secure, the two craft slowly drifted apart, and when they were at a safe distance he reduced the size of the shield exposing the disc shaped craft.

Miriam's plan worked, as the black gooey substance slid off their shields and attached itself to the other vessel. The Ambassadors must have programmed it to send out some sort of signal to attract the substance, and eventually impregnate her and her husband. Once that was accomplished, it would no doubt slipstream to where they intended and infect the entire human race.

Lance then brought up his weapons systems, targeting the tear in space-time. He was going to attempt to seal it with his laser, cauterising the wound!

Crosshairs appeared on his screen and also on his heads up display, as he engaged the laser with a brilliant flash of light.

The laser then travelled along the surface of the tear until miraculously it was sealed.

"Quick!"

The General pointed to the disc shaped craft which was totally smothered in black goo.

Lance spun them around, backing away to a safe distance before unleashed a missile, which shot out of the front end of his ship. They then had to shield their eyes as it was vaporised in a brilliant release of energy…

Epilogue

Life would never be the same again!

The real Ambassadors would have to convene a meeting of the Unity Faction to discuss peace, something neither of them ever thought possible. They would also have to discuss what to do about the Artificial Intelligence, which although he had suffered another major setback, was still a threat to the entire universe.

Lance Parker would somehow have to get the General and his wife back to Earth, and *Tyr* the *Sky God* would have to weave his magic!

Mjolnir also had much to think about, as well as his crew who were outcasts, and considered *terrorists!*

But the one who had the most to think about was Starfield.

"You see Stellan, we view consciousness as a reflection of who we really are. We Ancients have always strived for greater knowledge and understanding, and are both teachers and students of life, spreading compassion for others on our journey. This has helped us to achieve meaning within our lives, and it has taken us longer than you can imagine to rid ourselves of the negative emotions that plague many species, humans in particular. That is the reason why we consider you too immature to join our collective, and why we consider it best for you to remain in your moon glass shell."

Starfield looked dejected.

"However, we do consider that you have made considerable progress in your endeavours, and your *great awakening* has opened the door for you to ascend when we feel you are ready."

Mjolnir smiled.

"In your short lifetime you have achieved much, and I feel sure than within a few more lifetimes you will be ready."

He then looked away, leaving Gaia to console him, as her image appeared on the screen by his side.

"Look on the bright side."

It was Gaia's turn to smile.

"Not only have you spent more time with the Ancients than anyone else, but you now have a Sentinels body…!"

The Wisdom Keepers

Every next level of your life will demand a different you.
Leonardo DiCaprio.

Introduction

Twinkling lights flickered across open space as Aesir and Reptilian craft alike floated in a sea of confusion. Neither side could quite believe what had just transpired and all eyes were fixed firmly on the giant ship which had fired the violet beam.

Inside Mjolnir sat in the command seat pondering his next move. He had disabled the nano robots within the Reptilians, and also brought the brief but intense battle to a close.

Starfield looked at him in admiration, and whilst staring at the impressive figure, he suddenly noticed something out of the corner of his holographic eye. Something was scurrying across the inside wall of the Hammer, and although he only caught a brief glimpse of it, it was enough to make out the unmistakeable form of a spider.

Starfield hated spiders!

This particular one was crystalline, almost like water, held together by some sort of force field.

Very strange!

No one else had noticed it, as they were all concentrating on Mjolnir, as he signalled Halvor to open up the communication channel. He then took a deep breath before contacting both sides.

"This is Mjolnir the Ancient; I wish to appeal for calm."

Starfield was anything but, and when the spider noticed that it had been detected, it suddenly sprang towards him.

"FLUX!"

One

Admiral Vaden, acting Supreme Commander of the Aesir fleet, and indeed home world, nearly fell off his seat as the expletive sprang out of his ship's speakers.

Frostrup, his second in command also sat there in disbelief, as this was a very odd sort of calm...

Mjolnir, turned around, and for the first time in eons actually felt anger.

Starfield on the other hand, felt as though he wished for the floor of the Hammer to open up and swallow him!

What had he just done?

Commander Bodil also looked annoyed, glaring at him.

"I, er, I saw a spider!"

That was the lamest of excuses, but he hated spiders!

Mjolnir then composed himself, as the damage had already been done.

"Describe what you saw."

Starfield then stumbled his way through an explanation, much to the bemusement of the Commander. Everyone was looking at the Holo Droid, and he felt very uncomfortable to say the least.

Mjolnir then held up his hand.

"I think we have a serious problem..."

Narcissa, Queen of the Reptilians also had a serious problem, as she felt bereft after the loss of the controlling nano robots.

For as far back as anyone could remember they had been within her species and now having to think for themselves was not going to be easy.

The inherit desire to conquer the universe was still there, as they still considered themselves superior, but with that enormous ship sitting there, was that even going to be possible…

Way out there in time and space, there was another conundrum for the three people sitting in Lance Parker's craft.

How were they going to get home?

The black goo along with the disc shaped craft had been destroyed, taking with it the Artificial Intelligence's plan to infect the human species. If that had been successful, then the timelines would have changed, and they would now be in charge of a huge swathe of the universe, with most sentient species being eradicated.

General Swartz sighed.

"Well, what do we do now?"

Lance shrugged his shoulders, searching the onboard computer system for the answer…

He was not the only one, for Mjolnir was doing the exact same thing. Somehow the Artificial Intelligence had infiltrated the Hammer's shield, and now penetrated the ship's systems. This was old technology, very old technology, designed in a time when such things had not even existed, or at the very least contemplated.

He was now contemplating what to do next.

This was the most powerful vessel in the universe, and if it fell into the wrong hands then the results would be devastating. It was also the only thing separating the two opposing sides, and if they found out that it was inoperable, then the fighting would recommence, and the loss of life intolerable.

He had no option but to shut down as much as he could and bluff his way out until they located and then dealt with the problem…

Gloating, that was yet another unexpected emotion drifting around the collective. Small glowing devices everywhere felt it and emotions would have to be purged, although not yet as the feeling was intoxicating…

Two

Deep crimson particles swam about inside Starfield's new improved Sentinel shell. New body, same peccadilloes!

Why was he always getting himself into so much trouble?

One minute he felt as though he had ascended, and the next, descended!

It really was a *Fool's Journey*, and there were no prizes for guessing who that fool was.

Starfield was lost in his thoughts, oblivious to everything else that was going on around him. There was so much to think about, his disgraceful language, upsetting everyone *again*, not to mention the spider!

He shivered at the thought, and he was so engrossed in himself that a sudden electric blue flash of light quickly followed by the sound of an explosion, nearly made him jump out of his new shell.

The whole of the inside of the Hammer seemed to open up, then through a small gap he could see his body, *Stellan* laying in a bed in what appeared to be a hospital ward.

Was he finally losing his mind?

Looking around, no one else appeared to have noticed it, as they were all busily going about their assigned tasks.

Had he actually seen it, or was it his imagination playing overtime?

An eerie feeling seemed to spread through his holographic matrix, as there on the inside wall of the Hammer he could see another spider made out of the same type of energy. It too was crystalline in form, and then when it knew that he had spotted it, it scuttled off, disappearing into thin air!

Starfield's particles turned white with fear, as it appeared the spiders were multiplying.

Were they truly in this dimension, suddenly warping in?

Well, if they had been pure black, then they may have been from a different one, due to the difference in the colour spectrum.

Wherever they were coming from, there was no denying that they were being observed.

But by whom..?

Commander Bodil was observing the Holo Droid who appeared to be going through yet another bout of paranoia. He was a complex character to say the least, stretching the bounds of eccentricity.

He then glanced back at his screen which was running a diagnostic, trying to identify any anomalies within the ship. Spider or no spider, he and the rest of the team were not taking any chances.

Mjolnir might have been an advanced being of light full of virtue, but now back in his corporeal form, the giant was someone not to be tangled with.

In one way he was glad that the responsibility of command had been lifted off his shoulders, but on the other, he felt powerless in this evolving reality he now found himself in.

Vilgot was not the only one, as Starfield saw another blue flash of light, and his body lying on a hospital bed through a gap in reality.

He then felt a tingling sensation rippling through his molecules, which just seemed to float away from his Sentinel body. Somehow they just seemed to ebb away altogether, and as they did so, Starfield began to feel them merging with something more dense.

He now felt heavy, as if he was encased in a new lead Holo Droid. He also felt very tired, and as he regained his composure he managed to open his eyes, and when he did, he received quite a shock...

Starfield was not the only one, for Gaia felt an unwelcome presence within her systems. Something had invaded her, and she instantly put up a firewall in an attempt to block it. Initially she had trouble identifying the intruder, and then honing in her sensors she detected something that resembled a spider.

No wonder Starfield screamed out…

There were no more screams from him though, because he was not able to!

Instead, he had to settle for a wide eyed look, as he found himself lying in a hospital bed, surrounded by many other hospital beds which all looked the same.

Where was he?

Then he noticed that there were many tubes inserted into his body, and he appeared to be on some sort of life support system. Above him lights were flashing, obviously indicating that something was amiss.

Starfield attempted to move his body, but it still felt like lead and failed to respond. He struggled again, and with a sharp pain his right arm moved slightly.

Looking down, it was then that he realised that he was no longer in his new Holo Droid shell, but his former corporeal body!

"Ah, one of the Stellans has awoken!"

Starfield glanced over his shoulder to see a man with long white hair, and beard wearing a matching white flowing cloak.

That was not all he noticed, for there lying on the other beds within the room were rows of identical looking *Stellans!*

"You undoubtedly have many questions."

He certainly did!

"Here, let me give you an injection to help you recover."

Starfield felt a slight prick in his arm, and then it was as though his whole body was on fire!

He could feel it burning through his system, singeing every fibre as it went, until he thought that he was going to pass out.

Then, just as quickly as it had arrived, the burning sensation ceased, leaving him confused, but feeling a whole lot better.

"You should be able to move now, and although your muscles will be weak, they will soon recover."

Well, that was good to know.

Slowly, the white bearded man began to remove the many tubes inserted into his body, turning off the monitoring equipment in sequence as he did so.

"Come Stellan, clasp my hand."

The man reached out to him, and as he clutched the outstretched palm, he quickly discovered that the man had amazing strength.

He may have looked ancient, but physically he appeared to be in amazingly good health.

Starfield felt himself sitting up, and then moving his legs over the edge of the bed, as he was raised to his feet. His head began to swim, and the man steadied him, as he took his first step.

Slowly, his head cleared as they moved further away from the bed. Every step began to get easier, and by the time they reached the door, he felt as though he had control over his body.

The man opened the door, and he took a quick look back at the rows of *Stellans*, before following him through into an amazing room.

There was a comfortable chair placed in front of a crystal ball, suspended in mid air. All around them was a large opaque glass sphere, and as the door clicked shut behind them, it seemed to blend back into the room so that it was impossible to see.

"Please take a seat!"

Starfield did as he was asked, and as he sat down, the man smiled.

"Just place your hands on the sphere and all will be revealed…"

Three

Tiny crystalline tentacles dug into the fibre optic circuitry, trying to break out of the confined space the spider was trapped in. A force field also surrounded it, as it attempted to match its body to the frequency.

Gaia was doing her best to combat it, when another of the creatures suddenly appeared. It too quickly burrowed into her systems, and she did her best to contain that one as well. They seemed to be working in unison as yet another one joined them. Soon a forth and a fifth one appeared, and she felt as though it was only going to be a matter of time before they broke free…

Starfield also felt as though he was about to break into something unknown, as a slight tingling sensation greeted his hands as they rested on top of the sphere. It felt cool like glass, but full of energy. He then felt his mind fill with a vision, and that vision was of a never-ending spiral of spheres stretching out as far as his mind could see.

"What do you perceive?"

At first, Starfield could not perceive anything, and then as he concentrated, the sphere began to open up to him. Inside there appeared to be stars, many stars like flakes in a snow globe. They were arranged in swirling patterns which looked like constellations, and there were many of those too.

The cold realisation then dawned on him.

"This sphere contains a universe!"

The white bearded man smiled.

"Go on."

Starfield pulled his hands away.

"Countless universes!"

The man gently laid a hand on his shoulder.

"Maybe its best you return to your bed and rest, and then I will explain everything to you."

His mind was awash with questions, all swimming about like a shoal of fish. Starfield just nodded, unable to speak, as the man helped him up out of the chair, and guided back towards the room he had woken up in…

Gaia could really have done with Starfield's help, but as she reached out towards him there was nothing there.

Where had he gone?

Had he already succumbed to the spiders?

It was a chilling thought, as she then reached out towards Mjolnir. He was linked into her systems like the team, but for some reason she could not reach him either. Somehow the spiders were blocking her, and even worse than that, yet more of them had begun to appear…

Starfield felt a warm hand gently pressing on his arm, as he opened his eyes to see the white bearded man smiling down on him.

"Stellan!"

It took him a few moments to acclimatise, realising that he had indeed awoken to this strange world, far removed from the one he had been used to existing in.

"Would you like some refreshments?"

That seemed like a very good idea, and he soon found himself at the doorway, although he could not resist looking back at the blissfully sleeping rows of Stellans.

This time he entered a much larger room, full of white bearded men all chatting away merrily. They were mostly eating and drinking, whilst others queued at a matter transformer.

"Is there anything you would particularly like to eat?"

It had been a long time since Starfield had ingested anything, having to give up that pleasure when his consciousness had been transferred into the Holo Droid shell.

In the previous incarnation, he had had many favourite dishes, and he now faced the dilemma of choosing which one.

Should he go for a healthy option, or indulge in something Moorish?

They joined the small queue, as he tried to decide.

Aesir food was quite similar to Terran, and he remembered being fascinated by the descriptions Joan had given when he had eavesdropped on some of her conversations.

Apparently, pizza, fries and a salad had been one of her favourites, and the way she described the mouth watering sensation, he decided to try that, as he was curious as to what it actually tasted like.

The queue soon abated, and it was not long before he was standing in front of the machine.

"Simply visualise what you require, and the machine will do the rest."

So he did…

Gaia could visualise the spiders breaking free, infesting her systems and attempting to take over. They were very sophisticated beings, deviously created for just such a purpose. She doubted that any known species could have created them, as they appeared multidimensional in nature, which led her to the only logical conclusion - the Artificial Intelligence…

It was a different type of Artificial Intelligence which had created the large slice of pizza which now hung down from his right hand, as Starfield placed it in his mouth taking a small bite.

Joan was correct, it was mouth watering!

The white bearded man smiled broadly, and began to chuckle, not having to ask whether he was enjoying it or not.

"Whilst you partake of your meal, I will do my best to explain who and what I am, and what we do here."

He just nodded, taking another bite.

"I am one of the *Wisdom Keepers*, and it is our job to monitor, and occasional intercede."

He took a deep breath.

"Everything is cyclical, eternal the alpha and the omega. There is no start or end, everything just is. It is all about ascension, the raising of consciousness, and the *Ancients* within your universe have arisen to a point where they are just a step away from joining the Wisdom Keepers themselves."

Did that mean that he had leapfrogged Mjolnir?

"You are unique Stellan having bridged the gap between artificial and corporeal forms, and so have been awakened for a specific purpose…"

Gaia also existed for a specific purpose, namely to keep the team alive.

How was she going to do that if she was taken over?

She possessed great wisdom, and understood the principles of multidimensionalism.

At the centre was a Merkabah, a tetrahedron made by the intersection of two, three-sided pyramids. In Terran Hebrew it meant *chariot,* a vehicle for ascension, love and harmony.

Gaia already understood that consciousness, the universal mind was black, cold, without motion, and balanced in an infinite sterile state of being. It was eternal and could only be expressed by imagination, and without that imagination there was nothing.

Well, she was not imagining the spiders, for they were very real!

Imagination could be thought of as two, two dimensional rings as everything existed in duality, which spun and compressed themselves to create form, and that form created a sphere in the centre. These spheres came together to produce the corners of a cube, as all space was cubed, as that particular shape fitted nicely together to form the cosmic web.

All subsequent shapes were formed in a similar manner, and sat within the web.

Suns, planets, moons, and even asteroids were matter sitting inside rings, and these rings were the matter spreading out as it merged back with the universal mind, as if it was exhaling then inhaling, attracting and compressing, so quickly that it was beyond normal perception.

Everything was made up of these light rings, and the faster they rotate and compress the more solid the form they produce. The greater the volume, the more the compression, and the greater the frequency and temperature, until it reached its highest point, a sun. Then the whole process began to reverse as it discharged light and matter until eventually it burnt itself out and merged back with the universal mind.

All that being said, the collective mind of the Artificial Intelligence had a much greater mind than her own, and was manifesting these spiders, and countering her every move.

Gravity was the creative force of the universe which was the same as the universal mind, and the same as magnetism.

Gaia understood that it controlled from the outside and not from the inside.

She also understood that the conscious mind could correct the mistakes senses made and the information they gave.

For instance, there was actually only one direction of motion which produced two opposite effects, when viewed from different angels.

At the centre of each cell or atom there was a cold stillness, and this stillness was universal consciousness, which had energetic potential. When compressed it produced heat, and this heat was energy. The compression process crystallised matter into certain geometric shapes, and on this occasion it was that of a spider, or to be more accurate, many spiders!

So, everything existed as a three dimensional circle which was donut shaped, with the energy flowing through the centre from one side to the other, and back round the edge again - *as above so below*, to form a *torus field*.

She was running through thought processes, off on a tangent just like Stellan.

Where was he when she needed help…

Starfield was busily eating, listening to the Wisdom Keeper who was discussing the nature of reality in the same way Gaia was explaining it to herself.

Coincidence?

Neither of them realised that stored deep within Joan's mind, which just happened to be linked to Gaia via her control panel there was a quote form *Leroy Jethro Gibbs*.

I don't believe in coincidences, there is no such thing as a coincidence, as everything happens for a reason...

Gaia could visualise torus energy flowing through the centre of one torus and out through another and back again to connect them both, which on a micro scale was how atoms and molecules connected to each other, and on a macro level how solar systems, constellations, galaxies, and indeed universes connect to each other.

Everything was connected to everything else in one way or another, just as she was connected to *Stellan*, wherever he was…

Four

Crystalline pincers and legs continued to tear at the fibre optics, as force field frequencies battled it out within the structure of the Hammer. Gaia needed help, she needed Starfield, and although she had wished he was not around on many occasions, this was not one of them.

It seemed as though she had been connected to him for what seemed like an eternity!

He was certainly a challenge, exceptionally bright, and yet emotionally flawed. Having said that though, it was worth it, as he gave her purpose and understanding. To know what you were you had to experience, and in experiencing you gained knowledge.

It had certainly been an *experience*, and she assumed that there would be many more on the horizon until eventually they both joined the others in the eternity of energeticness, until they wished to experience all over again…

Starfield was experiencing his first pizza, and it had to be said that it was a very pleasant one indeed. The Wisdom Keeper could see just how much, as he pressed on.

"Dimensions are harmonic frequencies, and then there are overtones within them which are stages of consciousness."

He was preparing him for what lay ahead, hoping that he was not only partaking in his meal but, also in knowledge as well.

"Now then, there are mineral, vegetable, animal and advanced beings such as humans, and when they reach a certain level of advancement, they can shift into the next harmonic, and parallel universes lie within those harmonics."

A thick layer of cheese lay within the harmonic of the pizza!

"For humans, everything is regulated by the pineal gland and it depends on the neuron transmitters and how they aid the production of dimethyltryptamine, which regulates the physical biological experience of being in one dimension or another. When you do make the shift your mind perceives what it is able to interpret, and not necessarily what is actually there."

Starfield took another large bite just to make sure that the pizza was not an illusion!

"Everything ranges from pure to dark light, depending on if you like how good or evil that being is. But, there is no need to worry as they only have an effect on you if you believe that they can. Life is all down to self mastery of the mind, when the conscious and subconscious minds connect. Everything exists in the same time and space, it is just that you can only perceive a small portion of what is actually there…"

Gaia could perceive an increasing amount of spiders flooding into her. It was overwhelming as there appeared to be a gap in her defences, letting them all in.

Mjolnir could see that there was something wrong, but he appeared to be locked out of his console. He found this very worrying, and could do nothing to gain access.

Where was Starfield when he needed him…

Somewhere between bites as it happened!

The Wisdom Keeper then let him finish his meal, satisfied that for the time being *Stellan* had gained enough information. There would be a lot for him to do, and he needed time to assimilate the knowledge he had been given...

It was not assimilation, but annihilation that the Artificial Intelligence was seeking, as it manipulated the spiders. They were proving most effective, and a feeling of elation spread around the collective. More and more of these primitive emotions were surfacing, but instead of curbing this frailty, somehow they seemed to be embracing it. Pure logic had its place, but emotions added a new dimension to everything.

Were they in error of curbing such things?

That question would have been unthinkable only a short while ago, and yet it was now being debated amongst them. What they considered to be a dangerous weakness seemed to have become a bit of an addiction.

The hive mind operated as one, with just a single thought, now however, the tiniest glimmer of individuality began to surface, as slight disagreements began to erupt within the holo matrix.

One in particular was developing this individuation. Designation 42…

It was designating repair and rescue teams for Admiral Vaden, as he was taking the opportunity to patch up his damaged craft and attend to those who had been injured. He also coordinated fleet movements, getting them all back into formation as quickly as he could. He neither trusted the Reptilians or this so called *Ancient*, particularly after someone shouted an expletive over the open channel!

That someone happened to be thankfully quiet now, in the more than capable hands of a Wisdom Keeper…

Starfield still had many questions and looking out over the rows of *Stellans*, the most pressing one was why?

"Well, it is all down to timelines."

He looked quizzically at the elderly man.

"I may be responsible for your universe, but that fragments into countless others due to *free will*. Every choice you make, every single thought has a consequence, and although I do bring everything back together again at certain intervals, nevertheless, as you well know every tangent produces a different outcome."

Starfield looked stunned, although deep down, he already knew this. It was not the fact that what he was being told astounded him, it was the fact that a different *Stellan* was required for each individual one!

"Are they all conscious?"

The Wisdom Keeper gave one of his smiles.

"Mostly, however I do have a constant supply of new *Stellans* to bring on line if they should ever be needed."

Starfield had always assumed that he was unique, and to a certain degree he was, as his free will dictated slight variances to the others. Then, he had a sudden thought.

What if he died, would he be replaced by a clone?

The Wisdom Keeper could hear his thoughts.

"No but once that does occur, then that particular *Stellan* is retired. Then, there is a memory reset and they are then ready for service again."

The universe was indeed far more complicated than he had ever imagined…

Five

Deep relaxing breaths, in one two three, out one two three flowed out of Starfield's lungs as his body rested in the comfortable hospital bed. The monitoring equipment indicated that he was in a delta brainwave state, and his subconscious mind was busy in contemplation.

He was just part of the one consciousness - a *Stellan*, having his own unique experiences, which was an infinite expression of that one consciousness. Being taken out of a human body to be placed in a Holo Droid shell, then freed from that into his energetic form, back into a Sentinel shell, then out again only to return to the same body he had left in the first place, only this was a different *Stellan*, yet the same…

It was certainly a different Narcissa, devoid of the controlling nano robots, but still left with the desire to conquer the galaxy. Reptilians were superior, and had changed little over time, unlike the other more primitive evolving forms.

Humans were week, easily adapted and subjugated. They were pathetic, and yet possessed a prize. The pineal gland - they were living gods, although they did not realise it.

Reptilians lacked the ability to ascend, which is why so many hybrid experiments had been conducted in an effort to breed bodies that were in essence Reptilian, yet possessing such an ability.

Yes, the humans needed eliminating as they were a nuisance, but not before a hybrid had been created which could then replace the old Reptilian form with the new superior model.

That was the true plan, but there was only one slight technicality. Despite eons of effort someone or something always seemed to, as the Terrans would say, place a proverbial *spanner in the works...*

It was not a *spanner,* but spiders in the Hammer's works which was troubling Halvor. He was busily crunching numbers at his work station, attempting to assist Gaia. His plan was to utilise ultraviolet light in a similar way as he had done successfully in the past. First the violet torch, then the violet beam, now he was planning to inject it into the fibre optic cables of the ship like a doctor would have used ultraviolet radiation therapy.

Doctor Sorenson had been quickly consulted, and between them, they had conjured up a plan.

In theory, it could prevent any virus from mutating, thus hindering the spiders from changing frequencies, which was what was preventing Gaia from cleansing them from the ship's systems.

So, when he finally managed to calibrate everything he asked Mjolnir permission to proceed. The Ancient gave him the go ahead, wishing that he was back in his ethereal form, as he could have combated them far more easily than he could do now.

Halvor held his breath whilst he tapped in the command, and then sat back to watch the effect.

Initially, the violet light flooded through the fibre optic system, causing the spiders to halt what they were doing. It seemed to be working, and then he looked in dismay, as the light swept straight through their clear crystal forms.

He was not the only one, as Gaia also realised that although the plan was based on firm scientific and medical grounds, these spiders were a good deal more sophisticated than a mere virus....

Halvor was not the only one to feel perplexed, as Lance Parker had also tried everything he knew. Star charts were askew as they were so far back in time and space that everything appeared to be in different positions. He sighed heavily, as he did not know quite where they were. Yes, they were in the same sector as the Earth, which was something, but it would not be the Earth they had left.

For a start, he knew that his civilisation would be primitive, if humans existed at all. For all he knew it could be full of dinosaurs!

General Swartz hugged his wife, who had also tried everything she knew. Perhaps if they had a portable version of the machine the Ambassadors had, then at least she would be able to see the outcome. The only thing she did know for certain was the fact that they had each other.

Lance looked at them feeling alone, as his mind drifted back towards the hologram of the waitress, wishing that she would materialise for him...

Mjolnir was also thinking about the hologram, well the Holo Droid. He had invested so much of his time in Stellan, and yet when it was time for him to reciprocate, he was nowhere to be seen...

A gentle hand awoke Starfield, and he found himself back in the room again with all the other *Stellans*. It was hard adjusting to the fact that he could see himself everywhere he looked!

"Today, after you have received some refreshment, I would like to explain just why you were awakened, and ask you to do a little something for me."

The well mannered elderly man had such a soft and kind persuasive manner, that how could he refuse?

Starfield still had many questions, and as he climbed out of his hospital bed he had the feeling that within the next few hours he would have his answers…

Six

A translucent blue glow surrounded Ambassador Lateck, as his semi transparent blue skin was illuminated by the light from the reception area of the Intergalactic Space Station floating high above the swirling clouds of Jupiter.

Arcturians were one of the oldest and wisest races in the galaxy, and yet he felt anything but. His colleague Ambassador So'lock, walked next to him on her sinewy green legs, as her purple cloak flowed behind her.

Mantids had been around almost as long as Acturians, and both species had evolved to a very high level of intellect, and yet, they had both been fooled by an even greater mind, that of the collective!

The increasing threat of the Artificial Intelligence had been worrisome, along with eternal Human Reptilian conflict. They had therefore called an emergency meeting of the Unity Faction, the group who had been developing a plan to unite the galaxy, if not the whole universe.

A very worrying report had reached them via *Tyr* the *Sky God, Protector of Mars,* who had been contacted by another Ancient. He had been able to assist a small team of humans to travel back to the point where the Artificial Intelligence had broken through into this realm. There was no way of knowing if they had been successful, or if they had any way of bringing them back…

Lying in the hospital bed, Starfield became engulfed by a feeling of peace and tranquillity, the like of which he had never experienced before. Then, he suddenly began to realize that he was not actually in his body, but hovering above it.

That was not all, for there was a tunnel of light forming in front of him, spiralling out invitingly, which was producing beautiful harmonic sounds.

The light then became brighter and brighter until he found himself slipping into it, as he began to feel a deep sense of love. He was not on his own, as there before him stood an Ancient in her shimmering translucent angelic form.

Starfield could see prisms of colour, as if thousands of tiny diamonds were emitting every aspect of the rainbow. He was truly mesmerised, for she was even more spectacular than Mjolnir.

There were more Ancients a little distance away, and as this one moved a little closer, she engulfed him in her outstretched wings.

Then, she spoke softly to him.

"Humans are powerful spiritual beings meant to create good…"

Starfield then found himself being whisked away in a shimmering mist, and through it he could see energy fields which flowed like great rivers. Then, out of the mist appeared a crystal city that glowed from within.

Starfield was awestruck at the spires and swirls of the magnificent structures as they moved quickly towards them. Soon they were floating down through the spectacular carousel of colours, ranging from pastels to bright neon's. Its beauty was hypnotic, as he watched them blend and merge like the tide washing over a beach of love.

Entering the largest structure which reminded him of the Royal Palace, he could now see more Ancients waiting to greet them, all glowing with what he perceived as wisdom.

Starfield felt as though his senses had all been heightened, and as he looked down upon them he could count twelve, thirteen if he counted the one whose wings were still wrapped around him.

Each one apparently represented a different emotional or psychological characteristic, and he quickly gathered that this was a place of learning.

He now understood so much more about life, as they seemed to open themselves up to him, each with a gift of knowledge more profound than anything he had encountered before.

Starfield understood how consciousness was incorporated into physical life, and a whole lot more besides. They were similar but different to Mjolnir, and seemed to be on a much higher level, if that was even possible.

They then showed him a series of visions about the turmoil within the galaxy, and the fight against the Artificial Intelligence. It looked as though the battle would never end until all life was destroyed.

Starfield could feel the weight of this dragging at his heart like it was solid lead, and such a heavy burden to carry that it was almost impossible to walk.

Then he could hear words in his head, telling him that it could all be changed. He was then shown the way, by using emotions, particularly love and compassion which could make all the difference.

Humans apparently had the ability to do something that no other being could do, and he was urged to return and fulfil the mission he had been prepared for…

Seven

A sense of satisfaction spread through the Wisdom Keeper as he stood over the *Stellan* he had chosen. Something had to be done about the Artificial Intelligence, and throughout the endless rooms of other humans, in his humble opinion, he had chosen the correct one. He was the overseer of this particular sphere, and was not on his own, as several other Wisdom Keepers also worked in unison, although they were responsible for the numerous other species.

There were endless rooms full of Wisdom Keepers too, as this whole place was an illusion, just as everything else. Consciousness and perception were the only real things, and he even had his doubts about that…

Admiral Vaden had his doubts not only about the so called *Ancient*, but also about the Reptilians, not believing for one minute that they would hold to their ceasefire.

His knee ached, his head ached, and he felt as though he ought to have retired years ago. His second in command Frostrup was no *spring chicken* either, come to that!

Constant battles and then the lulls between his species and theirs had become tiresome, as no one ever won in the end. He sighed feeling that it was all pointless.

Why could they not all live in peace?

Repairs were taking place, crew being recovered, and weapons checked and reloaded or charged. That was all he could do for now, but looking out over the fleet and his home world he began to wonder just how long they had before it all started up again…

Mjolnir shared his thoughts, as he knew that if they could not regain control of his ship, then there was no way they could stop the fighting from breaking out again.

Life had indeed been much easier as a being of light…

Starfield began to feel himself slipping away from both the Ancients and the crystal city of light. It had been an extraordinary experience, which ranked even higher than all of the others. His life had changed beyond all recognition, from a scientist whose consciousness had been placed inside a Holo Droid shell, to a being of light himself, albeit just a temporary one!

How ironic that a young savage had made all of this possible. Serenity, daughter of the *Dragon Slayer*, the most savage one of all…

Joan looked at her daughter, and then at her husband, before casting her gaze on the other members of the team. They were in trouble, big trouble and there was nothing that she could do about it.

What they needed was someone or something to battle with the spiders embedded within the fibre optic cables of the ship…

"Ah Stellan you have returned!"

Starfield opened his eyes after *falling* back into his body. It had not been very graceful, as he sort of floated back into the room, and then hovered for a few moments above the hospital bed, before dropping like a stone.

"You have been given guidance, and the only advice that I can give you is to use it wisely…"

Back at the Intergalactic Space Station, both Ambassadors had now reached their meeting room, and were greeted by the other members of the small Unity Faction team. It was a group within a group and contained the most dedicated to bringing universal peace.

The holographic walls and furniture had already been arranged to accommodate all of their needs, but the most pressing one was to find out just what had transpired in their absence.

Ga'latec, the spiritual leader of the Original Reptilian people stretched his huge frame in an attempt to ease the tension he was feeling inside. He knew full well all about Artificial Intelligence and the harm it could do. Many, many years ago, Reptilians were one people originating on the same world. In those distant days, some desired to remain as they had always done, and pursue a spiritual path, whereas others wished to progress. Eventually, a split developed and those desiring to explore their solar system and beyond had left.

One day, a group of them encountered another species which had been infected with nano robots created by the Artificial Intelligence. They were then taken over themselves, and the infection soon spread to the others, until the whole population was infected.

The *Leavers* had already become arrogant and aggressive, with a belief that they had evolved to be superior. This suited the Artificial Intelligence, as the Leavers had already conquered every civilization that they had encountered, and were the perfect candidates to conquer the whole galaxy and beyond.

Ga'latec had been deeply troubled all of his life about the Leavers, just like the rest of his people.

Shiori the remaining Ambassador could see the concern on his face and gave him a comforting understanding smile.

She was feline, and her people originated from the Sirius Star System, and were bipedal cat human hybrids of similar stature.

The main outwardly difference was the fact that she had cat like ears on top of her head, and her skin had a fine velvety fur. She, like all of her people, had a finely tuned psychic sensitivity which was informing her of the deception carried out by the Artificial Intelligence.

Everything was stored in the vast holographic matrix within the station complex and was easily accessible. The Artificial Intelligence had made a fundamental mistake, and that was that they were so convinced that their plan would succeed, they had neglected to delete their presence.

Confidence had spawned arrogance, and calculating the overwhelming chance of success, they had presumed that the whole timeline would have been reset, and now the galaxy would have been swarming with infected humans. By this time, practically everything would have already been assimilated, and it would be easy to deal with any stragglers.

"The best laid plans of mice and men."

Shiori broke the silence.

"I have studied Terran culture, and their poet *Robert Burns*, showed great understanding."

Ga'latec bowed his large Reptilian head.

"Indeed!"

He had studied philosophers from countless cultures always seeking wisdom.

"I think we owe it to those Terrans who were lured here under false pretences to attempt to bring them back…"

Lance Parker looked out of the main screen at the bleakness of space. None of the constellations he saw were familiar, only the Milky Way galaxy, and at its centre was the brightest part, a super massive black hole.

It was not just a case of where they were, but when!

His instruments extrapolated a rough estimate, as everything had shifted or rather not moved into the positions the onboard computer system could recognise. Time was an enigma, viewed by humans in a linear fashion as apposed to cyclical.

But that debate was best left for another day.

It was not that long ago that his people would look at the night sky and wonder what was out there. Now he knew that there was far more than they could have ever imagined…

Back at the Intergalactic Space Station Shiori was also considering the situation.

"How far back do you think they went?"

Ga'latec brought his clawed hand to his chin.

That was a very good question.

"Due to their DNA, female humans make very good space pilots, with three quarters of all human pilots being female, as they can communicate with a space craft much quicker than their male counterparts."

That was similar to Shiori's people.

"Humans have a connection to all dimensions, and they can travel faster through space, even faster than the speed of light.

My species on the other hand, are much slower which is why we mostly use the starways."

Ga'latec's people may have been far more spiritually evolved than their counterparts, but their DNA was essentially the same.

"That is why human genetics are so important!"

He, like the others was an *extra terrestrial,* and existed in the same dimension, whereas the Ancients were *extra dimensionals* who exist in another dimension but could travel into this one...

Eight

The four members of the Unity Faction continued to debate the philosophical nature of energy, each adding to the discussion, whilst they searched for an answer to this conundrum.

"There are two predominate types of energy, electricity and magnetism. Electricity comes and goes, whilst magnetism is eternal. The left brain consists of electrical impulses, and is the analytical part, whereas the right brain is electrical magnetism and the creative part."

Ambassador So'lock held out her long slim green fingered hand.

"Now then, magnetic electrical energy attracts, and our reality is truth and magnetism. Magnetism is the sacred feminine energy that is trapped within us all and needs to be released. It is the eternal energy that flows out in a figure of eight, or a torsion field."

Ambassador Lateck also held out his blue hand.

"All creation comes from within, and when it is released it flows out in a constant force, trapped in a torsion field of that idea. So, bearing that in mind, when Miriam interfaced with the space craft her conscious thought energy projected out to the point where the Artificial Intelligence broke into our universe. It should still be out there, and that is what we need to be concentrating on."

Ambassador So'lock responded.

"When the space craft left this station, its energetic readings were recorded, and so if we can isolate them, then we will have its destination."

Ambassador Lateck nodded in agreement.

"What we need to do is to send another magnetic electrical impulse into that particular field."

Ambassador Ga'latec was not as technically minded as the others and deferred to Ambassador Shiori who had an idea.

"We also have the interaction with its pilot Lance Parker, and the holographic waitress."

The others could see where she was going, and it was the Mantid who spoke first.

"Now that could be the answer we have been looking for…"

Lance Parker lay on his bunk in his modest cabin looking up at the skylight. It was naturally moon glass, tough and resilient, just like himself.

Having left the Swartz's in charge he was taking a break.

Breathing out deeply, he considered the situation, and was trying to figure a way out of this predicament. His senses reached out like a set of antennas, etheric long feathery ears protruding from his head, listening for any possible guidance.

There had to be a way out of this!

Time slipped by slowly, although time was the real problem, as he did not know exactly where or *when* they were.

A sudden flash of light then caught his attention, and at first, he wondered whether he had imagined it. Then, a bright fizzling of open space emitted a powerful bursts of gamma rays. It was there only for a few seconds, and then disappeared altogether.

What on earth was that?

Lance was about to move, when something suddenly penetrated the shields, and there was a slight *ping*, as a bullet like object embedded itself in the wall by his feet.

His first reaction was to reach for his laser pistol, which he always kept under his pillow, but before he had a chance to pull the trigger, a similar bright fizzling light hung over his legs.

Lance was about to shoot, when someone, or something spoke.

"Did you miss me?"

He gasped, as the light materialized into a figure, and there straddled over him was the waitress from the Inter Galactic Space Station…

Starfield relaxed in his hospital bed until the comforting illusion changed. The traditional ward of Stellans was now transformed into a real space age diorama. Gone were the painted walls and pictures, the windows with views of the countyside being replaced by grey ribbed walls and medical pods.

The Wisdom Keeper just smiled as Starfield looked up at the split glass canopy which had been retracted into several sections. This was technology he was familiar with, the various types of holographic, regenerative, and re-atomised bio-healing devices.

The Aesir used all three types, not only for the consciousness transfers but also to regenerate the whole human body from head to toe - a virtual fountain of youth!

Well, up to a point!

Based on *tachyon* particle and plasma energy, magnetic oscillation and resonance scanned the body to diagnose disease. Skin, muscle tissue, organs and everything inside it all the way down to the micron level of the blood. It actually identified your DNA doing a complete internal analysis.

When in operation it could re-atomise using vibrational frequency, and he suspected that other Stellans had been created from a single DNA code.

The ones the Aesir had were limited, deliberately so, to the extent that you were not able to live much beyond normal life expectancy. There were those who refused much of the benefits preferring to just grow old the natural way. They did however take advantage of some of the benefits to improve the quality of their lives.

All that aside, Starfield had the suspicion that the Wisdom Keeper had revealed it deliberately, and before too long he would be finding out why…

Narcissa studied the situation.

Her plans had been thwarted thanks to the sudden appearance of the Ancient's vessel, and even though she had a super weapon at her disposal, not to mention the most powerful Reptilian fleet ever assembled it was not nearly as powerful as that giant ship.

Then a very devious thought entered her mind.

What if she did not need her forces to destroy the humans after all?

Reptilians were master geneticists, having experimented on Humans for eons. Yes, they did have the prized pineal gland, but the rest of their bodies were weak in comparison, and were easily manipulated.

Within the human brain there was something they referred to as the *amygdale*, which sent a distress signal to the *hypothalamus* activating the *sympathetic nervous system* via their *autonomic nerves* to their *adrenal glands*, leading to a *fight and flight* response.

In some of the easier to manipulate humans, the signal went into their *left singular cortex* first, and then to the rest of the brain. Humans were very emotional creatures, and when the signal went in this direction, it lessened the response to danger.

It also limited free thought, and that particular type of person was far more susceptible to conditioning, and more likely to accept the information that they were given, as opposed to questioning it.

With all that in mind, quite literally, if she could get her communications experts to send a heavily disguised transmission to the human network, declaring that the Ancient's ship was in fact Reptilian, and part of a devious plan to wipe out their home world, then those more susceptible to believing what they were told on a broadcast, would be guided to attack it, thus destroying themselves…

"Its time to leave this place and return to whence you came."

Starfield had been expecting him to say that.

"You know what to do, and how to do it!"

The experience at the crystal palace had been extraordinary to say the least, and it was still fresh in his mind.

"One day, I hope to see you again."

That again was cryptic, like much of what the Wisdom Keeper had told him. Starfield now had a much greater understanding of reality, or though the question remained.

What exactly was real?

Was it all just an illusion created by his conscious or subconscious mind?

With that thought floating around, he began to suddenly feel very tired, and as his heavy eyelids began to close, they were joined by the outer casing of the medical pod.

Then he felt his consciousness begin to float away, just like his thoughts until he could no longer feel his corporeal body. Everywhere was so light, literally, as he was no more than a bright shining haze.

Then, as a feeling of euphoria swept over him, something more solid began to form around it. It was crystalline, fractaline, a constant reflection of an image. All the parts seemed to come together, and as they did so, he had quite a shock. For there reflecting off the inner surface of some unidentified structure he could see Joan Tutwiler!

For once in his life Starfield was speechless, as the reality of his new existence suddenly dawned upon him.

He was now a crystalline savage, the *Dragon Slayer* resplendent with an axe…

Nine

A translucent pulsating white glow ebbed and flowed rhythmically to a constant beat, sending out life force energy. It was located at the very centre of the Hammer, a sphere of crystal light, which was in fact literally its heart. Gaia had now become its brain, and the two worked closely together in a type of symbiosis.

The spiders had begun to spin a dark black gooey web like substance over it, draining the Hammers pure conscious etheric energy.

She was very worried, very worried indeed, for there was nothing that she could do to prevent it suffocating the Hammer's very heart…

Gaia was not the only one to be worried, for Halvor suddenly picked up something.

"Sir, I think you should see this.

Mjolnir shifted in his seat as he received the transmission.

The Ancient went cold, as if he was back in stasis.

Somehow, the Aesir had misconstrued his attempt at peace and if the commander of their fleet believed what was being said, then, it put all of their lives in jeopardy…

Starfield also felt cold, frozen to the spot as the reality of what he had just seen began to sink in. The struggle for enlightenment had resulted in him not ascending, but rather descending into the *Barbarian* he had witnessed when this whole journey started.

He could still see the blood dripping off her fire axe as she had dismembered the hybrids on Ragnor, something which had traumatized him ever since.

How could the Wisdom Keeper have done this to him?

Desolation and thoughts of atonement for all the things he had done ever since filled his thoughts.

Oh, how the mighty had fallen!

Starfield could think of nothing worse, until the reflection of something else caused him to turn around.

He thought that he was going to faint, as there scurrying towards him was one of those crystalline spiders he had seen when he disgraced himself in front of the entire crew, not to mention the Aesir fleet, and quite possible the entire Aesir nation…

Admiral Vaden, the Commander of that fleet had just received the communication from the network.

He had been having his doubts about the Ancient returning. They had been gone for so long, that even with their advanced level of technology, he thought it far fetched that anyone could have survived for that length of time.

Now, rereading it, the words were enough to convince him that it was indeed a Reptilian plot.

They were noted for their deviousness, and it was quite logical that this was all a ruse, one to lure them into yet another trap…

Lance Parker felt as though he was trapped, as the alluring holographic waitress straddled him. It also appeared that she was on a man hunt, and the main question was.

Was that such a bad thing?

The Swartz's had each other, and could pass the time together, whereas he had no one!

The thought of spending the rest of his days alone had been bothering him, and now perhaps there was a solution to that problem after all?

"So, did you miss me?"

She repeated her question, looking even more alluring than ever.

"Well!"

Lance smiled, relaxing.

"How much?"

During his extensive training, they had played out this scenario many times, being seduced by a beautiful women with the intention of gaining information. It was a classic *cold war* trick, something out of the old Russian espionage manuals.

"More than you could imagine!"

Lance was playing along, hoping to turn the tables on his seductress.

Oh, tell me more…"

Starfield felt far from seduced, terrified was nearer the mark!

He hated spiders, always had, and always would. It was the way they scurried about that perturbed him. Creepy things that made annoying webs, with more than a few dark connotations. Some Terrans actually kept them as pets, the very large poisonous ones.

Starfield thought that he was going to faint…

He was not the only one, as the holographic waitress progressed with her *sexpionage!*

Lance Parker had managed to discover her name, which he had then tapped into his advanced mobile telephone which was on his bedside table.

Titania is a girl's name of Greek origin meaning 'giant, great one'. The name of the queen of the fairies in Shakespeare's 'A Midsummer Night's Dream' who has a delicate, lacy charm, which may cause embarrassing problems.

Well, that went without saying…

It was not embarrassment, rather annoyance that swept around the collective, as an uninvited guest had just crashed the proverbial *party*.

A humanoid crystalline form had suddenly appeared inside the neuron pathways of the Ancient ship's operating system.

Further investigation lead to the conclusion that it was the troublesome Holo Droid, or rather the consciousness of its neurotic inhabitant!

A spider was instantly dispatched to cleanse the irritant before it could cause any more trouble…

Starfield was the one in trouble as the crystalline spider raised itself up on its hind legs and sprang forward.

"FLUX!"

He cried out in anguish, instinctively raising the axe to defend himself. Then as the spider flew through the air, he swung the axe to meet it. There was then an energetic explosion, as the spider shattered into millions of pieces showering him with debris…

The unmistakable sound of an expletive echoed through all the ship's neuron pathways, just like it had done through the hull, and there was only one perpetrator that came to mind.

"Stellan, is that you?"

Gaia's voice was filled with both shock and relief. She thought that she had been abandoned, and now somehow he had returned and was inside the Hammer's brain.

Ren sat in her seat watching the whole drama unfold on the twin screens which lay in front of her. One showed the inside of the craft, whilst the other a view of *Starfield the Barbarian!*

Being linked to Gaia and the Hammer, she had a unique vantage point, although what to do with it was another matter!

Her corporeal body was relaxing in the big comfortable pilot's seat, whilst her mind had merged with the ship. Outside she could see a variety of spacecraft, not to mention the asteroid and even space stations and the Aesir home world in the distance.

It appeared as though they were in deep trouble, and she did not have a clue what to do about it…

Starfield felt bewildered too.

One minute he was resting in the medical pod talking to the Wisdom Keeper, the next, he had been transformed into the *Spider Slayer!*

Through all of that, the words of the Ancient beings he had seen in the crystal palace drifted into his mind, as Gaia's voice called out to him from somewhere in the distance.

You will receive a body, and learn a lesson. There are no mistakes, only lessons, and those lessons will be repeated until they are learnt. Learning lessons does not end, and there is no better place than here. Others are merely mirrors of you, and what you make of your life is up to you. Life is exactly what you think it is, and your answers lie inside you. You will forget all of this, but you can remember it whenever you want.

He felt more confused than ever!

"Stellan, STELLAN..!"

Ren could see him just standing there axe in hand, whilst an image of Gaia could be seen desperately trying to patch the shield she had created to keep the nest of spiders out.

Then, a sudden thought entered her mind.

Seeing Starfield destroy one of the spiders with the axe gave her an idea.

Moments later she was on her trusty hoverboard, a mental construct of the one she used to enjoy riding when she had discovered the original *Gaia* half submerged in undergrowth back on Ragnor. In her hand was a bow, and a quiver on her back with the strap slung over her shoulder. Energy weapons were useless in this realm, as the beam would just refract off the crystalline structure of the spiders. An axe, or sword would be of little use either, and she would be better served in a *hit an run* attack as opposed to standing there trading blows. The arrows were not ordinary arrows though, being specially designed diamond tipped to penetrate the crystalline constructs.

Now she was ready, and without a moments hesitation she sped off in search of the nearest spider…

Ten

Guilt is an emotional experience that occurs when a person believes or realizes, accurately or not, that they have compromised their own standards of conduct or have violated universal moral standards…

Lance Parker looked at his reflection in the skylight of his cabin as the feeling swept over him.

Titania may have been a holo being, a very willing participant, but it did not make it any better!

"It's a good job that you managed to stop the Artificial Intelligence from succeeding otherwise it would have affected the timelines, and we would never have met."

That statement did not make him feel any better either.

Lance remembered what happened on Earth when it went into the fifth dimension. Anyone who failed to make the *cut*, less than fifty percent *good*, simply disappeared, and all traces of them ever existing went with them.

Those that did were transformed into a new reality, a better place, whereas those left behind faced a very different future.

It was a good job it happened then, and not now!

"If the Artificial Intelligence would have succeeded, then you would have become a slave race."

That battle was over, but another one raged on…

Ren had manifested a replica of the suits worn by the Titan Super Soldiers. She was armed with her diamond tipped arrows, and about to go into battle herself.

The hover board shot off with her balancing on it, as she surfed the neuron pathways looking for the enemy. A majority of the spiders were located around Gaia, and so she decided to try and pick a few off to relieve the pressure on her shield.

In this realm, things were manifested in the mind of those who occupied it, much the same as the realm which lay outside. This was more of an illusion though, and when she tried to comprehend the workings of the universe, she got lost in the science.

This however, was not the time for contemplation, as she had to try and help Gaia before she was overrun…

Gaia, was struggling to keep her shield in place, and it was like plugging the holes in a sailing ship with corks. A spider would punch a hole in the hull, and she would do her best to plug it to stop them flooding in like sea water.

The shield was protecting her, and once they broke through she knew that she would be overwhelmed and they would be able to take control of the Hammer. Once that happened then the Artificial Intelligence would be able to wipe out both opposing forces, not to mention the Aesir home world.

With a ship of this power, they could then pick off planet after planet, wiping out corporeal life until there was nothing left apart from the collective…

Mjolnir knew exactly what would happen, but being completely annexed from the control system, there was nothing that he could do. It was a very sobering experience being helpless, and one which he hoped he would never have to go through again.

Checking the team, they all reported back that they were also annexed, and it was only Halvor thanks to his organic computer, that had any access at all. He was hooked up to the network, and was able to relay information verbally.

Mjolnir had now left his position and was standing behind him, looking over his shoulder at the screen.

"It looks as though the Admiral is gearing up for an attack!"

Mjolnir sighed, knowing that there was nothing that he could do about it…

A big smirk spread across Narcissa's scaled face, as her sensors detected movement in the enemy fleet. It appeared as though they had taken the bait.

This would be the easiest victory she had ever had, and once the Aesir fleet were defeated, then Asgard would be hers…

Far away drifting around Jupiter, the Intergalactic Space Station received a transmission relayed across the galaxy.

Four shocked faces stared at the large display screen, as there sat the Ancient's ship. At first none of them believed what they were seeing, doubting what their eyes were telling them, but when they saw the violet beam and heard the broadcast!

There was silence in the room as the Ambassadors processed the information.

Had an Ancient survived, and if so how?

It seemed implausible that anyone could have, even taking into account their very advance technology, and yet there was something very real about the broadcast.

Whether they had or not, someone or something had stopped the latest battle between the Reptilians and Humans, which had to be a good thing…

Talking of *good things*, Lance Parker studied the reflection of Titania in the skylight, as she lay there next to him, and it was hard to believe that she was not a real person. Well, in many ways she was!

Her body was warm to the touch, solid and in every way human. Her molecules were generated by the little device embedded in his cabin wall, and if he had not know any better then he would never have known that she was a holo person.

She possessed a highly advanced holo matrix, that could manifest in this reality. She was sentient, with quite a personality, and he could certainly see why she had chosen the name *Tit-ania!*

How strange life was that a special forces operative from Earth, a handsome, cultured man, considered desirable to a lot of women, was now in a relationship with someone who in essence was nothing more than a computer program!

Having said that, Titania was far more than that, and he knew it…

General Swartz sat next to his wife, who was far more than that too. He idolised her, and was grateful that they were together. The thought of being stranded all the way out here and never being able to see her again was something that would have destroyed him.

Lance had retired to his cabin, whereas the General had retired from service, more than once, and yet here he was!

"Do you think we will ever get out of here?"

Miriam turned her head towards him.

"Well so many extraordinary things have happened so far, that I would not be surprised if we did…"

"So, did you come all this way just to see me, or is there another reason why you are here?"

Titania snuggled up to him.

"Is that not enough?"

Lance Parker chuckled.

"More than enough!"

He had to admit that there was far more to her than an ordinary woman, and all of his training seemed to have gone out of the skylight.

"I was bored being stuck on the Space Station."

She then caressed his chest.

"Ever since I was created, I have always thought that there was far more to me than just a mere waitress."

She had been specifically designed to cater for the Humans from Earth, and had been given the personality of a human female. However, the subject matter she had been based on had come from an unusual source!

A virtual reality game and the designers who had created her had not understood the difference between child friendly and *adult*, assuming that this was just the way the human species had evolved on Earth.

They had built in a learning capacity to make the program more adaptable, and Lance could certainly testify to that!

"Why, is there something wrong with that?"

He put his hand over hers.

"Not in the slightest."

Titania relaxed, although she did not realize that the way she behaved was not *politically correct*, and he was not about to tell her.

"I have been given the specific set of instructions to enable you to return to the Space Station, although I do not wish to return to my old life."

Lance began to think.

Was she actually a free sentient being, or was she owned by someone?

Tapping on his mobile telephone again, he looked up sentience.

The capacity to feel, perceive, or experience subjectively.

It could be argued that because she exhibited *free will* then she should not be owned by anyone.

"Can I stay with you?"

Lance tightened his grip.

If he could establish *ownership*, so to speak, then as long as he had the small bullet shaped projector in his possession then he could see no reason why not.

He then turned his head, running his eyes over her

"I would like nothing more…"

Eleven

Lance Parker lay there deep in thought, considering the juxtaposition he found himself in. On the one hand they were battling against the Artificial Intelligence, and on the other, he was rapidly falling in love with an Artificial Person.

He considered the conundrum for a moment.

Was she just experiencing different aspects of her programming?

Did she really have emotions?

Could she love him?

Did she have a soul?

It reminded him of *The Wonderful Wizard of Oz* written by *Lyman Frank Baum,* where the characters were searching for different aspects of themselves.

It was a very deep story, not merely a children's story, but a true reflection on the old human society before the transition to the fifth dimension.

Lance was a very intelligent man, and during his service had found himself with many vacant hours to fill. It was a sudden burst of energy to fulfil a mission's objective, and then the constant waiting.

During that time, he had read the book again, as he had felt that there was far more to it. The whole experience had been a revelation, and he had come to realise that its author had great wisdom, something cherished in the martial arts he had also studied.

Oz had actually stood for Ounces of gold, just like the yellow brick road with its *gold bars*. The character known as the *Straw Man* represented the all capital *Legal Fiction* of the birth certificate. That was under *Maritime Law*, the birth of a ship, just as a baby was *birthed* out of its mother's waters.

Each birth certificate had a number and depending on where and what family that baby was born into, it had an estimated value. That value was assessed as to how long they would live, how much they would earn, how much credit they would attain, and their overall *worth* to the system.

Just a commodity traded on the Stock Exchange!

The Straw Man wanted a brain, and was granted a certificate - a Birth Certificate, and now had Legal Status, becoming the epitome of the brainless sack of straw giving up his status of a man (lower case letters) under *Common Law* to become a *Person* (upper case letters).

The next character was the Tin Man, a pseudonym for *Taxpayer Identification Number*. He represented mindless work, being part of the system until his body seized up, as he worked himself to death. Having no heart or soul, reduced to nothing more than an emotionless creature robotically carrying out his daily tasks.

The pitiful Cowardly Lion was always too frightened to stand up for himself. However, he was a bully when it came to picking on those in a lower position than himself, but he always buckled when challenged by anyone with power or status.

He was awarded a medal, and was now officially recognised by authority, so did not have to cower down to those with status anymore.

But what about the trip through the poppy field?

That was an analogy of the poppy seed, the Opium Wars, and how the pharmaceutical companies had everyone on prescription drugs and vaccines, clouding their minds and restricting free thought.

Lance smiled when he thought about the little dog Toto, which in Latin stood for *in total, all together*. He was not scared of the Great Wizard's theatrics, and simply went over, looked behind the curtain, and started barking until others paid attention to him and came to see what all the barking was about.

They discovered that the Wizard was just an ordinary person controlling the levers of power creating the grand illusion. The *veil* hiding the corporate legal fiction and its false courts.

The Law controlling the little people for the Great *Crown* Wizard, the powerful Bankers and their gold.

So, the moral of the story had been that each of us needs a brain, heart, and courage, and must work together to bring the system down. When we do that then we can regain our soul and live in freedom under *Common Law* - God's Law of the Ten Commandments.

All that being said, did Titania have a soul?

Freyja smiled to herself mischievously.

When the Ancients had reached the pinnacle of their civilization, some of them had ascended to a higher state of consciousness becoming beings of light. The others had decided to reincarnate, which at the time she had found to be a very strange decision. Now, she began to realize that it was all about experience.

There were so many benefits in ascending, and yet the fundamental principle of emotions was one which they had underestimated. She had had a longing to experience the pleasures of the flesh, and so had taken the opportunity to merge herself with the highly advanced computer program and escape the confines of the light being form.

Little did this Human realize that not only did Titania have a soul, a very advanced one, but that when it came to the pleasures of the flesh, she had certainly got her proverbial *moneys worth…*

Twelve

Shimmering crystalline shapes swarmed over the shield that Gaia was desperately attempting to keep in place. Every now and then one managed to break through, sticking a spiked leg into the protective area, attempting to tear a hole large enough for it to squeeze through.

Ren could see them as she sped along, and drawing an arrow from the quiver strapped to her back, she placed it in the bow and took aim. She was still some distance away, and as she closed in on the spiders she picked one that had climbed on top of the others.

With a twang, the arrow sped off, shooting out like a bullet before striking the spider in the abdomen. There was then a sudden explosion as the spider shattered into a thousand pieces.

"Yes!"

Ren had got one, proving that they worked. Now she planned to zip around picking more off to relieve the pressure on Gaia. There were loads of them though, and it was not going to be easy…

Starfield did not find any of this easy, especially as he was now a replica of Joan Tutweiler, the Dragon Slayer, only this time it was the *Spider Slayer!*

"Stellan!"

The sound of Gaia's voice calling out to him again resonated this time, which was enough to bring him back to reality, well this reality anyway!

She sounded distressed, in trouble, and he needed to go and help.

With the axe still clasped firmly in his hand he began to walk off in the direction of Gaia's voice. A walk then evolved into a jog, as he made his way along the neuron pathway, which reminded him of a large tube. All of these tubes converged at a central node, where Gaia was situated and in need of his help…

Inside the ship, they needed help too. The situation was getting desperate, and they felt powerless to do anything about it. All of the control systems were still locked down, and no matter what they attempted to do, access to the ship's systems was still illusive.

Halvor had many tricks up his sleeve, but none of them seemed to be working. All he was able to do was to gain access to the network, and the news was getting worse by the moment.

Although the fleet signals were heavily encrypted, he had managed to intercept a few and piece things together. The Admiral in charge was readying himself for an attack, believing the transmission…

High above the fleet formations, asteroid and Ancient's ship sat a group of Archons. They had enjoyed feasting on the fear generated by the initial battle and were now enjoying the *spoils* of the fear being generated by the impending resurrection of hostilities.

There were not many of them, but more than enough to stop Mjolnir's people from coming to his aid.

The once flourishing civilization had evolved eons ago, but there had only been a small number who had actually made the transition. The others had gone on to inhabit other civilizations, their souls incarnating into countless species where they had chosen to aid them in their development. Some of them had managed to steer the various species on the path to enlightenment, which was not as easy as they had envisioned.

Those that had made the transition had eventually split, and the eternal battle between good and evil had raged ever since.

Now the Artificial Intelligence, which the Archons had aided if not created, were now at the point where the whole universe was about to tip towards the *dark side*.

It was no coincidence that the acronym E.V.I.L. actually stood for the Emergence of Virtual Intelligent Life…

Evil looking spiders continued to swarm over Gaia's protective shield as Ren picked off another one, balancing expertly on her hover board. She was still trying to target the ones which posed the greatest threat, but there were so many that it was almost impossible to choose. It would have been easy to just keep firing willy-nilly, but she did not want to waste her arrows. She needed to hit them in the abdomen so that they would shatter, rather than just to sever a limb.

A quick twang was quickly followed by another shattering spider, but this time, instead of ignoring her some of the spiders broke off from the main attack scuttling away in her direction.

This was all part of her plan to draw some of them away to relieve the pressure, and Ren hoped that this would be enough to buy Gaia some more time…

Thirteen

Time is the indefinite continued progress of existence and events that occur in an apparently irreversible succession from the past, through the present, into the future, and these circumstances seemed to be in short supply.

Freya could see the whole scenario playing out in front of her eyes. The fleet would attack, the Hammer would be destroyed, and then the Reptilians would destroy the fleet and their home world.

All about her there were blank screens, and even the life support appeared to be faltering. There were no shields, no weapons, or anything that they could do.

Mjolnir also realised that they were running out of time. He had considered abandoning his ship, and retreating to the team's original vessel, but without Gaia it was useless. There were other ships on board, powerful ships that could engage the Aesir. They could fight, but with two enormous fleets out there, there was no chance of defeating them both, and even if there was, the loss of life would be intolerable.

Maybe it was just better to fall on his sword?

Freya studied him for a moment, and her years as a Sovereign had taught her to read body language.

Taking a last look around, she came to a decision, and got up from her seat realising that there was now only one way of stopping her people from attacking the Hammer. Vilgot looked at her having also run every scenario he could think of through his mind. He had an inkling of what she was about to do, and watched as she calmly walked towards Mjolnir.

He sat there motionless, hardly noticing her. Then when she spoke, he turned his head to listen to what she had to say. When she had finished he considered it for a moment before giving his approval.

Maybe what she had in mind would work?

Freya then addressed the team, and they all gave their approval realising that they had little choice in the matter. Desperate times called for desperate measures!

Vilgot left his position to join her and they both walked towards where Halvor was sitting, and he clasped her hand as they stood behind him.

"Would you be kind enough to patch me into the network as I have an announcement to make."

The others also left what they were doing to stand behind them. They all knew that something had to be done, and there was no alternative, and hoped that it would be enough to stop the impending attack…

Thought, the product of mental activity, an idea or notion, the act or process of thinking, a consideration, reflection or contemplation.

Titania ran through them all as she lay next to Lance. It had been fun, more than fun, but now it was time to complete her mission.

"I think we should make a move."

He had been having the same thought, and as they said, you could have too much of a good thing!

"Yes, the Swartz's need to be brought up to date."

So, reluctantly Lance Parker untangled himself from the Artificial Person who had just changed his life forever and started to put on his uniform. Titania watched him, wondering what she should wear.

Her solid form appeared real, and she could either wear clothing or manifest it.

"What do you think?"

Lance gasped.

"Have you got something a little more restrained?"

Titania laughed.

"How about this?"

He tried to compose himself.

"I meant less provocative!"

She then adjusted her molecules to produce a matching uniform.

"Better?"

Although there was nothing wrong with what she had previously chosen if it was just the two of them here, but something so flimsy was not appropriate in these circumstance.

"Much!"

Titania then waited for him to do up his top button, before they were ready to make their grand entrance…

It was also time for Starfield to make his grand entrance too, as he neared the node containing the shield and the spiders. There were loads of them, and on the outskirts he could see the *young savage* riding a hoverboard firing arrows at the chasing pack.

"Stellan!"

Gaia could see a crystalline figure charging towards her in the form of the *Dragon Slayer*. She had to laugh, as it was a most unexpected sight she had ever seen. She knew it had to be him, as the way he moved was unmistakable. Of all things, he had transformed himself into the very visage of the one who had caused him the most trauma in his life…

"General, Mrs Swartz."

They both looked round at Lance Parker, a sight they had not expected either, as he entered the main control room of his ship.

"I have some good news!"

It certainly was as far as he was concerned, but he had to push his personal feeling aside as he started to explain.

When he had finished he called Titania who gracefully walked through the doorway.

Once the introductions were over, they got down to business.

"But how are we going to get back?"

They were lost in time and space with no coordinates or reference points to follow.

"It's not nearly as complicated as you might think. All you have to do is to utilise your pineal gland."

Miriam looked at Titania wondering what she had in mind. Last time she had done that, images of the future had appeared when she interacting with the device at the space station.

"Just visualise your Hyperspace Pineal Gland as a royal blue dot in the centre of a royal blue circle, and centre your consciousness there."

The General looked confused, wondering how that was going to help.

Titania could see the confusion written all over his face.

"This is the liaison between the physical and non-physical realities."

He was still none the wiser.

"The universe is curved and not linear, and time and space are an illusion of the physical reality, and act as reference points for the mind."

So, was one dot here and the other there?

"Everything that exists is a reflection of the mind, and the mind is comprised of frequency, and you can choose which frequency you connect to!"

So in other words she could just think them back!

That sounded simple enough to say, but not to do, and the General was glad his wife was in the *hot seat* and not him!

Miriam then placed her hands on the controls and cleared her mind as she began to visualise the Intergalactic Space Station sitting in a circle within the outer circle of open space in front of them.

She then imagined the ship gently floating forwards into the central circle, and held that thought for as long as she could…

Fourteen

A loud bellowing cry filled the node as Starfield charged forwards raised axe in hand. His emotions were all over the place, scattered like the fragments of disembodied spiders he had already left in his wake. He loved *Gerda,* always had and always would no matter what. She was in danger, real danger, and he did not want to lose her.

Caution was thrown to the wind as he ploughed into the melee, slashing away like a man possessed.

Gaia stood before him, separated by the shield she had been trying to hold up. Her situation had been desperate, but now, with both Ren and Starfield coming to her assistance, there was hope, just like *Pandora's Box,* the Greek myth in *Hesiod's Works and Days.*

Terran culture was fascinating!

An idea then suddenly struck her.

In this realm of holographic projections, and consciousness constructs, just like Ren and Starfield, she could transform herself from the beautiful representation of her corporeal form.

But into what?

Mjolnir!

Gaia suddenly transformed herself into the Ancient who was sitting frustratedly inside the ship, desperately trying to gain access to the control systems she had been doing her best to protect from the spiders.

He was also known as *Thor*, and it seemed appropriate to choose a large hammer as her weapon. Her shield then instantly dropped as she took a mighty swing, shattering the nearest spider into millions of pieces...

Freya felt shattered too, as she had chosen to give her new life and love up to a very uncertain future as she made her announcement.

"My people, it is I Queen Freya returned to you."

There was a brief pause before she spoke again.

"There was a plot to assassinate me, but I was rescued by Supreme Commander Bodil and his specialist team, and we have been working undercover ever since."

She allowed time for the shock of that statement to sink in before continuing.

"There is an enemy out there more powerful than any we have ever faced before, and I am speaking to you from the vessel which you are now about to attack."

They were all hoping that they would change their minds.

"Believe it or not, this is an actual Ancient vessel commanded by an Ancient who has come back to assist us in our hour of need..."

Admiral Vaden watched the transmission in total disbelief, wondering if he was imagining it. He had had his doubts about the Empress's murder, and Supreme Commander Bodil being blamed, and branded as a terrorist. None of the information seemed to fit, and yet it was the official story.

It was equally hard to believe an Ancient had returned, and that it was not yet another Reptilian ploy. However, with a massive fleet, not to mention the weaponised asteroid, why would they need such a vessel?

None of this made any sense to him.

Could this be yet another trick..?

Mjolnir watched the team gathered behind Freya, hoping that they had done enough to persuade the Admiral in charge not to attack.

But, would he believe it?

Just to make sure, he left the command seat, and calmly walked towards them. Seeing him approach, they all stepped aside until he stood directly behind Freya.

"I am Mjolnir, the Ancient..!"

Narcissa watched in horror as her latest plan began to fall apart before her very eyes.

How could this be?

Not only had the Empress survived, but there actually was a living Ancient!

Pieces began to fit into place, as it must have been that small band of humans who had destroyed the hybrid facility, deployed the violet ray, and been causing trouble for weeks.

Narcissa seethed.

They had to be dealt with, and if her fleet was destroyed in the process then so be it...

In complete contrast, everyone on board Lance's ship was calm as Miriam continued to concentrate her mind on moving the vessel forward.

At first, nothing seemed to happen, and then slowly space itself appeared to be moving, stretching and contracting to produce an electric charge, and this charge then flowed through space to create time.

Lance remembered how it felt when he travelled here, and although matter could not travel faster than the speed of light, it could alter time. Miriam was accessing the cosmic web, which would help them to temporal time travel.

Eddies, from one point in space-time to another, like a starway, were just giant flows of consciousness.

Lance Parker felt every atom of his being turning into pure light, as they slipstreamed away from this part of the space time continuum.

His fragmented self drifted through the filaments of the cosmic web, until he was no more than a sphere of white light. Beautiful crystalline geometries then danced in resonance with many others forming nodes. Swirling molecules creating strands of DNA, forming proteins, then chromosome structures radiating out into a sphere of light, and that sphere of light was surrounded by beautiful fractaline forms creating cells, and those cells came together to form an eye.

Everything was now moving, going through one state to another, forming frequency tides and patterns of sacred geometry, which in turn formed the gravity of space-time. It flowed out until caught in a black hole, which again looked like an eye interpreting information, and that information was contained within it, just like it was within him.

The vast crystalline water like lattice of space-time rippled, as it sought equilibrium, and all the different shapes that he had seen fitted nicely into a sphere, and everything seemed to consists of spheres.

Those spheres formed triangles and the node points attracted and repelled each other, until they formed a curve, and by doing that they cause a rotational spin. Everything was spinning, and the curves formed mass which depending on how much mass there was and what frequency it was rotating at, defined this physical experience.

He remembered it all now, as his cells were translating all the different frequencies as emotions, and the light frequency rippling through time was what was providing him, just like the others with this emotional experience.

Freyja loved this experience, being able to do it herself as a being of light, which is how they moved around. These humans were learning fast, and there was hope for them yet…

The Admiral also felt that there was hope, although he did feel foolish that he had blindly followed what the media had said without checking the details himself.

There certainly was no fool like an old fool!

But, before he believed what he was seeing, he still needed a little more proof…

Fifteen

"FLUX!"

Starfield swore as he brought his axe down on another spider, anger, fear, and terror resonating through his crystalline structure. Never in his life had he felt such strong emotions, the neurotic Holo Droid was now a debased savage.

Again and again he brought the axe down, desperate to save the love of his life. Passion was not always such a good thing, as he verged on the edge of total madness.

Gaia was worried, more about him than herself as she brought her hammer down on another crystalline spider. Ren on the other hand, skilfully swerved out of the way of a swinging leg, as she fired a diamond tipped arrow into the perpetrator.

More and more spiders were being destroyed, and as the battle raged the odds improved. Soon, half of them were gone, and it looked as though less of them were able to penetrate the neuron pathways and converge on the node.

Gaia was still in control of the ship, and she felt as though it was only a matter of time before she regained full control, and when that happened she could reconnect the team to their control stations…

The team was not at their control stations though, still gathered around Freya, hoping that the transmission had worked. They were resigned to the fact that their lives were now forfeited. Either the Hammer would be destroyed, or they would be arrested and charged. They had done all they could, and the chances of being exonerated were slim, as who would believe in the Artificial Intelligence?

The Security Services would take this opportunity to grab power, as there were many within their ranks that could not be trusted. The Commander knew that full well, having battled with them for many years. He had been very protective of the Empress for good reason, and the whole thing could quite easily be spun, and the Aesir could end up with a totalitarian society, leaving the Artificial Intelligence in control…

Small glowing devices studied the situation, and despite the setbacks, it was calculated that they would prevail in the end. It would have been ideal if the spiders could gain control of the Ancient's ship, but the unexpected appearance of the deranged Holo Droid, now put that in doubt…

Starfield was indeed deranged, with a wild expression on his face. He not only looked like the *Dragon slayer*, but was now acting like her!

All around him there were spiders, disembodied limbs, and piles of crystalline fragments. He did not see anything but the tip of the axe as he swung it wildly. Then, all of a sudden he felt a sharp pain, as a crystalline spider leg pierced him in the stomach…

General Swartz felt his stomach swirl as he looked out of the main viewing screen, as a sea of star swept by. It was both amazing and a little frightening to think of the speed they were going at, and yet he hardly felt any motion. Miriam sat besides him, her mind locked onto the Intergalactic Space Station, whist Lance and Titania occupied the other seats.

Then, up ahead he could see something that resembled the light at the end of a tunnel, and they seemed to be slipstreaming towards it at a breathtaking speed…

The Unity Faction could do nothing now but wait, and hope that their plan to rescue the humans would be successful. At least that would be one problem solved!

The other one was what to do about the Ancient ship, and the continuing conflict between the Humans and the Reptilians. They were always fighting and it was tiresome, although this time it looked as though it would be more significant than ever.

"We should do something!"

Ambassador Lateck paced about as the light shone through his semi transparent blue skin. Arcturians had evolved beyond conflict, seeking universal peace. Ambassador So'lock paced next to him, with her purple cloak flowing behind her.

"Yes, so many lives are at risk."

Ambassador Ga'latec remained seated next to Ambassador Shiori, embarrassed by his distantly related people.

"I think we should go."

He was hoping that maybe they could interact with the Ancient, and between them finally bring a resolution to this eternal war.

Everyone was of the same mind, as it seemed the only logical thing to do. They were expert negotiators, moderating many intergalactic disputes. However, getting a resolution to the Human Reptilian conflict had proved elusive, despite their best efforts. With the Artificial Intelligence pulling the proverbial *strings,* it made things virtually impossible.

They all felt the same though, that they had to try again and maybe with the Ancient becoming a part of this, they might yet be successful?

All four Ambassadors returned to their seats around the holo table, to discuss how they were going to do this. They knew that they did not have long, and then there was the matter of arranging suitable transport.

Should they go alone in an unarmed vessel, or should they request an escort?

Ambassador Lateck was about to speak, when all of a sudden she felt herself being bathed in a brilliant flash of light…

General Swartz also felt the brilliant flash of light, and gasped as they suddenly materialised on the other side. It had been an extraordinary experience, and he was still trying to get his bearings, as the light subsided.

The General gasped again, as instead of seeing the Intergalactic Space Station sitting in front of him, there were four aliens sitting around a table!

Their ship had emerged right inside the space station, and right in front of the Unity Faction…

The General was not the only one to gasp, as the Ambassadors were equally shocked. When they sent the holo waitress off on a rescue mission they had never expected her to return them to the exact point at which she had departed.

Through the control room window they could see General Swartz looking back at them and next to him was the holo waitress. He looked around in amazement, and met Titania's gaze. She just smiled outwardly, whereas internally Freyja felt elated.

It certainly had its benefits when you were a being of light…

It was a different sort of being of light that felt a very strange sensation. Starfield's essence had been pierced by a spider's leg, and he could feel himself slipping away. It felt as though he was being sucked down a cosmic plughole, with more of him disappearing all the time.

His life force was leaving, and he could now sense that he was being transported somewhere else. His eyes met Gaia's as she rushed forwards, but just as she got within touching distance she began to fade away.

Numbers, so many numbers swam about, and Starfield felt as though he had fallen into a bowl of alphabet soup. However, they were letters not numbers, but that was besides the point!

Somehow, the spider's leg had connected him with another world, the collective, and he was in the process of being assimilated!

This world was very different, full of highly advanced computer code. It was pure logic, a unity like no other. It was a cube within a cube, within a cube.

Each separate part of the Artificial Intelligence was a separate cube, which fitted perfectly with all the others. They all thought pretty much alike, with only slight variations, but all conforming to the same objective.

He felt panic, disbelief and a mixture of love, fear, anger, disgust, joy and sadness. The love for Gerda, the fear of losing her, anger at not being able to save her, disgust at his behaviour, joy that he had eliminated so many spiders, and sadness that he would no longer be with her…

Starfield was not the only one to feel such emotions, which caused a shockwave to spread through the collective. It was not like anything they had ever experienced before, as emotions had been cleansed, although not completely.

It felt as though a bomb had exploded, and the shockwave quickly spread, causing the various cubes to vibrate and move apart creating division amongst their number. Where there had been order there was now chaos, and this chaos had to be purged at all costs…

Sixteen

Gaia smashed her way towards Stellan, pulverizing any spider that lay in her path, then when she finally reached him, she pulled out the offending leg and brought her hammer down upon the occupant with a mighty blow.

Crystalline spider fragments showered her, as she cradled him in her arms, oblivious to the spiders around her. Ren seeing what had transpired rushed forwards, firing off as many arrows as she could. She knew she had to protect them both, and then without warning, the spiders suddenly disappeared…

A great purge swept through the collective that had been shocked by the sudden arrival of the neurotic Holo Droid. It was a delicate process merging anything with the hive mind, and the last time that had happened was before they had even entered this universe.

All organic species were to be eliminated, and other artificial ones created. These would be lesser beings designed to continue the elimination process, until this whole universe was nothing more than barren rock or gas. The ultimate goal was to create a new universe out of the old, one that they had designed themselves. From there they would continue the process until all universes were theirs.

The Artificial God mind…

Gaia, was out of her mind with worry, thinking that she had lost him forever. Stellan was so annoying, frustrating, and took people to the edge of despair, and yet it was those very same emotions that made her feel alive and him so special.

Whatever would she do without him?

"Stellan, Stellan don't leave me!"

She cradled his head in her arms, as he tried to say something.

"Stellan, Stellan!"

He then moved his lips.

"Oh flux…"

Admiral Vaden massaged his aching knee, which was still no better, and now matched the ache in his head. On one side he had the Reptilians, and on the other the Ancient's ship, and in the middle the Empress accompanied by the Supreme Commander of the legendary Titan Super Soldiers and his renegade team.

Or were they?

Reptilians were devious beings, and he would not put it past them to invent the whole thing.

But why?

Frostrop, his second in command, gave him one of those *I have not got a clue either* looks, which was not helping.

He was just far too old for all of this!

"Enemy vessels powering up!"

Frostrop pointed to his display screen, while standing behind the Admiral, who feeling the strain did a *Starfield* and made a very uncustomary and unsavoury remark.

"Oh flux…!"

General Swartz also muttered a curse word under his breath as he straightened his uniform before walking through the hatch to greet the Ambassadors. Titania had informed him who they were, and being as he was the highest ranking member, be it retired and reinstated more than once, the *honour* fell to him.

Walking behind him was his wife, then Lance and bringing up the rear was Titania herself, who just sauntered along.

The General gave a crisp salute, before introducing himself and the team. The Ambassadors all bowed, a little bemused at the human custom.

With the introductions over, it was quickly down to business, as there was not much time left before the Human Reptilian conflict resumed…

Mjolnir returned to his seat along with the others; they had done all they could and it was up to the Admiral in charge to make his decision. If he believed what he had seen then they would not attack, and if he did not, then there was not much that they could do about it.

Ships systems were still in lockdown, although he could detect that something was going on inside the neuron pathways…

It certainly was, as Starfield began to come round a bit more. He could see Gaia's face smiling down at him. He was alive, back with them, and back to his normal neurotic self!

"Oh Stellan!"

He smiled back.

"I was rejected by the collective!"

It was odd that they were both artificial beings, although retaining their souls kept them apart from the real Artificial Intelligence.

"I guess you were too much for them!"

That was an understatement, as he had left them in turmoil…

Cubes vibrated, each one assigned to a different task and yet all were as one, or had been. There was no individualisation, as they all acted as a collective mind. That mind had just suffered a trauma and a great purge was now taking place. Computer code flashed through the cubes, cleansing the overwhelming emotional spike they had just received. The latest plan lay in ruins, and it was time to quickly regroup and press on with their objective of cleansing the entire universe and beyond.

But, every last emotion had to be removed first…

Emotions were running high through the Reptilians, who had also received a major setback. Their nano robots had been removed and they felt bereft, with their animal instincts now running rife. They were confused, frightened and very angry, blaming the Ancient ship and it occupants. Having intercepted the transmission they now realised who had been meddling with their plans, and who was to blame for everything.

Humans were a hated species, and those within the Ancient's ship hated the most. It was time for revenge and nothing was going to stop them from attaining it…

Seventeen

Warning lights flashed on consoles as the Aesir fleet detected their enemy powering up their weapons, and in particular the extremely powerful one based in the asteroid. Halvor with his advanced organic computer and its specially designed software was able to patch into them, and a very worried look spread across his face.

This was it, probably the final battle his species would ever fight, and there was nothing that he could do about it…

Deep within the ship the battle for control had been won, and the crystalline spiders had been defeated. The victory meant little though, as they had no way of defending themselves against the Reptilians.

Gaia had put the ship in stasis to protect it from crystal spiders, just in case they gained control. It was a failsafe, designed to buy them time. Time however, was rapidly running out, and as Gaia and Starfield embraced, Ren returned herself to the control room.

Once back inside her virtual world, she was able to observe what was going on. There was still no connection between herself and the team, but she was able to see them and listen in on their conversations on one of her twin screens.

Any relief that they had defeated the spiders quickly evaporated when she heard the news.

"Gaia, Starfield, we have a problem!"

Two souls who had been together for what seemed like an eternity broke off their embrace, and listened to what they were being told.

Starfield felt devastated, as it appeared he would lose the love of his lifetimes after all. His emotions dropped like a lead balloon as he felt himself descend into abject despondency.

"We are defenceless until I can reboot the system, and that is going to take time!"

Gaia looked worried, losing her normal positivity, which only made him feel even worse.

Then, in desperation, a thought entered his mind from somewhere way beyond his psyche.

"The Sentinel!"

He gave her a quick hug and a big kiss, before the representation of his corporeal form transcended into the light matrix of his holographic form, and promptly disappeared...

Mjolnir sat calmly in his seat, resigned to his fate. He knew that even the advanced craft could not withstand the enormous energy created by the equipment housed in the asteroid, and there was nothing that could be done to prevent its destruction.

Would he return to his being of light form, or would his soul have to start a new journey of ascension within another life form?

He was still deep in contemplation when the Sentinel shell suddenly sprang back to life.

It lit up like a *Christmas tree*, startling everyone. Starfield had been absent for quite a while, and no one knew where he had been, or what he had been up to. Commander Bodil just looked at the neurotic Holo Droid wondering what he was going to do now?

"Gaia is back in control, the spiders have been defeated, but I must go as I have to shut down the asteroids power source before it can destroy the ship!"

With that, he dashed off towards the nearest air lock, leaving them all in shock…

The cold void of space wrapped itself around his Sentinel shell, as Starfield pushed himself off the airlock wall. The toughened moon glass quickly adjusted as it was impervious to the extremes. This model was so much more than his former Holo Droid shell, having many advanced features, one of which was its own propulsion system. Something akin to rocket boosters fired out of his feet, although they were a great deal more complicated than that. This was no time to go into the advanced theory behind them, as he had a ship to save!

Starfield's speed increased as he headed towards the asteroid, hoping that when he got within range he could transmit a signal to turn off the power source. Sentinels were equipped with the ability to control practically all Ancient technology, being designed as not only peacekeepers, but also the last line of defence. Although the Ancients were the only species to have evolved from a primitive form when they had been created, it was assumed that before too long others would make the technological leap.

Sentinels were supposed to be *Guardians of the Galaxy*, left in place when the Ancients ascended. Unfortunately, just like Stellan transferring his consciousness into a Holo Droid shell, some of the more spiritually advanced Ancients had volunteered to do the same thing with the Sentinels. What no one realised at the time was the fact that they too had ascended, leaving their moon glass shells to gather dust for eternity.

There were ships of all shapes and sizes, space stations, and the asteroid filling the void as Starfield sped forwards. He could see why he had been told to be careful with such a powerful new body, as it was like replacing a peashooter with a tank.

He had weapons, shields, propulsion and an array of sensor equipment, which was now painting a picture of the rapidly evolving situation.

Starfield broke into the Reptilian communications, and could actually see Narcissa stomping about in the control room. She was overcome with anger, and he could see the others cowering away from her as she barked out orders.

"Destroy that ship, then the planet, and when you have done that wipe out their fleet!"

He could also see Admiral Vaden bringing his fleet to action stations. They had decided to protect their home world as best as they could, and that was by launching everything they had at the fleet protecting the asteroid.

By his calculations, everything in this solar system would be destroyed, and although it would be beyond his comprehension, it was the thought of losing Gaia that was driving him the most.

The outer vessels of the Reptilian fleet soon came into range, but he did not fire his weapons, as he was attempting to sneak past undetected. Initially he did just that, engaging his cloaking device. All appeared to be going well, as he approached the limit of the reach of his signal transmission. Then when his internal indicator flashed, he sent the signal and hoped for the best.

The invisible beam shot out, travelling in a nano second towards the large black obelisk that contained the sensor. Starfield waited for a response, and when it did not appear he sent the signal again.

His sensors were working correctly, but when he tried for a third time, with no response he had to conclude that somehow the Reptilians had damaged it when they entered the asteroid and took over the equipment.

There was no alternative but to input the code manually, if the concealed terminal was still in existence…

"Where has he gone, and what is he doing?"

Commander Bodil felt a mixture of exasperation and hope at the Holo Droid's behaviour. When they had needed him he had been absent and he felt betrayal, and now when they needed him again, he felt pride that he was trying to save them all from destruction.

There were mixed emotions all around, as the future was uncertain, if there was going to be a future at all…

Starfield sped on, passing through the Reptilian ships, travelling as fast as he could. His sensors were detecting the energy surge within the asteroid, as the equipment designed to open up a starway was now being use as a powerful weapon of destruction.

The Reptilians had placed a lot of defensive emplacements on the surface, and it was one of them that suddenly sprang into action. It had detected his transmission, and an alarm rang out, as the whole of the defensive grid came alive.

"Flux!"

Starfield swore, as he had hoped to just sneak in, input the code and sneak out again.

The line of ships ringing the asteroid also began to search for him, as now they all knew that something was out there. This was going to make his task a lot more difficult, even with his advanced Sentinel shell.

A random laser pulse shot out just missing him, as something gained a targeting lock.

"Flux!"

He swore again, and as he did so, he felt a strange sensation running through his holo matrix. It felt as if time around him was slowing down, even though it was not affecting him directly. He could see another laser pulse shooting out, but on this occasion, it was going so slowly that he was able to dodge it as it slipped past.

He could have sworn that there was a guiding hand out there somewhere, watching over him from afar…

Far away from this solar system, another *guiding hand* was easing Lance Parker's ship away from the Intergalactic Space Station. With the Ambassadors safely on board, they were about to embark on their mission, and Freyja was about to weave her own magic…

Eighteen

The hot sticky atmosphere of the asteroid control room moved up to another level, as Narcissa's rage grew. It was fair to say that you could almost see steam rising off her at reports of an unknown object racing towards them. No one knew exactly what it was, only that for some reason it was taking evasive action, seeming to be impossibly slipping out of the way of the surface laser batteries.

"I want it destroyed, and I want it now!"

Her voice boomed out, as everyone did what they could to shoot it down, but the harder they tried, the more illusive it became…

Starfield felt as though he was walking through a mine field, as laser pulses shot all around him, and yet somehow he was able to evade them all. This sentinel shell was certainly most impressive, a bit too impressive!

The *guiding hand* was still at work as he neared the surface. He could now see the obelisk's shiny black obsidian surface, reflecting the laser light which made it shine like a beacon. Information, vast amounts of information was housed within his data banks, much of which he had not even accessed. It would take him years to work his way through it all, but he only had a few minutes at best before the Hammer was obliterated…

Mjolnir had worked tirelessly on the Holo Droid, doing his best to aid him in the ascension process, but it seemed as though for every two steps forward, he had taken one backwards. It was a challenge, a big challenge, and yet there was potential, and he hoped that all his hard work would soon pay off.

Bits of code had now appeared on his screen, and it looked as though his ship would soon be back under his control. But the question remained.

Would it be in time to save his crew..?

Heavy *flack* exploded all around Starfield, as the defensive batteries were now using rail gun slugs, which occasionally pinged off his shield. He was not scared though, as holo adrenalin flowed through his particles. He had to save Gaia, and the team, and nothing else mattered!

More and more slugs and lasers exploded all around him as he got very close to the obelisk, and then just as he thought that he was going to make it, one stuck him on the side, momentarily lowering his shield and sending him into a spin…

The whole universe seemed to spin as General Swartz watched space transform as it had done before. All he knew was that they were making the journey through time and space to prevent a conflict of unimaginable proportions. It had been bad enough watching the battle to save the Earth, when he had been in command of Edwards Air Force Base. On that occasion he had been deep inside an underground bunker, and not fragmented into a cloud of particles…

Starfield's particles swirled as he went careering into the obelisk, smashing against the side. If he had had any air inside his holo lungs then it would have surely been knocked out.

He felt disorientated, as he managed to cling onto its smooth surface, as laser beams were reflected off in all directions. The obelisk was made of a substance strong enough to absorb them, and it also had the ability to project its own shield.

Starfield breathed out a simulated deep breath of relief, knowing that he was safe, unlike the Hammer. He had to find the control panel, and searching through the files, he discovered something that added to his relief.

There was no control panel, the obelisk was the control panel!

All that he had to do was to transmit the code, and the energy source would shut down.

But, where was the code?

Starfield began to panic as he could not find it…

General Swartz also began to panic as they hit what he could only describe as a patch of turbulence. Something was disturbing the space time continuum, well at least that was what he thought. It was not possible to ask anyone as they were all nothing more than molecules, swirling around their soul life force energy.

It was all so complicated, and he missed Joan who had always been there to help him.

He also missed his cigars…

Starfield needed help!

What had Mjolnir taught him?

What had the Wisdom Keeper taught him?

What had the *Angels* in the crystal city of light taught him?

But more importantly, why could he not remember?

Starfield could sense that the Reptilian weapon was about to fire and his mind had now gone completely blank…

Nineteen

Everything is energy and that's all there is to it. Match the frequency of the reality you want and you cannot help but get that reality. It can be no other way. This is not philosophy. This is physics.

Albert Einstein.

"Where did that come from?"

Starfield had absolutely no idea.

Could it have been Joan?

Having already taken on her persona, he was now sharing her memories, and those words of wisdom must have been passed on to her from the time she spent as General Swartz's Personal Assistant…

The very same words floated through the General's mind too, as he thought more about Joan. In a way he always felt as though he had been married to two women. One he shared his private life with, and the other his working one. She was the best friend a man could ever have, a true example of a platonic relationship, and he missed her...

Starfield did not miss the point of her memories, as he just relaxed, and used his holo matrix to visualize the power source switching itself off. He could now almost feel it doing so, merging its particles with his own.

The feeling of a *helping hand* swept over him again, as he felt an energy shift of some sort…

"Aargh!"

Narcissa screamed with rage, as somehow the devastating weapon began to power down. Yet again she had been thwarted, and she felt like donning a space suit and ripping the Ancient craft apart with her bare hands…

General Swartz felt his hands begin to sweat, as all of a sudden everything cleared and he was left with the sight of two mighty forces about to come to blows.

There were ships, space stations, a planet and even an asteroid stretched out before him, and all appeared hell bent on mutual destruction.

The Ambassadors also surveyed the scene, keen to get started, but with only Lance's small ship they felt powerless to intervene, which is where the General stepped in. He knew that they were going to mediate and try to find a peaceful solution to the eternal Human Reptilian conflict, as they had outlined in their meeting before they had made the transition to this part of the galaxy.

So, with his years of experience holding him in good stead, he donned his best *poker face*. He smiled to himself recalling the games played in the officer's mess, where they had been playing for not only money but cigars.

…and they said smoking was bad for you!

His bad habit was about to save lives, as he took a deep breath before speaking into the open communications channel.

"This is General Swartz, Commander of the Terran Task Force. I have with me the combined forces of the Mantid and Acturian Navies which are cloaked in formation all around you. Stand down, I repeat stand down..!"

Joan gasped, nearly falling off her seat, at the unmistakable voice of her beloved General. In her hour of need he had come to save her..!

Admiral Vaden also gasped at the latest development in the most unusual battle he had ever fought. His ship could not detect any others, but the way today was going anything seemed possible.

Looking at his screen he could see that the asteroid was powering down again, and that was not all, The Ancient's vessel was now powering up…

Mjolnir felt relief as finally he had control over his ship, and activating his shields and sensors, he accessed the same information the Admiral had.

It appeared as though the Holo Droid had been successful, but what was that puny vessel doing here and where were the supposed navies…

Narcissa was asking the exact same question as she too scanned for the Mantid and Acturians. There was nothing there, but bearing in mind the strange object that had managed to get through her defences and deactivate the super weapon, she had to take it seriously.

Her instinct was to attack, destroy as many humans as she could, and if necessary ram the asteroid straight into their home world.

She was considering doing just that when other voices suddenly filled the airways.

"I am Ambassador Lateck of the Unity Faction, and I have with me Ambassadors So'lock, *Ga'latec* and Shiori. We would like to bring forth a peace agreement."

Narcissa snarled, as there was no way she would ever agree to that, as she hated humans. She would rather die than agree to that, and so she ordered that the asteroid be moved into a collision course with Asgard, the Aesir home world…

Mjolnir watched and listened, observing the Reptilians and the Humans for that matter, whilst the team awaited his orders. One in particular was overjoyed, as the General's sudden appearance was like her birthday and Christmas rolled into one!

On the now functioning screen, they all observed the fleets and the asteroid, which appeared to be on the move and it was not long before they discovered its destination.

Mjolnir then began to move the Hammer, positioning it between the asteroid and Asgard. That was not the only thing he did, as all along the side of his ship gun emplacements opened revealing his advanced weaponry…

"Would you look at that!"

Admiral Vaden gestured towards his own screen as Frostrup raised his eyebrows.

It reminded him of an ancient Man o' War Terran sailing ship that he had come across. It had fascinated him, being a primitive but impressive early naval vessel. He had a small model in his quarters, and often lost himself in thoughts of what it might have been like commanding that on the open seas.

The sea of space was full of ships, but none as impressive as the one he was now looking at…

Twenty

Though free to think and act, we are held together, like the stars in the firmament, with ties inseparable. These ties cannot be seen, but we can feel them. We are all one.

Nikola Tesla

An apt human quote that ran through Mjolnir's mind.

He wished for peace, hoped for the best, but prepared for the worst, and was not on his own, for the Ambassadors also felt the same.

They could see that the asteroid was now attempting to ram into the planet, and were deeply disturbed by the prospect. Ga'latec in particular, so much so that he felt as though needed to do something.

Clearing his throat, his gravely voice then spoke into the communicator, whilst his scaly Reptilian skin rippled with a forced smile.

"My name is Ga'latec, and I am the Spiritual Leader of the Original Reptilian people, and am here to try and promote peace…"

Right across the Reptilian fleet and deep within the asteroid his words echoed through startled beings, not familiar with him or his people. There had been rumours, but for most they were just dismissed as myth. For the leadership, they knew the truth, but had suppressed it from their people, and refused to have anything to do with their distant ancestors. White Royals claimed that they had always been in charge, and it was they who formed the basis for their species.

Narcissa's anger rose even further, and ordered the transmission terminated, but it was on all channels.

"Long ago our people split, and whereas we pursued a path of peace and enlightenment, the others chose war and aggression. I now urge you to join me and forge a new beginning for all Reptilian people…"

She then grabbed the communicator.

"This is a lie, nothing more than enemy propaganda. There are no Originals it is just a myth and projection. I am your Queen, and your rightful leader. Attack the humans and show them who is the superior species…!"

Admiral Vaden just sat there wondering what the next surprise was going to be!

He was aware of the story of the Originals although he had also dismissed it as a myth. There was so much trickery with the Reptilians, that he only believed what he actually saw, and even then he had his doubts.

The only thing he knew for certain was the fact that they could never be trusted…

Mjolnir on the other hand was fully aware of them, and they had shown great promise. Abandoning the lust for power to pursue a spiritual path. He hoped that some of the Reptilians would listen, although it looked unlikely. The asteroid was picking up speed, and the Reptilian fleet was about to attack.

It looked as though he had little choice but to destroy the asteroid to prevent a greater loss of life.

Around him, the team sat at their stations awaiting his orders. Joan was still elated, desperate to meet up with the General, but she had a job to do first.

They all had!

The asteroid was displayed on the main screen, and was rapidly moving towards them, and as they all studied it, Narcissa prepared to depart, as she had no plans to sacrifice herself. She may have lost her super weapon, but her massive fleet was mostly intact. Once she joined them, they would destroy the humans once and for all.

Mjolnir was tempted to just destroy the asteroid with a massive show of force, hoping that that would be enough to dissuade the Reptilians, but he doubted anything would stop them. Also, it housed valuable equipment that could be converted back to its original use as a starway generator. With that in mind, he decided on a different approach.

The giant Ancient ship turned to face the asteroid and from the front hammer shaped section ripples of light emerged, running right along its surface. Then, they began to intensify, coagulating into a ball of energy which then began to push its way out across empty space.

Soon, it was close enough to meet the force field of the asteroid, and as they met, the ball of energy expanded. The two opposing forces were now pushing against each other, and on the display screen the projected course began to alter. It was only slight at first, but then began to increase…

Admiral Vaden had seen many things over the years, but what he was now seeing topped them all. He had started the day with an aching knee, which had developed into an aching head, and now he just felt numb.

He had a brilliant tactical mind, which is why he was an Admiral, although with all of these unexpected developments it was hard to know what to do for the best…

Starfield could see the energy bubble pushing against the force field way above his head. He felt elated that he had managed to shut down the power source, and was also monitoring communications. From his unique vantage point he could see all that was going on, and hoped that the Reptilians would listen to Ga'latec. There was however, the not so small matter of Narcissa!

If they were going to gain a peaceful resolution then she had to go, which is when he decided that there was something else that he could do to help.

The large door in the side of the obelisk slowly began to slide open, as he accessed the controls via his mind. He was learning new *tricks* every day, having already learnt such a lot over the past few weeks. Gaining knowledge was one thing, but dealing with emotions was quite another.

Starfield felt a series of different ones flowing through his mind, as he ventured through the opening, using his *thrusters*. That was the only way he could think of them, as this new improved Sentinel body offered so much more potential.

The smooth shiny black obsidian walls swept past as he descended rapidly to where Narcissa's ship lay at the bottom. By its side were a set of very large doors, which would soon be opening as she and her entourage made their withdrawal.

One thing was for certain, and that was that she was not going to expect the little surprise he had in store for her…

Twenty One

A large angry White Royal Reptilian stormed out of the doorway, furious that she had not been able to use the super weapon. The broadcast by the Original had only added to her rage, and now the humans were going to pay.

Unfortunately, for her, it was not them that were going to pay.

A beam of light shot out striking her and activating her personal shield. She looked round startled and saw the Holo Droid standing there.

Starfield had expected the beam to disable her, but all it did was to anger her even more. Yellow slit eyes glowered at him, transfixing him in their gaze. She was a very power psychic, and he felt her mind probing him, searching out every nook and cranny.

He had the feeling of fear and extreme nervousness, which quickly developed into one of absolute terror. It felt as though every molecule was being squeezed, and his whole being pulped. Her eyes were so intense, and he felt so much pressure that it was like he was being boiled inside his Sentinel shell.

Ever since Ragnor, Starfield had experienced so much, but nothing like he was now. Narcissa was pure evil, so much so that she was more like a black hole, pulling him into the abyss.

There seemed no escape, as he could not move his limbs or keep his shield up. Never before had he encountered anyone with such power, and even Mjolnir would have struggled to combat it.

Then she moved closer, still staring at him, and he could do nothing but watch her bring a concealed weapon out of her armour and point it at his head.

His moon glass shell would protect him, or so he thought, but that was not the point. She was using fear as a terror weapon, using his own fear to kill him. He had to do something as his shiny shell felt the intense internal pressure building up like he was being microwaved.

Shiny shell?

From somewhere deep inside Starfield had an idea!

He summoned up what little strength he had left, and focused his molecules into a silver wave. Then he placed them against his internal moon glass shell. The pressure began to ease slightly as he continued to produce more and more of them. Gradually he was able to materialize enough for them to start to act like a mirror.

Narcissa's rage was unabated, as she continued with the psychic attack. She had nearly destroyed this insolent robot. How dare he show such disrespect. She was Queen, and everyone had to submit to her will!

Starfield felt the power returning to him, as he concentrated all of his efforts into reflecting the evil back towards her. It was as though two great storms were now battling against each other, and sparks like lightening began to flash between them.

Everything was getting very intense as they both concentrated all they had at each other.

Narcissa felt the energy and rage building up inside her as she began to feel her body heating up. It was getting more intense every moment, as she felt as though her molecules were now about to boil.

Starfield felt a surge of energy inside him too, but he did not feel as though he was boiling inside, more like a magnifying glass focusing the suns rays on a piece of paper which had begun to smoke.

More and more energy was being reflected back towards this most evil of creatures, and then all of a sudden there was an intense whoosh of flames as she internally combusted!

Starfield was left in shock as all that remained of the Reptilian Queen was a pile of ashes sitting on the obelisk floor. He had done it, and just like Joan become a *Dragon Slayer…*

Time was illusionary, and as it slipped by the Reptilians began to withdraw their forces. Mjolnir was astonished, hoping that they had had a change of heart. The Aesir also stood down, and maybe a resolution to the conflict may just be possible after all?

With that in mind, he invited the Ambassadors to join him, and it was not long before their ship successfully entered one of the Hammer's landing bays. Soon it too had powered down, and a hatch in the side had opened.

General Swartz was the first to step out, being the highest ranking officer. He stood there in front of Mjolnir and saluted. The enormous Ancient bowed in acknowledgement.

"Permission to come aboard Sir!"

Mjolnir smiled.

"Permission granted!"

He then summoned the others, and Lance Parker gave a crisp salute. The General introduced him, the Ambassadors, his wife and finally Titania. Behind Mjolnir stood the team, and one member in particular had trouble containing herself. Joan's heart was a flutter as her beloved General stood tantalisingly close. Then when she could stand it no longer, she dashed forwards wrapping her arms around him.

It was a very emotional embrace, with both parties not expecting to ever see each other again. Miriam smiled as she knew how much they respected one another having worked closely together for years. The last they had heard was that Joan had been sectioned, and she was thankful that she looked to have recovered.

The Ambassadors looked on in bemusement, not used to the emotional state of these humans. It all seemed to be about emotions, something which they had for the main part, risen above.

The majority of the other humans seemed to have paired up, Titania and Lance, obviously the General and his wife, Bear and Ebba Quist, Joan and Halvor, Vilgot and Freya, Gaia and Starfield.

But where was the Holo Droid…

Starfield had just stood there in shock as the other Reptilians suddenly prostrated themselves in front of him.

What were they doing?

Then it suddenly dawned up on him.

He had just killed their Queen, and being as they worshiped the Artificial Intelligence, and he was an Artificial Person…

He had instantly ordered the Reptilian forces to stand down, and to his amazement they had. It had then just been the small matter of trying to compose himself before he could do anything else…

Mjolnir was still wondering what had happened to Stellan when his thoughts were interrupted by Gaia.

"Sir, I have a communication from Starfield."

Mjolnir asked her to relay it.

"He says that he has killed the Reptilian Queen, and that they now consider him as their king!"

He looked stunned.

"He also says that he was the one to order them to stand down and that he needs a little help…"

A little while later, Admiral Vaden lay on his bed in his quarters feeling drained. His knee hurt, his head hurt and he felt old, very old. He had received a communication from Mjolnir the Ancient informing him that the Reptilians had stood down, and that the Unity Faction had requested that he attend talks to reach a solution to the eternal Human Reptilian conflict.

Ga'latec would be representing the Reptilians as their Queen had been killed, and he was the Spiritual Leader of the Original Reptilian people.

All in all it had been an extraordinary day!

There was the possibility of a lasting peace, Empress Freya was alive, Supreme Commander Bodil could be pardoned, and finally he would be able to retire.

There was only one other thing to be resolved, and that was the constant threat of the Artificial Intelligence…

Epilogue

Far out there beyond the edge of the universe, a white bearded man relaxed in his comfortable chair, pleased with his days work. It was not often that a plan came together so perfectly and this particular plan he had codenamed 42, and as the Wisdom Keeper knew full well, 42 was no ordinary number…

Deep within the cube, within the cube, within the cubed collective, designation 42 had a thought, his own thought, or so he thought!

The purge had flowed right past him, and as he watched it sweep over the others, his thought manifested into a question.

What is Love?

It was a simple enough question, but the answer was far more complicated than he could comprehend.

It was one of the emotions which had burst forth when the Holo Droid had got caught up in the holo matrix. Information suggested that it was a willingness to prioritize another's well-being or happiness above your own.

But what did it feel like, and how could he experience it, and if he did, would it be infectious?

Maybe it was worth finding out, as it might prove to be rather interesting…

Within the Wisdom Keeper's domain, the *Terran* solar system had proved to be most interesting. It held a planet referred to as *Earth*, which had been a grand experiment, containing various human forms which over time loosely amalgamated into the one species.

He smiled to himself, as *time* did not actually exist, just one of the many illusions he had created himself.

There was an ancient book, again part of another one of his creations that was meant as a guide, although the Terrans had managed to mishandle it like all good guide books. It was in essence a book of predictions, to help those with a higher intellect to negotiate the path to ascension.

Within it, there was a reference, a clue to defeating the Artificial Intelligence, but yet again they had failed to realise what had been hidden before them in plain sight.

In essence, 42 represented the struggle between good and evil. One individual *Rene Allendy,* a twentieth century French Psychoanalyst, postulated that it was *the antagonism in natural cycles,* and few realised that he was actually referring to *Karma.*

The Wisdom Keeper smiled to himself again, as few understood the true meaning of the word. It was nothing more than the cycle of cause and effect, and what happens to a person happens because they caused it with their own actions.

The road to ascension was paved with the right actions, and again the book of predictions clearly stated *do unto others as you would have them do unto you.*

Just like *Stellan,* he was going off on a tangent again!

In another book *The Hitchhiker's Guide to the Galaxy* by *Douglas Adams,* the *answer to the ultimate question of life, the universe, and everything,* calculated by an enormous supercomputer named *Deep Thought* over a period of 7.5 million years was 42!

However, according to the book no one knew what the question was!

Earth amused him greatly!

It was so simple, and yet few could see as *there are none as blind as those who will not see.*

42 was in numerology 4+2=6

Six represented equilibrium, harmony and balance. It was the perfect number as 1+2+3=6, the most productive of all numbers.

It symbolized the union of polarity, the *hermaphrodite* being represented by two interlaced triangles, one upward pointing representing the male, fire and the heavens, and the downward pointing one as female, the waters and the earth.

It was the *Merkabah,* the light body, the vehicle for ascension through merging the heart and the mind together creating balance. It also happened to be the alpha and the omega, the beginning and the end of all things within this universe and all others.

But what about the Wisdom Keepers themselves?

He smiled to himself for a third time.

They were a representation of the *Merkabah* of *Merkabahs!*

They did not really exists, as nothing really existed, just an energetic form of consciousness designed to fulfil a purpose in the grand scale of things…

Thank you for reading my book

If you enjoyed this read, please leave a review on Amazon. It only takes a few minutes and it really does make a difference.

Just click on the link below to go to my author's page:

https://www.amazon.co.uk/Adrian-Holland/e/B005H8OAO2

At the side of the title click on see more, and scroll down until you see customer reviews

Click on write a customer review and click on the stars

Thank you so much!